背托福演講稿，一舉多得

　　托福測驗，現在已經全面電腦化，並且要求考生在 30 分鐘內，根據電腦隨機選取的作文題目，寫一篇作文，範圍是 185 個題目，學習出版公司已經出版「托福電腦作文 185 篇」，書中有 185 篇作文範例，及托福寫作評分介紹。

　　背作文很難背，很痛苦，但是如果改成「一口氣英語演講」的方式，就容易多了，我們精選 185 篇中的 36 篇，改寫成英文演講稿，以三句爲一組，九句爲一段，每篇演講稿可以講三分鐘，你可以選擇你所喜歡的題目，一篇接一篇地背下去，只要背了 20 篇，你就可以連續講英文一小時，你腦子裡有 1080 個句子，不管考什麼題目，你都可以排列組合，在規定的 30 分鐘之內，你就能文思泉湧，寫出道地的英文。

　　更棒的是，藉由準備托福的機會，你所背的演講，終生可以使用，在任何情況下，見到外國人，你都有很多話題，可以和他們深談。**背演講的祕訣就是，要背給別人聽**，你要找一些聽眾來協助你，或互相背，每天都要背，當每篇演講稿的速度背到一分鐘之內，就能變成直覺，從此終生不會忘記。

　　真巧，托福測驗明年起，就要做進一步的大改革，加考口試部分，現在，大家都了解，語言應該先學會口說表達能力。很慶幸，學習出版公司率先發明了「一口氣英語」和「一口氣英語演講」，從此解決了學英文的兩大困難：①背了會忘記；②沒有東西可背。

　　本書精選的 36 篇演講稿，每篇均附有中文翻譯及註釋，在編審及校對的每一階段，力求完善，但仍恐有疏漏之處，尚祈各界先進，不吝賜教。

劉 毅

本書製作過程

　　本書之所以完成，感謝林銀姿小姐擔任總指揮，也要感謝美籍老師 Edward Mcquire 與 Laura E. Stewart 編寫演講稿，Tony Chen 負責校訂，並且將這 36 篇演講稿改寫成作文，Andy Swarzman 最後校訂，也要感謝謝靜芳老師再三仔細校訂，白雪嬌小姐負責封面設計，黃淑貞小姐負責版面和目錄設計，葉家怡小姐協助本書的製作。

CONTENTS

1. Travel by Tour! Have the Time of Your Life!

Hello, Marco Polos!
Welcome future travelers!
Get ready for some travel advice.

Traveling is so popular these days.
It seems like everyone is going on a trip.
It's so important to travel smart.

I'm a tour advocate.
I'm convinced it's the best way to go.
Now, let me tell you why.

For starters, everything is pre-arranged.
There is no hassle with anything.
There is no wasting time with transportation
or accommodations.

---

travel by tour	*have the time of one's time*
Marco Polo	*these days*
smart (smɑrt)	advocate ('ædvəkɪt)
convinced (kən'vɪnst)	*for starters*
pre-arranged (ˌpriə'rendʒɪd)	hassle ('hæsḷ)
transportation (ˌtrænspɚ'teʃən)	
accommodations (əˌkɑmə'deʃənz)	

The tour guide does all "the dirty work."

Leave the reservations and negotiations
  to the guide.

Leave all the red tape and your frustrations
  behind.

A tour is carefree and relaxing.

A tour is more organized and efficient.

A tour offers many benefits that independent
  travel can't.

For instance, you have around-the-clock service.

You have a twenty-four hour source
  of information.

The guide tries to facilitate your every wish.

---

guide (gaɪd)	**dirty work**
reservation (ˌrɛzɚˈveʃən)	negotiation (nɪˌgoʃɪˈeʃən)
leave ~ behind	**red tape**
frustration (frʌsˈtreʃən)	carefree (ˈkɛrˌfri)
relaxing (rɪˈlæksɪŋ)	organized (ˈɔrgənˌaɪzd)
efficient (əˈfɪʃənt)	benefit (ˈbɛnəfɪt)
independent (ˌɪndɪˈpɛndənt)	**independent travel**
around-the-clock	source (sors, sɔrs)
facilitate (fəˈsɪləˌtet)	wish (wɪʃ)

You'll learn more in less time.
You'll feel pampered and privileged.
Your nose won't always be buried in a travel book.

Guides will answer any questions.
Guides will translate and give inside tips.
So don't worry about language barriers
   or getting ripped off.

In addition, tours are much safer.
Tours offer security and insurance.
No matter what happens, you're not alone.

Forget about pickpockets or weirdoes.
Forget about getting food poisoning from
   street food.
A tour protects you from many dangers!

---

pamper (ˈpæmpɚ)	privileged (ˈprɪvlɪdʒɪd)
bury one's nose in a book	translate (trænsˈlet)
inside (ˈɪnˈsaɪd)	tip (tɪp)
barrier (ˈbærɪɚ)	*rip off*
in addition	security (sɪˈkjʊrətɪ)
insurance (ɪnˈʃʊrəns)	alone (əˈlon)
pickpocket (ˈpɪkˌpɑkɪt)	weirdo (ˈwɪrdo)
poisoning (ˈpɔɪznɪŋ)	protect (prəˈtɛkt)

Put your mind at ease.

Put your worries to rest.

Traveling by tour will keep you out
   of trouble.

Finally, tours are more social and fun.

You'll make new friendships for sure.

You'll be interacting with people of similar
   interests.

The group enjoys a special comradery.

The group atmosphere is always festive.

Meals are often like mini-parties with lively
   conversations and jokes.

---

put (pʊt)	*at ease*
put···to rest	*keep···out of*
social ('soʃəl)	friendship ('frɛnd,ʃɪp)
for sure	interact (,ɪntə'ækt)
comradery (kəm'radərɪ)	atmosphere ('ætməs,fɪr)
festive ('fɛstɪv)	meal (mil)
mini- ('mɪnɪ)	lively ('laɪvlɪ)

The negative stereotypes about tours

  are hogwash!

Tours aren't boring; they're thrilling.

Tours aren't restrictive; they're often quite flexible.

In conclusion, take a tip from me.

Take a tour, and you'll still be free.

A tour is the best way to go.

It's the best of both worlds.

You can slip away and do your own thing.

You can follow the group and go with the flow.

Be a smart traveler.

Get the most out of every trip.

Joining a tour is the obvious choice.

---

negative ('nɛgətɪv)	stereotype ('stɛrɪəˌtaɪp)
hogwash ('hɑgˌwɑʃ)	thrilling ('θrɪlɪŋ)
restrictive (rɪ'strɪktɪv)	flexible ('flɛksəb!)
in conclusion	take (tek)
the best of both worlds	slip (slɪp)
go with the flow	*get the most out of*
obvious ('ɑbvɪəs)	

1. *Travel by Tour! Have the Time of Your Life!*
跟團旅行！享受人生最快樂的時光！

【演講解說】

Hello, Marco Polos!	哈囉，各位馬可波羅！
Welcome future travelers!	歡迎未來的旅行家！
Get ready for some travel advice.	準備聽聽一些旅行的建議。
Traveling is so popular these days.	最近旅行很受歡迎。
It seems like everyone is going on a trip.	似乎每個人都在旅行。
It's so important to travel smart.	做個聰明的旅行者非常重要。
I'm a tour advocate.	我是跟團旅遊的擁護者。
I'm convinced it's the best way to go.	我確信那是最好的旅遊方式。
Now, let me tell you why.	現在，讓我告訴你為什麼。
For starters, everything is pre-arranged.	首先，所有事情都預先安排好了。
There is no hassle with anything.	任何事情都不用麻煩。
There is no wasting time with transportation or accommodations.	不用浪費時間在交通和住宿的安排上。

** ————————————————

travel by tour 跟團旅行
have the time of one's life 享受一生中前所未有的快樂
Marco Polo 馬可波羅（1254?-1324?，義大利的旅行家）　　*these days* 最近
smart〔smɑrt〕*adv.* 聰明地　　advocate〔'ædvəkɪt〕*n.* 擁護者
convinced〔kən'vɪnst〕*adj.* 確信的　　*for starters* 作為開始；首先
pre-arranged〔͵priə'rendʒɪd〕*adj.* 預先安排好的
hassle〔'hæs!〕*n.* 麻煩　　transportation〔͵trænspə'teʃən〕*n.* 交通運輸
accommodations〔ə͵kɑmə'deʃənz〕*n. pl.* 住宿設備

The tour guide does all "the dirty work."	導遊會做所有的苦差事。
Leave the reservations and negotiations to the guide.	把預訂和協調的工作留給導遊。
Leave all the red tape and your frustrations behind.	將所有繁瑣的手續和沮喪全拋在腦後。
A tour is carefree and relaxing.	跟團旅行是無憂無慮、輕鬆自在的。
A tour is more organized and efficient.	跟團旅行比較有組織、有效率。
A tour offers many benefits that independent travel can't.	跟團旅行提供許多自助旅行享受不到的好處。
For instance, you have around-the-clock service.	例如，你有日夜無休的服務。
You have a twenty-four hour source of information.	你有二十四小時的資訊來源。
The guide tries to facilitate your every wish.	導遊會努力達成你的每一項要求。

**

guide〔gaɪd〕*n.* 導遊　　*dirty work* 討厭做的工作
reservation〔͵rɛzɚ'veʃən〕*n.* 預訂
negotiation〔nɪ͵goʃɪ'eʃən〕*n.* 談判；協商
leave~behind 留下~；將~拋在腦後　　*red tape* 繁瑣的手續；官僚作風
frustration〔frʌs'treʃən〕*n.* 挫折　　carefree〔'kɛr͵fri〕*adj.* 無憂無慮的
relaxing〔rɪ'læksɪŋ〕*adj.* 令人輕鬆的
organized〔'ɔrgən͵aɪzd〕*adj.* 有組織的；有條理的
efficient〔ə'fɪʃənt〕*adj.* 有效率的　　benefit〔'bɛnəfɪt〕*n.* 好處
independent〔͵ɪndɪ'pɛndənt〕*adj.* 獨立的　　*independent travel* 自助旅行
around-the-clock 二十四小時不斷的　　source〔sors,sɔrs〕*n.* 來源
facilitate〔fə'sɪlə͵tet〕*v.* 使便利；使容易　　wish〔wɪʃ〕*n.* 希望；要求

You'll learn more in less time.

你將在更短的時間內學到更多東西。

You'll feel pampered and
　privileged.

你將會覺得受到呵護、享有特權。

Your nose won't always be buried
　in a guidebook.

你不用一直埋頭閱讀旅行指南。

Guides will answer any questions.

導遊會回答任何問題。

Guides will translate and give
　inside tips.

導遊會做翻譯，並提供內部情報。

So don't worry about language
　barriers or getting ripped off.

所以不用擔心有語言障礙或是被敲竹槓。

In addition, tours are much safer.

此外，跟團旅行安全多了。

Tours offer security and insurance.

跟團旅行提供安全和保險。

No matter what happens, you're
　not alone.

不論發生什麼事情，你都不孤單。

**

pamper〔ˈpæmpɚ〕*v.* 嬌寵；溺愛
privileged〔ˈprɪvɪlɪdʒɪd〕*adj.* 享有特權的；幸運的
bury* one's *nose in a book 埋頭看書
guidebook〔ˈgaɪd,buk〕*n.* 旅行指南　　translate〔trænsˈlet〕*v.* 翻譯
inside〔ɪnˈsaɪd〕*adj.* 內部的；內幕的
tip〔tɪp〕*n.* 內部情報；祕密消息；建議
barrier〔ˈbærɪɚ〕*n.* 障礙　　***rip off*** 欺騙；敲竹槓
in addition 此外　　security〔sɪˈkjurətɪ〕*n.* 安全
insurance〔ɪnˈʃurəns〕*n.* 保險　　alone〔əˈlon〕*adj.* 獨自的；單獨的

Forget about pickpockets or weirdoes.	不用擔心遇到扒手或怪胎。
Forget about getting food poisoning from street food.	不用擔心吃路邊攤而食物中毒。
A tour protects you from many dangers!	跟團旅行保護你免受許多危險！
Put your mind at ease.	放鬆心情。
Put your worries to rest.	忘卻煩惱。
Traveling by tour will keep you out of trouble.	跟團旅行將使你遠離麻煩。

Finally, *tours are more social and fun*.
最後，跟團旅行比較能和別人來往，而且有趣。

You'll make new friendships for sure.	你一定會結交到新朋友。
You'll be interacting with people of similar interests.	你將會和興趣相投的人產生互動。

The group enjoys a special comradery.	團體享有一種特別的同伴之誼。
The group atmosphere is always festive.	團體氣氛往往是歡樂的。
Meals are often like mini-parties with lively conversations and jokes.	吃飯常常就像在開小型派對，穿插著活潑熱烈的對話和笑話。

**

pickpocket〔'pɪk,pɑkɪt〕*n.* 扒手　weirdo〔'wɪrdo〕*n.* 怪胎（= *weirdie*）
poisoning〔'pɔɪznɪŋ〕*n.* 中毒　protect〔prə'tɛkt〕*v.* 保護 <*from*>
put〔put〕*v.* 使…成爲（某種狀態）　*at ease* 放鬆地；自在地
put…to rest 忘卻…（= *lay…to rest*）　*keep…out of* 使…不受（危險等）
social〔'soʃəl〕*adj.* 社交的　friendship〔'frɛnd,ʃɪp〕*n.* 友誼
for sure 必定　interact〔,ɪntɚ'ækt〕*v.* 互動 <*with*>
comradery〔kəm'rɑdɚɪ〕*n.* 同伴之誼；友誼
atmosphere〔'ætməs,fɪr〕*n.* 氣氛　festive〔'fɛstɪv〕*adj.* 歡樂的
mini-〔'mɪnɪ〕*adj.* 小型的　lively〔'laɪvlɪ〕*adj.* 活潑的；熱烈的

The negative stereotypes about
   tours are hogwash!

Tours aren't boring; they're
   thrilling.

Tours aren't restrictive; they're
   often quite flexible.

In conclusion, take a tip from me.

Take a tour, and you'll still be free.

A tour is the best way to go.

It's the best of both worlds.

You can slip away and do your
   own thing.

You can follow the group and go
   with the flow.

Be a smart traveler.

Get the most out of every trip.

Joining a tour is the obvious choice.

有關跟團旅行的負面刻板印象是
一派胡言！

跟團旅行不會無聊；跟團旅行是
令人興奮的。

跟團旅行不會限制重重；跟團旅
行通常是相當具有彈性的。

總之，聽我的建議。

如果你跟團旅行，你還是能自由
自在。

跟團旅行是最好的方式。

可以享受兩者的優點。

你可以溜走，做自己的事情。

你可以跟著團，跟著大家走。

作個聰明的旅行者。

充分把握每一次的旅行。

跟團旅行顯然是你該做的選擇。

**

negative (ˈnɛgətɪv) *adj.* 負面的   stereotype (ˈstɛrɪə,taɪp) *n.* 刻板印象
hogwash (ˈhɑg,wɑʃ) *n.* 廢話；無聊的話
thrilling (ˈθrɪlɪŋ) *adj.* 令人興奮的   restrictive (rɪˈstrɪktɪv) *adj.* 限制的
flexible (ˈflɛksəbl) *adj.* 有彈性的   ***in conclusion*** 總之
take (tek) *v.* 選用；採用   ***the best of both worlds*** 兩者之優點
slip (slɪp) *v.* 溜走 <*away*>
go with the flow 跟著大家走（含有「隨波逐流」的被動意味）
get the most out of 充分利用；儘量利用 (=*make the most of*)
obvious (ˈɑbvɪəs) *adj.* 明顯的；無疑的

【托福作文範例】

1. Travel by Tour

There are so many things to see around the world and even in our own backyards! But not everybody takes the time to explore this great planet we live on, because they feel they have no time. Well, I have a solution and that is to go on a tour. Let me tell you why tours are so great.

First, everything is pre-arranged on a tour. You don't have to waste time planning transportation or accommodations. All the details are taken care of by a tour. *Second*, a tour is carefree and relaxing because it's more organized and efficient. You have a twenty-four hour source of information in your tour guide to answer any questions, help with translation and give inside tips. *In addition*, tours are much safer. You will be traveling in a group so you need not worry about pickpockets or weirdoes. And if you get sick from eating the local food, you have somebody there to take care of you.

Finally, you will make new friends on a tour. You will be among people with similar interests and the group atmosphere is always so lively. *In conclusion*, a tour is the best way to travel. So go join a tour today!

1. 跟團旅行

　　世界上有很多的事物等著我們去看，甚至連我們自家的後院都有！但是並非每個人都會花時間，去探索我們所居住的這個很棒的星球，因為他們覺得沒有時間。嗯，我有一個解決方法，那就是跟團旅行。讓我告訴你跟團旅行為什麼這麼棒。

　　第一，旅行的所有的事務都事先安排好了。你不需要浪費時間去計劃交通或住宿。所有的細節都交由旅行團來幫你處理。第二，參加旅行團是無憂無慮而且輕鬆的，因為旅行團比較有組織，而且也較有效率。你的導遊更是你二十四小時的資訊來源，能回答你所有的問題，也可以提供語言翻譯的協助，更可以給你一些內幕消息。此外，旅行團安全多了。你將會以團體的方式旅行，所以你不必擔心有扒手或是遇到怪胎。而且如果你因為吃了當地的食物而生病了，也會有人照顧你。

　　最後，你可以在旅行團中結交新朋友。你將會與和你興趣相投的人相處在一起，而且團體總是充滿著非常活潑熱烈的氣氛。總之，跟團旅行是旅遊的最佳方式。所以今天就去參加一個旅行團吧！

【托福作文原試題】

Do you agree or disagree with the following statement? The best way to travel is in a group led by a tour guide. Use specific reasons and examples to support your answer.

2. *Difficult Experiences Are the Best Lessons in Life*

Good day, everyone.
I'm so glad you're here.
I have some useful advice about life.

We all know life isn't easy.
We know it's full of hardship and strife.
We should also know that's what makes
   life great!

Difficult times are valuable lessons.
Difficult times are the best teachers.
Here are four points you should know
   and remember.

---

lesson ('lɛsn̩)	*good day*
advice (əd'vaıs)	*be full of*
hardship ('hɑrdʃɪp)	strife (straıf)
valuable ('væljuəbl̩)	point (pɔınt)

First, adversity is part of life.

Accept it but try to change it.

Accept it, deal with it and overcome it.

Never quit or give up.

Tough times are only temporary.

Tough times don't last, but tough people do.

Life is not a picnic.

Don't expect it to be easy.

Don't expect anything worthwhile without effort.

Second, the benefits of hardship are many.

Difficulty strengthens and toughens you up.

Difficulty makes you grow and improve.

---

adversity (əd'vɜsətɪ)

deal with

quit (kwɪt)

tough (tʌf)

last (læst)

worthwhile ('wɜθ'hwaɪl)

strengthen ('strɛŋθən)

toughen sb. up

(a) part of

overcome (ˌovə·'kʌm)

give up

temporary ('tɛmpəˌrɛrɪ)

picnic ('pɪknɪk)

benefit ('bɛnəfɪt)

toughen ('tʌfn̩)

You learn patience and endurance.

You learn perseverance and desire.

You develop determination and diligence, too.

Difficulty demands that you give more effort.

Difficulty helps you appreciate the little things.

Success is born from difficulty.

Third, *difficult times are a window of opportunity*.

They are a challenge and a springboard.

They lead to bigger and better things.

Great people rise above adversity.

Great people use it to change and get better.

Like Einstein said, "Adversity offers opportunity."

---

patience ('peʃəns)

perseverance (ˌpɝsə'vɪrəns)

develop (dɪ'vɛləp)

determination (dɪˌtɝmə'neʃən)

demand (dɪ'mænd)

window('wɪndo)

springboard ('sprɪŋˌbord)

rise above

endurance (ɪn'djurəns)

desire (dɪ'zaɪr)

diligence ('dɪlədʒəns)

appreciate (ə'priʃɪˌet)

challenge ('tʃælɪndʒ)

lead to

Einstein ('aɪnstaɪn)

For example, look at the Chinese character
　　for crisis.
It consists of two characters.
It has the dual meaning of opportunity and danger!

Finally, *you learn from difficulties*.
Every trouble is a valuable experience.
Every tough break can teach you a lot.

You learn to believe in yourself.
You learn to rely on yourself.
You become a "top student" in the "school of
　　hard knocks."

Remember what you learn.
Store it away like money.
Save it all up for a rainy day.

---

character ('kærɪktɚ)	crisis ('kraɪsɪs)
consist of	dual ('d(j)uəl)
break (brek)	*tough break*
believe in	*rely on*
top (tɑp)	knock (nɑk)
hard knocks	store (stor)
save (sev)	*a rainy day*

In conclusion, welcome challenging times.

They are often blessings in disguise.

They often sow the seeds of success.

Be thankful for setbacks.

They give us new focus and knowledge.

They motivate us to try harder.

That which doesn't break us, only

   builds us up.

That which doesn't kill us, only makes

   us stronger.

Turn difficulty into an advantage and you'll

   go far!

---

in conclusion

blessing ('blɛsɪŋ)

a blessing in disguise

seed (sid)

setback ('sɛt,bæk)

motivate ('motə,vet)

build sb. up

advantage (əd'væntɪdʒ)

challenging ('tʃælɪndʒɪŋ)

disguise (dɪs'gaɪz)

sow (so)

thankful ('θæŋkfəl)

focus ('fokəs)

break (brek)

turn···into ~

go far

2. *Difficult Experiences Are the Best Lessons in Life*
困難的經驗是人生最好的教訓

【演講解說】

Good day, everyone.　　　　　　大家好。

I'm so glad you're here.　　　　很高興你們能來到這裡。

I have some useful advice　　　我有一些關於人生有用的建

　　about life.　　　　　　　　議。

We all know life isn't easy.　　　我們全都知道人生絕非易事。

We know it's full of hardship　　我們知道人生充滿艱難和

　　and strife.　　　　　　　衝突。

We should also know that's what　我們也應該知道就是因為如

　　makes life great!　　　　此，生命才變得偉大！

Difficult times are valuable lessons.　困難的日子是寶貴的教訓。

Difficult times are the best teachers.　困難的日子是最好的老師。

Here are four points you should　這裡有四個你們應該知道並

　　know and remember.　　　牢記的要點。

**

lesson (ˈlɛsn̩) *n.* 教訓　　***good day*** 日安！；您好！

advice (ədˈvaɪs) *n.* 勸告；建議　***be full of*** 充滿

hardship (ˈhɑrdʃɪp) *n.* 艱難；困苦　　strife (straɪf) *n.* 衝突

valuable (ˈvæljuəbl̩) *adj.* 珍貴的　　point (pɔɪnt) *n.* 要點

First, adversity is part of life.　　　第一，逆境是人生的一部份。

Accept it but try to change it.　　　接受它，但是要努力改變它。

Accept it, deal with it and　　　接受它、處理它，並克服它。
　　overcome it.

Never quit or give up.　　　絕對不要放棄。

Tough times are only temporary.　　　艱苦的日子只是暫時的。

Tough times don't last, but tough　　　艱苦的日子不會一直持續下去，
　　people do.　　　但是不屈不撓的人會堅持到底。

Life is not a picnic.　　　人生不是輕鬆的事。

Don't expect it to be easy.　　　不要期待人生是輕輕鬆鬆的。

Don't expect anything worthwhile　　　不要期待任何值得做的事情是不
　　without effort.　　　需要努力的。

Second, the benefits of hardship　　　第二，逆境的好處很多。
　　are many.

Difficulty strengthens and toughens　　　困難能使你更堅強。
　　you up.

Difficulty makes you grow and　　　困難能讓你成長和進步。
　　improve.

**

adversity〔əd'vɝsətɪ〕*n.* 逆境；厄運　　*deal with* 處理
overcome〔͵ovə'kʌm〕*v.* 克服　　quit〔kwɪt〕*v.* 放棄（*= give up*）
tough〔tʌf〕*adj.* 困難的；不幸的；（人）不屈不撓的
temporary〔'tɛmpə͵rɛrɪ〕*adj.* 暫時的　　last〔læst〕*v.* 持續
picnic〔'pɪknɪk〕*n.* 愉快的事；輕鬆的工作
worthwhile〔'wɝθ'hwaɪl〕*adj.* 值得的　　benefit〔'bɛnəfɪt〕*n.* 好處
strengthen〔'strɛŋθən〕*v.* 加強　　toughen〔'tʌfn̩〕*v.* 使堅強
toughen sb. up 使某人更堅強

You learn patience and endurance.　　你學到耐心和耐力。

You learn perseverance and desire.　　你學到毅力和渴望。

You develop determination and　　你也培養出決心和勤勉。
　　diligence, too.

Difficulty demands that you give　　困難要求你付出更多努力。
　　more effort.

Difficulty helps you appreciate the　　困難有助於你感激小事情。
　　little things.

Success is born from difficulty.　　成功來自困難。

Third, difficult times are a window　　第三點，困難的日子是開向機
of opportunity.　　會的窗口。

They are a challenge and a springboard.　　它們是挑戰也是立足點。

They lead to bigger and better　　一步步將你引向越來越大、越來
　　things.　　越好的事情。

Great people rise above adversity.　　偉人克服逆境。

Great people use it to change and　　偉人利用逆境改變、求進步。
　　get better.

Like Einstein said, "Adversity offers　　就如愛因斯坦說：「逆境提供
　　opportunity."　　機會。」

**

---

patience ('peʃəns) n. 耐心　　endurance (ɪn'djʊrəns) n. 耐力

perseverance (,pɜsə'vɪrəns) n. 毅力　　desire (dɪ'zaɪr) n. 渴望

develop (dɪ'vɛləp) v. 培養　　determination (dɪ,tɜmə'neʃən) n. 決心

diligence ('dɪlədʒəns) n. 勤勉　　demand (dɪ'mænd) v. 要求

appreciate (ə'priʃɪ,et) v. 感激　　window ('wɪndo) n. 窗子；往外開的東西

challenge ('tʃælɪndʒ) n. 挑戰　　springboard ('sprɪŋ,bord) n. 跳板；立足點

lead to 通往；導致　　**rise above** 克服

Einstein ('aɪnstaɪn) n. 愛因斯坦（1879-1955，生於德國的美籍物理學家，
　　為相對論的提出者）

For example, look at the Chinese character for crisis.	例如，看看中文字「危機」。
It consists of two characters.	是由兩個字所組成的。
It has the dual meaning of opportunity and danger!	具有機會和危險的雙重意義！
Finally, you learn from difficulties.	最後一點，你從困難中學習。
Every trouble is a valuable experience.	每一次的困難都是寶貴的經驗。
Every tough break can teach you a lot.	每一次的不幸都可以教導你許多。
You learn to believe in yourself.	你學會相信自己。
You learn to rely on yourself.	你學會依賴自己。
You become a "top student" in the "school of hard knocks."	你要成為「艱苦學校」的「高材生」。
Remember what you learn.	記住你所學到的東西。
Store it away like money.	儲存起來，就像存錢一樣。
Save it all up for a rainy day.	全部存起來，以備不時之需。

**

character〔ˈkærɪktə〕*n.* 文字　　crisis〔ˈkraɪsɪs〕*n.* 危機

consist of 由…組成　　dual〔ˈdj(u)əl〕*adj.* 雙重的

break〔brek〕*n.* 機會；運氣　　***tough break*** 厄運；不幸

believe in 相信　　***rely on*** 依靠　　top〔tɑp〕*adj.* 最頂尖的；最優良的

knock〔nɑk〕*n.* 不幸；艱苦　　***hard knocks*** 艱苦；挫折

store〔stor〕*v.* 儲存＜*away*＞　　save〔sev〕*v.* 儲蓄；存錢＜*up*＞

a rainy day 將來可能有的苦日子；不時之需

In conclusion, welcome challenging times.	總之,欣然接受具有挑戰性的時刻。
They are often blessings in disguise.	它們往往是塞翁失馬、禍中得福。
They often sow the seeds of success.	它們往往種下成功的種子。
Be thankful for setbacks.	對每一次的挫敗心存感激。
They give us new focus and knowledge.	它們為我們帶來新的關注和知識。
They motivate us to try harder.	它們激勵我們要更努力。
That which doesn't break us, only builds us up.	不會打倒我們的東西,只會讓我們進步。
That which doesn't kill us, only makes us stronger.	不會殺死我們的東西,只會讓我們更堅強。
Turn difficulty into an advantage and you'll go far!	把困難轉化為有利的條件,你就會因此而成功!

**

in conclusion 總之　　challenging〔ˋtʃælɪndʒɪŋ〕*adj.* 具有挑戰性的
blessing〔ˋblɛsɪŋ〕*n.* 幸運;幸福　　disguise〔dɪsˋgaɪz〕*n.* 偽裝
a blessing in disguise 先前看似不幸,後來卻變為幸運之事;塞翁失馬;
　　禍中得福　　sow〔so〕*v.* 播(種)　　seed〔sid〕*n.* 種子
thankful〔ˋθæŋkfəl〕*adj.* 感激的 < *for* >
setback〔ˋsɛt͵bæk〕*n.* 挫折
focus〔ˋfokəs〕*n.* 焦點;(注意、活動等的)中心;重點
motivate〔ˋmotə͵vet〕*v.* 激勵　　break〔brek〕*v.* 毀滅(人)
build up 增進　　*turn…into~* 使…轉變成~
advantage〔ədˋvæntɪdʒ〕*n.* 有利條件;優勢
go far 成功(= *go a long way*)

【托福作文範例】

2. Difficult Experiences Are the Best Lessons in Life

Many times when people are faced with adversity in life they just give up. But difficult experiences offer some of the best lessons in life. Here are four points you should know and remember about difficult times.

First, adversity is part of life. Accept it and deal with it. Never quit or give up. Tough times are only temporary. Tough times don't last, but tough people do. *Second*, there are many benefits to hardships. Difficulty strengthens your resolve; it makes you grow and improve. You learn perseverance and determination. Difficulty helps you appreciate the little things. *Third*, difficult times are like a springboard leading to bigger and better things. Great people use difficulty to change and get better. Like Einstein said, "Adversity offers opportunity." *Finally*, you learn from difficulties. Every trouble is a valuable experience as you learn to believe in yourself.

In conclusion, welcome challenging times for they are often blessings in disguise. Just remember: that which doesn't break us only builds us up and that which doesn't kill us, only makes us stronger. So the next time you encounter difficulties, just keep your head up and believe everything will be okay in the end.

2. 困難的經驗是人生最好的教訓

　　很多時候，當人在面對生命中的逆境時，就只是放棄。但是困難的經驗提供了人生中一些最好的教訓。這裡有四個關於困境的要點，是你應該知道並且牢記的。

　　第一點，逆境是人生的一部份。要接受它並且處理它。絕對不要放棄。艱苦的日子只是暫時的。艱苦的日子不會一直持續下去，但是不屈不撓的人會堅持到底。第二點，困境有很多好處。困難可以加強你的決心；使你成長進步。你學到毅力與決心。困難幫助你感激小事情。第三點，困難的時光就像跳板一樣，將你一步步引向越來越大、越來越好的事情。偉人利用困境來進行改變、求進步。就像愛因斯坦說的：「逆境提供了機會。」最後一點，你從困難中學習。當你學會相信自己，所有的困難都是寶貴的經驗。

　　總之，要欣然接受充滿挑戰的時刻，因為這往往是塞翁失馬、禍中得福。只要記住：不會打倒我們的東西，只會讓我們進步，不會殺死我們的東西，只會讓我們更堅強。所以下次你遇到困難的時候，不要垂頭喪氣，要相信凡事到最後都會沒問題的。

───【托福作文原試題】───

Do you agree or disagree with the following statement? Most experiences in our lives that seemed difficult at the time become valuable lessons for the future. Use reasons and specific examples to support your answer.

3. *A Live Performance Is Best!*

Thank you all for being here.
I hope you enjoy my talk.
I'll be discussing the best way to view
  performances.

Some prefer the comfort of staying at home.
They prefer the convenience of watching TV.
They say it's more relaxing and saves money.

I don't see things that way.
I love to see events in person.
Let me tell you why.

First, nothing beats the atmosphere of a live
  performance.
All my senses come alive.
All my feelings and emotions are more intense.

---

live (laɪv)	performance (pɚˈfɔrməns)
view (vju)	comfort (ˈkʌmfɚt)
relaxing (rɪˈlæksɪŋ)	event (ɪˈvɛnt)
in person	beat (bit)
atmosphere (ˈætməsˌfɪr)	sense (sɛns)
come alive	emotion (ɪˈmoʃən)
intense (ɪnˈtɛns)	

You can feel the energy in the air.

It's like an electric current flowing around.

It's a very stimulating experience.

It's thrilling to be there in person.

It's exciting to be in the audience.

It's a lot of fun to be in the crowd!

Second, *going out is a special occasion!*

Going to public events is a real treat.

It's not something we can do every day.

It's an opportunity to learn something new.

It's a privilege I value a lot.

It's both eye-opening and mind-opening to me.

---

energy ('ɛnɚdʒɪ)　　　　*in the air*
electric (ɪ'lɛktrɪk)　　　current ('kɝənt)
flow (flo)　　　　　　　stimulating ('stɪmjə,letɪŋ)
thrilling ('θrɪlɪŋ)　　　　audience ('ɔdɪəns)
crowd (kraʊd)　　　　　occasion (ə'keʒən)
public ('pʌblɪk)　　　　　treat (trit)
privilege ('prɪvlɪdʒ)　　　value ('væljʊ)
eye-opening ('aɪ,opənɪŋ)
mind-opening ('maɪnd,opənɪŋ)

Live performances are special memories.

Watching one on a screen just can't compare.

Watching at home is just a passive, vicarious
experience.

Third, *a live event is a more personal*
experience.

You can interact in a much closer way.

You can connect with and relate to the
performers.

The action is right there in front of you.

You can almost reach out and touch it.

You feel like you're part of it all.

---

memory ('mɛmərɪ)	screen (skrin)
compare (kəm'pɛr)	passive ('pæsɪv)
vicarious (vaɪ'kɛrɪəs)	personal ('pɝsn̩l)
interact (ˌɪntə-'ækt)	connect (kə'nɛkt)
relate (rɪ'let)	action ('ækʃən)
reach out	*(a) part of*

You become more involved.

The experience leaves a greater impression on you.

The live performance is more enjoyable
   entertainment.

Fourth, a live event has fewer distractions.

It's easier to pay attention.

It's also easier to catch more details.

You don't have any household disturbances.

You don't have to worry about anything.

You have no one to please but yourself!

There are no family members to bother you.

There are no noisy neighbors or telephones.

There is no homework nearby to make you
   feel guilty.

---

involved (ɪn'vɑlvd)

enjoyable (ɪn'dʒɔɪəb!)

entertainment (ˌɛntɚ'tenmənt)

distraction (dɪ'strækʃən)

detail ('ditel)

disturbance (dɪ'stɝbəns)

member ('mɛmbɚ)

nearby ('nɪr,baɪ)

impression (ɪm'prɛʃən)

catch (kætʃ)

household ('haʊs,hold)

please (pliz)

bother ('bɑðɚ)

guilty ('gɪltɪ)

In conclusion, let me summarize.

I'm a big fan of live events!

I like to experience things in person.

It might cost a substantial fee.

It might require more effort and planning.

I still believe it's definitely worth it.

Live performances are wonderful memories.

They might last your whole life long.

They are magical and unforgettable to me!

---

in conclusion

fan (fæn)

substantial (səb'stænʃəl)

require (rɪ'kwaɪr)

worth (wɝθ)

last (læst)

unforgettable (ˌʌnfɚ'gɛtəbl̩)

summarize ('sʌməˌraɪz)

experience (ɪk'spɪrɪəns)

fee (fi)

definitely ('dɛfənɪtlɪ)

memory ('mɛmərɪ)

magical ('mædʒɪkl̩)

3. A Live Performance Is Best!
現場表演最棒！

【演講解說】

Thank you all for being here.	感謝大家全都來到這裡。
I hope you enjoy my talk.	我希望你們喜歡我的演說。
I'll be discussing the best way to view performances.	我將要討論觀看表演的最佳方式。
Some prefer the comfort of staying at home.	有些人比較喜歡待在家裡，享受舒適的感覺。
They prefer the convenience of watching TV.	他們比較喜歡看電視的便利性。
They say it's more relaxing and saves money.	他們說那樣比較輕鬆，而且省錢。
I don't see things that way.	我不是那樣想的。
I love to see events in person.	我喜歡看現場。
Let me tell you why.	讓我告訴你為什麼。

**

live〔laɪv〕*adj.* 現場的　performance〔pɚˈfɔrməns〕*n.* 表演
view〔vju〕*v.* 觀看　comfort〔ˈkʌmfɚt〕*n.* 舒適
relaxing〔rɪˈlæksɪŋ〕*adj.* 令人輕鬆的
event〔ɪˈvɛnt〕*n.* 事件；（比賽、節目中的）項目；大事；令人高興的事
in person 親自；本人

First, nothing beats the atmosphere of a live performance.	首先，什麼都比不上現場表演的氣氛。
All my senses come alive.	我所有的感官全都活躍起來。
All my feelings and emotions are more intense.	我所有的感覺和情緒都變得更加強烈。
You can feel the energy in the air.	你可以感受到空氣中充滿著活力。
It's like an electric current flowing around.	就像是電流在周圍流動。
It's a very stimulating experience.	那是個非常刺激的經驗。
It's thrilling to be there in person.	親自參與現場令人興奮。
It's exciting to be in the audience.	坐在觀眾席很刺激。
It's a lot of fun to be in the crowd!	坐在人群當中很好玩！
Second, going out is a special occasion!	第二，外出是一件特別的大事！
Going to public events is a real treat.	參加公開活動真的是難得的樂事。
It's not something we can do every day.	這可不是每天都有的。

**

beat〔bit〕*v.* 打敗；勝過　atmosphere〔'ætməsˌfɪr〕*n.* 氣氛
sense〔sɛns〕*n.* 感官　***come alive*** 活躍起來
emotion〔ɪ'moʃən〕*n.* 情緒　intense〔ɪn'tɛns〕*adj.* 強烈的
energy〔'ɛnədʒɪ〕*n.* 活力　***in the air*** 在空中
electric〔ɪ'lɛktrɪk〕*adj.* 電的　current〔'kɝənt〕*n.* 電流
flow〔flo〕*v.* 流動　stimulating〔'stɪmjəˌletɪŋ〕*adj.* 使人興奮的；刺激的
thrilling〔'θrɪlɪŋ〕*adj.* 令人興奮的　audience〔'ɔdɪəns〕*n.* 觀眾
crowd〔kraʊd〕*n.* 人群　occasion〔ə'keʒən〕*n.* 場合；大事
public〔'pʌblɪk〕*adj.* 公開的　treat〔trit〕*n.* 難得的樂事

It's an opportunity to learn something new.　那是學習新東西的機會。

It's a privilege I value a lot.　是我非常重視的特別機會。

It's both eye-opening and mind-opening to me.　它能讓我大開眼界，也擴展視野。

Live performances are special memories.　現場表演是特別的回憶。

Watching one on a screen just can't compare.　只透過電視螢幕觀看，根本就比不上。

Watching at home is just a passive, vicarious experience.　在家看電視只是被動、想像別人感受的經驗。

Third, a live event is a more personal experience.　第三，現場活動是更直接的體驗。

You can interact in a much closer way.　你可以以更靠近的方式產生互動。

You can connect with and relate to the performers.　你可以和演出者產生連結、加強和演出者之間的關聯。

**

privilege (`'prɪvlɪdʒ`) n. (個人的) 恩典　value (`'vælju`) v. 重視；珍惜
eye-opening (`'aɪˌopənɪŋ`) adj. 讓人大開眼界的
mind-opening (`'maɪndˌopənɪŋ`) adj. 讓人擴展視野的；讓人增廣見聞的
memory (`'mɛmərɪ`) n. 回憶　screen (`skrin`) n. (電視) 螢幕
compare (`kəm'pɛr`) v. 相比　passive (`'pæsɪv`) adj. 被動的
vicarious (`vaɪ'kɛrɪəs`) adj. (藉想像) 體驗他人經驗的；產生同感或共鳴的
personal (`'pɝsn̩l`) adj. 個人的；(本人) 直接的
interact (`ˌɪntɚ'ækt`) v. 互動　connect (`kə'nɛkt`) v. 連接 <with>
relate (`rɪ'let`) v. 使有關係 <to>

The action is right there in front of you.　活動就在你眼前進行。

You can almost reach out and touch it.　你幾乎可以伸手摸到。

You feel like you're part of it all.　你會覺得自己好像是全體的
一部份。

You become more involved.　你會變得更有參與感。

The experience leaves a greater
impression on you.　這個經驗會留給你更深刻的
印象。

The live performance is more enjoyable
entertainment.　現場表演是更令人開心的娛
樂。

***Fourth, a live event has fewer
distractions.***　第四，現場活動比較少有令
人分心的事物。

It's easier to pay attention.　比較容易專心。

It's also easier to catch more details.　也比較容易掌握細節。

You don't have any household
disturbances.　沒有任何家庭事務的干擾。

You don't have to worry about anything.　你不用擔心任何事情。

You have no one to please but
yourself!　除了自己之外，你不需要討
好任何人！

**

action ('ækʃən) n. 活動　　***reach out*** 伸出手　　***(a) part of*** …的一部份
involved (ɪn'vɑlvd) adj. (對事件等) 有關係的；投入的
impression (ɪm'prɛʃən) n. 印象 < on >
enjoyable (ɪn'dʒɔɪəbl) adj. 令人愉快的
entertainment (,ɛntə'tenmənt) n. 娛樂
distraction (dɪ'strækʃən) n. 使人分心的事物　　catch (kætʃ) v. 捕捉；獲得
detail ('ditel) n. 細節　　household ('haʊs,hold) adj. 家庭的
disturbance (dɪ'stɜbəns) n. 擾亂　　please (pliz) v. 討好

There are no family members to
  bother you.

沒有家庭成員會煩你。

There are no noisy neighbors or
  telephones.

沒有吵鬧的鄰居或電話。

There is no homework nearby to make
  you feel guilty.

沒有功課在旁邊,讓你覺得
有罪惡感。

In conclusion, *let me summarize*.

總之,讓我作個總結。

I'm a big fan of live events!

我是現場活動的超級愛好者!

I like to experience things "in person."

我喜歡「親自」感受事物。

It might cost a substantial fee.

現場表演可能要花一大筆錢。

It might require more effort and
  planning.

可能需要更多努力和計劃。

I still believe it's definitely worth it.

我仍然相信絕對值回票價。

Live performances are wonderful
  memories.

現場表演是美好的回憶。

They might last your whole life long.

這些回憶可能會延續一輩子。

They are magical and unforgettable
  to me!

對我而言,它們是神奇而且
令人難忘的回憶!

**

member ('mɛmbɚ) n. 成員   bother ('bɑðɚ) v. 煩擾;打擾
nearby ('nɪr,baɪ) adv. 在附近   guilty ('gɪltɪ) adj. 內疚的
in conclusion 總之   summarize ('sʌmə,raɪz) v. 總結
substantial (səb'stænʃəl) adj. 多的;大量的   fee (fi) n. 費用
require (rɪ'kwaɪr) v. 需要   definitely ('dɛfənɪtlɪ) adv. 肯定地;當然
worth (wɝθ) adj. 值得 (做…) 的   last (læst) v. 持續
magical ('mædʒɪkl̩) adj. 有魔力的;神奇的
unforgettable (,ʌnfɚ'gɛtəbl̩) adj. 令人難忘的

【托福作文範例】

3. A Live Performance Is Best!

Nothing beats watching your favorite band perform live or catching a baseball game at a stadium. Some people like to stay in the comfort of their home to watch these events but not me. Let me tell you why.

First, nothing beats the atmosphere of a live performance. You can feel the energy in the air, the intense electrifying experience of all the people cheering. *Second*, going out to public events is a special occasion. It's refreshing and both eye-opening and mind-opening. *Third*, live events are a more personal experience. The action is right there in front of you, watching it on screen just can't compare. You become involved with the performers and they leave a lasting impression on you. *Fourth*, a live event has fewer distractions. There are no family members bothering you; no noisy neighbors or telephones. You can just concentrate on the performance.

In conclusion, I am a big fan of live events. They may cost more but they're definitely worth it. So I hope everybody can go attend a live performance today!

3. 現場表演最棒!

　　沒有事情比得上觀看你最喜愛的樂團現場表演,或是在體育場觀看棒球比賽。有些人喜歡待在家裡,享用舒適的設備來觀賞表演,但我可不喜歡。讓我告訴你為什麼。

　　第一點,沒有事情比得上現場表演的氣氛。你可以感受到空氣中充滿著活力,所有人一起歡呼,這種令人振奮的強烈感受。第二點,外出參與公開活動是一件特殊的大事。那是一件使人提振精神的事情,同時也會使我們大開眼界及增廣見聞。第三點,現場演出是一種更直接的經驗。活動就在你的眼前進行,只透過電視螢幕觀賞,根本就比不上。你和演出者產生連結,而他們也在你心中留下了持久的印象。第四點,看現場演出,比較少有令人分心的事物。沒有家庭成員會煩擾你;沒有吵鬧的鄰居或電話。你只需要專心看表演。

　　總之,我是現場表演的狂熱支持者。也許會花費較多,但是絕對值回票價。所以我希望每個人今天都能去參加現場表演!

【托福作文原試題】

> *Do you agree or disagree with the following statement?*
> *Attending a live performance (for example, a play,*
> *concert, or sporting event) is more enjoyable than*
> *watching the same event on television. Use specific*
> *reasons and examples to support your opinion.*

4. A Reliable Friend Is Best!

Welcome one and all.
I'm so happy to be here.
I hope you enjoy my speech.

I'd like to talk about friends.
We have so many kinds of friends.
We should all know what kind of friend is the best.

I say reliable friends are the best.
I value reliability more than anything.
Let me tell you why.

First of all, a reliable friend will always
  be there.
A reliable friend will always stand by you.
He will support you no matter what.

---

reliable (rɪˈlaɪəbḷ)	*one and all*
value (ˈvælju)	reliability (rɪˌlaɪəˈbɪlətɪ)
stand by	support (səˈport)
no matter what	

Reliable friends are very dependable.

They won't run and hide.

They're around when you need them.

They are not "fair-weather" friends.

They are friends for all seasons.

A reliable friend is as good as gold.

Second, a reliable friend will never let you down.

A reliable friend never disappoints you.

He or she is as trustworthy as can be.

Reliable friends keep their promises.

They also keep your secrets.

They share your hopes and dreams.

---

dependable (dɪ'pɛndəbḷ)	fair-weather ('fɛr,wɛðɚ)
as good as	*let sb. down*
disappoint (ˌdɪsə'pɔɪnt)	trustworthy ('trʌst,wɝðɪ)
as…as can be	*keep one's promise*
secret ('sikrɪt)	share (ʃɛr)

Reliable friends are good communicators.

They give sound advice and opinions.

They only have your best interests in mind.

Third, *reliable friends always tell you*
  ***the truth*.**

They will always be honest with you.

They are sincere and straightforward pals.

They are sensitive and understanding.

They are sympathetic and big-hearted.

They are always patient and forgiving.

---

communicator (kə'mjunəˌ ketə)   sound (saʊnd)

advice (əd'vaɪs)   ***have···in mind***

interest ('ɪnt(ə)rɪst)   sincere (sɪn'sɪr)

straightforward (ˌstret'fɔrwəd)   pal (pæl)

sensitive ('sɛnsətɪv)

understanding (ˌʌndə'stændɪŋ)

sympathetic (ˌsɪmpə'θɛtɪk)

big-hearted ('bɪgˌhɑrtɪd)   patient ('peʃənt)

forgiving (fə'gɪvɪŋ)

Reliable friends aren't judgmental.

They accept you no matter what.

They will always give you the benefit of the doubt.

***Finally, reliable friends are forever*.**

Their friendship is everlasting.

Their friendship will endure the test of time.

They are friends for a lifetime.

They won't slowly slip away.

They will remain loyal through the years.

A reliable friend is a lifelong gift.

It's a relationship that won't fade.

It's a trust that will always survive.

---

judgmental (dʒʌdʒˈmɛntḷ)　　benefit (ˈbɛnəfɪt)

give sb. the benefit of the doubt

forever (fəˈɛvə)　　everlasting (ˌɛvəˈlæstɪŋ)

endure (ɪnˈdjur)　　test (tɛst)

lifetime (ˈlaɪfˌtaɪm)　　slip (slɪp)

loyal (ˈlɔɪəl)　　lifelong (ˈlaɪfˌlɔŋ)

relationship (rɪˈleʃənˌʃɪp)　　fade (fed)

survive (səˈvaɪv)

In conclusion, be a reliable friend.

That will ensure that you have one, too.

That is all you need to be happy.

Reliable friends can be anyone of any age.

They can be classmates or neighbors.

They can even be family members.

Choose reliable people to befriend.

Reliable friends make life worth living.

Thank God for reliable friends.

---

in conclusion

befriend (bɪ'frɛnd)

ensure (ɪn'ʃur)

worth (wɝθ)

4. *A Reliable Friend Is Best!*
可靠的朋友最好！

【演講解說】

Welcome one and all.	歡迎大家來到這裡。
I'm so happy to be here.	我非常高興能夠來到這裡。
I hope you enjoy my speech.	我希望你們喜歡我的演講。

I'd like to talk about friends.	我想要談論朋友。
We have so many kinds of friends.	我們有很多不同種類的朋友。
We should all know what kind of friend is the best.	我們全都應該知道怎麼樣的朋友最好。

I say reliable friends are the best.	我說可靠的朋友最好。
I value reliability more than anything.	我重視可靠度，甚於其他。
Let me tell you why.	讓我告訴你爲什麼。

First of all, a reliable friend will always be there.	首先，可靠的朋友永遠都在。
A reliable friend will always stand by you.	可靠的朋友總是支持你。
He will support you no matter what.	不論發生什麼事情，他都會支持你。

** ────────────

reliable〔rɪ'laɪəbḷ〕*adj.* 可靠的　　***one and all*** 全部；大家
value〔'væljʊ〕*v.* 重視　　reliability〔rɪ,laɪə'bɪlətɪ〕*n.* 可靠性
stand by 站在旁邊；支持　　support〔sə'port〕*v.* 支持
no matter what 不論什麼

Reliable friends are very dependable.	可靠的朋友非常值得信賴。
They won't run and hide.	他們不會跑掉躲起來。
They're around when you need them.	在你有需要的時候，他們就在身旁。
They are not "fair-weather" friends.	他們不是「酒肉」朋友。
They are friends for all seasons.	他們一年春夏秋冬都是朋友。
A reliable friend is as good as gold.	可靠的朋友就如同黃金一般。
Second, a reliable friend will never let you down.	第二，可靠的朋友絕對不會讓你失望。
A reliable friend never disappoints you.	可靠的朋友絕對不會使你失望。
He or she is as trustworthy as can be.	他或她是非常值得信賴的。
Reliable friends keep their promises.	可靠的朋友信守承諾。
They also keep your secrets.	他們也替你保守秘密。
They share your hopes and dreams.	他們會分享你的希望和夢想。

** ———————————————————

dependable〔dɪ'pɛndəbḷ〕adj. 可靠的
fair-weather〔'fɛr,wɛðɚ〕adj. 只能同安樂不能共患難的
as good as 和…幾乎一樣　　**let sb. down** 使某人失望
disappoint〔,dɪsə'pɔɪnt〕v. 使失望
trustworthy〔'trʌst,wɝðɪ〕adj. 值得信賴的；可靠的
as…as can be 非常…　　**keep one's promise** 信守承諾
secret〔'sikrɪt〕n. 秘密　　share〔ʃɛr〕v. 分享

Reliable friends are good communicators.	可靠的朋友是擅長溝通的人。
They give sound advice and opinions.	他們能提供明智的忠告和意見。
They only have your best interests in mind.	他們只想到要為你最大的利益著想。
Third, reliable friends always tell you the truth.	第三，可靠的朋友永遠告訴你實話。
They will always be honest with you.	他們會永遠對你誠實。
They are sincere and straightforward pals.	他們是真誠坦率的好朋友。
They are sensitive and understanding.	他們既敏感，又善解人意。
They are sympathetic and big-hearted.	他們富有同情心、而且心胸寬大。
They are always patient and forgiving.	他們總是很有耐心、而且寬宏大量。

** ――――――――――――――――――

communicator〔kə'mjunə,ketə〕n. 溝通者

sound〔saund〕adj. 合理的；明智的　　advice〔əd'vaɪs〕n. 忠告；建議

have…in mind 想到…　　interest〔'ɪnt(ə)rɪst〕n. 利益

sincere〔sɪn'sɪr〕adj. 真誠的

straightforward〔,stret'fɔrwəd〕adj. 坦率的　　pal〔pæl〕n. 好友

sensitive〔'sɛnsətɪv〕adj. 敏感的

understanding〔,ʌndə'stændɪŋ〕adj. 體諒的

sympathetic〔,sɪmpə'θɛtɪk〕adj. 有同情心的

big-hearted〔'bɪg,hɑrtɪd〕adj. 心胸寬大的

patient〔'peʃənt〕adj. 有耐心的　　forgiving〔fə'gɪvɪŋ〕adj. 寬容的

Reliable friends aren't judgmental.	可靠的朋友不會過於主觀。
They accept you no matter what.	不論發生什麼事情，他們都會接受你。
They will always give you the benefit of the doubt.	他們總是會先假定你沒有錯。
***Finally**, **reliable friends are forever**.*	最後，可靠的朋友是永遠的。
Their friendship is everlasting.	他們的友誼是恆久的。
Their friendship will endure the test of time.	他們的友誼經得起時間的考驗。
They are friends for a lifetime.	他們是一輩子的朋友。
They won't slowly slip away.	他們不會逐漸消逝。
They will remain loyal through the years.	他們歷經多年都依然忠誠。
A reliable friend is a lifelong gift.	可靠的朋友是終身的禮物。
It's a relationship that won't fade.	那是永不消失的關係。
It's a trust that will always survive.	那是永遠都會存在的信任。

**

judgmental〔dʒʌdʒˈmɛntḷ〕*adj.* (不一定客觀、帶衝動地) 判定的；過於主觀的
benefit〔ˈbɛnəfɪt〕*n.* 利益；好處
give sb. the benefit of the doubt 假定某人是無辜的
forever〔fɚˈɛvɚ〕*adv.* 永遠　　everlasting〔͵ɛvɚˈlæstɪŋ〕*adj.* 永遠的
endure〔ɪnˈdjʊr〕*v.* 忍耐；忍受　　test〔tɛst〕*n.* 考驗
lifetime〔ˈlaɪf͵taɪm〕*n.* 一生　　slip〔slɪp〕*v.* 溜走＜*away*＞
loyal〔ˈlɔɪəl〕*adj.* 忠誠的　　lifelong〔ˈlaɪf͵lɔŋ〕*adj.* 終身的；一輩子的
relationship〔rɪˈleʃən͵ʃɪp〕*n.* (人際) 關係　　fade〔fed〕*v.* 逐漸消失
survive〔səˈvaɪv〕*v.* 殘留；繼續存在

In conclusion, be a reliable friend.　總之，要做個可靠的朋友。

That will ensure that you have one, too.　那會保證你也會結交到可靠的朋友。

That is all you need to be happy.　那就是你想快樂所需要的東西。

Reliable friends can be anyone of any age.　可靠的朋友可以是各種年齡層的人。

They can be classmates or neighbors.　他們可能是同學或是鄰居。

They can even be family members.　他們甚至可能是家人。

Choose reliable people to befriend.　選擇可靠的人做朋友。

Reliable friends make life worth living.　可靠的朋友讓生命更有價值。

Thank God for reliable friends.　感謝上帝賜給我們可靠的朋友。

**

in conclusion 總之　　ensure〔ɪnˈʃʊr〕v. 保證
befriend〔bɪˈfrɛnd〕v. 和…交朋友
worth〔wɝθ〕*adj.* 值得（做…）的

【托福作文範例】

4. A Reliable Friend Is Best!

Everybody has friends. There are many kinds of friends but how many of these friends are reliable? Reliability is an important trait in a friend and I think reliable friends are the best. Now let me tell you why.

First, a reliable friend will always be there. He will always stand by you and support you no matter what happens. Reliable friends won't run and hide but are around when you need them. *Second*, reliable friends will never let you down because they are trustworthy. Reliable friends keep promises and your secrets. They also give good advice and opinions because they have your best interests in mind. *Third*, reliable friends will always tell you the truth. They will always be honest with you because they are sincere and straightforward. They are sensitive and understanding. They have a big heart and are always patient and forgiving. *Finally*, reliable friends last forever. They are friends for life; they won't slip away with time.

In conclusion, be a reliable friend because that will ensure that you have one, too. Reliable friends can be anybody. They can be classmates or your neighbors; they can even be family members. So start making reliable friends today!

4. 可靠的朋友最好！

　　每個人都有朋友。朋友有各式各樣的類型，但他們之中，有多少人是可靠的呢？可靠性是朋友的一個重要特質，而且我認為可靠的朋友是最好的。現在就讓我告訴你為什麼。

　　第一，可靠的朋友會永遠都在。無論發生什麼事，他總是會陪在你身旁，支持你。當你需要他們的時候，可靠的朋友會留在你身邊，不會逃跑和躲藏。第二，可靠的朋友絕對不會讓你失望，因為他們是值得信任的。可靠的朋友會信守諾言，並且保守秘密。他們也能夠提供明智的建議及看法，因為他們總是為你的最大利益著想。第三，可靠的朋友總是會跟你說實話。他們永遠對你誠實，因為他們既誠懇又坦率。他們很敏銳而且善解人意。他們擁有寬大的心胸，而且總是有耐心又寬容。最後一點，可靠的朋友是會永遠存在的。他們是一輩子的朋友；他們不會隨著時間而消失。

　　總之，要做個可靠的朋友，因為這樣也能保證你也交到這種朋友。可靠的朋友可以是任何人。他們可以是同班同學或是你的鄰居；他們甚至可以是你家庭中的成員。所以今天就開始結交可靠的朋友吧！

【托福作文原試題】

*What do you want **most** in a friend — someone who is intelligent, or someone who has a sense of humor, or someone who is reliable?　Which **one** of these characteristics is most important to you?　Use reasons and specific examples to explain your choice.*

5. *Classmates Are the Biggest Influence*

Ladies and gentlemen:
Dear students of all ages.
Welcome here today.

I'd like to talk about classmates.

Classmates influence us a lot.

Classmates are an even bigger influence than
   our parents.

They affect our attitude and behavior.

They affect our performance and future success.

Here's why our classmates are so influential.

First of all, classmates are our peer group.

Classmates are the social group we belong to.
We crave and desire their acceptance.

---

influence ('ɪnfluəns)
attitude ('ætə,tjud)
performance (pə'fɔrməns)
peer (pɪr)
belong to
desire (dɪ'zaɪr)

affect (ə'fɛkt)
behavior (bɪ'hevjə)
influential (,ɪnflu'ɛnʃəl)
social ('soʃəl)
crave (krev)
acceptance (ək'sɛptəns)

We rely and depend on them.

We want their respect and approval.

They can make us feel safe and secure.

We try hard to be like our classmates.

We try to conform and fit in.

It is essential for us to get along with them.

Second, we spend most of our time with classmates.

We're with classmates all day long.

We're with classmates much more than with our
families.

Classmates are like our family away from home.

Classmates help shape our self-image and
self-worth.

Our relationships with classmates are so important.

---

rely on	*depend on*
approval (ə'pruvḷ)	secure (sɪ'kjur)
conform (kən'fɔrm)	*fit in*
essential (ə'sɛnʃəl)	*get along with*
all day long	shape (ʃep)
self-image ('sɛlf'ɪmɪdʒ)	self-worth ('sɛlf'wɝθ)
relationship (rɪ'leʃən,ʃɪp)	

We learn a lot from classmates.

We interact and exchange ideas.

Our viewpoints often mesh.

Third, *we communicate more easily with*

** *classmates*.**

We relate to them very well.

We seem to trust them more than anyone.

We feel comfortable with classmates.

We have no big age difference with them.

Unlike with our parents, there is no generation gap.

We learn and grow together.

We share opinions and perspectives.

Our knowledge and experiences are shaped by

  each other.

---

interact (ˌɪntɚˈækt) exchange (ɪksˈtʃendʒ)

viewpoint (ˈvjuˌpɔɪnt) mesh (mɛʃ)

communicate (kəˈmjunəˌket) relate (rɪˈlet)

generation (ˌdʒɛnəˈreʃən) gap (gæp)

generation gap

perspective (pɚˈspɛktɪv)

**Fourth, classmates certainly affect
our success.**
They help set the standards we aspire to.
They influence our future hopes and dreams.

Classmates can reinforce our good behavior.
Classmates can support and motivate us.
Their influence on our lives is great.

Classmates can improve us in many ways.
Classmates can make us work harder.
They can also weaken us with bad habits.

---

set (sɛt)   standard ('stændɚd)
aspire (ə'spaɪr)   reinforce (,riɪn'fɔrs)
support (sə'port)   motivate ('motə,vet)
improve (ɪm'pruv)   weaken ('wikən)

In conclusion, classmates are our number one

  influence.

They help form our character.

They help determine our future success.

Classmates are role models.

Classmates are advisors and confidants.

They are closer to us than anybody.

You can't choose your classmates.

You can, however, select the ones you hang

  out with.

Pick the ones who are honest, kind, diligent

  and true.

---

in conclusion

form (fɔrm)

determine (dɪ'tɜmɪn)

advisor (əd'vaɪzə)

confidant ('kɑnfə,dænt , ,kɑnfə'dænt)

close (klos)

hang out with sb.

honest ('ɑnɪst)

true (tru)

number one

character ('kærɪktə)

role model

select (sə'lɛkt)

pick (pɪk)

diligent ('dɪlədʒənt)

5. *Classmates Are the Biggest Influence*
同班同學具有最大的影響力

【演講解說】

Ladies and gentlemen:	各位先生，各位女士：
Dear students of all ages.	各個年齡層親愛的同學們：
Welcome here today.	歡迎你們今天來到這裡。
I'd like to talk about classmates.	我想要討論同班同學。
Classmates influence us a lot.	同班同學影響我們很多。
Classmates are an even bigger influence than our parents.	同班同學的影響力甚至比父母還來得大。
They affect our attitude and behavior.	他們影響我們的態度和行為。
They affect our performance and future success.	他們影響我們的表現和未來的成功。
Here's why our classmates are so influential.	以下就是為什麼我們的同班同學會這麼有影響力的原因。

**

influence (ˋɪnfluəns) *n.* 有影響力的人；影響（力） *v.* 影響
affect (əˋfɛkt) *v.* 影響　　attitude (ˋætə,tjud) *n.* 態度
behavior (bɪˋhevjɚ) *n.* 行為　　performance (pɚˋfɔrməns) *n.* 表現
influential (,ɪnfluˋɛnʃəl) *adj.* 有影響力的

First of all**, **classmates are our
***peer group**.*　　　　　　　　　首先，同班同學是我們的同儕。

Classmates are the social group
　　we belong to.　　　　　　　同班同學是我們所屬的社會團體。

We crave and desire their
　　acceptance.　　　　　　　　我們渴望獲得他們的認同。

We rely and depend on them.　　我們依賴他們。

We want their respect and
　　approval.　　　　　　　　　我們想要得到他們的尊敬和贊同。

They can make us feel safe and
　　secure.　　　　　　　　　　他們可以讓我們有安全感，而且安
　　　　　　　　　　　　　　　心。

We try hard to be like our
　　classmates.　　　　　　　　我們努力要和我們的同班同學一
　　　　　　　　　　　　　　　樣。

We try to conform and fit in.　　我們努力要適應、和他們一致。

It is essential for us to get along
　　with them.　　　　　　　　和他們和睦相處，對我們而言是
　　　　　　　　　　　　　　　很重要的。

**

peer〔pɪr〕n. 同儕　　social〔'soʃəl〕adj. 社會的

belong to 屬於；是…的成員　　crave〔krev〕v. 渴望（= *desire*）

acceptance〔ək'sɛptəns〕n. 接受　　***rely on*** 依賴（= *depend on*）

approval〔ə'pruvl̩〕n. 贊成；肯定

secure〔sɪ'kjur〕adj. 安全的；安心的；無憂無慮的

conform〔kən'fɔrm〕v. 與…一致；適應　　***fit in*** 與…一致

essential〔ə'sɛnʃəl〕adj. 必要的　　***get along with*** 與…和睦相處

Second, we spend most of our time with classmates.

We're with classmates all day long.

We're with classmates much more than with our families.

Classmates are like our family away from home.

Classmates help shape our self-image and self-worth.

Our relationships with classmates are so important.

We learn a lot from classmates.

We interact and exchange ideas.

Our viewpoints often mesh.

Third, we communicate more easily with classmates.

We relate to them very well.

We seem to trust them more than anyone.

第二，我們和同班同學共度大部分的時間。

我們整天和同班同學在一起。

我們和同班同學在一起的時間，比和家人在一起的時間還多。

同班同學就像是我們在外的家人。

同班同學有助於塑造我們的自我形象和自我價值。

我們和同班同學的關係是非常重要的。

我們從同班同學身上學到很多。

我們產生互動，並且交換想法。

我們的觀點往往不謀而合。

第三，我們和同班同學比較容易溝通。

我們和他們處得非常好。

我們似乎最信任他們。

**

all day long 一整天 (= *all day*)

shape (ʃep) *v.* 使成形；塑造   self-image ('sɛlf'ɪmɪdʒ) *n.* 自我形象

self-worth ('sɛlf'wɜθ) *n.* 自尊 (心) (= *self-esteem*)

relationship (rɪ'leʃən,ʃɪp) *n.* (人際) 關係   interact (,ɪntə'ækt) *v.* 互動

exchange (ɪks'tʃendʒ) *v.* 交換   viewpoint ('vju,pɔɪnt) *n.* 觀點

mesh (mɛʃ) *v.* (想法等) 完全相合

communicate (kə'mjunə,ket) *v.* 溝通   relate (rɪ'let) *v.* 相處 < *to* >

We feel comfortable with classmates.	我們和同班同學在一起，覺得很舒服。
We have no big age difference with them.	我們和他們沒有很大的年齡差距。
Unlike with our parents, there is no generation gap.	那和與父母相處不一樣，沒有代溝問題。
We learn and grow together.	我們一起學習和成長。
We share opinions and perspectives.	我們分享意見和看法。
Our knowledge and experiences are shaped by each other.	我們彼此建構知識和經驗。

***Fourth**, **classmates certainly affect our success**.*	第四，同班同學一定會影響我們成功與否。
They help set the standards we aspire to.	他們有助於設定我們渴望追求的標準。
They influence our future hopes and dreams.	他們影響我們未來的希望和夢想。
Classmates can reinforce our good behavior.	同班同學能夠強化我們良好的行為。
Classmates can support and motivate us.	同班同學能夠支持和激勵我們。
Their influence on our lives is great.	他們對我們的人生造成的影響非常大。

**

generation〔͵dʒɛnə'reʃən〕*n.* 世代　　gap〔gæp〕*n.* 隔閡；差距
generation gap 代溝　　perspective〔pə'spɛktɪv〕*n.* 看法
set〔sɛt〕*v.* 設定　　standard〔'stændəd〕*n.* 標準
aspire〔ə'spaɪr〕*v.* 渴望　　reinforce〔͵riɪn'fɔrs〕*v.* 強化
support〔sə'port〕*v.* 支持　　motivate〔'motə͵vet〕*v.* 激勵

Classmates can improve us in many ways.	同班同學使我們在許多方面獲得改善。
Classmates can make us work harder.	同班同學可以讓我們更努力。
They can also weaken us with bad habits.	他們可能也會用壞習慣使我們變得軟弱。
***In conclusion*, *classmates are our number one influence*.**	總之,同班同學是對我們最具影響力的人。
They help form our character.	他們有助於塑造我們的性格。
They help determine our future success.	他們有助於決定我們未來的成就。
Classmates are role models.	同班同學是榜樣。
Classmates are advisors and confidants.	同班同學是提供意見的人,也是知己。
They are closer to us than anybody.	他們和我們最親近。
You can't choose your classmates.	你無法選擇同班同學。
You can, however, select the ones you hang out with.	然而你可以選擇和你在一起的同班同學。
Pick the ones who are honest, kind, diligent and true.	要選擇誠實、親切、勤奮,和忠實的同班同學。

**　　　——————————

improve〔ɪmˋpruv〕v. 改善　　weaken〔ˋwikən〕v. 使變弱
number one 第一的　　form〔fɔrm〕v. 形成
character〔ˋkærɪktə〕n. 性格　　determine〔dɪˋtɜmɪn〕v. 決定
role model 榜樣;模範　　advisor〔ədˋvaɪzə〕n. 提供意見者;顧問
confidant〔ˋkɑnfə͵dænt,͵kɑnfəˋdænt〕n. 知己;密友
select〔səˋlɛkt〕v. 選擇　　***hang out with sb.*** 和某人在一起
pick〔pɪk〕v. 選擇　　honest〔ˋɑnɪst〕adj. 誠實的
diligent〔ˋdɪlədʒənt〕adj. 勤奮的　　true〔tru〕adj. 忠實的;忠誠的

【托福作文範例】

5. Classmates Are the Biggest Influence

There are influences everywhere; influences from our parents to our friends to television. But the biggest influence of all is our classmates. They affect our attitude and behavior and here's why.

First, classmates are our peer group. They are the social group we belong to, so we crave their acceptance. We rely and depend on them because they can make us feel safe and secure. *Second*, we spend most of our time with classmates. We are with them more than our families so that's why our relationships with classmates are so important. *Third*, we communicate more easily with classmates because we relate to them very well. We feel comfortable around them; unlike our parents, there is no generation gap. *Fourth*, classmates affect our success. Classmates can reinforce our good behavior through support and motivation. They can improve us in many ways.

In conclusion, classmates are our number one influence. They help form our character and determine our future success. Classmates are advisors and confidants. So pick the right ones who are honest, kind, diligent and true.

5. 同班同學具有最大的影響力

　　到處都充滿了能影響我們的人或事物；從我們的父母、朋友到電視，都對我們具有影響力。但其中最大的影響力，莫過於我們的同班同學。他們影響了我們的態度和行為，而以下就是原因。

　　第一，同班同學是我們的同儕團體。他們是我們所屬的社會團體，所以我們渴望得到他們的認同。我們非常依賴他們，因為他們可以讓我們有安全感，而且安心。第二，我們大部分的時間是和同班同學一起渡過的。我們和他們在一起相處的時間，比和家人還多，這就是為什麼我們和同班同學的關係會如此重要。第三，我們和同班同學比較容易溝通，因為我們和他們處得非常好。我們在同班同學身邊會覺得自在，不像是和我們的父母相處，完全沒有代溝的問題。第四，同班同學影響了我們的成功。同班同學可以透過支持及激勵，強化我們的良好行為。他們使我們在許多方面獲得改善。

　　總之，同班同學對我們的影響力最大。他們有助於我們人格的形成，以及決定我們未來的成就。同班同學是提供忠告的人，也是我們的知己。所以挑選正確的人做朋友，找誠實、親切、勤奮而且忠實的人。

【托福作文原試題】

Do you agree or disagree with the following statement? Classmates are a more important influence than parents on a child's success in school. Use specific reasons and examples to support your answer.

6. I'd Like to Study World Religions

Welcome dear listeners.
Thank you for being here.
I hope you enjoy this talk.

My topic today is world religions.
It's a fascinating area of study.
It's very useful and important to know.

Religion is a neglected area of knowledge.
Religion is seldom taught in many schools.
Here are some advantages of studying world
  religions.

First, you'll learn more about history.
Studying world religions helps explain history.
Studying religions really helps explain the past.

---

listener ('lɪsn̩ə)   talk (tɔk)
religion (rɪ'lɪdʒən)   fascinating ('fæsn̩,etɪŋ)
area ('ɛrɪə)   neglected (nɪ'glɛktɪd)
advantage (əd'væntɪdʒ)   explain (ɪk'splen)

Many historical events have religious origins.
Many historical leaders were influenced by religion.
Religion and history are very interrelated.

Studying religions also teaches us about other
  cultures.
Religion is a reflection of other cultures.
Religions reveal customs, values and traditions.

Second, you'll learn more about human nature.
You'll learn about human motivations.
Studying religions is like sociology
  and psychology put together.

It tells us what people live for.
It tells us what people die for.
It explains what people believe about life.

---

religious (rɪˈlɪdʒəs)　　　　origin (ˈɔrədʒɪn)
leader (ˈlidɚ)　　　　　　　influence (ˈɪnfluəns)
interrelated (ˌɪntɚrɪˈletɪd)　　culture (ˈkʌltʃɚ)
reflection (rɪˈflɛkʃən)　　　　reveal (rɪˈvil)
values (ˈvæljuz)　　　　　　*human nature*
motivation (ˌmotəˈveʃən)　　sociology (ˌsoʃɪˈalədʒɪ)
psychology (saɪˈkalədʒɪ)　　*put together*

We can learn many interesting beliefs.
We can evaluate and compare them together.
Studying religions is an opportunity to explore
great mysteries.

***Third, it can help us understand current world
affairs.***
It helps explain what's happening today.
It gives insight and background into why people
can't get along.

Many conflicts are caused by religious
disagreements.
Many international problems have religion
as the cause.
It's a shame that religion is misinterpreted.

---

belief (bə'lif)
compare (kəm'pɛr)
mystery ('mɪstrɪ)
affairs (ə'fɛrz)
background ('bæk,graund)
conflict ('kɑnflɪkt)
disagreement (,dɪsə'grimənt)
international (,ɪntɚ'næʃənl̩)
misinterpret (,mɪsɪn'tɝprɪt)

evaluate (ɪ'vælju,et)
explore (ɪk'splor)
current ('kɝənt)
insight ('ɪn,saɪt)
get along
cause (kɔz)

shame (ʃem)

Religion often motivates political actions.
Many world leaders are influenced by religion.
Many governments act according to religious
  beliefs.

**Finally, studying religions could help promote
world peace.**
It could lead to better communication among
  people.
It could lead to less conflict and strife.

Religion teaches us more tolerance and respect.
Religion teaches us peaceful coexistence.
Studying religions has many benefits.

---

motivate ('motə,vet)	political (pə'lıtıkḷ)
action ('ækʃən)	act (ækt)
according to	promote (prə'mot)
peace (pis)	*lead to*
communication (kə,mjunə'keʃən)	strife (straıf)
tolerance ('talərəns)	peaceful ('pisfəl)
coexistence (,koıg'zıstəns)	benefit ('bɛnəfıt)

Every student should study world religions.

Every school should include it in its curriculum.

We could learn a lot from the wisdom and morals
 of religion.

In conclusion, world religion deserves careful study.

It is such an important part of human society.

It is too important to be neglected.

The world we live in is changing fast.

The bad news seems to get worse every day.

It's time for everyone to learn from religion.

We must learn about truth and respect.

We must all learn to solve problems together.

Studying world religions would be one step
 in the right direction.

---

curriculum (kə'rɪkjələm)

morals ('mɔrəlz)

deserve (dɪ'zɜv)

solve (sɑlv)

direction (də'rɛkʃən)

wisdom ('wɪzdəm)

in conclusion

too…to V.

step (stɛp)

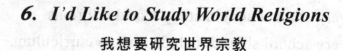

6. I'd Like to Study World Religions
我想要研究世界宗教

【演講解說】

Welcome dear listeners. 　歡迎各位親愛的聽眾。
Thank you for being here. 　謝謝你們來到這裡。
I hope you enjoy this talk. 　我希望你們喜歡這次的演講。

My topic today is world religions. 　我今天的主題是世界宗教。
It's a fascinating area of study. 　那是個迷人的研究領域。
It's very useful and important to know. 　非常有用，而且十分重要。

Religion is a neglected area of
knowledge. 　宗教是被忽略的知識領域。
Religion is seldom taught in many
schools. 　宗教在很多學校很少被教到。
Here are some advantages of studying
world religions. 　以下是研讀世界宗教的一些好處。

**First, you'll learn more about
history.** 　首先，你將學到更多關於歷史的事情。
Studying world religions helps
explain history. 　研究世界宗教有助於解讀歷史。
Studying religions really helps explain
the past. 　研究宗教真的有助於解讀過去。

**　——————————————

listener (ˈlɪsnɚ) n. 聽眾　　talk (tɔk) n. 演講
religion (rɪˈlɪdʒən) n. 宗教　　fascinating (ˈfæsn̩ˌetɪŋ) adj. 迷人的
area (ˈɛrɪə) n. 領域　　neglected (nɪˈglɛktɪd) adj. 被忽視的
advantage (ədˈvæntɪdʒ) n. 好處　　explain (ɪkˈsplen) v. 解釋

Many historical events have religious origins. | 許多歷史事件的起源和宗教有關。

Many historical leaders were influenced by religion. | 許多歷史上的領導者都受到宗教的影響。

Religion and history are very interrelated. | 宗教和歷史習習相關。

Studying religions also teaches us about other cultures. | 研究宗教也教導我們認識其他文化。

Religion is a reflection of other cultures. | 宗教是其他文化的反映。

Religions reveal customs, values and traditions. | 宗教展現了習俗、價值觀和傳統。

Second, you'll learn more about human nature. | 第二，你將會更加認識人性。

You'll learn about human motivations. | 你將知道人類動機爲何。

Studying religions is like sociology and psychology put together. | 研究宗教就像是把社會學和心理學結合在一起。

It tells us what people live for. | 宗教讓我們知道人類爲何而活。

It tells us what people die for. | 宗教告訴我們人類爲何而死。

It explains what people believe about life. | 它可以解釋人們對人生的看法。

**

religious〔rɪˋlɪdʒəs〕adj. 宗教的　　origin〔ˋɔrədʒɪn〕n. 起源
leader〔ˋlidɚ〕n. 領袖　　influence〔ˋɪnfluəns〕v. 影響
interrelated〔ͺɪntərɪˋletɪd〕adj. 互相關聯的　　culture〔ˋkʌltʃɚ〕n. 文化
reflection〔rɪˋflɛkʃən〕n. 反映　　reveal〔rɪˋvil〕v. 顯示
values〔ˋvæljuz〕n. pl. 價值觀　　***human nature*** 人性
motivation〔ͺmotəˋveʃən〕n. 動機　　sociology〔ͺsoʃɪˋalədʒɪ〕n. 社會學
psychology〔saɪˋkalədʒɪ〕n. 心理學　　***put together*** 把…放在一起；組合

We can learn many interesting beliefs.

We can evaluate and compare them together.

Studying religions is an opportunity to explore great mysteries.

我們可以學到很多有趣的信仰。

我們可以把它們加以評估和比較。

研究宗教是探索偉大神秘事物的機會。

Third, it can help us understand current world affairs.

第三，它可以有助於我們了解當今的世界局勢。

It helps explain what's happening today.

It gives insight and background into why people can't get along.

它有助於解釋現今所發生的事情。

它提供洞察力和背景知識，使我們了解人類為何無法和睦相處。

Many conflicts are caused by religious disagreements.

Many international problems have religion as the cause.

It's a shame that religion is misinterpreted.

許多衝突是因為宗教上的不合所引發的。

許多國際問題起因於宗教。

宗教遭受誤解是件可惜的事。

**

belief〔bə'lif〕n. 信仰　　evaluate〔ɪ'vælju,et〕v. 評估

compare〔kəm'pɛr〕v. 比較　　explore〔ɪk'splor〕v. 探索

mystery〔'mɪstrɪ〕n. 神祕的事物；奧秘　　current〔'kɝənt〕adj. 目前的

affairs〔ə'fɛrz〕n. pl. 事務　　insight〔'ɪn,saɪt〕n. 洞察力 < into >

background〔'bæk,graʊnd〕n. 背景　　***get along*** 和睦相處

conflict〔'kɑnflɪkt〕n. 衝突　　cause〔kɔz〕v. 引起　n. 原因

disagreement〔,dɪsə'grimənt〕n. 不一致；意見不合

international〔,ɪntɚ'næʃənḷ〕adj. 國際的　　shame〔ʃem〕n. 可惜的事

misinterpret〔,mɪsɪn'tɝprɪt〕v. 誤解

Religion often motivates political actions.	宗教通常是政治活動的動機所在。
Many world leaders are influenced by religion.	許多世界上的領導者都受到宗教的影響。
Many governments act according to religious beliefs.	許多政府會根據宗教信仰來行事。
Finally, *studying religions could help promote world peace*.	最後，唸宗教可以有助於促進世界和平。
It could lead to better communication among people.	可以使人們進行更良好的溝通。
It could lead to less conflict and strife.	它可以減少衝突和紛爭。
Religion teaches us more tolerance and respect.	宗教教導我們要更加寬容和尊重。
Religion teaches us peaceful coexistence.	宗教教導我們要和平共存。
Studying religions has many benefits.	研究宗教有許多好處。

**

motivate (ˈmotəˌvet) v. 給…動機；激勵

political (pəˈlɪtɪkl̩) adj. 政治的　　action (ˈækʃən) n. 行動；活動

act (ækt) v. 行動；做事　　*according to* 根據

promote (prəˈmot) v. 促進　　peace (pis) n. 和平

lead to 導致　　communication (kəˌmjunəˈkeʃən) n. 溝通

strife (straɪf) n. 衝突　　tolerance (ˈtɑlərəns) n. 寬容

peaceful (ˈpisfəl) adj. 和平的　　coexistence (ˈkoɪgˈzɪstəns) n. 共存

benefit (ˈbɛnəfɪt) n. 好處

Every student should study world religions.	每個學生都應該研讀世界宗教。
Every school should include it in its curriculum.	每個學校都應該將它納入課程。
We could learn a lot from the wisdom and morals of religion.	我們可以從宗教的智慧和行為準則學到許多。
In conclusion, world religion deserves careful study.	總之，世界宗教值得好好研究。
It is such an important part of human society.	它是人類社會中重要的一部份。
It is too important to be neglected.	它太重要了，不能忽略。
The world we live in is changing fast.	我們所生存的世界變動快速。
The bad news seems to get worse every day.	壞消息似乎每天越來越嚴重。
It's time for everyone to learn from religion.	該是每個人從宗教中學習的時候了。
We must learn about truth and respect.	我們必須知道真理和尊重。
We must all learn to solve problems together.	我們全都必須學習共同解決問題。
Studying world religions would be one step in the right direction.	研究世界宗教就是朝正確的方向向前邁進了一步。

** ———————————————

curriculum (kə'rɪkjələm) *n.* 課程　　wisdom ('wɪzdəm) *n.* 智慧
morals ('mɔrəlz) *n. pl.* 道德觀；行為準則　　***in conclusion*** 總之
deserve (dɪ'zɝv) *v.* 應得　　***too…to V.*** 太⋯以致於不~
solve (salv) *v.* 解決　　step (stɛp) *n.* (接近目標的) 一步
direction (də'rɛkʃən) *n.* 方向

【托福作文範例】

6. I'd Like to Study World Religions

There are many religions in the world. Most people believe in one form of religion or another so it is very important and useful to know about religion. Religion is a neglected area of knowledge so here are some advantages of studying world religions.

First, you'll learn more about history. Studying world religions helps explain history because many historical events have religious origins. Religion is also a reflection of other cultures because it reveals customs, values and traditions. *Second*, you'll learn more about human nature. Religion tells us what people live and die for. It explains what people believe about life. We can learn many interesting beliefs and compare them. *Third*, religion can help us understand current world affairs. It gives insight and background into why people can't get along. Many conflicts are caused by religious disagreements. Religion often motivates political actions because many world leaders are influenced by religion. *Finally*, studying religions could help promote world peace by leading to better communication among people. Religion teaches us more tolerance and respect.

In conclusion, studying world religions is very important to human society. We must learn about truth and respect and how to solve problems together.

6. 我想要研究世界宗教

世界上有很多宗教。大多數的人會信仰某種宗教,所以認識宗教是非常重要而且有用的。宗教是被忽略的一個知識領域,所以以下就是學習世界宗教的好處。

第一,你將學習到更多和歷史有關的事情。學習世界宗教會幫助你解讀歷史,因為很多歷史事件都起因於宗教。宗教同時也能反映其他的文化,因為它能顯示各種不同的習俗、價值觀及傳統。第二,你會對人性更加瞭解。宗教告訴我們人類為了什麼而活,又為了什麼而死。宗教解釋了人們對人生的看法。我們可以得知許多有趣的信仰,並且加以比較。第三,宗教可以幫助我們了解現今的世界局勢。它使我們具備洞察力及背景知識,因而了解人們為何無法和平相處。許多的衝突都起因於在宗教上的意見不合。宗教常常引發政治活動,因為許多世界領袖都深受宗教的影響。最後一點,研讀宗教可以使人與人之間有更良好的溝通,並藉此促進世界和平。宗教教導我們要更寬容與尊重。

總之,研讀世界宗教對人類社會是非常重要的。我們一定要知道真理和尊重,以及如何共同解決問題。

【托福作文原試題】

If you could study a subject that you have never had the opportunity to study, what would you choose? Explain your choice, using specific reasons and details.

7. *Be Your Own Boss*

Good day, everybody.
I appreciate your being here.
I'd like to share a dream with you.

I want to be my own boss!
I want to control my own destiny.
I plan to be self-employed.

The advantages are many.
The benefits are great.
Here's why you should be your own boss.

First, you can make your own decisions.
You get to call the shots.
Everything depends on you.

---

good day	appreciate (ə'priʃɪˌet)
destiny ('dɛstənɪ)	self-employed (ˌsɛlfɪm'plɔɪd)
advantage (əd'væntɪdʒ)	benefit ('bɛnəfɪt)
get to V.	shot (ʃɑt)
call the shots	*depend on*

There is no miscommunication.

There is no waiting for slowpokes.

You are not constrained by others.

The foul-ups are fewer.

The chain of command is clear.

You have no one to blame but yourself.

Second, the rewards are greater.

The opportunities are more numerous!

The risks and challenges are more intense.

You reap what you sow.

You get what you deserve.

You are responsible for whatever happens.

---

miscommunication ﹝ˌmɪskəˌmjunə'keʃən﹞

slowpoke ﹝'slo͵pok﹞　　　　constrain ﹝ kən'stren ﹞

foul-up ﹝'faul͵ʌp ﹞　　　　chain ﹝ tʃen ﹞

command ﹝ kə'mænd ﹞　　　blame ﹝ blem ﹞

reward ﹝ rɪ'wɔrd ﹞　　　　numerous ﹝'njumərəs ﹞

risk ﹝ rɪsk ﹞　　　　　　challenge ﹝'tʃælɪndʒ ﹞

intense ﹝ ɪn'tɛns ﹞　　　　reap ﹝ rip ﹞

sow ﹝ so ﹞　　　　　　　responsible ﹝ rɪ'spansəbḷ ﹞

deserve ﹝ dɪ'zɝv ﹞

The feeling of achievement is stronger.

The feeling of satisfaction is sweet.

The perks and salary can't be beat.

Third, self-employment is more flexible.

You can set your own working hours.

You determine daily output and objectives.

You can work overtime.

You can take a day off.

The self-employed are totally free.

---

achievement (ə'tʃivmənt)

satisfaction (ˌsætɪs'fækʃən)　sweet (swit)

perks (pɜks)　salary ('sælərɪ)

beat (bit)

self-employment (ˌsɛlfɪm'plɔɪmənt)

flexible ('flɛksəbl̩)　set (sɛt)

hours (aʊrz)　determine (dɪ'tɜmɪn)

output ('aʊtˌpʊt)　objective (əb'dʒɛktɪv)

overtime ('ovəˌtaɪm)　_take ~ off_

the self-employed　totally ('totl̩ɪ)

The self-employed have more options.

They can experiment and try new things.

They can adjust and make corrections right away.

Fourth, *self-employment develops leadership*.

You learn how to make decisions.

You gain competence and knowledge fast.

You develop confidence and courage.

Being a boss requires dedication and hard work.

Being a boss is being a leader.

You call the shots.

You run the show.

You get to control everything.

---

option (ˈɑpʃən)

experiment (ɪkˈspɛrəmənt)　　　adjust (əˈdʒʌst)

correction (kəˈrɛkʃən)　　　*right away*

develop (dɪˈvɛləp)

leadership (ˈlidəˌʃɪp)　　　gain (gen)

competence (ˈkɑmpətəns)

confidence (ˈkɑnfədəns)　　　require (rɪˈkwaɪr)

dedication (ˌdɛdəˈkeʃən)　　　leader (ˈlidə)

show (ʃo)　　　*run the show*

In conclusion, be your own boss!

Be in control of your life.

Being self-employed is the best way to go.

You only live once.

Try to follow your dreams!

Try to rely on yourself!

You'll be the king of your castle.

You'll have autonomy and freedom.

You'll have an exciting life for sure!

---

in conclusion

follow ('falo)

castle ('kæsl)

freedom ('fridəm)

for sure

in control of

rely on

autonomy (ɔ'tɑnəmɪ)

exciting (ɪk'saɪtɪŋ)

7. *Be Your Own Boss*
自己做老闆

【演講解說】

Good day, everybody.	大家好。
I appreciate your being here.	我很感謝你們來到這裡。
I'd like to share a dream with you.	我想和你們分享一個夢想。

I want to be my own boss!	我想要自己做老闆！
I want to control my own destiny.	我想要掌握自己的命運。
I plan to be self-employed.	我打算從事自由業。

The advantages are many.	好處很多。
The benefits are great.	優點很棒。
Here's why you should be your own boss.	以下就是為什麼你應該自己當老闆的原因。

First, you can make your own decisions.	第一，你可以自己做決定。
You get to call the shots.	你可以發號施令。
Everything depends on you.	每件事情都仰賴你自己做決定。

** ─────────────

good day 日安；您好（白天見面或告別時的招呼語）
appreciate〔əˈpriʃɪˌet〕v. 感激
self-employed〔ˌsɛlfɪmˈplɔɪd〕adj. 自僱的；自由業的（如作家等，不受雇於別人的）
advantage〔ədˈvæntɪdʒ〕n. 好處（= benefit〔ˈbɛnəfɪt〕）
get to V. 得以～；能夠～   shot〔ʃɑt〕n. 射擊
call the shots 發號施令；控制局面（源自「下令射擊」之義）
depend on 依靠

There is no miscommunication. | 沒有溝通不良的問題。
There is no waiting for slowpokes. | 不用等動作慢吞吞的人。
You are not constrained by others. | 你不用受到別人的限制。

The foul-ups are fewer. | 亂七八糟的狀況會比較少。
The chain of command is clear. | 命令傳遞的過程很清楚。
You have no one to blame but yourself. | 除了自己之外，你沒有人可以責怪。

***Second**, **the rewards are greater**.* | 第二，報酬會比較多。
The opportunities are more numerous! | 機會也會更多！
The risks and challenges are more intense. | 承擔的風險和面臨的挑戰更高。

You reap what you sow. | 種瓜得瓜，種豆得豆。
You get what you deserve. | 你得到你應得的東西。
You are responsible for whatever happens. | 不論發生什麼事，你都要負起責任。

**

miscommunication〔͵mɪskə͵mjunəˋkeʃən〕*n.* 溝通不良
slowpoke〔ˋslo͵pok〕*n.* 動作特別慢的人
constrain〔kənˋstren〕*v.* 限制；束縛
foul-up〔ˋfaul͵ʌp〕*n.*（由於疏忽、笨拙所造成的）混亂
chain〔tʃen〕*n.* 一連串；連續＜*of*＞　command〔kəˋmænd〕*n.* 命令
blame〔blem〕*v.* 責備　reward〔rɪˋwɔrd〕*n.* 報酬
numerous〔ˋnjumərəs〕*adj.* 許多的　risk〔rɪsk〕*n.* 風險
challenge〔ˋtʃælɪndʒ〕*n.* 挑戰　intense〔ɪnˋtɛns〕*adj.* 強烈的
reap〔rip〕*v.* 收割；收穫　sow〔so〕*v.* 播（種）
You reap what you sow.【諺】種瓜得瓜，種豆得豆。
deserve〔dɪˋzɝv〕*v.* 應得　responsible〔rɪˋspɑnsəbḷ〕*adj.* 應負責的

The feeling of achievement is stronger.

成就感會更強烈。

The feeling of satisfaction is sweet.

滿足感會更窩心。

The perks and salary can't be beat.

額外補貼和薪水是最高的。

Third, self-employment is more flexible.

第三，自由業比較有彈性。

You can set your own working hours.

你可以自己設定工作時間。

You determine daily output and objectives.

你決定每天的產量和目標。

You can work overtime.

你可以加班。

You can take a day off.

你可以放假一天。

The self-employed are totally free.

自己開業的人完全是自由的。

**

achievement〔ə'tʃivmənt〕*n.* 成就

satisfaction〔,sætɪs'fækʃən〕*n.* 滿意；滿足

sweet〔swit〕*adj.* 甜美的；愉快的　　perks〔pɝks〕*n. pl.* 額外補貼

salary〔'sælərɪ〕*n.* 薪水　　beat〔bit〕*v.* 打敗；勝過

self-employment〔,sɛlfɪm'plɔɪmənt〕*n.* 自由業

flexible〔'flɛksəbl̩〕*adj.* 有彈性的　　set〔sɛt〕*v.* 設定

hours〔aʊrz〕*n. pl.* 上班時間　　determine〔dɪ'tɝmɪn〕*v.* 決定

output〔'aʊt,pʊt〕*n.* 產量　　objective〔əb'dʒɛktɪv〕*n.* 目標

overtime〔'ovɚ,taɪm〕*adv.* 加班地　　***take~off*** 休假~

the self-employed 自由業者（集合稱，當複數用）（= *self-employed people*）

totally〔'totl̩ɪ〕*adv.* 完全

The self-employed have more options. | 從事自由業的人有更多選擇。

They can experiment and try new things. | 他們可以試驗和嘗試新事物。

They can adjust and make corrections right away. | 他們可以立刻調整和修正。

Fourth, *self-employment develops leadership*. | 第四，從事自由業可以培養領導能力。

You learn how to make decisions. | 你學會如何做決定。

You gain competence and knowledge fast. | 你很快就能獲得能力和知識。

You develop confidence and courage. | 你會培養自信和勇氣。

Being a boss requires dedication and hard work. | 當老闆需要投入和努力。

Being a boss is being a leader. | 當老闆就是要做個領導者。

You call the shots. | 你發號施令。

You run the show. | 你管理事務。

You get to control everything. | 你可以控制每件事情。

**

option ('ɑpʃən) *n.* 選擇　　experiment (ɪk'spɛrəmənt) *v.* 試驗
adjust (ə'dʒʌst) *v.* 調整；適應　　correction (kə'rɛkʃən) *n.* 修正
right away 馬上　　develop (dɪ'vɛləp) *v.* 培養
leadership ('lidɚ,ʃɪp) *n.* 領導能力　　gain (gen) *v.* 獲得
competence ('kɑmpətəns) *n.* 能力
confidence ('kɑnfədəns) *n.* 自信心　　require (rɪ'kwaɪr) *v.* 需要
dedication (,dɛdə'keʃən) *n.* 專心致力；投入　　leader ('lidɚ) *n.* 領導者
show (ʃo) *n.* (正在發生的) 事情　　*run the show* 管理或主持事務

In conclusion, be your own boss!　　　　　總之，自己當老闆！

Be in control of your life.　　　　　　　　　支配自己的人生。

Being self-employed is the best　　　　　　　自己開業是最好的一條路。

　　way to go.

You only live once.　　　　　　　　　　　　人只能活一次。

Try to follow your dreams!　　　　　　　　　努力追求你的夢想！

Try to rely on yourself!　　　　　　　　　　試著靠自己！

You'll be the king of your castle.　　　　　你將成為自己的城堡的國王。

You'll have autonomy and freedom.　　　　　你將擁有自主性和自由。

You'll have an exciting life　　　　　　　　你一定會擁有刺激的人生！

　　for sure!

** ─────────────────────────────

　　in conclusion 總之　　*in control of* 支配

　　follow〔'falo〕v. 追求　　*rely on* 依靠

　　castle〔'kæsḷ〕n. 城堡　　autonomy〔ɔ'tɑnəmɪ〕n. 自治（權）；自主性

　　freedom〔'fridəm〕n. 自由

　　exciting〔ɪk'saɪtɪŋ〕adj. 刺激的；令人興奮的　　*for sure* 一定

【托福作文範例】

7. Be Your Own Boss

Ask any person if they would rather work for someone or be their own boss, I am confident the answer will be that they want to be self-employed. There are many advantages to being your own boss and here's why.

First, you call the shots. There is no miscommunication, fewer foul-ups and everything depends on you. *Second*, the rewards are greater. The risks and challenges are more intense but you reap what you sow. *Third*, self-employment is more flexible. You can set your own working hours. You determine how hard you want to work each day and can take off whenever you want. The self-employed have more options to experiment with new things. *Fourth*, self-employment develops leadership. You learn how to make decisions and gain competence and knowledge fast. You develop confidence and courage. Being a boss requires dedication and hard work. Being a boss is being a leader because you call the shots and run the show.

In conclusion, be your own boss! You will be in charge of your own destiny and follow your dreams instead of others'. It will be very exciting.

7. 自己做老闆

　　隨便問任何一個人，問他們寧願為別人工作或者是自己做老闆，我有信心，答案都會是想要從事自由業。自己做老闆的好處很多，而以下就是原因。

　　首先，你能夠掌控全局。不會有溝通不良的情況，事情比較不容易被搞砸，而且所有事情都仰賴你的決定。第二，你所得到的報酬會更多。你承擔的風險和面臨的挑戰更高，但是種瓜得瓜，種豆得豆。第三，從事自由業比較有彈性。你可以設定自己的工作時間。你可以決定每天要多努力工作，而且可以隨時放假。從事自由業將讓你有更多機會去實驗新事物。第四，從事自由業可以培養領導能力。你會學會如何做決定，如何很快地獲得能力和知識。你會培養出自信及勇氣。當老闆必須要投入並且努力工作。當老闆就是當領導者，因為你必須發號施令並且掌控全局。

　　總之，自己當老闆吧！你將能掌控自己的命運，並且追求屬於你自己而非他人的夢想。這將會是非常令人興奮的。

【托福作文原試題】

> *Some people prefer to work for themselves or own a business. Others prefer to work for an employer. Would you rather be self-employed, work for someone else, or own a business? Use specific reasons to explain your choice.*

8. *Experience Counts the Most*

Ladies and gentlemen:
I appreciate your being here.
It's an honor to speak with you.

I'd like to talk about experience.
It's the most valuable quality to have.
It's more important than just about anything.

Experience is the best teacher in life.
Experience comes from learning life's lessons.
Here's why employers hire the more experienced.

First, experience assures quality.
Experienced workers do a better job.
Experienced people have learned from years
   of trial and error.

---

count (kaʊnt)	*good day*
appreciate (əˈpriʃɪˌet)	honor (ˈɑnɚ)
valuable (ˈvæljəbl̩)	quality (ˈkwɑlətɪ)
just about	lesson (ˈlɛsn̩)
employer (ɪmˈplɔɪɚ)	assure (əˈʃʊr)
trial and error	

Experienced people have more skills.

They have higher standards.

They have higher expectations and more
   maturity, too.

Experienced workers contribute right away.

They perform well from the start.

They are better prepared and more disciplined.

Second, *experienced people benefit everybody*.

They are like role models and teachers.

They inspire everyone around them to do better.

Experienced workers are better problem solvers.

They are full of information and advice.

Their insight and wisdom are invaluable.

---

standard ('stændə d)

maturity (mə't(j)urətɪ)

right away

from the start

benefit ('bɛnəfɪt)

inspire (ɪn'spaɪr)

wisdom ('wɪzdəm)

expectation (ˌɛkspɛk'teʃən)

contribute (kən'trɪbjut)

perform (pə'fɔrm)

disciplined ('dɪsəplɪnd)

role model

insight ('ɪnˌsaɪt)

invaluable (ɪn'væljuəbl̩)

Experienced workers are independent.

They require less direction.

They can also be selfless team players.

Third, *experienced employees save the*

   company money.

They save on training costs.

They also save by making fewer mistakes.

Experienced workers are a better investment.

Experienced workers do cost a little more.

But their higher salary will return more

   dividends in the long run.

---

independent (ˌɪndɪˈpɛndənt)

direction (dəˈrɛkʃən)   selfless (ˈsɛlflɪs)

team player   employee (ɪmˈplɔɪ·i)

training (ˈtrenɪŋ)   costs (kɔsts)

investment (ɪnˈvɛstmənt)   salary (ˈsælərɪ)

return (rɪˈtɜn)

dividend (ˈdɪvəˌdɛnd)   *in the long run*

With experienced workers, you receive
   quality work.
With experienced workers, you get excellent
   results.
With experience, you get what you pay for.

Finally, the experienced are dependable.
They have been tried and tested.
They are a proven talent.

Experience means "know-how."
Experienced workers have more knowledge.
They are competent and efficient at what they do.

They don't waste time.
They seldom disappoint you.
Experienced workers rarely let you down.

---

receive (rɪ'siv)	*pay for*
dependable (dɪ'pɛndəbḷ)	try (traɪ)
test (tɛst)	proven ('pruvən)
talent ('tælənt)	know-how ('no,haʊ)
competent ('kɑmpətənt)	efficient (ə'fɪʃənt, ɪ-)
disappoint (,dɪsə'pɔɪnt)	rarely ('rɛrlɪ)
let sb. down	

In conclusion, always rely on the experienced.

Experience counts the most.

Experience is a top asset to have.

Experience benefits all.

Experience is the best teacher.

Try to get as much experience as you can.

Trust the experienced.

Choose experienced people.

Experience is the mother of wisdom.

---

in conclusion	*rely on*
top (tɑp)	asset ('æsɛt)
as⋯as one can	mother ('mʌðɚ)

8. *Experience Counts the Most*
經驗最重要

【演講解説】

Ladies and gentlemen:	各位先生，各位女士：
I appreciate your being here.	感謝你們能夠來到這裡。
It's an honor to speak with you.	我很榮幸能和你們談談。
I'd like to talk about experience.	我想要討論經驗。
It's the most valuable quality to have.	那是最寶貴的特質。
It's more important than just about anything.	那幾乎比任何東西都重要。
Experience is the best teacher in life.	經驗是人生最好的老師。
Experience comes from learning life's lessons.	經驗來自學習人生獲取的教訓。
Here's why employers hire the more experienced.	以下就是為什麼雇主要僱用比較有經驗的員工。
First, experience assures quality.	首先，經驗是品質的保證。
Experienced workers do a better job.	有經驗的員工表現較出色。
Experienced people have learned from years of trial and error.	有經驗的人在多年不斷摸索的過程中學習。

** ————————————

count〔kaʊnt〕v. 重要　　*good day* 日安；您好（白天見面或告別時的招呼）
appreciate〔əˋpriʃɪͺet〕v. 感激　　honor〔ˋɑnɚ〕n. 光榮的事
valuable〔ˋvæljəbl̩〕adj. 珍貴的　　quality〔ˋkwɑlətɪ〕n. 特質　adj. 優質的
just about 幾乎（= almost）　　lesson〔ˋlɛsn̩〕n. 教訓
employer〔ɪmˋplɔɪɚ〕n. 雇主　　assure〔əˋʃʊr〕v. 確保
trial and error 反覆試驗；不斷摸索（試了錯，錯了再試）

Experienced people have more skills.	有經驗的人有更多的技術。
They have higher standards.	他們的水準較高。
They have higher expectations and more maturity, too.	他們的期望較高，也展現較高的成熟度。
Experienced workers contribute right away.	有經驗的員工能馬上有所貢獻。
They perform well from the start.	他們從一開始就表現出色。
They are better prepared and more disciplined.	他們準備更充分，更訓練有素。
Second, experienced people benefit everybody.	第二，有經驗的人能讓大家受益。
They are like role models and teachers.	他們就如同模範榜樣和老師。
They inspire everyone around them to do better.	他們能激勵周圍的每個人表現得更好。

** ─────────────

standard (ˈstændə·d) *n.* 水準　　expectation (ˌɛkspɛkˈteʃən) *n.* 期待
maturity (məˈt(j)urətɪ) *n.* 成熟　　contribute (kənˈtrɪbjut) *v.* 貢獻
right away 馬上　　perform (pə·ˈfɔrm) *v.* 表現
from the start 從一開始　　disciplined (ˈdɪsəplɪnd) *adj.* 受過訓練的
benefit (ˈbɛnəfɪt) *v.* 對…有益　　*role model* 模範；榜樣
inspire (ɪnˈspaɪr) *v.* 激勵

Experienced workers are better problem
solvers.

有經驗的員工比較擅長解決問題。

They are full of information and advice.

他們有豐富的資訊和建議。

Their insight and wisdom are invaluable.

他們的深入見解和智慧是無價的。

Experienced workers are independent.

有經驗的員工很獨立。

They require less direction.

他們比較不需要指導。

They can also be selfless team
players.

他們也可以是很有團隊精神的人。

Third, experienced employees save the
company money.

第三,有經驗的員工會替公司省錢。

They save on training costs.

他們節省了訓練費用。

They also save by making fewer
mistakes.

他們也因為比較不會犯錯而省錢。

Experienced workers are a better
investment.

有經驗的員工是較好的投資。

Experienced workers do cost a little
more.

有經驗的員工的確貴了一點。

But their higher salary will return
more dividends in the long run.

但是他們較高的薪水終究會產生更多的效益。

**

insight ('ɪn,saɪt) n. 深入的見解　wisdom ('wɪzdəm) n. 智慧
invaluable (ɪn'væljʊəbḷ) adj. 無價的;珍貴的
independent (,ɪndɪ'pɛndənt) adj. 獨立的　direction (də'rɛkʃən) n. 指導
selfless ('sɛlflɪs) adj. 無私的　**team player** 有團隊精神的人
employee (ɪm'plɔɪ·i) n. 員工　training ('trenɪŋ) n. 訓練
costs (kɔsts) n. pl. 費用　investment (ɪn'vɛstmənt) n. 投資
salary ('sælərɪ) n. 薪水　return (rɪ'tɝn) v. 回報;獲得 (利潤等)
dividend ('dɪvə,dɛnd) n. 紅利;效益　**in the long run** 最終

With experienced workers, you receive quality work. 　　僱用有經驗的員工，你得到高品質的工作成果。

With experienced workers, you get excellent results. 　　僱用有經驗的員工，你得到極好的結果。

With experience, you get what you pay for. 　　如果有經驗，那麼你所付出的，將會得到等值的回報。

Finally, the experienced are dependable. 　　最後，有經驗的人是可靠的。

They have been tried and tested. 　　他們都經過磨練和考驗。

They are a proven talent. 　　他們被證明是有才幹的人。

Experience means "know-how." 　　經驗代表「實際知識」。

Experienced workers have more knowledge. 　　有經驗的員工有更多的知識。

They are competent and efficient at what they do. 　　他們可以勝任工作，而且做事效率高。

**　　　　receive** (rɪˈsiv) *v.* 得到　　***pay for*** 爲…付出（金錢或代價）
dependable (dɪˈpɛndəbḷ) *adj.* 可靠的　　**try** (traɪ) *v.* 磨練
test (tɛst) *v.* 考驗　　**proven** (ˈpruvən) *adj.* 經過證明的
talent (ˈtælənt) *n.* 有才能的人
know-how (ˈnoˌhau) *n.* 實際知識；技術
competent (ˈkɑmpətənt) *adj.* 有能力的；能勝任的
efficient (əˈfɪʃənt,ɪ-) *adj.* 有效率的

They don't waste time.	他們不會浪費時間。
They seldom disappoint you.	他們很少讓你感到失望。
Experienced workers rarely let you down.	有經驗的員工幾乎不會讓你失望。
In conclusion, always rely on the experienced.	總之，永遠信賴有經驗的人。
Experience counts the most.	經驗最重要。
Experience is a top asset to have.	經驗是最大的資產。
Experience benefits all.	經驗讓所有人受益。
Experience is the best teacher.	經驗是最好的老師。
Try to get as much experience as you can.	竭盡所能，努力累積經驗。
Trust the experienced.	信任有經驗的人。
Choose experienced people.	選擇有經驗的人
Experience is the mother of wisdom.	經驗乃智慧之母。

**　　**

disappoint (ˌdɪsəˈpɔɪnt) *v.* 使失望
rarely (ˈrɛrlɪ) *adv.* 很少 (= *seldom*)　　　*let sb. down* 讓某人失望
in conclusion 總之　　*rely on* 信任
top (tɑp) *adj.* 最高的；最優良的
asset (ˈæsɛt) *n.* 資產；有利或有用的人或物
as…as one can 儘量…　　mother (ˈmʌðɚ) *n.* 根源 < *of* >

8. Experience Counts the Most

There are many qualities that employers look for in a new hire. *Above all*, experience counts the most because it's the most valuable quality to have. Here's why employers hire the more experienced.

First, experience assures quality. Experienced workers do a better job because they have learned from years of trial and error. They have more skills and higher standards. *Second*, experienced people benefit everybody. They are like role models and teachers. Experienced workers are better problem solvers as well. *Third*, experienced workers save the company money because they are independent. They require less direction so they save on training costs. They also save by making fewer mistakes. Experienced employees are a better investment because you receive quality work. With experience, you get what you pay for. *Finally*, the experienced are dependable. They have been tried and tested. They are a proven talent and don't waste time. Experienced workers seldom disappoint you.

In conclusion, always rely on the experienced. Experience counts the most and it is a top asset to have. Trust the experienced and go hire someone with experience today!

8. 經驗最重要

　　雇主在僱用新員工時，要注意的特質有很多。最重要的是經驗，因為那是最有價值的特質。以下就是為何雇主要僱用比較有經驗的人的理由。

　　首先，經驗能確保品質。有經驗的員工能將工作做得更好，因為他們已經從多年的嘗試錯誤中學習。他們有更多的技巧及更高的水準。第二，有經驗的人能使所有人受益。他們就像楷模榜樣和老師。有經驗的員工同時也較擅長解決問題。第三，有經驗的員工能替公司省錢，因為他們比較獨立。他們不太需要指導，因此能省下訓練的開銷。他們也因為較少犯錯，能替公司省錢。僱用有經驗的員工將會是較好的投資，因為你能夠得到高品質的工作成果。有經驗的話，那麼你所付出的，將會得到等值的回報。最後一點，有經驗的人是值得信賴的。他們已經通過過磨練及考驗。他們被證明是有才幹的人，而且不會浪費時間。有經驗的員工很少會讓你失望。

　　總之，永遠信賴有經驗的人。經驗是最重要的，而且是我們能擁有的最好的資產。相信有經驗的人，今天就去僱用一個吧！

【托福作文原試題】

If you were an employer, which kind of worker would you prefer to hire: an inexperienced worker at a lower salary or an experienced worker at a higher salary? Use specific reasons and details to support your answer.

9. *We Must Preserve Historic Buildings*

Welcome everybody!
Thank you for being here.
Thank you for this opportunity to speak.

I'm here on a mission.
I have a message to deliver.
We must preserve our historic buildings!

We should cherish our past.
We should learn from these structures.
Here are some good reasons why.

First, these buildings are a valuable part
  of our heritage.
They are true symbols of the past.
They remind us of where we came from.

---

preserve (prɪ'zɜv)   historic (hɪs'tɔrɪk)
mission ('mɪʃən)   message ('mɛsɪdʒ)
deliver (dɪ'lɪvɚ)   cherish ('tʃɛrɪʃ)
structure ('strʌktʃɚ)   valuable ('væljuəbḷ)
heritage ('hɛrətɪdʒ)   symbol ('sɪmbḷ)
remind sb. of sth.   *come from*

These buildings are true landmarks.

They reflect the glory of the past.

They represent the best of that culture.

We have inherited these buildings.

They have been passed down to us.

They are a gift from a past generation.

Second, they have historical significance.

Many things can be learned from them.

Many important events occurred in them.

These buildings are living history.

They are legacies full of tradition.

They characterize the spirit of our ancestors.

---

landmark ('lænd,mɑrk)   reflect (rɪ'flɛkt)

glory ('glorɪ)   represent (,rɛprɪ'zɛnt)

culture ('kʌltʃɚ)   inherit (ɪn'hɛrɪt)

pass down   generation (,dʒɛnə'reʃən)

historical (hɪs'tɔrɪkl̩)   significance (sɪg'nɪfəkəns)

event (ɪ'vɛnt)   living ('lɪvɪŋ)

legacy ('lɛgəsɪ)   **be full of**

tradition (trə'dɪʃən)   characterize ('kærɪktə,raɪz)

spirit ('spɪrɪt)   ancestor ('ænsɛstɚ)

These structures are like museums.

They are full of fascinating stories.

If we demolish them, we will bury the past.

Third, historic buildings are beautiful.

Historic buildings are like art.

They are a splendid sight to see.

They are fascinating to look at.

They are magical to walk through.

It's like going back in time.

They make our city more attractive.

They deserve our upkeep and respect.

To tear them down would be a crime.

---

fascinating ('fæsn,etɪŋ)	demolish (dɪ'malɪʃ)
bury ('bɛrɪ)	splendid ('splɛndɪd)
sight (saɪt)	magical ('mædʒɪkl̩)
go back	attractive (ə'træktɪv)
deserve (dɪ'zɜv)	upkeep ('ʌp,kip)
tear down	crime (kraɪm)

Finally, _their architecture is unique_.

Their design and style are rare.

Historic buildings are like monuments

  of art.

These buildings are true originals.

These buildings are invaluable and priceless.

We can never let them be destroyed.

We can learn from old styles.

We can integrate them with the new.

They help us to appreciate the progress

  we've made.

---

architecture ('ɑrkə,tɛktʃɚ)   unique (ju'nik)

design (dɪ'zaɪn)   rare (rɛr)

monument ('mɑnjəmənt)   original (ə'rɪdʒənḷ)

invaluable (ɪn'væljuəbḷ)   priceless ('praɪslɪs)

destroy (dɪ'strɔɪ)   integrate ('ɪntə,gret)

appreciate (ə'priʃɪ,et)   progress ('prɑgrɛs)

In conclusion, we must preserve old buildings.

We have a duty to maintain them.

They are an important part of our past.

I beg you all to support me.

Please take my words to heart.

Please don't let our past be erased.

Let's honor our cultural heritage.

Let's honor and cherish our ancestors.

Let's preserve and care for all historic
  buildings.

---

in conclusion	duty ('djutɪ)
maintain (men'ten)	beg (bɛg)
support (sə'port)	*take ~ to heart*
erase (ɪ'res)	honor ('ɑnɚ)
cultural ('kʌltʃərəl)	*care for*

9. We Must Preserve Historic Buildings

我們必須保存具有歷史價值的建築物

【演講解說】

Welcome everybody!	歡迎大家！
Thank you for being here.	謝謝你們來到這裡。
Thank you for this opportunity to speak.	謝謝你們給我這個機會發表演說。
I'm here on a mission.	我在此有一項使命。
I have a message to deliver.	我有一個訊息要傳達。
We must preserve our historic buildings!	我們必須保存我們具有歷史價值的建築物！
We should cherish our past.	我們應該珍惜過去。
We should learn from these structures.	我們應該從這些建築中學習。
Here are some good reasons why.	以下就是為什麼要這麼做的充分理由。

** ——————————————

preserve〔prɪˈzɝv〕v. 保存

historic〔hɪsˈtɔrɪk〕adj. 有歷史性的；具有重大歷史意義的

mission〔ˈmɪʃən〕n. 任務；使命

message〔ˈmɛsɪdʒ〕n. 訊息　　deliver〔dɪˈlɪvɚ〕v. 發表；說

cherish〔ˈtʃɛrɪʃ〕v. 珍惜　　structure〔ˈstrʌktʃɚ〕n. 建築物

First, these buildings are a valuable part of our heritage.	首先，這些建築物是我們的遺產中珍貴的一部份。
They are true symbols of the past.	它們是過去的真正象徵。
They remind us of where we came from.	它們提醒我們自己根在何處。
These buildings are true landmarks.	這些建築物是真正的地標。
They reflect the glory of the past.	它們反映過去的光榮。
They represent the best of that culture.	它們代表某個文化的最好部分。
We have inherited these buildings.	我們繼承了這些建築物。
They have been passed down to us.	它們被傳承下來給我們。
They are a gift from a past generation.	它們是上個世代所留下來的禮物。
Second, they have historical significance.	第二，它們具有重大的歷史意義。
Many things can be learned from them.	從它們身上可以學到很多。
Many important events occurred in them.	很多重要的事件發生在其中。

＊＊

valuable (ˈvæljʊəbḷ) adj. 珍貴的　　heritage (ˈhɛrətɪdʒ) n. 遺產
symbol (ˈsɪmbḷ) n. 象徵　　*remind sb. of sth.* 提醒某人某事
come from 來自　　landmark (ˈlænd͵mɑrk) n. 地標
reflect (rɪˈflɛkt) v. 反映　　glory (ˈglorɪ) n. 光榮
represent (͵rɛprɪˈzɛnt) v. 代表　　culture (ˈkʌltʃə) n. 文化
inherit (ɪnˈhɛrɪt) v. 繼承（傳統、遺產等）
pass down 傳下來　　generation (͵dʒɛnəˈreʃən) n. 世代
historical (hɪsˈtɔrɪkḷ) adj. 歷史上的
significance (sɪgˈnɪfəkəns) n. 意義；重要性　　event (ɪˈvɛnt) n. 事件

These buildings are living history.

這些建築物是活生生的歷史。

They are legacies full of tradition.

它們是富有傳統精神的遺產。

They characterize the spirit of our ancestors.

它們代表了我們祖先的精神。

These structures are like museums.

這些建築物就像是博物館。

They are full of fascinating stories.

它們充滿了許多迷人的故事。

If we demolish them, we will bury the past.

如果我們破壞它們，我們就會湮沒過去。

Third, historic buildings are beautiful.

第三，歷史建築很美。

Historic buildings are like art.

歷史建築就像藝術品一樣。

They are a splendid sight to see.

它們是絕佳的景色。

They are fascinating to look at.

它們看起來十分迷人。

They are magical to walk through.

走過其中會覺得十分神奇。

It's like going back in time.

就像是回到過去。

** ──────────

living (ˈlɪvɪŋ) *adj.* 活的；現存的　　legacy (ˈlɛgəsɪ) *n.* 遺產
be full of 充滿　　tradition (trəˈdɪʃən) *n.* 傳統
characterize (ˈkærɪktəˌraɪz) *v.* 是…的特色
spirit (ˈspɪrɪt) *n.* 精神　　ancestor (ˈænsɛstə) *n.* 祖先
fascinating (ˈfæsn̩ˌetɪŋ) *adj.* 迷人的
demolish (dɪˈmɑlɪʃ) *v.* 拆毀；破壞　　bury (ˈbɛrɪ) *v.* 埋葬
splendid (ˈsplɛndɪd) *adj.* 壯麗的　　sight (saɪt) *n.* 景色
magical (ˈmædʒɪkl̩) *adj.* 有魔力的；神奇的　　***go back*** 回去；追溯

They make our city more attractive. | 它們讓我們的城市更有吸引力。
They deserve our upkeep and respect. | 它們值得我們的維護和尊敬。
To tear them down would be a crime. | 將它們拆毀是個罪過。

**Finally, *their architecture is
　unique*.** | 最後一點，它們的建築風格是
獨一無二的。
Their design and style are rare. | 它們的設計和風格是少見的。
Historic buildings are like
　monuments of art. | 歷史建築物就像是不朽的藝術
品。

These buildings are true originals. | 這些建築物是真正的創作。
These buildings are invaluable and
　priceless. | 這些建築物是無價之寶。
We can never let them be destroyed. | 我們絕對不能讓它們遭到破壞。

＊＊

attractive〔ə'træktɪv〕*adj.* 有吸引力的
deserve〔dɪ'zɝv〕*v.* 應得　　upkeep〔'ʌp,kip〕*n.* 保養；維修
tear down 拆除　　crime〔kraɪm〕*n.* 罪過
architecture〔'ɑrkə,tɛktʃɚ〕*n.* 建築式樣；建築風格
unique〔ju'nik〕*adj.* 獨特的
design〔dɪ'zaɪn〕*n.* 設計　　rare〔rɛr〕*adj.* 罕見的
monument〔'mɑnjəmənt〕*n.* 紀念碑；不朽的作品
original〔ə'rɪdʒənl〕*n.* 原物；創作作品
invaluable〔ɪn'væljuəbl〕*adj.* 無價的（= priceless〔'praɪslɪs〕）
destroy〔dɪ'strɔɪ〕*v.* 破壞

We can learn from old styles.	我們可以從舊式風格中學習。
We can integrate them with the new.	我們可以將它們和新的風格相融合。
They help us to appreciate the progress we've made.	它們有助於我們了解自己的進步。
In conclusion, we must preserve old buildings.	總之，我們必須保存古老的建築。
We have a duty to maintain them.	我們有責任維護它們。
They are an important part of our past.	它們是我們過去很重要的一部份。
I beg you all to support me.	我懇請大家支持我。
Please take my words to heart.	請認真思考我所說的話。
Please don't let our past be erased.	請不要讓我們的過去被抹滅。
Let's honor our cultural heritage.	讓我們尊重我們的文化遺產。
Let's honor and cherish our ancestors.	讓我們尊重並且珍惜我們的祖先。
Let's preserve and care for all historic buildings.	讓我們好好保存所有具有歷史價值的建築物。

**

integrate (ˈɪntəˌgret) v. 整合　　appreciate (əˈpriʃɪˌet) v. 了解
progress (ˈprɑgrɛs) n. 進步　　*in conclusion* 總之
duty (ˈdjutɪ) n. 責任　　maintain (menˈten) v. 保持；維持
beg (bɛg) v. 請求；懇求　　*take~to heart* 認真考慮~
erase (ɪˈres) v. 抹去；消除　　honor (ˈɑnɚ) v. 尊敬
cultural (ˈkʌltʃərəl) adj. 文化的　　*care for* 照料

【托福作文範例】

9. We Must Preserve Historic Buildings

Many old and historic buildings are being torn down to make room for new and modern buildings. But we must preserve our historic buildings because we have to cherish our past. Here are some good reasons why.

First, these buildings are a valuable part of our heritage. They are symbols of the past because they remind us of where we came from. We have inherited these buildings as a gift from a past generation. *Second*, they have historical significance. Many things can be learned from them because many important events occurred in them. These buildings are true living history. They are like museums full of fascinating stories. *Third*, historic buildings are beautiful. They are like pieces of art and a sight to behold. They make our cities more attractive so to tear them down would be a great shame. *Finally*, their architecture is unique. These buildings are original in every aspect. We can learn a lot from their old styles and can integrate them with the new.

In conclusion, we must preserve old buildings. We have a duty to maintain them. Let's honor our cultural heritage and cherish our ancestors by preserving historic buildings.

9. 我們必須保存具有歷史價值的建築物

　　爲了挪出空間給新式的現代建築，許多老舊而且具有歷史價值的建築物都被拆除了。但是我們應該保存這些具有歷史性的建築物，因爲我們必須珍惜我們的過去。以下就是爲什麼要這麼做的一些很好的理由。

　　首先，這些建築物是我們的遺產中寶貴的一部份。它們是過去的象徵，因爲他們提醒了我們自己來自何處。我們所繼承的這些建築物，是上個世代所留下來的禮物。第二，他們具有重大的歷史意義。從它們身上我們可以學到很多，因爲曾經有許多重要的事件都發生在裡面。這些建築物就像活生生的歷史。它們就像是充滿了迷人故事的博物館。第三，具有歷史價值的建築物非常美麗。他們就像是藝術品和可供人觀賞的名勝。它們使我們的城市更加吸引人，所以將它們拆毀會是一件非常可惜的事情。最後一點，它們的建築風格十分獨特。這些建築物在各方面都具有原創性。我們可以從這些舊式風格中學習到許多，並且可以和新的風格相融合。

　　總之，我們必須保存古老的建築。我們有責任要維護它們。讓我們一起來尊重我們的文化遺產，並且珍惜我們的祖先，就從保存這些具有歷史價值的建築物做起吧。

【托福作文原試題】

Should a city try to preserve its old, historic buildings or destroy them and replace them with modern buildings? Use specific reasons and examples to support your opinion.

10. Computers Make Life So Much Better!

Greetings, ladies and gentlemen.
I warmly welcome you here today.
I hope you enjoy my speech.

My topic is computers.
Computers are the greatest advancement.
Computers have made our world a much
   better place.

They have changed the way we work.
They have changed the way we communicate
   and live.
Here's why I think computers are wonderful.

First, computers make communication easy.
Computers have revolutionized communications.
We can now transfer information in seconds!

---

greetings ('gritɪŋz)

advancement (əd'vænsmənt)

communicate (kə'mjunə,ket)

revolutionize (,rɛvə'luʃən,aɪz)

communication (kə,mjunə'keʃən)

warmly ('wɔrmlɪ)

transfer (træns'fɝ)

The Internet has emerged as an electronic highway.
The World Wide Web is our main source of
information.
Thanks to computerized satellites, communication
is fast and efficient.

We can email classmates with questions.
We can email pen pals around the world.
We can send messages to anyone, anytime,
anywhere.

Second, computers benefit our global village.
They help us advance in every technological field.
They also make great contributions to medicine
and science.

Internet ('ɪntɚˌnɛt)

electronic (ɪˌlɛk'trɑnɪk)

World Wide Web

source (sors , sɔrs)

computerized (kəm'pjutəˌraɪzd)

efficient (ə'fɪʃənt , ɪ-)

pen pal

global ('globl)

advance (əd'væns)

technological (ˌtɛknə'lɑdʒɪkl)

contribution (ˌkɑntrə'bjuʃən)

emerge (ɪ'mɝdʒ)

highway ('haɪˌwe)

main (men)

thanks to

satellite ('sætlˌaɪt)

email ('iˌmel)

benefit ('bɛnəfɪt)

global village

field (fild)

Computers are used to save lives in hospitals.
They find new sources of energy.
They forecast and protect us from dangerous
   weather patterns.

Computers allow businesses to function more
   efficiently.
Computers help reduce costs for consumers.
They are responsible for greater productivity
   worldwide.

Third, *computers improve our communities*.
Computers bring us closer together.
They also make us a lot safer.

---

energy ('ɛnɚdʒɪ)

protect (prə'tɛkt)

allow (ə'laʊ)

reduce (rɪ'djus)

be responsible for

productivity (ˌprodʌk'tɪvətɪ)

community (kə'mjunətɪ)

forecast (for'kæst, fɔr-)

pattern ('pætən)

function ('fʌŋkʃən)

consumer (kən's(j)umɚ)

worldwide ('wɜld'waɪd)

They assist the police in protecting us.
They aid the fire department with surveillance.
Computers make emergency management
   more efficient.

Computers are terrific for our schools.
Computers improve learning in many ways.
Because of computers, students today have
   many wonderful opportunities.

Finally, computers empower individuals.
They give us more freedom and autonomy.
They make our lives more convenient in many
   ways.

Computers allow some people to work at home.
Computers save a great deal of time.
They are the greatest time-saver ever invented.

---

assist (ə'sɪst)   aid (ed)
fire department   surveillance (sə'veljəns)
emergency (ɪ'mɝdʒənsɪ)
management ('mænɪdʒmənt)   terrific (tə'rɪfɪk)
empower (ɪm'pauɚ)   individual (ˌɪndə'vɪdʒuəl)
autonomy (ɔ'tɑnəmɪ)   ***a great deal of***
time-saver ('taɪmˌsevɚ)

People can shop or pay bills.

People can keep financial records or store
  information "online."

Through computers, home-users have access to a
  wealth of information.

***In conclusion**, **computers make us smarter**.*

Computers keep us better informed.

The computer is our "brain machine."

The advantages are too numerous to count.

Computer technology is increasing every year.

Computers will continue to benefit us even more.

We live in an information society.

We must know more to do more.

I'm confident computers will make the future
  even better!

---

shop (ʃɑp)

store (stor)

access ('æksɛs)

in conclusion

advantage (əd'væntɪdʒ)

count (kaʊnt)

financial (fə'nænʃəl ,faɪ-)

on line

wealth (wɛlθ)

informed (ɪn'fɔrmd)

numerous ('njumərəs)

confident ('kɑnfədənt)

10. *Computers Make Life So Much Better!*
電腦讓生活更好！

【演講解説】

Greetings, ladies and gentlemen.	各位先生，各位女士，大家好。
I warmly welcome you here today.	我熱烈地歡迎你們今天來到這裡。
I hope you enjoy my speech.	我希望你們喜歡我的演講。
My topic is computers.	我的主題是電腦。
Computers are the greatest advancement.	電腦是最偉大的進步。
Computers have made our world a much better place.	電腦已經使我們的世界成爲更美好的地方。
They have changed the way we work.	它們已經改變了我們的工作方式。
They have changed the way we communicate and live.	它們已經改變了我們通訊和生活的方式。
Here's why I think computers are wonderful.	以下就是爲什麼我認爲電腦很棒的原因。
First, computers make communication easy.	第一點，電腦讓通訊變得更容易。
Computers have revolutionized communications.	電腦已經讓通訊設備產生重大變革。
We can now transfer information in seconds!	我們現在可以在數秒鐘之內傳遞資訊！

** ————————

greetings ('gritɪŋz) *n. pl.* 問候語　　warmly ('wɔrmlɪ) *adv.* 熱烈地
advancement (əd'vænmənt) *n.* 進步
communicate (kə'mjunəˌket) *v.* 通訊
revolutionize (ˌrɛvə'luʃənˌaɪz) *v.* 在…方面有突破性的大變革
communication (kəˌmjunə'keʃən) *n.* 通訊；(*pl.*) 通訊設備
transfer (træns'fɝ) *v.* 轉移；傳遞

The Internet has emerged as an electronic highway.

網際網路以電子公路之姿出現。

The World Wide Web is our main source of information.

全球資訊網是我們資訊的主要來源。

Thanks to computerized satellites, communication is fast and efficient.

幸虧有電腦化的人造衛星，通訊才能既快速又有效率。

We can email classmates with questions.

我們可以寄電子郵件問同學問題。

We can email pen pals around the world.

我們可以寄電子郵件給全世界的筆友。

We can send messages to anyone, anytime, anywhere.

我們可以隨時隨地傳送訊息給任何人。

Second, computers benefit our global village.

第二點，電腦有助於地球村的發展。

They help us advance in every technological field.

它們幫助我們在各個科技領域中進步。

They also make great contributions in medicine and science.

它們也在醫學及科學方面有極大的貢獻。

＊＊

Internet ('ɪntə,nɛt) *n.* 網際網路　　emerge (ɪ'mɝdʒ) *v.* 出現
electronic (ɪ,lɛk'trɑnɪk) *adj.* 電子的　　highway ('haɪ,we) *n.* 公路
World Wide Web 全球資訊網　　main (men) *adj.* 主要的
source (sors,sɔrs) *n.* 來源　　***thanks to*** 幸虧
computerized (kəm'pjutə,raɪzd) *adj.* 電腦化的
satellite ('sætl̩,aɪt) *n.* 人造衛星　　efficient (ə'fɪʃənt ,ɪ-) *adj.* 有效率的
email ('i,mel) *v.* 寄電子郵件　　***pen pal*** 筆友
benefit ('bɛnəfɪt) *v.* 對…有益　　global ('globl̩) *adj.* 全球的；全世界的
global village 地球村 (由於大眾傳播普及，時空縮短，世界如一村)
advance (əd'væns) *v.* 進步　　technological (,tɛknə'lɑdʒɪkl̩) *adj.* 科技的
field (fild) *n.* 領域　　contribution (,kɑntrə'bjuʃən) *n.* 貢獻

Computers are used to save lives in hospitals.	電腦在醫院被用來拯救生命。
They find new sources of energy.	它們找到新的能量來源。
They forecast and protect us from dangerous weather patterns.	它們預測並且保護我們免受危險的天氣型態的傷害。
Computers allow businesses to function more efficiently.	電腦讓企業更有效率地運作。
Computers help reduce costs for consumers.	電腦有助於減少消費者的開銷。
They are responsible for greater productivity worldwide.	它們是全世界生產力提高的原因。
Third, computers improve our communities.	第三點，電腦改善我們的社區。
Computers bring us closer together.	電腦把我們拉得更近。
They also make us a lot safer.	它們也讓我們更加安全。

** ───────────────────

energy (ˈɛnədʒɪ) *n.* 能量   forecast (forˈkæst, fɔr-) *v.* 預測
protect (prəˈtɛkt) *v.* 保護 <*from*>
pattern (ˈpætən) *n.* 型態   allow (əˈlaʊ) *v.* 使成為可能
function (ˈfʌŋkʃən) *v.* 運作   reduce (rɪˈdjus) *v.* 減少
consumer (kənˈs(j)umə) *n.* 消費者   **_be responsible for_** 是…的原因
productivity (ˌprodʌkˈtɪvətɪ) *n.* 生產力
worldwide (ˈwɜldˈwaɪd) *adv.* 在世界各地；在全世界
community (kəˈmjunətɪ) *n.* 社區

They assist the police in protecting us. | 它們協助警方保護我們。
They aid the fire department with surveillance. | 它們協助消防隊做好監視的工作。
Computers make emergency management more efficient. | 電腦使緊急情況的管理更有效率。

Computers are terrific for our schools. | 電腦對我們的學校而言很棒。
Computers improve learning in many ways. | 學習的許多方面因為電腦而獲得改善。
Because of computers, students today have many wonderful opportunities. | 因為電腦，現在的學生有許多很棒的機會。

Finally, computers empower individuals. | 最後一點，電腦讓每個人有更大的權力。
They give us more freedom and autonomy. | 它們賦予我們更多的自由和自主性。
They make our lives more convenient in many ways. | 它們讓我們的生活在很多方面更方便。

Computers allow some people to work at home. | 電腦使某些人可以在家裡工作。
Computers save a great deal of time. | 電腦省下了許多時間。
They are the greatest time-saver ever invented. | 它們是有史以來最偉大的節省時間裝置。

**

assist〔ə'sɪst〕v. 協助（= aid〔ed〕）
fire department 消防隊　　surveillance〔sə'veljəns〕n. 監視
emergency〔ɪ'mɝdʒənsɪ〕n. 緊急情況
management〔'mænɪdʒmənt〕n. 管理　　terrific〔tə'rɪfɪk〕adj. 非常好的
empower〔ɪm'pauɚ〕v. 授權　　individual〔ˌɪndə'vɪdʒuəl〕n. 個人
autonomy〔ɔ'tɑnəmɪ〕n. 自治（權）；自主性　　*a great deal of* 大量的
time-saver〔'taɪmˌsevɚ〕n. 節省時間的事物（或人）

People can shop or pay bills.　　　　人們可以購物或付清帳單。

People can keep financial records　　人們可以記錄金錢方面的往來，
　　or store information "online."　　或是「在線上」儲存資訊。

Through computers, home-users have　透過電腦，家庭個人電腦的使
　　access to a wealth of information.　用者有管道接收豐富的資訊。

In conclusion, computers make us　總之，電腦讓我們更聰明。
　　smarter.

Computers keep us better informed.　電腦使我們見聞更廣博。

The computer is our "brain machine."　電腦是我們的「腦部機器」。

The advantages are too numerous　　電腦的好處多到數不完。
　　to count.

Computer technology is increasing　　電腦科技每年都在增進。
　　every year.

Computers will continue to benefit　　電腦將繼續造福我們更多。
　　us even more.

We live in an information society.　　我們活在一個資訊社會。

We must know more to do more.　　我們必須知道更多，才能做更多。

I'm confident computers will make　　我確信電腦將讓未來更加美好！
　　the future even better!

**

shop〔ʃɑp〕*v.* 購物　　financial〔fəˈnænʃəl, faɪ-〕*adj.* 金融的
store〔stor〕*v.* 貯存　　online〔ˈɑnˈlaɪn〕*adv.* 在線上；在網路上
access〔ˈæksɛs〕*n.* 接近或使用權 < *to* >
wealth〔wɛlθ〕*n.* 豐富；大量 < *of* >　　***in conclusion*** 總之
informed〔ɪnˈfɔrmd〕*adj.* 有知識的；見聞廣的
advantage〔ədˈvæntɪdʒ〕*n.* 優點；好處
numerous〔ˈnjumərəs〕*adj.* 為數眾多的　　count〔kaunt〕*v.* 數
confident〔ˈkɑnfədənt〕*adj.* 有信心的；確信的

【托福作文範例】

10. Computers Make Life So Much Better!

Computers have revolutionized our world. Today, we cannot imagine what it would be like without computers. They have changed the way we work, communicate and live. Here are some reasons why I think computers are wonderful.

First, computers make communication easy. Computers have revolutionized communications and we can now transfer information in seconds. The Internet has become an electronic highway and the World Wide Web is our main source of information. *Second*, computers benefit our world. They help us advance in every technological field with great contributions to medicine and science. Computers are used to save lives in hospitals. They forecast and protect us from dangerous weather. They are responsible for greater productivity worldwide. *Third*, computers improve our communities by bringing us together. They assist the police in protecting us by making emergency management more efficient. *Finally*, computers empower individuals. They give us more freedom and make our lives more convenient by letting us pay bills or shop online.

In conclusion, computers make us smarter. In this information society, computers keep us better informed. There are too many advantages to computers to count. Why don't you use a computer today?

10. 電腦讓生活更好！

　　電腦已經徹底改革了我們的世界。現在，我們無法想像沒有電腦的生活會變成什麼樣子。電腦已經改變了我們工作、溝通，以及生活的方式。以下就是我為什麼認為電腦非常棒的原因。

　　首先，電腦讓溝通更容易。電腦已經造成通訊設備的大變革，我們現在可以在數秒鐘之內傳輸資訊。網路已經成為電子公路，而全球資訊網是我們資訊取得的主要來源。第二點，電腦對我們的世界有益。它們幫助我們在各個科技領域中進步，並因此在醫學及科學方面都有極大的貢獻。電腦被用來在醫院拯救性命。它們會預告危險的天氣並保護我們不受威脅。它們也是導致全世界生產力更為提高的原因。第三點，藉由將大家連結在一起，電腦改善了我們的社區。因為電腦使緊急情況的管理變得更有效率，所以能協助警方保護我們。最後，電腦授與個人更大的權力。它讓我們能夠線上付帳或是購物，因此也賦予我們更多的自由，使生活更便利。

　　總之，電腦讓我們變得更聰明。在這個資訊社會裡，電腦使我們見聞更廣博。電腦的好處實在是多到數不清。你何不今天就馬上來用電腦呢？

【托福作文原試題】

> *Some people say that computers have made life easier and more convenient. Other people say that computers have made life more complex and stressful. What is your opinion? Use specific reasons and examples to support your answer.*

11. *The Automobile: A Most Important Invention*

The auto is amazing!
It's an incredible machine!
It's a truly remarkable invention!

Welcome everyone!
Thank you for coming.
I'm here to praise the automobile!

It's changed our world.
It's transformed our lives.
Here are some reasons why.

First, the auto has revolutionized transportation.
Traveling is now faster and cheaper.
Traveling is more efficient and accessible to all.

---

automobile ('ɔtəmə,bil ,ɔtə'mobil) (= auto ('ɔto))

most (most)   amazing (ə'mezɪŋ)
incredible (ɪn'krɛdəbḷ)   truly ('trulɪ)
remarkable (rɪ'mɑrkəbḷ)   praise (prez)
transform (træns'fɔrm)
revolutionize (,rɛvə'luʃən,aɪz)
transportation (,trænspə'teʃən) efficient (ə'fɪʃənt)
accessible (æk'sɛsəbḷ)

The auto created a boom in road construction.
It stimulated the development of highway systems.
It changed travel from a burden to an adventure.

The car's invention led to better public
　transportation.
Now anyone can go anywhere.
Now any person can work, attend school
　or travel.

***Second*, *the auto helped modernize industry
　and business*.**
Its development initiated new methods of
　production.
It improved manufacturing techniques in
　many ways.

---

boom (bum)　　　　　　　　construction (kən'strʌkʃən)
stimulate ('stɪmjə,let)　　　highway ('haɪ,we)
burden ('bɝdn̩)　　　　　　adventure (əd'vɛntʃɚ)
lead to　　　　　　　　attend (ə'tɛnd)
modernize ('mɑdən,aɪz)　　industry ('ɪndəstrɪ)
initiate (ɪ'nɪʃɪ,et)　　　　production (prə'dʌkʃən)
manufacturing (,mænjə'fæktʃərɪŋ)
technique (tɛk'nik)

With its invention, came the assembly line.
This was a breakthrough discovery in efficiency.
This forever changed the way that work
   was done.

The auto itself has helped mobilize countries.
The auto industry has energized whole
   economies.
Its effect on employment and labor has been
   immense.

Third, the auto is responsible for great social
   movement.
The auto has given many people greater freedom.
The car has been a liberating force.

---

assembly (ə'sɛmblɪ)

breakthrough ('brek͵θru)

mobilize ('mobl͵aɪz)

economy (ɪ'kɑnəmɪ)

employment (ɪm'plɔɪmənt)

immense (ɪ'mɛns)

social ('soʃəl)

liberate ('lɪbə͵ret)

assembly line

efficiency (ə'fɪʃənsɪ)

energize ('ɛnə͵dʒaɪz)

effect (ɪ'fɛkt)

labor ('lebə)

be responsible for

movement ('muvmənt)

force (fors)

It has sparked the expansion of suburban life.

It's created greater employment opportunities.

It's given many a chance to move up and improve.

The auto has also created more leisure time.

Every social class has benefited.

Every income group has improved because
 of the car.

Finally, the auto has challenged mankind.

It has introduced new problems.

It has threatened our global environment.

We now have an air pollution dilemma.

We have a dangerous appetite for oil.

The automobile is the major culprit.

---

spark〔spɑrk〕

suburban〔sə'bɝbən〕

move up

class〔klæs〕

income〔'ɪn,kʌm〕

mankind〔mæn'kaɪnd〕

threaten〔'θrɛtn̩〕

dilemma〔də'lɛmə〕

oil〔ɔɪl〕

culprit〔'kʌlprɪt〕

expansion〔ɪk'spænʃən〕

many a

leisure〔'liʒɚ〕

benefit〔'bɛnəfɪt〕

challenge〔'tʃælɪndʒ〕

introduce〔,ɪntrə'djus〕

global〔'globl̩〕

appetite〔'æpə,taɪt〕

major〔'medʒɚ〕

We are researching solutions.

We are closely monitoring gas emissions.

The auto has forced us to start protecting the planet.

In conclusion, the car is responsible for great progress.

It's improved the world in many ways.

It's also created new challenges for the future.

The auto has created lots of pleasure.

The auto has changed the way we live.

It's one of the most important inventions ever.

We should appreciate the car.

We shouldn't take it for granted.

The auto has added so much to our lives.

---

research (rɪ'sɝtʃ , 'risɝtʃ)

closely ('kloslɪ)

gas (gæs)

protect (prə'tɛkt)

in conclusion

pleasure ('plɛʒɚ)

take…for granted

solution (sə'luʃən)

monitor ('manətɚ)

emission (ɪ'mɪʃən)

planet ('plænɪt)

progress ('pragrɛs)

appreciate (ə'priʃɪ,et)

add (æd)

11. *The Automobile: A Most Important Invention*
汽車:一項非常重要的發明

【演講解說】

The auto is amazing!	汽車真是驚人!
It's an incredible machine!	它是一部不可思議的機器!
It's a truly remarkable invention!	它真的是非常了不起的發明!
Welcome everyone!	歡迎各位!
Thank you for coming.	謝謝你們前來。
I'm here to praise the automobile!	我在此要讚揚汽車!
It's changed our world.	它改變了我們的世界。
It's transformed our lives.	它改變了我們的生活。
Here are some reasons why.	以下就是部分的原因。
First, the auto has revolutionized transportation.	首先,汽車造成交通運輸徹底的改革。
Traveling is now faster and cheaper.	現在旅行變得更快速、更便宜。
Traveling is more efficient and accessible to all.	旅行變得更有效率,而且人人都可以旅行。

** ————————————————

automobile ('ɔtəmə,bil,,ɔtə'mobil) *n.* 汽車 (= auto ('ɔto))
most (most) *adv.* 非常   incredible (ɪn'krɛdəbḷ) *adj.* 難以置信的
truly ('trulɪ) *adv.* 非常   remarkable (rɪ'mɑrkəbḷ) *adj.* 非凡的;驚人的
transform (træns'fɔrm) *v.* 改變
revolutionize (,rɛvə'luʃən,aɪz) *v.* 徹底改革
transportation (,trænspə'teʃən) *n.* 運輸
efficient (ə'fɪʃənt) *adj.* 有效率的
accessible (æk'sɛsəbḷ) *adj.* 可得到的

The auto created a boom in road construction.

It stimulated the development of highway systems.

It changed travel from a burden to an adventure.

汽車創造了道路建設的榮景。

它刺激公路系統的發展。

它把旅行從負擔變成冒險的經歷。

The car's invention led to better public transportation.

Now anyone can go anywhere.

Now any person can work, attend school or travel.

汽車的發明造成更好的大眾交通運輸。

現在任何人都可以到任何地方。

現在任何人都可以工作、上學或是旅行。

***Second*, *the auto helped modernize industry and business*.**

Its development initiated new methods of production.

It improved manufacturing techniques in many ways.

第二，汽車有助於工商業的現代化。

它的發展促使新的生產方法的出現。

它改善很多方面的製造技術。

**

boom〔bum〕*n.* (商業等的) 景氣；繁榮
construction〔kən'strʌkʃən〕*n.* 建造；建設
stimulate〔'stɪmjə,let〕*v.* 刺激　　highway〔'haɪ,we〕*n.* 公路
burden〔'bɝdn̩〕*n.* 負擔　　adventure〔əd'vɛntʃɚ〕*n.* 冒險活動 (或經歷)
lead to 導致　　attend〔ə'tɛnd〕*v.* 上 (學)
modernize〔'mɑdɚn,aɪz〕*v.* 使現代化　　industry〔'ɪndəstrɪ〕*n.* 工業
initiate〔ɪ'nɪʃɪ,et〕*v.* 創始　　production〔prə'dʌkʃən〕*n.* 生產
manufacturing〔,mænjə'fæktʃərɪŋ〕*adj.* 製造的
technique〔tɛk'nik〕*n.* 技術

With its invention, came the assembly line.	由於汽車的發明，裝配線就跟著出現了。
This was a breakthrough discovery in efficiency.	這是效能的突破性發現。
This forever changed the way that work was done.	永遠改變了進行生產工作的方式。
The auto itself has helped mobilize countries.	汽車本身促進了全國性的流動。
The auto industry has energized whole economies.	汽車工業刺激整體經濟的發展。
Its effect on employment and labor has been immense.	它對於工作和勞動的影響非常廣泛。
Third, the auto is responsible for great social movement.	第三，汽車是造成社會大幅度流動的原因。
The auto has given many people greater freedom.	汽車讓許多人享有更多的自由。
The car has been a liberating force.	汽車已經成為解放的力量。

** ────────────

assembly (ə'sɛmblɪ) *n.* 裝配　***assembly line*** 裝配線
breakthrough ('brek,θru) *n.* 突破性進展
efficiency (ə'fɪʃənsɪ) *n.* 效率　mobilize ('mobḷ,aɪz) *v.* 使流通
energize ('ɛnə,dʒaɪz) *v.* 供給…能量；激勵
economy (ɪ'kɑnəmɪ) *n.* 經濟（情況）　effect (ɪ'fɛkt) *n.* 影響 < *on* >
employment (ɪm'plɔɪmənt) *n.* 職業；工作　labor ('lebə) *n.* 勞動
immense (ɪ'mɛns) *adj.* 廣大的　***be responsible for*** 是…的原因
social ('soʃəl) *adj.* 社會的
movement ('muvmənt) *n.* 移動；（人口之）流動
liberate ('lɪbə,ret) *v.* 解放　force (fors) *n.* 力量　*v.* 迫使

It has sparked the expansion of
suburban life.

It's created greater employment
opportunities.

It's given many a chance to move up
and improve.

它帶動了郊區生活的發展。

它創造了更多的就業機會。

它提供了許多向上提昇和進步
的機會。

The auto has also created more
leisure time.

Every social class has benefited.

Every income group has improved
because of the car.

汽車也帶來了更多的休閒時間。

所有的社會階級皆因此受益。

每個收入階層皆因為汽車而獲
得改善。

***Finally, the auto has challenged
mankind***.

It has introduced new problems.

It has threatened our global environment.

最後，汽車對人類而言也是一
項挑戰。

它引發了新的問題。

它對我們全球的環境造成威脅。

We now have an air pollution dilemma.

We have a dangerous appetite for oil.

The automobile is the major culprit.

我們現在面臨空氣污染的兩難。

我們過度開發石油。

汽車是主要的元兇。

**　——————————————————

spark (spɑrk) *v.* 成為…的導火線；發動
expansion (ɪk'spænʃən) *n.* 擴展　　suburban (sə'bɝbən) *adj.* 郊區的
many a 許多的　　***move up*** 提升　　leisure ('liʒɚ) *adj.* 空閒的
class (klæs) *n.* 階級　　benefit ('bɛnəfɪt) *v.* 得益　　income ('ɪn,kʌm) *n.* 收入
income group 收入階層（按照年收入分成高、中、低三階層）
challenge ('tʃælɪndʒ) *v.* 向…挑戰　*n.* 挑戰
mankind (mæn'kaɪnd) *n.* 人類　　introduce (,ɪntrə'djus) *v.* 提出
threaten ('θrɛtn̩) *v.* 威脅　　global ('globḷ) *adj.* 全球的
dilemma (də'lɛmə) *n.* 進退兩難　　appetite ('æpə,taɪt) *n.* 慾望 <*for*>
oil (ɔɪl) *n.* 石油　　major ('medʒɚ) *adj.* 主要的
culprit ('kʌlprɪt) *n.* 被控犯罪的人

We are researching solutions.	我們正在研究解決方法。
We are closely monitoring gas emissions.	我們正在嚴密監控汽油排放廢氣。
The auto has forced us to start protecting the planet.	汽車也迫使我們開始保護地球。
In conclusion, the car is responsible for great progress.	總之,汽車是重大進步的主因。
It's improved the world in many ways.	它在很多方面改善了全世界。
It's also created new challenges for the future.	它也為未來創造了新的挑戰。
The auto has created lots of pleasure.	汽車也創造了許多樂趣。
The auto has changed the way we live.	汽車也改變了我們生活的方式。
It's one of the most important inventions ever.	它是有史以來最重要的發明之一。
We should appreciate the car.	我們應該感謝汽車的發明。
We shouldn't take it for granted.	我們不應該將它視為理所當然。
The auto has added so much to our lives.	汽車使我們的生活更加豐富。

＊＊

research (rɪ'sɛtʃ , 'risɜtʃ) v. 研究　　solution (sə'luʃən) n. 解決之道
closely ('kloslɪ) adv. 嚴密地　　monitor ('manətə) v. 監視
gas (gæs) n. 汽油　　emission (ɪ'mɪʃən) n. 排出物 (從汽車的);排氣
protect (prə'tɛkt) v. 保護　　planet ('plænɪt) n. 行星 (在此是指地球)
in conclusion 總之　　progress ('prɑgrɛs) n. 進步
appreciate (ə'priʃɪ,et) v. 感激
take…for granted 視…為理所當然　　add (æd) v. 增加 < to >

【托福作文範例】

11. The Automobile: A Most Important Invention

Of all the great inventions of the past century, perhaps the most important is the automobile. It's changed our world and transformed our lives. Here are some reasons why.

First, the auto revolutionized transportation. Traveling is now faster and cheaper. Traveling has become more efficient and accessible to all. The car's invention led to better public transportation. Now anyone can go anywhere. *Second*, the auto helped modernize industry and business. Its development created new methods of production and improved manufacturing techniques in many ways. *Third*, the auto is responsible for great social mobility. The car has been a liberating force by sparking the expansion of suburban life. It gave many people a chance to move up and improve. The auto has created more leisure time and every social class has benefited. *Finally*, the auto has challenged mankind. The auto introduced new problems like air pollution and dependence on oil. But we are now researching solutions and closely monitoring gas emissions. The auto has forced us to start protecting the planet.

In conclusion, the car is responsible for great progress. It has created lots of pleasure and changed the way we live. We should appreciate the car and not take it for granted.

11. 汽車：一項非常重要的發明

在前一個世紀的所有偉大發明之中，最重要的也許就是汽車了。它已經改變了我們的世界及我們的生活。以下就是一些原因。

首先，汽車徹底改革了交通運輸。旅遊在現今是既快速又便宜。旅遊已經變得更加有效率，而且人人都可以旅遊。汽車的發明促成了更完善的大眾運輸系統。現在每個人都可以到達任何地方。第二，汽車有助於工商業的現代化。它的發展創造了新的生產方法，而且也在各方面改善了生產製造的技術。第三，汽車讓社會有更大的流動性。藉由帶動郊區生活的擴張，汽車已經成為一股解放的力量。它讓許多人有機會向上提升，獲得進步。汽車也創造了更多的休閒時間，而且所有的社會階級都因此受惠。最後一點，汽車也成為人類的一項挑戰。它帶來了許多新的問題，像是空氣污染和對石油的依賴。但我們現在正在研究解決的方法，同時也嚴密監控廢氣的排放。汽車已經迫使我們開始保護地球了。

總之，汽車是我們大幅進步的原因。它創造了許多樂趣，也改變了我們的生活方式。我們應該對此心存感激，而非視其為理所當然。

【托福作文原試題】

Some people think that the automobile has improved modern life. Others think that the automobile has caused serious problems. What is your opinion? Use specific reasons and examples to support your answer.

12. The Advantages of a Less Demanding Job

Welcome everybody.
I have some useful advice.
I'm going to tell it to you right now.

Don't let money run your life!
Don't let your work control you!
Don't be a slave to your job!

Choose a job very carefully.
Choose a less demanding job.
Here's why I believe that's wise.

First, you'll have more personal time.
You'll have more free time with loved ones.
You'll have time to pursue your own interests.

---

advantage (əd'væntɪdʒ)

demanding (dɪ'mændɪŋ)

run (rʌn)

wise (waɪz)

loved ones

interest ('ɪntrɪst)

advice (əd'vaɪs)

slave (slev)

free time

pursue (pɚ'su)

Relationships are very important.

Relationships bring happiness in life.

We all need time to be with friends.

My first priority is my family.

My family comes before my job.

Quality time with family is precious to me.

Second, you'll be healthier.

You'll have more energy.

You'll look and feel better, too.

Demanding jobs can ruin your health.

Demanding jobs can run you down.

They can really wipe you out.

---

relationship (rɪ'leʃən,ʃɪp)

come before

precious ('prɛʃəs)

ruin ('ruɪn)

wipe out

priority (praɪ'ɔrətɪ)

quality ('kwɑlətɪ)

energy ('ɛnə·dʒɪ)

run down

A less demanding job is less stressful.

You'll feel less worry and less pressure.

You'll feel more in control of your life.

Third, you won't waste money.

You'll be more frugal.

You'll be more careful with your cash.

A moderate salary is enough.

A lower salary isn't a disgrace.

It might be a blessing in disguise.

It could help you save money.

You'll prioritize your needs.

You'll be a better money manager, too.

---

stressful ('strɛsfəl)

in control of

cash (kæʃ)

salary ('sælərɪ)

blessing ('blɛsɪŋ)

a blessing in disguise

prioritize (praɪ'ɔrətaɪz)

pressure ('prɛʃɚ)

frugal ('frugḷ)

moderate ('mɑdərɪt)

disgrace (dɪs'gres)

disguise (dɪs'gaɪz)

manager ('mænɪdʒɚ)

Finally, you'll have a more balanced life.

You should have well-rounded lives.

You shouldn't be workaholics.

Every day should be balanced.

Every day should offer variety.

Every day should have some peaceful

   moments, too.

We should balance work and play.

We must keep things in perspective.

We'll be happier and live longer if we do.

---

balanced ('bælənst)

well-rounded ('wɛl'raʊndɪd)

workaholic (ˌwɜkə'halɪk)　　variety (və'raɪətɪ)

peaceful ('pisfəl)　　balance ('bæləns)

perspective (pə'spɛktɪv)　　***keep sth. in perspective***

In conclusion, *choose the right job for you*.

Choose a less demanding job.

You'll have more time for a quality life.

Work is only one part of life.

Don't let it control you.

Don't let it consume your life.

Think about what's important.

Think about your family and your future.

I hope you make the right choice!

---

in conclusion

consume (kən's(j)um)

12. The Advantages of a Less Demanding Job
工作較輕鬆的好處

【演講解說】

Welcome everybody.	歡迎大家。
I have some useful advice.	我有一些有用的建議。
I'm going to tell it to you right now.	我現在就要告訴你們。
Don't let money run your life!	不要讓金錢支配你的人生！
Don't let your work control you!	不要讓你的工作控制你！
Don't be a slave to your job!	不要成為工作的奴隸！
Choose a job very carefully.	小心謹慎地選擇工作。
Choose a less demanding job.	選擇一個較輕鬆的工作。
Here's why I believe that's wise.	以下就是為什麼我覺得那是明智之舉的理由。
First, you'll have more personal time.	首先，你將擁有更多的個人時間。
You'll have more free time with loved ones.	你將擁有更多的空閒時間和親人相處。
You'll have time to pursue your own interests.	你將有時間追求自己的興趣。

**

advantage〔əd'væntɪdʒ〕*n.* 優點
demanding〔dɪ'mændɪŋ〕*adj.* 要求過多的；苛求的
advice〔əd'vaɪs〕*n.* 建議　　run〔rʌn〕*v.* 支配
slave〔slev〕*n.* 奴隸般受控制的人＜*to*＞　　*loved ones* 親人
pursue〔pə'su〕*v.* 追求　　interest〔'ɪntrɪst〕*n.* 興趣

Relationships are very important.	人際關係非常重要。
Relationships bring happiness in life.	人際關係帶來生命的快樂。
We all need time to be with friends.	我們全都需要時間和朋友在一起。
My first priority is my family.	我的第一優先順位是我的家人。
My family comes before my job.	我的家人比工作更重要。
Quality time with family is precious to me.	和家人擁有優質的相處時間對我而言是珍貴的。
Second, you'll be healthier.	第二，你會更健康。
You'll have more energy.	你會擁有更多精力。
You'll look and feel better, too.	你也會看起來、感覺起來更好。
Demanding jobs can ruin your health.	要求高的工作會破壞你的健康。
Demanding jobs can run you down.	要求高的工作會耗損你的身心。
They can really wipe you out.	它們真的會徹底摧毀你。

**

relationship (rɪ'leʃənˌʃɪp) *n.* (人際) 關係
priority (praɪ'ɔrətɪ) *n.* 優先考慮的事
come before 比…重要　　quality ('kwɑlətɪ) *adj.* 優質的
precious ('prɛʃəs) *adj.* 珍貴的
energy ('ɛnədʒɪ) *n.* 精力　　ruin ('ruɪn) *v.* 毀壞
run down 耗損；用壞　　***wipe out*** 徹底摧毀

A less demanding job is less stressful.	較不費力的工作比較沒有壓力。
You'll feel less worry and less pressure.	你將會感受到較少的憂慮和壓力。
You'll feel more in control of your life.	你將會覺得更能掌握自己的人生。
Third, you won't waste money.	第三，你不會浪費錢。
You'll be more frugal.	你會更節儉。
You'll be more careful with your cash.	你會更小心運用現金。
A moderate salary is enough.	適量的薪水就夠了。
A lower salary isn't a disgrace.	薪水較低並非是丟臉的事。
It might be a blessing in disguise.	那可能是塞翁失馬，焉知非福的事情。

**

stressful (ˈstrɛsfəl) *adj.* 緊張的；壓力大的

pressure (ˈprɛʃɚ) *n.* 壓力   ***in control of*** 控制；支配

frugal (ˈfrugl̩) *adj.* 節約的   cash (kæʃ) *n.* 現金

moderate (ˈmɑdərɪt) *adj.* 適度的；中等的

salary (ˈsælərɪ) *n.* 薪水

disgrace (dɪsˈgres) *n.* 丟臉的事

blessing (ˈblɛsɪŋ) *n.* 幸福   disguise (dɪsˈgaɪz) *n.* 偽裝

a blessing in disguise 先前看似不幸，後來卻變為幸運之事；
    塞翁失馬，焉知非福；禍中得福

It could help you save money. | 它可以幫你省錢。
You'll prioritize your needs. | 你會依照優先順序來處理你的需求。
You'll be a better money manager, too. | 你也會成為更有能力的理財者。

***Finally*, *you'll have a more balanced life*.** | 最後，你將擁有更均衡發展的人生。

You should have well-rounded lives. | 你應該擁有多元發展的生活。

You shouldn't be workaholics. | 你不應該成為工作狂。

Every day should be balanced. | 每天都應該均衡發展。

Every day should offer variety. | 每天都應該有變化。

Every day should have some peaceful moments, too. | 每天也都應該有些平靜的時刻。

** ———————————

prioritize〔praɪ'ɔrətaɪz〕*v.* 按優先順序處理
manager〔'mænɪdʒɚ〕*n.* 處理事物者；理財者
balanced〔'bælənst〕*adj.* 均衡的
well-rounded〔'wɛl'raundɪd〕*adj.* 多元發展的
workaholic〔ˌwɝkə'hɔlɪk〕*n.* 工作狂
variety〔və'raɪətɪ〕*n.* 變化；多樣性
peaceful〔'pisfəl〕*adj.* 平靜的；安寧的

We should balance work and
　　play.

我們應該在工作和玩樂之間找到
平衡點。

We must keep things in perspective.

我們必須對事物抱持正確的眼光。

We'll be happier and live longer if
　　we do.

如此我們將會更快樂，而且活得
更久。

*In conclusion, **choose the right job
for you***.

總之，為自己選擇適當的工作。

Choose a less demanding job.

選擇比較輕鬆的工作。

You'll have more time for a quality
　　life.

你將會有更多時間享有高品質的
生活。

Work is only one part of life.

工作只是生活的一部份。

Don't let it control you.

不要讓它控制你。

Don't let it consume your life.

不要讓它消耗你的生活。

Think about what's important.

想想看什麼是重要的。

Think about your family and your
　　future.

想想看你的家人和你的未來。

I hope you make the right choice!

我希望你做出正確的選擇！

**　**　———————————————

balance〔'bæləns〕*v.* 使平衡
perspective〔pɚ'spɛktɪv〕*n.* 正確的眼光
keep sth. in perspective 以正確地眼光看待某事
in conclusion 總之
consume〔kən's(j)um〕*v.* 消耗

【托福作文範例】

12. The Advantages of a Less Demanding Job

You work hard to make money. But don't let money control your life and don't let your work control you! When given a choice, choose a less demanding job with less pay and here is why I believe you should do so.

First, you'll have more personal time. You will get to spend time with your loved ones and have more leisure time to pursue your own interests. *Second*, you'll be healthier. You'll have more energy. Instead of spending all your time at the office, you can be outside enjoying life. A less demanding job is less stressful so you'll look and feel better. *Third*, you won't waste money. You'll be more frugal because you have less money. A less demanding job pays less but that's okay. It might even be a blessing in disguise. You'll prioritize your needs and become a better money manager. *Finally*, you'll have a more balanced life. You should lead well-rounded lives. You shouldn't be workaholics. You should balance work and play because you will be happier and live longer if you do.

In conclusion, choose the right job for you. Don't choose a job where you will end up spending all your time in the office. Think about what's important.

12. 工作較輕鬆的好處

　　你為了賺錢，努力工作。但是不要讓金錢控制你的生活，也不要讓工作控制你！當你有選擇權時，要選擇一個較輕鬆、薪水較低的工作，以下就是我認為為什麼你應該這麼做的原因。

　　第一，你將會擁有更多屬於你自己的時間。你將能夠有時間與親人相處，也會有更多的空閒時間追求你自己的興趣。第二，你會更健康。你將擁有更多的精力。你可以到戶外享受生活，而非將你的所有時間，都花在辦公室裡。一個較輕鬆的工作壓力較小，所以你不論看起來或是感覺上都會比較好。第三，你不會浪費錢。你將會更節儉，因為你所擁有的錢比較少。較輕鬆的工作薪水較低，不過沒關係。這有可能是一件塞翁失馬，焉知非福的事情。你將會把你的需求排出優先順序，並且成為一個更有能力的理財者。最後，你會擁有一個較為均衡的生活。你應該過著多元發展的生活。你不應該當一個工作狂。你應該在工作及玩樂中取得平衡，因為如果你這麼做，你就會更快樂並且活得較長久。

　　總之，選擇對你而言適當的工作。不要選擇一個會讓你整天待在辦公室裡面的工作。想想看什麼才是重要的。

【托福作文原試題】

Which would you choose: a high-paying job with long hours that would give you little time with family and friends or a lower-paying job with shorter hours that would give you more time with family and friends? Explain your choice, using specific reasons and details.

13. *Homework Must Be Practical*

Ladies and gentlemen:
Dear students and friends.
Welcome one and all.

I'd like to talk about homework.
I think it's essential and beneficial.
But educators are going about it the
   wrong way.

Homework should serve a good purpose.
Homework should further a student's
   understanding.
Here are some areas in which I advocate
   reform.

---

practical ('præktɪkl̩)

essential (ə'sɛnʃəl)

educator (ˌɛdʒə'ketə)

serve (sɜv)

further ('fɜðə)

advocate ('ædvəˌket)

one and all

beneficial (ˌbɛnə'fɪʃəl)

go about

purpose ('pɜpəs)

area ('ɛrɪə)

reform (rɪ'fɔrm)

First, stop the mindless assignments.

Stop giving homework out of habit.

This monotony is a big waste of time.

Make homework meaningful.

Make it interesting and useful.

Homework should be practical and applicable
  to learning.

Assign homework appropriately.

Assign it to reinforce learning.

It's time we stopped giving students busywork.

Second, let's give students more time for homework.

Quality homework takes time.

Quality assignments require thoughtful work.

---

mindless ('maɪndlɪs)　　　　assignment (ə'saɪnmənt)

out of　　　　　　　　　　monotony (mə'natn̩ɪ)

meaningful ('minɪŋfəl)　　　applicable ('æplɪkəbl̩)

assign (ə'saɪn)　　　　　appropriately (ə'proprɪɪtlɪ)

reinforce (,rɪɪn'fors)　　　busywork ('bɪzɪ,wɜk)

quality ('kwɑlətɪ)　　　　take (tek)

require (rɪ'kwaɪr)　　　　thoughtful ('θɔtfəl)

Any meaningful work requires more time.

It demands careful effort and planning.

It's not a one night race to complete.

More study time should be given.

There should be a daily study hall.

There should be extra help available to

   all students.

Third, students need less homework.

Teachers shouldn't pile it on.

Teachers should only assign reasonable amounts.

Homework should be supplementary.

Homework shouldn't overwhelm students.

Two or three hours a night is enough.

---

demand (dɪ'mænd)

complete (kəm'plit)

study hall

available (ə'veləbḷ)

reasonable ('riznəbḷ)

supplementary (ˌsʌplə'mɛntərɪ)

overwhelm (ˌovɚ'hwɛlm)

race (res)

daily ('delɪ)

extra ('ɛkɛstrə)

pile on

amount (ə'maʊnt)

Too much homework is detrimental.
Students need time for other activities.
Students deserve time for hobbies and sports.

Fourth, *forget about giving homework every day*.
Try two or three times a week.
Try giving more creative and challenging tasks.

Students need more stimulating assignments.
Students need more opportunity and flexibility.
Small projects, research and group assignments
   would be perfect.

Allow a few days for each assignment.
Allow students to get together during school.
Let students have more interaction time to
   solve problems.

---

detrimental (ˌdɛtrə'mɛntḷ)   deserve (dɪ'zɜv)
creative (krɪ'etɪv)   challenging ('tʃælɪndʒɪŋ)
task (tæsk)   stimulating ('stɪmjəˌletɪŋ)
flexibility (ˌflɛksə'bɪlətɪ)   project ('prɑdʒɛkt)
research ('risɜtʃ , rɪ'sɜtʃ)   allow (ə'lau)
get together   interaction (ˌɪntɚ'ækʃən)

In conclusion, focus on quality not quantity.

Students deserve meaningful homework.

Students should be given enough time to
  do a quality job.

Let's stop wasting valuable time.

Let's make homework worthwhile
  and productive.

Let's give students the skill-building tasks
  they deserve.

Thank you all for listening.

I hope you agree with me.

Homework policies are in need of reform!

---

in conclusion
quantity ('kwɑntətɪ)
worthwhile ('wɜθ'hwaɪl)
productive (prə'dʌktɪv)
skill-building ('skɪl,bɪldɪŋ)
in need of

focus on
valuable ('væljuəbḷ)

policy ('pɑləsɪ)

13. *Homework Must Be Practical*
回家作業必須實用

【演講解説】

Ladies and gentlemen:	各位先生、各位女士：
Dear students and friends.	親愛的學生和朋友。
Welcome one and all.	歡迎大家。
I'd like to talk about homework.	我想要討論回家作業。
I think it's essential and beneficial.	我認為那是必要而且有益的。
But educators are going about it the wrong way.	但是教育者運用回家作業的方法不對。
Homework should serve a good purpose.	回家作業應該符合正確的用途。
Homework should further a student's understanding.	回家作業應該促進學生的了解。
Here are some areas in which I advocate reform.	某些方面我主張改革。

** ──────────────────────────

practical (ˈpræktɪkl̩) *adj.* 實用的　　***one and all*** 全部
essential (əˈsɛnʃəl) *adj.* 必要的　　beneficial (ˌbɛnəˈfɪʃəl) *adj.* 有益的
educator (ˌɛdʒəˈketɚ) *n.* 教育者；教師　　***go about*** 著手處理；做
serve (sɝv) *v.* 符合　　purpose (ˈpɝpəs) *n.* 用途；目的
further (ˈfɝðɚ) *v.* 促進　　area (ˈɛrɪə) *n.* 範圍；方面
advocate (ˈædvəˌket) *v.* 提倡；主張　　reform (rɪˈfɔrm) *n.* 改革

First, stop the mindless assignments. 　第一，不要出欠缺考慮的作業。

Stop giving homework out of habit. 　停止出於習慣而給作業。

This monotony is a big waste of
　　time. 　這種單調無味的事情大大浪費了時間。

Make homework meaningful. 　讓回家作業有意義。

Make it interesting and useful. 　讓它有趣而且有用。

Homework should be practical and
　　applicable to learning. 　回家作業應該實用而且可以適用於學習。

Assign homework appropriately. 　適當地分派回家作業。

Assign it to reinforce learning. 　分派作業來加強學習。

It's time we stopped giving students
　　busywork. 　應該是我們停止給學生讓他們不致於空閒而故意外加的作業。

Second, *let's give students more time
　　for homework*. 　第二，我們給學生更多時間做作業吧。

Quality homework takes time. 　優質的回家作業需要時間。

Quality assignments require
　　thoughtful work. 　優質的作業需要思考。

**

mindless ('maɪndlɪs) *adj.* 欠缺考慮的
assignment (ə'saɪnmənt) *n.* 作業；功課　　*out of* 由於（原因、動機）
monotony (mə'nɑtnɪ) *n.* 單調　　meaningful ('minɪŋfəl) *adj.* 有意義的
applicable ('æplɪkəbḷ) *adj.* 適用的 < *to* >
assign (ə'saɪn) *v.* 分派；指定　　appropriately (ə'propriɪtlɪ) *adv.* 適當地
reinforce (,riɪn'fors) *v.* 加強　　*It's time* + 假設語氣 該是做～的時候了
busywork ('bɪzɪ,wɜk) *n.* 外加作業（使學生不致於空閒而故意外加的作業）
quality ('kwɑlətɪ) *adj.* 優質的　　take (tek) *v.* 需要
require (rɪ'kwaɪr) *v.* 需要　　thoughtful ('θɔtfəl) *adj.* 富有思想的

Any meaningful work requires more time.	任何有意義的事情都需要多一點的時間。
It demands careful effort and planning.	需要細心和規劃。
It's not a one night race to complete.	並不是一個晚上就可以完成的競賽。
More study time should be given.	學生應該擁有更多的唸書時間。
There should be a daily study hall.	應該設有每天開放的自習教室。
There should be extra help available to all students.	應該提供所有學生額外的協助。
***Third*, *students need less homework*.**	第三，學生需要較少的回家作業。
Teachers shouldn't pile it on.	老師不應該出成堆的功課。
Teachers should only assign reasonable amounts.	老師應該只指派合理的功課量。
Homework should be supplementary.	回家作業應該是輔助性的。
Homework shouldn't overwhelm students.	回家作業不應該壓垮學生。
Two or three hours a night is enough.	每晚兩三個小時就夠了。

**

demand〔dɪ'mænd〕v. 要求　　race〔res〕n. 賽跑；比賽
complete〔kəm'plit〕v. 完成　　daily〔'delɪ〕adj. 每天的
study hall 自修教室　　extra〔'ɛkstrə〕adj. 額外的
available〔ə'veləbļ〕adj. 可獲得的＜to＞　　*pile on* 堆積
reasonable〔'riznəbļ〕adj. 合理的　　amount〔ə'maʊnt〕n. 數量
supplementary〔ˌsʌplə'mɛntərɪ〕adj. 補充的
overwhelm〔ˌovɚ'hwɛlm〕v. 淹沒；使受不了

Too much homework is detrimental. | 過多的回家作業是有害的。
Students need time for other activities. | 學生需要時間從事其他活動。
Students deserve time for hobbies and sports. | 學生應該有時間從事嗜好和運動。

***Fourth**, **forget about giving homework every day**.* | 第四，不要每天都出回家作業。
Try two or three times a week. | 試試每個禮拜給兩三次作業。
Try giving more creative and challenging tasks. | 試試出些更有創意和更具挑戰性的作業。

Students need more stimulating assignments. | 學生需要更有刺激性的作業。
Students need more opportunity and flexibility. | 學生需要更多機會和彈性。
Small projects, research and group assignments would be perfect. | 小計劃、研究和團體作業都是理想的選擇。

Allow a few days for each assignment. | 每次作業給學生幾天的時間完成。
Allow students to get together during school. | 允許學生在在校時間可以聚在一起。
Let students have more interaction time to solve problems. | 讓學生有更多的互動時間來解決問題。

** ——————————————

detrimental (ˌdɛtrəˈmɛntl̩) *adj.* 有害的
deserve (dɪˈzɝv) *v.* 應得　　creative (krɪˈetɪv) *adj.* 有創意的
challenging (ˈtʃælɪndʒɪŋ) *adj.* 有挑戰性的　　task (tæsk) *n.* 任務；作業
stimulating (ˈstɪmjəˌletɪŋ) *adj.* 刺激的；激勵的
flexibility (ˌflɛksəˈbɪlətɪ) *n.* 彈性　　project (ˈprɑdʒɛkt) *n.* 計劃
research (ˈrisɝtʃ, rɪˈsɝtʃ) *n.* 研究　　allow (əˈlaʊ) *v.* 允許；給予
get together 聚集　　interaction (ˌɪntɚˈækʃən) *n.* 互動

In conclusion, focus on quality not quantity.　　總之，要重質不重量。

Students deserve meaningful homework.　　學生應該得到有意義的回家作業。

Students should be given enough time to do a quality job.　　學生應該擁有足夠的時間去做有品質的作業。

Let's stop wasting valuable time.　　讓我們停止浪費寶貴的時間。

Let's make homework worthwhile and productive.　　讓我們把回家作業變得值得做，而且有收穫。

Let's give students the skill-building tasks they deserve.　　讓我們給學生增進技巧的作業，這是他們應得的。

Thank you all for listening.　　謝謝你們的聆聽。

I hope you agree with me.　　我希望你們同意我的說法。

Homework policies are in need of reform!　　回家作業的政策需要改革！

** ————————————————

in conclusion 總之　　*focus on* 把焦點集中於

quantity (ˋkwɑntətɪ) *n.* 量

valuable (ˋvæljuəbḷ) *adj.* 寶貴的

worthwhile (ˋwɝθˋhwaɪl) *adj.* 值得做的

productive (prəˋdʌktɪv) *adj.* 富有成效的；有收穫的

skill-building (ˋskɪl͵bɪldɪŋ) *adj.* 建立技巧的

policy (ˋpɑləsɪ) *n.* 政策　　*in need of* 需要

【托福作文範例】

13. Homework Must Be Practical

Students always complain that they are being assigned too much useless homework. I agree. I think homework is essential and beneficial but there are some areas that need reform.

First, stop the mindless assignments. Stop giving homework for the sake of giving homework. Make homework meaningful, interesting and useful. Assign homework appropriately to reinforce learning. *Second*, give students more time for homework. Quality homework takes time and requires thoughtful work. It demands careful effort and planning. More study time should be given. *Third*, students need less homework. Teachers shouldn't pile it on but assign only reasonable amounts. Homework should be supplementary. Too much homework is detrimental. Students need time for other activities like hobbies and sports. *Fourth*, don't give homework every day. Try two or three times a week. Students need more stimulating assignments like group research projects. Allow a few days for each assignment. Let the students have more interaction time to solve problems.

In conclusion, focus on quality not quantity. Students deserve meaningful homework. Students should be given enough time to do a good job. Let's give students skill-building tasks they deserve.

13. 回家作業必須實用

　　學生們總是抱怨他們被指定了太多沒有用的回家作業。我同意。我認爲回家作業是必要的，並且是有益的，但還是有一些需要改革的地方。

　　首先，停止指定一些欠缺考慮的作業。不要再爲了出作業而出作業。要讓回家作業變得有意義、具有趣味性並且實用。適當地指派作業來加強學習的效果。第二，給學生更多的時間來完成回家作業。有品質的回家作業需要花費時間及思考。需要細心及規劃。因此他們應該被給予更多的學習時間。第三，學生需要的是更少的作業。老師不應該給他們成堆的作業，應該只給他們合理的份量。回家作業應該是輔助性的。太多的作業是有害的。學生需要時間來從事其他的活動，像是嗜好或運動。第四，不要每天給作業。嘗試一個禮拜出兩三次的作業。學生需要更多具有刺激性的作業，像是小組研究計劃。讓他們能夠有幾天的時間來完成每一項作業。讓學生彼此之間有更多的時間互動，解決問題。

　　總之，要重質不重量。學生應該得到有意義的回家作業。學生也應該被給予足夠的時間來把作業做好。讓我們給學生增進技巧的作業，這是他們應得的。

【托福作文原試題】

Many teachers assign homework to students every day. Do you think that daily homework is necessary for students? Use specific reasons and details to support your answer.

14. *Grades Encourage Students to Learn*

What a great looking audience!
What a pleasure to be here!
Welcome one and all.

My speech today is about grades.
Grades are the marks we get in school.
Grades are such a big influence in our lives.

Many experts criticize our grading system.
Many educators respectfully disagree.
Let me tell you how I feel about grades.

---

grade (gred)

great looking

one and all

influence ('ɪnfluəns)

criticize ('krɪtə‚saɪz)

educator ('ɛdʒə‚ketɚ , 'ɛdʒu-)

respectfully (rɪ'spɛktfəlɪ)

looking ('lʊkɪŋ)

audience ('ɔdɪəns)

mark (mɑrk)

expert ('ɛkspɜt)

Let me start with a definition.

Grades can be numbers, letters or even symbols.

Grades indicate a student's level of achievement.

Grades are evaluations.

They are ratings on our efforts.

They are valuable feedback from our teachers.

A numerical grade is called a score.

A general grade is called a mark.

All grades are either passing or failing.

Everyone knows that grades are important.

They determine our future success.

They are a good indicator of how well we'll do.

---

start with   definition (ˌdɛfəˈnɪʃən)

letter (ˈlɛtɚ)   symbol (ˈsɪmbḷ)

indicate (ˈɪndəˌket)   level (ˈlɛvḷ)

achievement (əˈtʃivmənt)   evaluation (ɪˌvæljuˈeʃən)

rating (ˈretɪŋ)   valuable (ˈvæljuəbḷ)

feedback (ˈfidˌbæk)   numerical (njuˈmɛrɪkḷ)

score (skor)   indicator (ˈɪndəˌketɚ)

High marks can win you scholarships.

High scores can win admissions to the best schools.

Better grades mean better opportunities.

Grades carry great weight.

Grades affect us in many ways.

Every student, parent and employer knows
  this is true.

Grades are a good way to measure intelligence.

Grades efficiently reflect performance.

Grades are the best evaluating method.

The grading system is convenient for educators.

Scores are calculated with uniform standards.

Scores give objective, clear-cut results.

---

scholarship ('skɑlə͵ʃɪp)   admission (əd'mɪʃən)

carry ('kærɪ)   weight (wet)

employer (ɪm'plɔɪɚ)   measure ('mɛʒɚ)

intelligence (ɪn'tɛlədʒəns)   efficiently (ə'fɪʃəntlɪ, ɪ-)

reflect (rɪ'flɛkt)   performance (pɚ'fɔrməns)

evaluate (ɪ'vælju͵et)   calculate ('kælkjə͵let)

uniform ('junə͵fɔrm)   standard ('stændɚd)

objective (əb'dʒɛktɪv)   clear-cut ('klɪr'kʌt)

The grading system isn't perfect.

The grading system has its flaws.

But it is the best way developed so far.

Grades really do motivate.

They provide great incentive.

They inspire students to excel.

Students yearn for perfect scores.

Students desire top grades.

This is our system's number one goal.

Grades are why students work hard.

Grades impel students to sacrifice.

Good grades are a powerful psychological force.

---

flaw (flɔ)

so far

incentive (ɪn'sɛntɪv)

excel (ɪk'sɛl)

desire (dɪ'zaɪr)

number one

impel (ɪm'pɛl)

psychological (ˌsaɪkə'lɑdʒɪkl̩)

develop (dɪ'vɛləp)

motivate ('motə,vet)

inspire (ɪn'spaɪr)

yearn (jɜn)

top (tɑp)

goal (gol)

sacrifice ('sækrə,faɪs)

force (fors)

In conclusion, let me summarize.

Grades are a great motivator.

Grades really serve a useful purpose.

They are worthwhile and necessary.

They inform us of our progress.

They encourage us to study hard.

Thank you all for listening.

I wish you the best of luck.

Get good grades for a wonderful life!

---

in conclusion   summarize ('sʌmə,raɪz)

motivator ('motə,vetɚ)   serve (sɝv)

purpose ('pɝpəs)   worthwhile ('wɝθ'hwaɪl)

inform (ɪn'fɔrm)   progress ('prɑgrɛs)

14. *Grades Encourage Students to Learn*
分數鼓勵學生學習

【演講解説】

What a great looking audience!	看起來都很棒的聽衆們！
What a pleasure to be here!	很榮幸能夠來到這裡！
Welcome one and all.	歡迎大家。
My speech today is about grades.	今天我的演說是關於成績。
Grades are the marks we get in school.	成績是我們在學校得到的分數。
Grades are such a big influence in our lives.	成績在我們的人生中具有非常大的影響力。
Many experts criticize our grading system.	許多專家批評我們的評分制度。
Many educators respectfully disagree.	許多教育者愼重地提出反對意見。
Let me tell you how I feel about grades.	讓我告訴你我對成績的感覺。

＊＊ ──────────────

grade〔gred〕*n.* 分數；成績（＝mark〔mɑrk〕＝score〔skor〕） *v.* 評分
looking〔'lukɪŋ〕*adj.* 有…樣子的；看起來…的（常用以構成複合詞）
great looking 看起來很棒的　　audience〔'ɔdɪəns〕*n.* 聽衆
one and all 全部；大家　　influence〔'ɪnfluəns gred〕*n.* 影響力
expert〔'ɛkspɝt〕*n.* 專家　　criticize〔'krɪtə,saɪz〕*v.* 批評
educator〔'ɛdʒə,ketə,'ɛdʒʊ-〕*n.* 教育者
respectfully〔rɪ'spɛktfəlɪ〕*adv.* 恭敬地；鄭重地

Let me start with a definition.　　　讓我先從下定義開始。

Grades can be numbers, letters or　　　成績可以是數字、字母，或甚
  even symbols.　　　至是符號。

Grades indicate a student's level　　　成績表示學生的學業成就程度
  of achievement.　　　有多高。

Grades are evaluations.　　　成績是評價。

They are ratings on our efforts.　　　它們是對我們努力程度的評分。

They are valuable feedback from　　　它們是老師給的珍貴意見。
  our teachers.

A numerical grade is called a score.　　　數字形式的成績叫做分數。

A general grade is called a mark.　　　一般的成績（grade）叫做成
  績（mark）。

All grades are either passing or　　　所有的成績，不是及格，就是
  failing.　　　不及格。

Everyone knows that grades are　　　每個人都知道成績很重要。
important.

They determine our future success.　　　它們決定我們未來成功與否。

They are a good indicator of how　　　它們是我們未來會多好的有效
  well we'll do.　　　指標。

**

start with 以…開始　　definition〔͵dɛfə'nɪʃən〕*n.* 定義
letter〔'lɛtɚ〕*n.* 字母　　symbol〔'sɪmbl̩〕*n.* 符號
indicate〔'ɪndə͵ket〕*v.* 指出；表示　　level〔'lɛvl̩〕*n.* 程度
achievement〔ə'tʃivmənt〕*n.* 成就　　evaluation〔ɪ͵vælju'eʃən〕*n.* 評價
rating〔'retɪŋ〕*n.* 評分　　valuable〔'væljuəbl̩〕*adj.* 珍貴的
feedback〔'fid͵bæk〕*n.* 反饋；意見反應
numerical〔nju'mɛrɪkl̩〕*adj.* 以數字表示的
general〔'dʒɛnərəl〕*adj.* 一般的　　indicator〔'ɪndə͵ketɚ〕*n.* 指標

High marks can win you
　　scholarships.

High scores can win admissions to
　　the best schools.

Better grades mean better
　　opportunities.

高分可以替你贏得獎學金。

分數高可以讓你進入頂尖學校
就讀。

成績比較好表示會更有機會。

Grades carry great weight.

Grades affect us in many ways.

Every student, parent and employer
　　knows this is true.

成績非常重要。

成績在許多方面影響我們。

每個學生、父母和雇主都知道
這是事實。

***Grades are a good way to measure
　　intelligence.***

Grades efficiently reflect
　　performance.

Grades are the best evaluating
　　method.

成績是測量智能的有效方式。

成績能有效率地反映表現。

成績是最佳的評估方法。

**

scholarship ('skɑlə,ʃɪp) *n.* 獎學金
admission (əd'mɪʃən) *n.* (入學) 許可 < *to* >
carry ('kærɪ) *v.* 具有　　weight (wet) *n.* 重要性
measure ('mɛʒə) *v.* 測量；衡量
intelligence (ɪn'tɛlədʒəns) *n.* 智能
efficiently (ə'fɪʃəntlɪ,ɪ-) *adv.* 有效率地
reflect (rɪ'flɛkt) *v.* 反映　　performance (pə'fɔrməns) *n.* 表現
evaluate (ɪ'væljuˌet) *v.* 評估

The grading system is convenient
for educators.

評分制度對教育者而言是方便
的。

Scores are calculated with uniform
standards.

成績以相同的標準來計算。

Scores give objective, clear-cut
results.

成績提供了客觀明確的結果。

The grading system isn't perfect.

這個評分制度並不完善。

The grading system has its flaws.

這個評分制度有其缺陷。

But it is the best way developed
so far.

但是這是到目前為止所研發出
最好的方式。

Grades really do motivate.

成績真的具有激勵作用。

They provide great incentive.

它們提供強大的動機。

They inspire students to excel.

它們激勵學生要追求卓越。

Students yearn for perfect scores.

學生渴望完美的成績。

Students desire top grades.

學生渴望得到最高的成績。

This is our system's number one goal.

此為我們這個制度的首要目標。

_____

calculate (ˈkælkjəˌlet) v. 計算　　uniform (ˈjunəˌfɔrm) adj. 相同的
standard (ˈstændəd) n. 標準　　objective (əbˈdʒɛktɪv) adj. 客觀的
clear-cut (ˈklɪrˈkʌt) adj. 明確的；清楚的　　flaw (flɔ) n. 缺點
develop (dɪˈvɛləp) v. 研發　　***so far*** 到目前為止
motivate (ˈmotəˌvet) v. 激勵；使 (學生等) 產生學習之興趣或動力
incentive (ɪnˈsɛntɪv) n. 刺激；動機　　inspire (ɪnˈspaɪr) v. 激勵
excel (ɪkˈsɛl) v. 突出；勝過他人　　yearn (jɜn) v. 渴望 < *for* >
desire (dɪˈzaɪr) v. 渴望　　top (tɑp) adj. 最高的；最優良的
number one 第一的　　goal (gol) n. 目標

Grades are why students work hard.	成績是學生為什麼努力唸書的原因。
Grades impel students to sacrifice.	成績驅使學生要犧牲。
Good grades are a powerful psychological force.	好成績是強大的心理力量。
In conclusion, let me summarize.	總之，讓我來作個總結。
Grades are a great motivator.	成績是很好的驅策力。
Grades really serve a useful purpose.	成績真的很有用。
They are worthwhile and necessary.	它們是值得而且必要的。
They inform us of our progress.	它們讓我們知道自己進步了多少。
They encourage us to study hard.	它們鼓勵我們要努力唸書。
Thank you all for listening.	謝謝你們的聆聽。
I wish you the best of luck.	我祝你們好運。
Get good grades for a wonderful life!	能得到好成績，擁有美好的人生！

**

impel〔ɪmˈpɛl〕v. 驅使；激勵　　sacrifice〔ˈsækrəˌfaɪs〕v. 犧牲

psychological〔ˌsaɪkəˈlɑdʒɪkḷ〕adj. 心理的　　force〔fors〕n. 力量

in conclusion 總之　　summarize〔ˈsʌməˌraɪz〕v. 總結

motivator〔ˈmotəˌvetɚ〕n. 驅策者　　serve〔sɝv〕v. 適合

purpose〔ˈpɝpəs〕n. 用途；目的　　worthwhile〔ˈwɝθˈhwaɪl〕adj. 值得的

inform〔ɪnˈfɔrm〕v. 通知 <*of*>　　progress〔ˈprɑgrɛs〕n. 進步

【托福作文範例】

14. Grades Encourage Students to Learn

Nothing is more important to a student than getting good grades. Many experts may criticize our grading system while educators disagree. Let me tell you how I feel about grades.

Let me start by defining grades. Grades can be numbers, letters or even symbols. Grades indicate a student's level of achievement. They are evaluations of a student's effort and provide feedback from teachers. Everyone knows that grades are important. They determine a student's future success and are often a good indicator of how well we'll do. High marks can get you scholarships and win admission to the best schools. Better grades often mean better opportunities. Grades carry great weight and affect us in many ways. Grades are a good way to measure intelligence. Grades efficiently reflect performance and are the best evaluating method. The grading system is convenient for educators. Scores give objective, clear-cut results. Grades motivate students by providing an incentive to excel. Students yearning for top scores will study harder to get them.

In conclusion, I think grades are a great motivator. They inform us of our progress and encourage us to study hard.

14. 分數鼓勵學生學習

　　對學生而言，沒有什麼事情會比得到好成績要來得更重要。許多專家也許會批評我們的評分制度，然而教育者並不同意他們的看法。讓我來告訴你們我對成績的感覺。

　　讓我先從定義「成績」開始。成績可以是數字、字母或甚至是符號。成績表示學生的學業成就程度有多高。它們是對於學生努力的評估，也提供了老師對於學生的意見。所有人都知道，成績是很重要的。它們決定了學生未來成功與否，而且常常是學生未來成就的良好指標。成績高可以讓你得到獎學金，並且贏得最好學校的入學許可。較好的成績通常代表了機會比較大。成績非常重要，而且在許多方面影響我們。成績是測量智能的好方法。成績能夠有效地反應出我們的表現，是一個最佳的評量方式。評分制度對於教育者而言，是相當方便的。成績提供了客觀及明確的結果。成績能激勵學生，提供他們追求卓越的動力。渴望能夠得到頂尖成績的學生，會為此而更加努力學習。

　　總之，我認為成績是一個很棒的驅策力。它們能讓我們了解自己進步了多少，並且鼓勵我們努力唸書。

【托福作文原試題】

Do you agree or disagree with the following statement? Grades (marks) encourage students to learn. Use specific reasons and examples to support your opinion.

15. *Coeducation: Learning Together Is Best*

Ladies and gentlemen:
Greetings and welcome.
My topic is coeducation.

Coeducation means males and females
  studying together.
It's boys and girls attending the same schools.
It's having diversity and equal opportunity in school.

I'm a strong advocate of coeducation.
I think its advantages are many.
Here is why I support coeducation.

First, coeducation increases competition.
Students improve by interacting.
Students perform better when challenged by
  each other's talents.

---

greetings ('gritɪŋz)

male (mel)

diversity (də'vɜsətɪ ,daɪ-)

advocate ('ædvəkɪt)

support (sə'port)

interact (,ɪntə'ækt)

coeducation (,koɛdʒə'keʃən)

female ('fimel)

equal ('ikwəl)

advantage (əd'væntɪdʒ)

competition (,kɑmpə'tɪʃən)

challenge ('tʃælɪndʒ)

Competition between the sexes is good.

Competition is natural and healthy.

It's been proven to raise learning standards.

Coeducation provides a higher level
   of learning.

Coeducation produces quality results.

It's beneficial for boys and girls to compete
   against each other.

***Second, coeducation teaches valuable
   social skills.***

The interaction improves interpersonal skills.

The co-ed environment creates a more balanced
   gender perspective.

---

sex (sɛks)	natural ('nætʃərəl)
raise (rez)	standard ('stændəd)
level ('lɛvḷ)	quality ('kwɑlətɪ)
beneficial (ˌbɛnə'fɪʃəl)	compete (kəm'pit)
valuable ('væljuəbḷ)	social ('soʃəl)
interaction (ˌɪntə'ækʃən)	interpersonal (ˌɪntə'pɜsṇl)
co-ed ('ko'ɛd)	balanced ('bælənst)
gender ('dʒɛndə)	perspective (pə'spɛktɪv)

Students are more sensitive and mature.

Students are more respectful and considerate.

Coeducation increases mutual awareness
 and understanding.

Students actually treat each other better.

Coeducation encourages courtesy.

Coeducation requires learning good manners
 and being polite.

**Third, coeducation better prepares students
 for the future.**

Co-ed classes prepare students for the workplace.

Coexistence is a reality of our culture.

Coeducation is a reflection of society.

The real world is coeducational.

The everyday interaction of both sexes is normal.

---

sensitive ('sɛnsətɪv)   mature (mə'tjʊr)
respectful (rɪ'spɛktfəl)   considerate (kən'sɪdərɪt)
mutual ('mjutʃʊəl)   awareness (ə'wɛrnɪs)
encourage (ɪn'kɜɪdʒ)   courtesy ('kɜtəsɪ)
manners ('mænəz)   workplace ('wɜk,ples)
coexistence (,koɪg'zɪstəns)   reality (rɪ'ælətɪ)
reflection (rɪ'flɛkʃən)   coeducational (,koɛdʒə'keʃənḷ)
everyday ('ɛvrɪ'de)   normal ('nɔrmḷ)

Integration is simple common sense.

Young boys and girls should learn together.

Young people should interact with each other
  as they grow up.

**Finally, I'd like to refute a critique
  of coeducation.**

Some experts say it's a distraction on learning.

Some say students focus more on each other
  than curriculum.

I don't think that's true at all.

Single sex classrooms are too isolated.

Single sex classrooms are a cocoon-like
  environment.

---

integration (ˌɪntəˈgreʃən)   **common sense**
refute (rɪˈfjut)   critique (krɪˈtik)
expert (ˈɛkspɜt)   distraction (dɪˈstrækʃən)
focus on   curriculum (kəˈrɪkjələm)
not…at all   single (ˈsɪŋɡḷ)
isolated (ˈaɪsḷˌetɪd)   cocoon (kəˈkun)
cocoon-like

Co-ed schools do, however, have additional challenges.
Co-ed school teachers might have stricter
  disciplinary guidelines to follow.
Students at co-ed schools have no trouble
  concentrating whatsoever!

In conclusion, *coeducation offers equal opportunities*.
Coeducation is better for both males and females.
Coeducation is a reality we must accept.

Males and females must work together in life.
Males and females need each other to succeed.
Students need coeducation to really succeed.

Both sexes have much to learn from each other.
I think everyone in this room will agree.
I hope you'll all help promote coeducation with me.

---

additional (ə'dɪʃənḷ)   challenge ('tʃælɪndʒ)
disciplinary ('dɪsəplɪn‚ɛrɪ)   guideline ('gaɪd‚laɪn)
have trouble + *V-ing*   concentrate ('kɑnsn‚tret)
whatsoever (‚whatso'ɛvɚ)   *in conclusion*
promote (prə'mot)

15. *Coeducation: Learning Together Is Best*
男女合校：共同學習最好

【演講解說】

Ladies and gentlemen:	各位先生、各位女士：
Greetings and welcome.	歡迎大家。
My topic is coeducation.	我的主題是男女合校。
Coeducation means males and females studying together.	男女合校表示男女一起讀書。
It's boys and girls attending the same schools.	男生和女生上同樣的學校。
It's having diversity and equal opportunity in school.	學校裡會有多樣性和平等的機會。
I'm a strong advocate of coeducation.	我是男女同校的強烈擁護者。
I think its advantages are many.	我認為其優點很多。
Here is why I support coeducation.	以下是為什麼我支持男女合校。
First, coeducation increases competition.	第一，男女合校能增加競爭。
Students improve by interacting.	學生透過互動而進步。
Students perform better when challenged by each other's talents.	學生會挑戰彼此的才能，因而表現更好。

**

greetings〔'gritɪŋz〕*n. pl.* 問候語
coeducation〔ˏkoɛdʒə'keʃən〕*n.* 男女合校的教育；男女合校
male〔mel〕*n.* 男性   female〔'fimel〕*n.* 女性
diversity〔də'vɝsətɪ,daɪ-〕*n.* 多樣性   equal〔'ikwəl〕*adj.* 相等的
advocate〔'ædvəkɪt〕*n.* 擁護者   advantage〔əd'væntɪdʒ〕*n.* 優點
support〔sə'port〕*v.* 支持   competition〔ˏkampə'tɪʃən〕*n.* 競爭
interact〔ˏɪntə'ækt〕*v.* 交互作用；互相影響   challenge〔'tʃælɪndʒ〕*v. n.* 挑戰

Competition between the sexes is good.	兩性之間的競爭是好的。
Competition is natural and healthy.	競爭是自然而且健康的。
It's been proven to raise learning standards.	經過證實可以提高學習水準。
Coeducation provides a higher level of learning.	男女合校提供更高層次的學習。
Coeducation produces quality results.	男女合校造成優值的結果。
It's beneficial for boys and girls to compete against each other.	男女生彼此競爭是有益的。
Second, coeducation teaches valuable social skills.	第二，男女合校教導珍貴的社交技巧。
The interaction improves interpersonal skills.	互動有助於人際技巧。
The co-ed environment creates a more balanced gender perspective.	男女合校的環境創造出更均衡的性別觀點。

**

sex〔sɛks〕*n.* 男性；女性　　natural〔'nætʃərəl〕*adj.* 自然的
raise〔rez〕*v.* 提高　　standard〔'stændəd〕*n.* 水準
level〔'lɛvl̩〕*n.* 程度　　quality〔'kwalətɪ〕*adj.* 優質的
beneficial〔͵bɛnə'fɪʃəl〕*adj.* 有益的　　compete〔kəm'pit〕*v.* 競爭
valuable〔'væljuəbl̩〕*adj.* 珍貴的　　social〔'soʃəl〕*adj.* 社交的
interaction〔͵ɪntə'ækʃən〕*n.* 交互作用
interpersonal〔͵ɪntə'pɝsn̩l̩〕*adj.* 人與人之間的；人際關係的
co-ed〔'ko͵ɛd〕*adj.* 男女合校的　　balanced〔'bælənst〕*adj.* 均衡的
gender〔'dʒɛndə〕*n.* 性別　　perspective〔pə'spɛktɪv〕*n.* 觀點

Students are more sensitive and mature.	學生會更敏感與成熟。
Students are more respectful and considerate.	學生會更尊重別人與體貼。
Coeducation increases mutual awareness and understanding.	男女合校讓人更注意到彼此，而且更能互相了解。
Students actually treat each other better.	學生實際上對彼此更好。
Coeducation encourages courtesy.	男女合校讓大家更有禮貌。
Coeducation requires learning good manners and being polite.	男女合校需要學習良好的禮節並且有禮貌。
Third, coeducation better prepares students for the future.	第三，男女合校更能幫助學生對未來做準備。
Co-ed classes prepare students for the workplace.	男女合班讓學生為職場做準備。
Coexistence is a reality of our culture.	共存是我們文化的現實情況。

＊＊————————————————

sensitive (ˈsɛnsətɪv) *adj.* 敏感的　　mature (məˈtjʊr) *adj.* 成熟的
respectful (rɪˈspɛktfəl) *adj.* 尊敬的
considerate (kənˈsɪdərɪt) *adj.* 體貼的　　mutual (ˈmjutʃuəl) *adj.* 互相的
awareness (əˈwɛrnɪs) *n.* 意識　　encourage (ɪnˈkɜɪdʒ) *v.* 促進
courtesy (ˈkɜtəsɪ) *n.* 禮貌　　manners (ˈmænəz) *n. pl.* 禮貌；規矩
workplace (ˈwɜk,ples) *n.* 工作場所
coexistence (ˌkoɪgˈzɪstəns) *n.* 共存
reality (rɪˈælətɪ) *n.* 現實；實際存在的事物

Coeducation is a reflection of society. 　男女合校能反映社會。
The real world is coeducational. 　現實的世界是男女合校的。
The everyday interaction of both 　兩性日常的互動是正常的。
　　sexes is normal.

Integration is simple common sense. 　融合是簡單的常識。
Young boys and girls should learn 　年輕的男生和女生應該一起學習。
　　together.
Young people should interact with 　年輕人長大後應該彼此互動。
　　each other as they grow up.

Finally, I'd like to refute a critique 　最後一點，我相要反駁一項對男
of coeducation. 　女合校的批評。
Some experts say it's a distraction 　有些專家說，那會造成學習上的
　　on learning. 　分心。
Some say students focus more on 　有些人說學生比較注意彼此，比
　　each other than curriculum. 　較不注重課程。

I don't think that's true at all. 　我完全不認為那是真的。
Single sex classrooms are too isolated. 　單一性別的教室太孤立了。
Single sex classrooms are a cocoon- 　單一性別的教室，就像繭一般的
　　like environment. 　環境，與外界隔絕。

** ————————————————

reflection〔rɪˈflɛkʃən〕*n.* 反映
coeducational〔ˌkoɛdʒəˈkeʃənḷ〕*adj.* 男女合校的
everyday〔ˈɛvrɪˌde〕*adj.* 日常的　　normal〔ˈnɔrmḷ〕*adj.* 正常的
integration〔ˌɪntəˈgreʃən〕*n.* 整合；融合
common sense 常識　　refute〔rɪˈfjut〕*v.* 反駁
critique〔krɪˈtik〕*n.* 批評　　expert〔ˈɛkspɜt〕*n.* 專家
distraction〔dɪˈstrækʃən〕*n.* 使人分心的事物　***focus on*** 專注於
curriculum〔kəˈrɪkjələm〕*n.* 課程　***not…at all*** 一點也不
single〔ˈsɪŋḷ〕*adj.* 單一的　　isolated〔ˈaɪsḷˌetɪd〕*adj.* 孤立的
cocoon〔kəˈkun〕*n.* 繭　***cocoon-like*** 如繭一般隔絕的

Co-ed schools do, however, have additional challenges.	不過男女合校還是有其他的挑戰。
Co-ed school teachers might have stricter disciplinary guidelines to follow.	男女合校的老師可能要遵守更嚴格的紀律指導方針。
Students at co-ed schools have no trouble concentrating whatsoever!	男女合校的學生沒有專不專心之類的問題！
In conclusion, coeducation offers equal opportunities.	總之，男女合校提供相等的機會。
Coeducation is better for both males and females.	男女合校對男女都更好。
Coeducation is a reality we must accept.	男女合校是我們必須接受的現實。
Males and females must work together in life.	男女在生活上必須一起合作。
Males and females need each other to succeed.	男女需要彼此才能成功。
Students need coeducation to really succeed.	學生需要男女合校，才能真正成功。
Both sexes have much to learn from each other.	兩性彼此要互相學習的地方很多。
I think everyone in this room will agree.	我認為在場的每個人都會同意。
I hope you'll all help promote coeducation with me.	我希望你們全都能夠協助我，提倡男女合校。

** ─────────────

additional (əˋdɪʃənḷ) *adj.* 附加的
disciplinary (ˋdɪsəplɪnˏɛrɪ) *adj.* 紀律的　guideline (ˋgaɪdˏlaɪn) *n.* 指導方針
have trouble + V-ing 做…有困難　　concentrate (ˋkɑnsnˏtret) *v.* 專心
whatsoever (ˏwhɑtsoˋɛvɚ) *pron.* 無論什麼 (whatever 的強調型)
in conclusion 總之　　promote (prəˋmot) *v.* 提倡

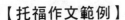

【托福作文範例】

15. Coeducation

Some schools insist on separating the student population into males and females. But I think that's wrong. I am an advocate of coeducation, which is boys and girls studying together, and I will tell you why.

First, coeducation increases competition. Students improve by interacting which leads to competition. Competition between the sexes is good. It's natural and healthy. *Second*, coeducation teaches valuable social skills. The co-ed environment creates a more balanced gender perspective. Students are more respectful and considerate. Coeducation encourages courtesy. *Third*, coeducation better prepares students for the future. Coexistence is a reality of our culture and a reflection of society. The everyday interaction of both sexes is normal. *Finally*, there is a critique of coeducation that I disagree with. Some experts say it's distracting and that students will focus more on each other than curriculum. I don't think that's true. Single sex classrooms are too isolated. It's not an effective learning environment.

In conclusion, coeducation offers equal opportunities. Coeducation is better for both males and females. Both sexes have much to learn from each other. So support coeducation today.

15. 男女合校

　　有些學校堅持要將學生分為男性及女性兩群。但我認為那是不對的。我是一個男女合校的擁護者，也就是男生和女生要在一起學習，讓我告訴你們原因。

　　第一，男女合校能增加競爭。學生藉由互動帶來的競爭而進步。兩性之間的競爭是有益的。那是相當自然而且健康的。第二，男女合校能夠教導學生珍貴的社交技巧。男女合校的環境能夠創造出一個更為均衡的性別觀點。學生會變得更加尊重他人而且體貼。男女合校能讓人更有禮貌。第三，男女合校使學生對未來有更充分的準備。男女共存是我們文化中的現況，也反映了社會。兩性之間日常的互動是正常的。最後一點，有一個對男女合校的批評是我不同意的。有些專家說，男女合校會讓學生分心，他們會比較專注於彼此，比較不專心於課業。我不認為這是真的。單一性別的教室太過於孤立了。那不會是一個有效果的學習環境。

　　總之，男女合校提供了平等的機會。男女合校無論對於男性或是女性而言，都會比較好。兩性彼此有很多地方可以互相學習。所以現在就支持男女合校吧。

【托福作文原試題】

Do you agree or disagree with the following statement? Boys and girls should attend separate schools. Use specific reasons and examples to support your answer.

16. *A Comprehensive Education Is Best*

Welcome everybody.
I'm delighted you're here.
I hope you'll enjoy my speech.

My topic today is education.
My main point is that a comprehensive education
  is best.
I plan to explain why in this speech.

Some universities require students to specialize
  in one subject.
Some require students to take classes in many
  subjects.
Here's why I support the latter.

---

comprehensive (ˌkɑmprɪ'hɛnsɪv)
delighted (dɪ'laɪtɪd)   *main point*
require (rɪ'kwaɪr)   specialize ('spɛʃəlˌaɪz)
support (sə'port)   *the latter*

***First, taking many classes develops well-rounded
individuals.***

Students can gain more knowledge.

Students can learn a wider range of things.

It's better to study many things.

It gives students a broad base of knowledge.

They can be a "Jack of all trades" in many
different areas.

This type of education is more balanced.

It provides lots of more general information.

It makes students more flexible, too.

---

well-rounded ('wɛl'raʊndɪd) individual (‚ɪndə'vɪdʒʊəl)

gain (gen) range (rendʒ)

broad (brɔd) base (bes)

trade (tred) *Jack of all trades*

area ('ɛrɪə) balanced ('bælənst)

general ('dʒɛnərəl) flexible ('flɛksəbļ)

***Second, taking many classes creates a solid
  knowledge foundation***.
It's kind of like building a pyramid.
It's compiling information, like blocks on top
  of blocks.

Knowledge builds on top of knowledge.
The more you learn, the more you can learn.
The more you know, the more you can know.

Old knowledge clarifies new knowledge.
General knowledge facilitates learning.
General knowledge also enhances creativity.

Third, taking many classes strengthens your mind.
Taking many classes opens your mind.
You'll grasp more ideas and do more intellectual
  work.

---

solid (ˈsɑlɪd)   foundation (faʊnˈdeʃən)
kind of   pyramid (ˈpɪrəmɪd)
compile (kəmˈpaɪl)   block (blɑk)
on top of   clarify (ˈklærə͵faɪ)
facilitate (fəˈsɪlə͵tet)   enhance (ɪnˈhæns)
creativity (͵krieˈtɪvətɪ)   strengthen (ˈstrɛŋθən)
grasp (græsp)   intellectual (͵ɪntl̩ˈɛktʃʊəl)

Your mind is like a muscle.

You must exercise it a lot.

You must challenge it to make it stronger.

A comprehensive education stimulates
　　your mind.

It presents many new ideas.

It provides you with new tools for understanding.

Finally, taking many classes will help you to
　　discover your true interests.

It will help you to select a major.

It will assist you in finding a suitable career.

You'll have tried many subjects.

You'll have tested many areas.

You'll have a good idea of what you like.

---

muscle (ˈmʌsḷ)	exercise (ˈɛksɚˌsaɪz)
challenge (ˈtʃælɪndʒ)	stimulate (ˈstɪmjəˌlet)
present (prɪˈzɛnt)	select (səˈlɛkt)
major (ˈmedʒɚ)	assist (əˈsɪst)
suitable (ˈsutəbḷ)	career (kəˈrɪr)
test (tɛst)	

It's not a waste of time.

It's a precious experience that you'll gain.

You'll have a much better focus on the future.

In conclusion, you'll be happier and smarter.

They say that variety is the spice of life.

They also say that knowledge is power.

Taking many classes will make you more
  intelligent.

A general knowledge is your best asset.

A comprehensive education is the best.

Believe me everybody!

Believe it because it's true.

Now God bless you all and happy learning.

---

precious ('prɛʃəs)

in conclusion

spice (spaɪs)

intelligent (ɪn'tɛlədʒənt)

bless (blɛs)

focus ('fokəs)

variety (və'raɪətɪ)

power ('pauɚ)

asset ('æsɛt)

happy ('hæpɪ)

16. *A Comprehensive Education Is Best*
多元化的教育最好

【演講解説】

Welcome everybody.	歡迎大家。
I'm delighted you're here.	我很高興你們能夠來到這裡。
I hope you'll enjoy my speech.	我希望你們喜歡我的演說。
My topic today is education.	我今天的主題是教育。
My main point is that a comprehensive education is best.	我的重點是多元化的教育是最好的。
I plan to explain why in this speech.	我打算在這次的演講中說明原因。
Some universities require students to specialize in one subject.	有些大學要求學生專攻單一學科。
Some require students to take classes in many subjects.	有些大學要求學生修許多不同學科的課程。
Here's why I support the latter.	以下就是為什麼我支持後者的原因。

** ————————————————————

comprehensive〔͵kɑmprɪˈhɛnsɪv〕*adj.* 全面的;廣泛的
delighted〔dɪˈlaɪtɪd〕*adj.* 高興的   *main point* 重點
require〔rɪˈkwaɪr〕*v.* 要求   specialize〔ˈspɛʃəl͵aɪz〕*v.* 專攻 *< in >*
support〔səˈport〕*v.* 支持   *the latter* 後者

*First, taking many classes develops
　well-rounded individuals*.
Students can gain more knowledge.
Students can learn a wider range of
　things.

It's better to study many things.
It gives students a broad base of
　knowledge.
They can be a "Jack of all trades" in
　many different areas.

This type of education is more balanced.
It provides lots of more general
　information.
It makes students more flexible, too.

*Second, taking many classes creates a
　solid knowledge foundation*.
It's kind of like building a pyramid.
It's compiling information, like blocks
　on top of blocks.

首先，選修許多不同的學科能培
養出通才。
學生可以得到更多知識。
學生可以學習到更廣泛的事物。

學習許多不同的事物比較好。
能提供學生更廣泛的知識基礎。

他們可以成爲許多不同領域的
「萬事通」。

這樣的教育比較均衡發展。
它能提供更多的一般資訊。

也讓學生適應力更強。

第二，選修許多不同的課程能
建立堅實的知識基礎。
有點像是在蓋金字塔。
這就是收集資訊，就像是一塊
石頭之上再蓋一塊。

** ——————————————

well-rounded ('wɛl'raundɪd) *adj.* (知識、經驗等) 涵蓋多方面的；廣泛的
individual (,ɪndə'vɪdʒəl) *n.* 個人　　range (rendʒ) *n.* (知識等的) 範圍
broad (brɔd) *adj.* 廣泛的　　base (bes) *n.* 基礎　　trade (tred) *n.* 技藝
Jack of all trades 萬事通　　area ('ɛrɪə) *n.* 領域
balanced ('bælənst) *adj.* 均衡的　　general ('dʒɛnərəl) *adj.* 一般的
flexible ('flɛksəbḷ) *adj.* 有彈性的；有適應性的　　solid ('salɪd) *adj.* 穩固的
foundation (faun'deʃən) *n.* 基礎　　*kind of* 有點
pyramid ('pɪrəmɪd) *n.* 金字塔　　compile (kəm'paɪl) *v.* 收集 (資料等)
block (blɑk) *n.* (木或石等的) 一塊　　*on top of* 在…上面

Knowledge builds on top of knowledge.	知識是累積而成的。
The more you learn, the more you can learn.	你學的越多,你就擁有更多學習的能力。
The more you know, the more you can know.	你知道的越多,你能知道的東西就越多。
Old knowledge clarifies new knowledge.	固有的知識能釐清新的知識。
General knowledge facilitates learning.	一般性的知識能促進學習。
General knowledge also enhances creativity.	一般性的知識也能提昇創造力。
Third, taking many classes strengthens your mind.	第三,選修許多不同的課程,以加強你的心智。
Taking many classes opens your mind.	選修許多不同的課程,能擴展你的視野。
You'll grasp more ideas and do more intellectual work.	你將會理解更多知識,而且更常動腦筋思考。

** ――――――――――――――――

clarify (ˈklærəˌfaɪ) v. 澄清;闡明
facilitate (fəˈsɪləˌtet) v. 促進;幫助
enhance (ɪnˈhæns) v. 提高;增進   creativity (ˌkrieˈtɪvətɪ) n. 創造力
strengthen (ˈstrɛŋθən) v. 加強   grasp (græsp) v. 理解
intellectual (ˌɪntlˈɛktʃuəl) adj. 需要智力的;要用腦筋的

Your mind is like a muscle. | 你的心智就像是肌肉。
You must exercise it a lot. | 你必須常常運用它。
You must challenge it to make it stronger. | 你必須刺激它，讓它更加強壯。

A comprehensive education stimulates your mind. | 多元化的教育能刺激你的心智。
It presents many new ideas. | 它提供許多新的想法。
It provides you with new tools for understanding. | 它提供你新的理解工具。

Finally, *taking many classes will help you to discover your true interests*. | 最後，選修許多不同的課程將有助於你發現自己真正的興趣。
It will help you to select a major. | 它將協助你選擇主修課程。
It will assist you in finding a suitable career. | 它將協助你找到合適的職業生涯。

You'll have tried many subjects. | 你將已經嘗試過許多不同的學科。
You'll have tested many areas. | 你將已經測試過許多不同的領域。
You'll have a good idea of what you like. | 你將會更了解自己喜歡的是什麼。

**

muscle (ˈmʌsḷ) *n.* 肌肉　　exercise (ˈɛksɚˌsaɪz) *v.* 運動；運用
challenge (ˈtʃælɪndʒ) *v.* 刺激；激發　　stimulate (ˈstɪmjəˌlet) *v.* 刺激
present (prɪˈzɛnt) *v.* 提供　　select (səˈlɛkt) *v.* 選擇
major (ˈmedʒɚ) *n.* 主修科目　　assist (əˈsɪst) *v.* 幫助
suitable (ˈsutəbḷ) *adj.* 合適的　　career (kəˈrɪɚ) *n.* 職業
test (tɛst) *v.* 測試

It's not a waste of time.	那不是浪費時間。
It's a precious experience that you'll gain.	那是你會獲得的寶貴經驗。
You'll have a much better focus on the future.	你對未來的焦點將會更加清楚。
In conclusion, you'll be happier and smarter.	總之，你將會更快樂、更聰明。
They say that variety is the spice of life.	大家都說變化是生活的香料。
They also say that knowledge is power.	大家也說知識就是力量。
Taking many classes will make you more intelligent.	選修很多不同的課程將讓你更聰明。
A general knowledge is your best asset.	一般性的知識是你最佳的資產。
A comprehensive education is the best.	多元化的教育是最恰當的。
Believe me everybody!	大家相信我吧！
Believe it because it's true.	相信它，因為那是真的。
Now God bless you all and happy learning.	現在願上帝祝福你們大家，並祝你們快樂地學習。

**

precious (ˈprɛʃəs) *adj.* 寶貴的　　focus (ˈfokəs) *n.* 焦點
in conclusion 總之　　variety (vəˈraɪətɪ) *n.* 變化；多樣性
spice (spaɪs) *n.* 香料；調味品
Variety is the spice of life. 【諺】變化是生活的香料；變化是生活的調味品。
power (ˈpaʊɚ) *n.* 力量　　***Knowledge is power.*** 【諺】知識就是力量。
intelligent (ɪnˈtɛlədʒənt) *adj.* 聰明的
asset (ˈæsɛt) *n.* 資產　　bless (blɛs) *v.* 祝福
happy (ˈhæpɪ) *adj.*【用作祝賀用語】恭賀…；祝你…快樂

【托福作文範例】

16. A Comprehensive Education Is Best

There are many types of education a student can get at a university. Some universities require students to specialize in one subject; others require students to take classes in many subjects. Here is why I support a comprehensive education.

First, taking many classes develops well-rounded individuals. Students can gain more knowledge and learn a wider range of things. It's better to study many things so they can be a "Jack of all trades" in many different areas. *Second*, taking many classes creates a solid knowledge foundation. It's like building a pyramid as knowledge builds on top of knowledge. The more you learn, the more you can learn. *Third*, taking many classes strengthens your mind. You'll grasp more ideas and do more intellectual work. Your mind is a muscle that needs exercise as well. A comprehensive education stimulates your mind. It provides you with new tools for understanding. *Finally*, taking many classes will help you to discover your true interests and help you select a major.

In conclusion, the more you know, the better you can prepare yourself for the world. You'll have tried many subjects and tested many areas and you'll have a good idea of what you like.

16. 多元化的教育最好

　　學生在大學裡可以接受到各種不同類型的教育。有些大學要求學生專攻一個學科；有些則要求學生修習各種不同的學科。以下是我支持多元化教育的原因。

　　首先，修習許多不同的課程能培養出通才。學生可以得到更多的知識，並且學習到更廣泛的事物。學習許多事物是比較好的，因為學生才能在許多不同的領域中成為「萬事通」。第二，選修許多課程建立堅實的知識基礎。知識的累積其實就像在蓋金字塔。你學的越多，你就擁有更多學習的能力。第三，選修許多不同的課程能夠增強你的心智。你會得到更多的想法，並且常動腦筋思考。你的心智就和肌肉一樣，也需要運動。多元化教育能夠刺激你的心智。它會提供你新的理解知識的工具。最後，選修許多課程將有助於你發現自己真正的興趣，並幫助你選擇主修科目。

　　總之，你知道的越多，你面對這個世界所做的準備就越完善。你將已經嘗試過許多科目，並試驗過許多不同的領域，而且會更清楚自己喜歡的是什麼。

【托福作文原試題】

Some universities require students to take classes in many subjects. Other universities require students to specialize in one subject. Which is better? Use specific reasons and examples to support your answer.

17. *Second Language Acquisition for Kids:*
The Sooner, the Better

I'd like to welcome you all here.
I'm delighted to see you.
It's an honor to speak with you today.

I will be talking about language education.
My topic is second language acquisition for kids.
My main theme is this: "The sooner kids start
　　to learn, the better it is."

Acquiring a second language is so valuable.
I believe parents are responsible and should
　　take the initiative.
I'm going to share some beneficial suggestions
　　right now.

---

second language　　　　acquisition (ˌækwə'zɪʃən)
main (men)　　　　　　　theme (θim)
acquire (ə'kwaɪr)　　　　valuable ('væljuəbḷ)
responsible (rɪ'spɑnsəbḷ)　initiative (ɪ'nɪʃɪˌetɪv)
take the initiative　　　beneficial (ˌbɛnə'fɪʃəl)
suggestion (sə'dʒɛstʃən)　**right now**

First, start teaching kids early.

Start early, start now!

Start them learning as soon as you can.

Don't wait for any specific age to start.

Don't wait for your kids to start school.

Don't rely on teachers or so-called experts.

A child's parents are the most effective teachers.

The best time to learn is now.

"The earlier, the better" is always true.

Second, realize childhood is the optimum time
   to learn.

The brain is still growing and developing.

The brain is able to absorb and retain a lot.

---

as⋯as one can	specific (spɪˈsɪfɪk)
rely on	so-called (ˈsoˈkɔld)
expert (ˈɛkspɝt)	effective (əˈfɛktɪv, ɪ-)
optimum (ˈɑptəməm)	develop (dɪˈvɛləp)
absorb (əbˈsɔrb)	retain (rɪˈtən)

Children have the most learning potential.
Children learn faster and more efficiently.
Youth is the great window of opportunity.

Kids' minds are like sponges.
They can soak up information like water.
They have an unlimited capacity to learn.

Third, remember children are ideal learners.
They are more relaxed learners.
They aren't afraid to make mistakes.

Lang. learning is fun for kids.
Lang. learning is like a game to them.
It's an enjoyable and interesting task.

---

potential (pə'tɛnʃəl)
efficiently (ə'fɪʃəntlɪ,ɪ-)
window ('wɪndo)
soak up
capacity (kə'pæsətɪ)
relaxed (rɪ'lækst)
enjoyable (ɪn'dʒɔɪəbḷ)

youth (juθ)
sponge (spʌndʒ)
unlimited (ʌn'lɪmɪtɪd)
ideal (aɪ'diəl)
lang. (læŋ)
task (tæsk)

Kids don't get distracted like adults.

Kids don't get as embarrassed as adults.

Kids are optimal learning machines.

Finally, bilingualism will soon be the norm.

It's becoming essential to learn a second
  language.

It's especially true for non-native English
  speakers.

Today's world is quickly becoming a
  global village.

English is the most dominant and most popular
  language.

English is the international language.

---

distracted (dɪ'stræktɪd)

embarrassed (ɪm'bærəst)　　optimal ('ɑptəməl)

bilingualism (baɪ'lɪŋgwəl͵ɪzəm)

norm (nɔrm)　　essential (ə'sɛnʃəl)

non-native (nɑn'netɪv)　　speaker ('spikɚ)

global ('globḷ)　　*global village*

dominant ('dɑmənənt)

international (͵ɪntɚ'næʃənḷ)

Speaking two languages is so important.

Having a second language ability is a great asset.

Having another "tongue" brings many advantages.

***In conclusion, children shouldn't wait for school
  to learn a second language.***

Children are never too young to learn.

They should start learning as early as they can.

Language is the key to communication.

Communication skills determine success.

Communication skills can never be taught too early.

Thanks for listening everybody.

I wish you all the best.

I hope you enjoyed my short speech!

---

asset ('æsɛt)   tongue (tʌŋ)

advantage (əd'væntɪdʒ)

in conclusion   key (ki)

communication (kə͵mjunə'keʃən)

determine (dɪ'tɜmɪn)   ***all the best***

17. *Second Language Acquisition for Kids: The Sooner, the Better*
小孩學習第二外語：越早越好

【演講解說】

I'd like to welcome you all here.	我要歡迎在場的各位。
I'm delighted to see you.	我很高興可以看到你們。
It's an honor to speak with you today.	今天向你們演說眞是我的榮幸。

I will be talking about language education.	我將要談論語言教育。
My topic is second language acquisition for kids.	我的主題是小孩學習第二外語。
My main theme is this: "The sooner kids start to learn, the better it is."	我的主題是：「小孩越早開始學習越好。」

Acquiring a second language is so valuable.	學會第二外語是非常有用的。
I believe parents are responsible and should take the initiative.	我相信父母對此都有責任，並且應該採取主動。
I'm going to share some beneficial suggestions right now.	現在我將與你們分享一些有益的建議。

**

second language （母語以外所學的）第二種語言
acquisition〔͵ækwə`zɪʃən〕*n.* 學習；習得　　main〔men〕*adj.* 主要的
theme〔θim〕*n.* 主題　　acquire〔ə`kwaɪr〕*v.* 學得（知識等）
valuable〔`væljuəbḷ〕*adj.* 有用的；有價值的
responsible〔rɪ`spɑnsəbḷ〕*adj.* 應負責任的
initiative〔ɪ`nɪʃɪ͵etɪv〕*n.* 率先；主動（權）　　*take the initiative* 採取主動
beneficial〔͵bɛnə`fɪʃəl〕*adj.* 有益的；有利的
suggestion〔sə`dʒɛstʃən〕*n.* 建議　　*right now* 現在

First, *start teaching kids early*.	首先，早點開始教導小孩。
Start early, start now!	早點開始，現在就開始吧！
Start them learning as soon as you can.	儘量趁早讓他們開始學習。
Don't wait for any specific age to start.	不用等到任何特定的年齡再開始。
Don't wait for your kids to start school.	不用等到小孩開始上學。
Don't rely on teachers or so-called experts.	不要依賴老師及那些所謂的專家。
A child's parents are the most effective teachers.	小孩的父母就是最有效的老師。
The best time to learn is now.	最好的學習時機就是現在。
"The earlier, the better" is always true.	「越早學習越好」是永遠不變的眞理。
Second, *realize childhood is the optimum time to learn*.	第二，要知道童年時期是最理想的學習時機。
The brain is still growing and developing.	此時大腦仍在成長發育。
The brain is able to absorb and retain a lot.	大腦能夠吸收並且記憶很多事物。

＊＊————————————————————————————————

as…as one can 儘量…　　specific (spɪˈsɪfɪk) *adj.* 特定的
rely on 依賴；信任　　so-called (ˈsoˈkɔld) *adj.* 所謂的
expert (ˈɛkspɝt) *n.* 專家　　effective (əˈfɛktɪv, ɪ-) *adj.* 有效的
optimum (ˈɑptəməm) *adj.* 最理想的　　develop (dɪˈvɛləp) *v.* 發展；發育
absorb (əbˈsɔrb) *v.* 吸收　　retain (rɪˈten) *v.* 保留；記憶

Children have the most learning potential. 小孩有最豐富的學習潛能。

Children learn faster and more efficiently. 小孩學習更快、更有效率。

Youth is the great window of opportunity. 青少年時期是創造機會的絕佳窗口。

Kids' minds are like sponges. 小孩的心智就像是海綿。

They can soak up information like water. 它們能夠像吸收水一般,吸收資訊。

They have an unlimited capacity to learn. 他們有無限的學習能力。

Third, remember children are ideal learners. 第三,記住小孩是理想的學習者。

They are more relaxed learners. 他們是比較放鬆的學習者。

They aren't afraid to make mistakes. 他們不會害怕犯下較多的錯誤。

Lang. learning is fun for kids. 學習語言對小孩而言是有趣的。

Lang. learning is like a game to them. 學習語言對他們而言就像是玩遊戲。

It's an enjoyable and interesting task. 那是快樂而有趣的事情。

**

potential〔pəˈtɛnʃəl〕*n.* 潛力　efficiently〔əˈfɪʃntlɪ, ɪ-〕*adv.* 有效率地
youth〔juθ〕*n.* 青少年時期　window〔ˈwɪndo〕*n.* 往外開的東西;窗子
sponge〔spʌndʒ〕*n.* 海綿　***soak up*** 吸收(液體)
unlimited〔ʌnˈlɪmɪtɪd〕*adj.* 無限制的　capacity〔kəˈpæsətɪ〕*n.* 能力
ideal〔aɪˈdiəl〕*adj.* 理想的　relaxed〔rɪˈlækst〕*adj.* 放鬆的
lang.〔læŋ〕*n.* 語言(language 的縮寫)
enjoyable〔ɪnˈdʒɔɪəbḷ〕*adj.* 快樂的;有樂趣的　task〔tæsk〕*n.* 任務;工作

Kids don't get distracted like adults.	小孩不像大人，不會受到太多干擾。
Kids don't get as embarrassed as adults.	小孩不會和大人一樣不好意思。
Kids are optimal learning machines.	小孩是最理想的學習機器。
Finally*, *bilingualism will soon be the norm.	最後一點，擁有雙語能力不久就將成為常規。
It's becoming essential to learn a second language.	學習第二外語越來越必要。
It's especially true for non-native English speakers.	對母語不是英語的人來說，特別是如此。
Today's world is quickly becoming a global village.	現今的世界很快就要成為地球村。
English is the most dominant and most popular language.	英文是最強勢，也是使用最普遍的語言。
English is the international language.	英文是國際性的語言。

** ————————————

distracted (dɪ'stræktɪd) *adj.* 分心的
embarrassed (ɪm'bærəst) *adj.* 不好意思的
optimal ('ɑptəməl) *adj.* 最理想的
bilingualism (baɪ'lɪŋgwəl‚ɪzəm) *n.* 能用兩種語言
norm (nɔrm) *n.* 標準　essential (ə'sɛnʃəl) *adj.* 必要的
non-native (nɑn'netɪv) *adj.* 非本地的
speaker ('spikɚ) *n.* 講（某種）語言的人　global ('globḷ) *adj.* 全球的
global village 地球村（由於大眾傳播普及，時空縮短，世界如一村）
dominant ('dɑmənənt) *adj.* 佔優勢的；支配的
international (‚ɪntɚ'næʃənḷ) *adj.* 國際性的

Speaking two languages is so important.	會說兩種語言是非常重要的。
Having a second language ability is a great asset.	具有第二外語的能力是一大資產。
Having another "tongue" brings many advantages.	會說另一種「語言」會帶來許多好處。
In conclusion, children shouldn't wait for school to learn a second language.	總之，小孩不應該等到上學才開始學習第二外語。
Children are never too young to learn.	小孩學東西永遠不嫌早。
They should start learning as early as they can.	他們應該儘早開始學習。
Language is the key to communication.	語言是溝通的關鍵。
Communication skills determine success.	溝通技巧決定成功與否。
Communication skills can never be taught too early.	學習溝通技巧永遠都不嫌早。
Thanks for listening everybody.	謝謝大家的聆聽。
I wish you all the best.	我祝福你們一切順利。
I hope you enjoyed my short speech!	我希望你喜歡我簡短的演說！

** ————————————————

asset〔'æsɛt〕*n.* 資產
tongue〔tʌŋ〕*n.* 舌頭；語言　　advantage〔əd'væntɪdʒ〕*n.* 好處
in conclusion 總之　　key〔ki〕*n.* 關鍵 < *to* >
communication〔kə,mjunə'keʃən〕*n.* 溝通
determine〔dɪ'tɜmɪn〕*v.* 決定
all the best（祝酒、告別等時說）祝一切順利

【托福作文範例】

17. Second Language Acquisition for Kids

In today's global village, language has become a very important part of education. That is why I believe the sooner kids start to learn, the better it is. I am going to share some beneficial insights about learning a second language at an early age.

First, start teaching kids early. Start early and start now! Don't wait for any specific age to start. Don't wait for your kids to start school. *Second*, realize childhood is the optimum time to learn. The brain is still growing and developing. The brain is able to absorb and retain a lot. Children have the most learning potential and they learn faster and more efficiently. *Third*, remember children are ideal learners. They are more relaxed and are not afraid to make mistakes. Language learning is fun for kids because it's like a game to them. It's an enjoyable and interesting task. *Finally*, bilingualism will soon be the norm. It's becoming essential to know a second language, especially for non-native English speakers. English is the international language and can be advantageous to know.

In conclusion, children shouldn't wait for school to learn a second language. They should start learning as early as they can. So go enroll your children in a language school today!

17. 小孩學習第二外語

　　在現今的地球村中，語言已經成為教育中非常重要的一部份。那也就是為什麼我相信，小孩子越早開始學習越好的原因。我將與你們分享一些幼年時期學習第二外語的有益見解。

　　首先，及早開始教導小孩。早一點開始，現在就開始！不要等到任何特定的年齡再開始。不用等到你的小孩開始上學。第二，要知道童年時期是學習的最佳時段。此時大腦仍然在成長發育。大腦能夠吸收並且記憶很多事物。小孩子擁有最豐富的學習潛能，而且他們學得更快、更有效率。第三，要記得小孩是理想的學習者。他們比較能夠放鬆，而且不害怕犯錯。語言學習對孩子來說是有趣的，因為對他們來說就像是玩遊戲。那是一個快樂而且有趣的事情。最後一點，能用兩種語言不久就會成為常規。尤其對於母語並非是英文的人來說，具有第二外語的能力越來越必要了。英文是國際性的語言，懂英文是非常有幫助的。

　　總之，孩子不應該等到上學才開始學習第二外語。他們應該要儘早開始學習。所以現在就帶著你的孩子去語言學校註冊吧！

【托福作文原試題】

Do you agree or disagree with the following statement? Children should begin learning a foreign language as soon as they start school. Use specific reasons and examples to support your position.

18. *Teamwork Is the Best Way to Succeed*

Welcome ladies and gentlemen.
It's an honor to be here.
It's a pleasure to speak with you.

I'm here to advocate teamwork.
I know teamwork is essential for success.
You can't go far in life without being a
   team player.

Working together "makes the world go around."
Working together and cooperation is the name of
   the game.
Here's why teamwork is the best way to succeed.

First, "no man is an island."
No one person can achieve all alone.
Everyone needs someone sometimes.

---

teamwork ('tim,wɜk)	honor ('ɑnɚ)
pleasure ('plɛʒɚ)	advocate ('ædvə,ket)
essential (ə'sɛnʃəl)	*go far*
a team player	*work together*
go around	cooperation (ko,ɑpə'reʃən)
the name of the game	island ('aɪlənd)
achieve (ə'tʃiv)	

Everyone needs occasional support.

Everyone needs guidance and encouragement.

Assistance is a prerequisite for success.

It might be your parents helping you.

It might be a teacher or friend.

No matter what, you can't succeed by yourself.

Second, *"two heads are better than one."*

The benefits include shared knowledge and
  experience.

The benefits include better decision-making,
  better problem solving, and greater motivation.

Teamwork means better quality results.

Teamwork means more efficient production.

This results in great production numbers.

---

occasional (ə'keʒənḷ)   guidance ('gaɪdns)
assistance (ə'sɪstəns)
prerequisite (pri'rɛkwəzɪt)   benefit ('bɛnəfɪt)
decision-making (dɪ'sɪʒən͵mekɪŋ)
motivation (͵motə'veʃən)   quality ('kwɑlətɪ)
efficient (ə'fɪʃənt)
production (prə'dʌkʃən)   ***result in***

A team gets things done faster.

A team can save money and time.

A group effort to achieve a common goal is
a powerful force.

Third, teamwork enhances individual skills.

Teamwork enhances independent
working ability.

Teamwork and individuality are not
incompatible.

Group members learn from each other.

Group dynamics encourage interaction
and healthy competition.

Teamwork fosters self-improvement.

---

enhance (ɪnˈhæns)　　　　　individual (ˌɪndəˈvɪdʒuəl)

independent (ˌɪndɪˈpɛndənt)

individuality (ˌɪndə,vɪdʒuˈælətɪ)

incompatible (ˌɪnkəmˈpætəbḷ)

dynamics (daɪˈnæmɪks)　　　interaction (ˌɪntəˈækʃən)

competition (ˌkɑmpəˈtɪʃən)　foster (ˈfɔstə)

self-improvement (ˌsɛlfɪmˈpruvmənt)

You can hone individual skills in a group setting.

You can make speedy self progress.

You don't have to totally sacrifice individuality
   for the sake of the team.

Finally, being a team player is a prerequisite
   to finding employment.

The corporate world demands employees
   practice teamwork.

The business community emphasizes the spirit
   of working together.

Employers know team players are the best workers.

They know team players have character
   and loyalty.

They realize team players maximize total potential.

---

hone〔hon〕	setting〔'sɛtɪŋ〕
speedy〔'spidɪ〕	*self progress*
totally〔'totḷɪ〕	sacrifice〔'sækrə,faɪs〕
for the sake of	employment〔ɪm'plɔɪmənt〕
corporate〔'kɔrpərɪt〕	demand〔dɪ'mænd〕
community〔kə'mjunətɪ〕	emphasize〔'ɛmfə,saɪz〕
spirit〔'spɪrɪt〕	character〔'kærɪktɚ〕
loyalty〔'lɔɪəltɪ〕	maximize〔'mæksə,maɪz〕
total〔'totḷ〕	potential〔pə'tɛnʃəl〕

Most companies won't hire a "lone wolf."

Most companies won't hire an independent superstar.

Companies want dynamos who can share, motivate,
   teach and benefit everyone.

In conclusion, it's more important to be able to
   work in a group.

Working independently can only take you so far.

Working together is the best way to get ahead.

Remember there is no "I" in team.

Remember team skills must come first.

Individual accomplishments will inevitably follow.

Being independent is not the best way.

Being a team player is the way to succeed.

Thank you all for listening.

---

lone wolf	dynamos ('daɪnəˌmo)
motivate ('motəˌvet)	*in conclusion*
so far	*get ahead*
accomplishment (ə'kɑmplɪʃmənt)	
inevitably (ɪn'ɛvətəblɪ)	follow ('fɑlo)

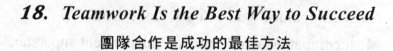

18. *Teamwork Is the Best Way to Succeed*

團隊合作是成功的最佳方法

【演講解說】

Welcome ladies and gentlemen.	歡迎各位先生、各位女士。
It's an honor to be here.	很榮幸能來到這裡。
It's a pleasure to speak with you.	很高興能和你們聊聊。

I'm here to advocate teamwork.	我在這裡要提倡團隊合作。
I know teamwork is essential for success.	我知道團隊合作是成功的必要條件。
You can't go far in life without being a team player.	如果無法成為有團隊精神的人,你的人生就無法成功。

Working together "makes the world go around."	一起工作「讓世界運轉」。
Working together and cooperation is the name of the game.	一起工作和合作是最要緊的。
Here's why teamwork is the best way to succeed.	以下就是團隊合作是成功的最佳方法的原因。

** ————————————

teamwork (ˈtimˌwɝk) *n.* 團隊合作　　honor (ˈɑnɚ) *n.* 光榮的事
pleasure (ˈplɛʒɚ) *n.* 樂事　　advocate (ˈædvəˌket) *v.* 擁護;提倡
essential (əˈsɛnʃəl) *adj.* 必要的　　*go far* 成功
a team player 有團隊精神的人　　*work together* 合作
go around 環繞;運行　　cooperation (koˌɑpəˈreʃən) *n.* 合作
the name of the game 最要緊的東西;實質

First, "*no man is an island.*"	首先，「沒有人是一座孤島」。
No one person can achieve all alone.	沒有人可以獨自完成所有的事情。
Everyone needs someone sometimes.	每個人有時候都會需要別人。
Everyone needs occasional support.	每個人偶爾都需要支持。
Everyone needs guidance and encouragement.	每個人都需要引導和鼓勵。
Assistance is a prerequisite for success.	協助是成功的必要條件。
It might be your parents helping you.	可能是你的父母幫忙你。
It might be a teacher or friend.	可能是老師或是朋友。
No matter what, you can't succeed by yourself.	不論是什麼，你都無法獨自一個人成功。
Second, "*two heads are better than one.*"	第二，「三個臭皮匠，勝過一個諸葛亮」。
The benefits include shared knowledge and experience.	好處包括知識和經驗共享。
The benefits include better decision-making, better problem solving, and greater motivation.	好處包括在決策及解決問題方面，能夠有更加完善的結果，以及具有更強烈的動機。

**

island ('aɪlənd) *n.* 島

No man is an island. 【諺】沒有人是一座孤島；沒有人是孤立的。
　(出自 John Donne 的詩句，描述人與社會休戚與共的關係)

achieve (ə'tʃiv) *v.* 完成；實現　　occasional (ə'keʒən!) *adj.* 偶爾的

guidance ('gaɪdn̩s) *n.* 指導；引導　　assistance (ə'sɪstəns) *n.* 協助

prerequisite (pri'rɛkwəzɪt) *n.* 必要條件；前提 <*for/to*>

Two heads are better than one. 【諺】集思勝於獨斷；三個臭皮匠，
　勝過一個諸葛亮。　　benefit ('bɛnəfɪt) *n.* 好處　*v.* 使獲益

decision-making (dɪ'sɪʒən,mekɪŋ) *n.* 決策

motivation (,motə'veʃən) *n.* 動機

Teamwork means better quality results.	團隊合作意味著更高品質的結果。
Teamwork means more efficient production.	團隊合作意味著更有效率的生產模式。
This results in great production numbers.	這導致生產量的成長。

A team gets things done faster.	團隊讓事情加速完成。
A team can save money and time.	團隊可以節省金錢和時間。
A group effort to achieve a common goal is a powerful force.	集體努力完成共同的目標是一個強大的力量。

Third, teamwork enhances individual skills.	第三，團隊合作增進個人技巧。
Teamwork enhances independent working ability.	團隊合作增進獨立作業的能力。
Teamwork and individuality are not incompatible.	團隊合作和個人特質並非是互不相容的。

Group members learn from each other.	團隊中的成員彼此學習。
Group dynamics encourage interaction and healthy competition.	團隊的合作過程刺激互動和良性的競爭。
Teamwork fosters self-improvement.	團隊合作能促進自我改善。

** ——————————

quality ('kwɑlətɪ) adj. 有品質的　　efficient (ə'fɪʃənt) adj. 有效率的
production (prə'dʌkʃən) n. 生產；產量　***result in*** 導致
enhance (ɪn'hæns) v. 增進　　individual (ˌɪndə'vɪdʒʊəl) adj. 個人的
independent (ˌɪndɪ'pɛndənt) adj. 獨立的
individuality (ˌɪndəˌvɪdʒʊ'ælətɪ) n. (個人的) 特性；特質
incompatible (ˌɪnkəm'pætəbḷ) adj. 不相容的
dynamics (daɪ'næmɪks) n. pl. 變動 (過程)
interaction (ˌɪntə'ækʃən) n. 互動
competition (ˌkɑmpə'tɪʃən) n. 競爭　　foster ('fɔstə) v. 培養；促進
self-improvement (ˌsɛlfɪm'pruvmənt) n. 自我改善

You can hone individual skills in a group setting. | 你可以在團隊的環境中，磨練個人的技巧。

You can make speedy self progress. | 你可以迅速地自我進步。

You don't have to totally sacrifice individuality for the sake of the team. | 你不需要爲了團隊，而完全犧牲個人特質。

Finally, being a team player is a prerequisite to finding employment. | 最後一點，做一個有團隊精神的人是求職的必要條件。

The corporate world demands employees practice teamwork. | 企業界要求員工做到團隊合作。

The business community emphasizes the spirit of working together. | 工商界強調合作的精神。

Employers know team players are the best workers. | 雇主知道有團隊精神的人是最好的員工。

They know team players have character and loyalty. | 他們知道有團隊精神的人有品格和忠誠度。

They realize team players maximize total potential. | 他們知道有團隊精神的人會將全體的潛能發揮至最大極限。

** ――――――――――――――――――

hone (hon) *v.* 磨練（技術等）
setting (ˋsɛtɪŋ) *n.* 環境；背景　　speedy (ˋspidɪ) *adj.* 迅速的
self progress 自我進步　　totally (ˋtotl̩) *adv.* 完全地
sacrifice (ˋsækrə͵faɪs) *v.* 犧牲　　*for the sake of* 爲了…的緣故
employment (ɪmˋplɔɪmənt) *n.* 工作；職業
corporate (ˋkɔrpərɪt) *adj.* 公司的
community (kəˋmjunətɪ) *n.* 共同社會；共同體
demand (dɪˋmænd) *v.* 要求　　emphasize (ˋɛmfə͵saɪz) *v.* 強調
spirit (ˋspɪrɪt) *n.* 精神　　character (ˋkærɪktɚ) *n.* 人格
loyalty (ˋlɔɪəltɪ) *n.* 忠誠　　maximize (ˋmæksə͵maɪz) *v.* 使增加至最大限度
total (ˋtotl̩) *adj.* 全體的　　potential (pəˋtɛnʃəl) *n.* 潛力

Most companies won't hire a "lone wolf."	大多數的公司不會僱用一個「獨行俠」。
Most companies won't hire an independent superstar.	大多數的公司不會僱用獨來獨往的超級明星。
Companies want dynamos who can share, motivate, teach and benefit everyone.	公司行號希望僱用精力充沛的人,能夠分享、激勵、指導,並且有益於大家的人。
***In conclusion*, *it's more important to be able to work in a group*.**	總之,具有在團隊中工作的能力是比較重要的。
Working independently can only take you so far.	獨立工作只能夠讓你發揮到某個程度。
Working together is the best way to get ahead.	合作是成功的最佳方式。
Remember there is no "I" in team.	要記住,在團隊中沒有「個人」。
Remember team skills must come first.	要記住,團隊技巧一定最重要。
Individual accomplishments will inevitably follow.	個人的成就自然而然會產生。
Being independent is not the best way.	獨立作業不是最好的方式。
Being a team player is the way to succeed.	做一個有團隊精神的人,是成功之道。
Thank you all for listening.	謝謝你們大家的聆聽。

** ────────────────────

lone wolf 獨來獨往的人　　dynamo ('daɪnə‚mo) *n.* 精力充沛的人
motivate ('motə‚vet) *v.* 激勵　　*in conclusion* 總之
so far 到有限的範圍或程度　　*get ahead* 成功
accomplishments (ə'kamplɪʃmənts) *n. pl.* 成就
inevitably (ɪn'ɛvətəblɪ) *adv.* 無法避免地;必定
follow ('falo) *v.* 隨之而來

【托福作文範例】

18. Teamwork Is the Best Way to Succeed

Everybody knows the word teamwork, but not everybody knows it's one of the best ways to accomplish something and the following reasons are why teamwork is the best way to succeed.

First, no man is an island. No one person can achieve all alone. Everyone needs occasional support. Everyone needs guidance and encouragement. *Second*, two heads are better than one. The benefits of teamwork include shared knowledge and experience. They also include better decision-making, better problem solving and greater motivation. A team gets things done faster and saves money and time. *Third*, teamwork enhances individual skills by improving independent working ability. Group members learn from each other. Group dynamics encourage interaction and healthy competition. *Finally*, being a team player is a prerequisite to finding employment. The corporate world demands employees practice teamwork. Most companies won't hire a "lone wolf." Companies want individuals who can share, teach, motivate and benefit everyone.

In conclusion, it's more important to be able to work in a group. There is no "I" in team and remember, team skills come first. Individual accomplishments will follow with teamwork. So go join a team today!

18. 團隊合作是成功的最佳方法

　　每個人都知道「團隊合作」這個字，但是並非每個人都知道這是完成某件事情的最佳方法之一，以下就是爲什麼團隊合作是成功的最佳方法的理由。

　　首先，沒有人是一座孤島。沒有人可以獨自完成所有的事情。每個人偶爾都需要協助。每個人都需要指引和鼓勵。第二，三個臭皮匠，勝過一個諸葛亮。團隊合作的好處包括了知識與經驗的共享。也包括了在決策及解決問題方面，能夠有更加完善的結果，以及具有更強烈的動機。團隊能夠讓事情更快完成，節省金錢與時間。第三，藉由增進獨立作業的能力，團隊合作加強個人的技巧。團隊成員能夠彼此學習。團隊的合作過程促進了互動以及良性的競爭。最後一點，做一個有團隊精神的人，是求職的必要條件。企業界要求員工能夠做到團隊合作。大多數的公司不會僱用一個「獨行俠」。公司需要的是一個能夠分享、指導、激勵並且有益於大家的人。

　　總之，具有在團體中工作的能力是比較重要的。在團隊中沒有「個人」，要記住團隊技巧最重要。個人的成就會隨著團隊合作而來。所以今天就去加入一個團隊吧！

【托福作文原試題】

Is it more important to be able to work with a group of people on a team or to work independently? Use reasons and specific examples to support your answer.

19. *Confucius: The Moral Foundation of China*

Greetings and welcome.
It's an honor to be here.
It's a great pleasure to speak with you.

I'm here to salute a great man.
I'm here to praise and honor Confucius.
His many contributions to Chinese civilization
   and culture are unsurpassed.

Confucius was more than a brilliant scholar.
Confucius was more than an insightful philosopher.
Let me illustrate his genius by mentioning four
   areas where his greatness was exceptional.

Confucius (kən'fjuʃəs)
foundation (faʊn'deʃən)
honor ('ɑnɚ)
contribution (ˌkɑntrə'bjuʃən)
unsurpassed (ˌʌnsɚ'pæst)
scholar ('skɑlɚ)
philosopher (fə'lɑsəfɚ)
genius ('dʒinɪəs)
exceptional (ɪk'sɛpʃənḷ)

moral ('mɔrəl)
greetings ('gritɪŋz)
salute (sə'lut)
civilization (ˌsɪvḷə'zeʃən)
brilliant ('brɪljənt)
insightful ('ɪnˌsaɪtfʊl)
illustrate ('ɪləstret)
area ('ɛrɪə)

First, Confucius was devoted to education and
learning.
He was passionate about knowledge acquisition.
He was the ultimate teacher's teacher.

His main goal was personal and moral cultivation.
His method of learning was strict and meticulous.
He used the ancient classics for textbooks and
stressed self-enlightenment.

Confucius was the first to advocate education
for all.
Confucius advocated equal opportunity
education without class distinction.
He was truly the founding father of education
in China.

---

devoted (dɪ'votɪd)　　　　passionate ('pæʃənɪt)
acquisition (,ækwə'zɪʃən)　ultimate ('ʌltəmɪt)
cultivation (,kʌltə'veʃən)　cultivation (,kʌltə'veʃən)
meticulous (mə'tɪkjələs)　ancient ('enʃənt)
classics ('klæsɪks)　　　　stress (strɛs)
self-enlightenment ('sɛlfɪn'laɪtn̩mənt)
advocate ('ædvə,ket)　　　equal ('ikwəl)
class (klæs)　　　　　　distinction (dɪ'stɪŋkʃən)
founding ('faundɪŋ)　　　***founding father***

Second, Confucius was deeply concerned with
individual and social morality.
He wanted the total cultivation of personal character.
He wanted all relationships and actions based
　on social ethics.

Confucius emphasized the concept of "Ren,"
　which means benevolence.
Ren includes love, wisdom and courage.
Ren also includes generosity, respect and filial piety.

Confucius strived for a pure conscience and an
　ideal society.
He hoped we could all trust each other.
He hoped we could comfort the old and cherish
　the young.

---

be concerned with
total ('totl̩)
relationship (rɪ'leʃən,ʃɪp)
ethics ('ɛθɪks)
concept ('kɑnsɛpt)
benevolence (bə'nɛvələns)
filial ('fɪlɪəl)
filial piety
pure (pjʊr)
comfort ('kʌmfət)

morality (mɔ'rælətɪ,mə-)
character ('kærɪktə)
be based on
emphasize ('ɛmfə,saɪz)
Ren
generosity (,dʒɛnə'rɑsətɪ)
piety ('paɪətɪ)
strive (straɪv)
conscience ('kɑnʃəns)
cherish ('tʃɛrɪʃ)

Third, *Confucius was a political genius*.

Confucius was a leadership expert.

He knew the basis of political legitimacy lies
    in virtue.

He stated that a ruler must lead and guide
    by virtue.

He maintained that every leader should care
    about the people's welfare.

Every government must serve the people.

A leader must set the example.

A leader must be a good role model.

Leaders must be kind to subjects, avoid
    violence and maintain a stable society.

---

political (pə'lɪtɪkḷ)	leadership ('lidɚ،ʃɪp)
expert ('ɛkspɝt)	legitimacy (lɪ'dʒɪtəməsɪ)
lie in	virtue ('vɝtʃu)
state (stet)	ruler ('rulɚ)
guide (gaɪd)	maintain (men'ten)
care about	welfare ('wɛl،fɛr)
serve (sɝv)	*set the example*
role model	subject ('sʌbdʒɪkt)
violence ('vaɪələns)	stable ('stebḷ)

Fourth, *Confucius advocated the idea of social*
  justice.

He insisted that people come first.
He yearned for improvement in the livelihood
  of common people.

All his ideas were based on compassion.
All his efforts were towards benefiting people.
Confucius preached that people are the most
  important consideration.

Confucius opposed exploitation of any kind.
He criticized overtaxation.
He thought all activities should benefit everyone.

---

justice ('dʒʌstɪs)   insist (ɪn'sɪst)
yearn (jɜn)   improvement (ɪm'pruvmənt)
livelihood ('laɪvlɪˌhʊd)   common ('kɑmən)
compassion (kəm'pæʃən)
towards (tordz ,tə'wordz)
benefit ('bɛnəfɪt)   preach (pritʃ)
consideration (kənˌsɪdə'reʃən)
oppose (ə'poz)   exploitation (ˌɛksplɔɪ'teʃən)
overtaxation ('ovəˌtæk'seʃən)

In conclusion, I'd like to make a proposal.

I propose building a statue to honor Confucius.

I can think of no better role model to venerate.

He was and still is a great inspiration.

We must remember and carry on his philosophy.

We must perpetuate all that he stood for to the
    next generation.

The thought and philosophy of Confucius have
    eternal value.

The Confucian way promotes virtue, love, ethics
    and morality.

What a great formula for saving the human race!

---

in conclusion

propose (prə'poz)

think of

inspiration (,ɪnspə'reʃən)

philosophy (fə'lɑsəfɪ)

stand for

eternal (ɪ'tɜnl̩)

Confucian (kən'fjuʃən)

formula ('fɔrmjələ)

human race

proposal (prə'pozl̩)

statue ('stætʃu)

venerate ('vɛnəˌret)

carry on

perpetuate (pɚ'pɛtʃuˌet)

generation (,dʒɛnə'reʃən)

value ('vælju)

promote (prə'mot)

race (res)

19. *Confucius: The Moral Foundation of China*

孔子：中國的道德基礎

【演講解說】

Greetings and welcome.	大家好，歡迎大家。
It's an honor to be here.	很榮幸能來到這裡。
It's a great pleasure to speak with you.	非常高興可以和你們談談。
I'm here to salute a great man.	在此我要向一位偉人致敬。
I'm here to praise and honor Confucius.	在此我要讚賞和敬仰孔子。
His many contributions to Chinese civilization and culture are unsurpassed.	他對中國文明和文化的眾多貢獻是別人無法超越的。
Confucius was more than a brilliant scholar.	孔子不僅是一位傑出的學者。
Confucius was more than an insightful philosopher.	孔子不僅是一位富有洞察力的哲學家。
Let me illustrate his genius by mentioning four areas where his greatness was exceptional.	讓我提出四個他特別偉大的地方，來說明他的才能。

** ———————————————————

Confucius (kənˈfjuʃəs) *n.* 孔子 (551-479 B.C.，中國的思想家，儒家的始祖)
moral (ˈmɔrəl) *adj.* 道德 (上) 的　　foundation (faʊnˈdeʃən) *n.* 基礎
greetings (ˈgritɪŋz) *n. pl.* 問候語　　honor (ˈɑnə) *n.* 光榮的事　*v.* 向…表示敬意
salute (səˈlut) *v.* 向…致敬　　contribution (ˌkɑntrəˈbjuʃən) *n.* 貢獻 < to >
civilization (ˌsɪvḷəˈzeʃən) *n.* 文明　　unsurpassed (ˌʌnsəˈpæst) *adj.* 未被超越的
more than 不僅是　　brilliant (ˈbrɪljənt) *adj.* 傑出的　　scholar (ˈskɑlə) *n.* 學者
insightful (ˈɪnˌsaɪtfʊl) *adj.* 富於洞察力的　　philosopher (fəˈlɑsəfə) *n.* 哲學家
illustrate (ˈɪləstret) *v.* 說明　　genius (ˈdʒiniəs) *n.* 非凡的才能；天才
area (ˈɛrɪə) *n.* 領域　　exceptional (ɪkˈsɛpʃənḷ) *adj.* 特別的；非凡的

First, Confucius was devoted to education and learning.	首先，孔子致力於教育和學習。
He was passionate about knowledge acquisition.	他熱中於追求知識。
He was the ultimate teacher's teacher.	他是至聖先師。
His main goal was personal and moral cultivation.	他的主要目標是個人和道德上的培養。
His method of learning was strict and meticulous.	他的學習方法是嚴格而一絲不苟的。
He used the ancient classics for textbooks and stressed self-enlightenment.	他利用古代的文學經典做為教科書，並且強調自我敎化。
Confucius was the first to advocate education for all.	孔子是第一個倡導有敎無類的人。
Confucius advocated equal opportunity education without class distinction.	孔子倡導平等的敎育機會，不要有階級的區別。
He was truly the founding father of education in China.	他的確是中國敎育的創始者。

** ─────────────

devoted (dɪ'votɪd) *adj.* 獻身的；專心致力的 < *to* >
passionate ('pæʃənɪt) *adj.* 熱情的　　acquisition (,ækwə'zɪʃən) *n.* 獲得
ultimate ('ʌltəmɪt) *adj.* 最好的　　cultivation (,kʌltə'veʃən) *n.* 培養；敎養
meticulous (mə'tɪkjələs) *adj.* 一絲不苟的；嚴密的
ancient ('enʃənt) *adj.* 古代的
classics ('klæsɪks) *n. pl.* 古典文學　　stress (strɛs) *v.* 強調
self-enlightenment ('sɛlfɪn'laɪtṇmənt) *n.* 自我敎化；自我啓蒙
advocate ('ædvə,ket) *v.* 擁護；提倡　　equal ('ikwəl) *adj.* 平等的
class (klæs) *adj.*) 階級的　　distinction (dɪ'stɪŋkʃən) *n.* 區別
founding ('faundɪŋ) *adj.* 創辦的；發起的　　***founding father*** 創始人

Second, Confucius was deeply concerned with individual and social morality.	第二，孔子深切地關心個人品德和社會道德。
He wanted the total cultivation of personal character.	他希望全面培養個人的品格。
He wanted all relationships and actions based on social ethics.	他希望所有的人際關係和行為是建立在社會倫理的基礎上。
Confucius emphasized the concept of "Ren," which means benevolence.	孔子強調「仁」的觀念，也就是仁慈。
Ren includes love, wisdom and courage.	仁包括了愛、智慧和勇氣。
Ren also includes generosity, respect and filial piety.	仁也包括了慷慨、尊敬和孝順。
Confucius strived for a pure conscience and an ideal society.	孔子努力追求清白的良心，以及一個理想的社會。
He hoped we could all trust each other.	他希望我們全都能夠信任彼此。
He hoped we could comfort the old and cherish the young.	他希望我們能夠安慰年老的人，珍愛年幼的人。

** ─────────────────────────

be concerned with 關心
morality (mɔ'rælətɪ,mə-) *n.* 品德；道德
total ('totḷ) *adj.* 全體的　　character ('kærɪktɚ) *n.* 人格；品行
relationship (rɪ'leʃən,ʃɪp) *n.* (人際)關係　　***be based on*** 以⋯為基礎
ethics ('ɛθɪks) *n.* 倫理觀；道德標準　　emphasize ('ɛmfə,saɪz) *v.* 強調
concept ('kɑnsɛpt) *n.* 觀念　　***Ren*** 仁
benevolence (bə'nɛvələns) *n.* 仁慈　　generosity (,dʒɛnə'rɑsətɪ) *n.* 慷慨
filial ('fɪlɪəl) *adj.* 子女的；孝順的　　piety ('paɪətɪ) *n.* 孝順；恭敬
filial piety 孝道　　strive (straɪv) *v.* 努力 <*for*>
pure (pjʊr) *adj.* 純潔的　　conscience ('kɑnʃəns) *n.* 良心
comfort ('kʌmfɚt) *v.* 安慰　　cherish ('tʃɛrɪʃ) *v.* 珍愛

Third, Confucius was a political genius.　　第三，孔子是政治上的天才。

Confucius was a leadership expert.　　孔子是領導專家。

He knew the basis of political legitimacy lies in virtue.　　他知道政權正當性的基礎是在於美德。

He stated that a ruler must lead and guide by virtue.　　他說統治者必須以美德來領導和引導他人。

He maintained that every leader should care about the people's welfare.　　他主張每一位領導者都應該關心人民的福祉。

Every government must serve the people.　　每一個政府都必須為人民服務。

A leader must set the example.　　領導者必須立下榜樣。

A leader must be a good role model.　　領導者必須是好的典範。

Leaders must be kind to subjects, avoid violence and maintain a stable society.　　領導者必須對臣民仁慈，避免暴力，並且維持社會穩定。

**　　——————————————

political (pə'lɪtɪkl) *adj.* 政治的
leadership ('lidə,ʃɪp) *n.* 領導（才能）　　expert ('ɛkspɝt) *n.* 專家
legitimacy (lɪ'dʒɪtɪməsɪ) *n.* 合法（性）；正統（性）　　*lie in* 在於
virtue ('vɝtʃu) *n.* 美德；德性　　state (stet) *v.* 陳述；聲明
ruler ('rulə) *n.* 統治者　　guide (gaɪd) *v.* 引導
maintain (men'ten) *v.* 堅持；主張；維持　　*care about* 關心
welfare ('wɛl,fɛr) *n.* 福利　　serve (sɝv) *v.* 為…服務
set the example 樹立榜樣；作為表率　　*role model* 楷模；典範
subject ('sʌbdʒɪkt) *n.* (國王、君主之下的) 臣民
violence ('vaɪələns) *n.* 暴力　　stable ('stebl) *adj.* 穩定的

**Fourth, Confucius advocated the
idea of social justice.**

He insisted that people come first.

He yearned for improvement in the
livelihood of common people.

第四，孔子提倡社會正義的觀
念。

他堅持人民優先。

他渴望平民百姓的生活能夠獲
得改善。

All his ideas were based on
compassion.

All his efforts were towards
benefiting people.

Confucius preached that people are
the most important consideration.

他所有的思想皆建立在憐憫的
基礎上。

他所有的努力皆以助人為目標。

孔子倡導應將人民列為最重要的
考量。

Confucius opposed exploitation of
any kind.

He criticized overtaxation.

He thought all activities should
benefit everyone.

孔子反對任何形式的剝削。

他批評課稅過重。

他認為所有的活動都應該要造福
每一個人。

**

justice〔'dʒʌstɪs〕*n.* 正義　　insist〔ɪn'sɪst〕*v.* 堅持

yearn〔jɝn〕*v.* 渴望；嚮往 *< for >*

improvement〔ɪm'pruvmənt〕*n.* 改善

livelihood〔'laɪvlɪ,hud〕*n.* 生活；生計　　common〔'kɑmən〕*adj.* 普通的

compassion〔kəm'pæʃən〕*n.* 同情（心）；憐憫

towards〔tordz,tə'wordz〕*prep.* 為；有助於；用於

benefit〔'bɛnəfɪt〕*v.* 有益於　　preach〔pritʃ〕*v.* 倡導

consideration〔kən,sɪdə'reʃən〕*n.* 需要考慮的事

oppose〔ə'poz〕*v.* 反對　　exploitation〔,ɛksplɔɪ'teʃən〕*n.* 剝削

overtaxation〔'ovɚ,tæk'seʃən〕*n.* 課稅過重

In conclusion, I'd like to make a proposal.	總之，我想要提出一個建議。
I propose building a statue to honor Confucius.	我提議興建一座雕像來向孔子致敬。
I can think of no better role model to venerate.	我想不到還有誰比他更適合做為崇敬的楷模。
He was and still is a great inspiration.	從當時一直到現在，他都是鼓舞人心的偉人。
We must remember and carry on his philosophy.	我們必須記得，並且繼續奉行他的哲學。
We must perpetuate all that he stood for to the next generation.	我們必須永久留存他擁護的全部思想到下一個世代。
The thought and philosophy of Confucius have eternal value.	孔子的思想和哲學有不朽的價值。
The Confucian way promotes virtue, love, ethics and morality.	孔子之道提倡美德、愛、倫理和道德。
What a great formula for saving the human race!	眞是拯救人類的偉大準則！

** ───────────

in conclusion 總之　　proposal〔prə'pozḷ〕*n.* 提議

propose〔prə'poz〕*v.* 提議　　statue〔'stætʃu〕*n.* 雕像

think of 想出　　venerate〔'vɛnəret〕*v.* 崇敬

inspiration〔ˌɪnspə'reʃən〕*n.* 鼓舞人心的人（或事物）

carry on 繼續　　philosophy〔fə'lɑsəfɪ〕*n.* 哲學

perpetuate〔pə'pɛtʃuˌet〕*v.* 使…永遠存在　　*stand for* 主張；擁護

generation〔ˌdʒɛnə'reʃən〕*n.* 世代

eternal〔ɪ'tɝnḷ〕*adj.* 永恆的；不朽的　　value〔'vælju〕*n.* 價值

Confucian〔kən'fjuʃən〕*adj.* 孔子的；儒家的

promote〔prə'mot〕*v.* 提倡　　formula〔'fɔrmjələ〕*n.* 準則

race〔res〕*n.*（生物的）種類　　*human race* 人類

【托福作文範例】

19. Confucius: The Moral Foundation of China

Perhaps the greatest Chinese philosopher that ever lived was Confucius. His many contributions to Chinese civilization and culture remain unsurpassed to this day. Let me tell you a little more about his genius by discussing four areas where his influence was the greatest.

First, Confucius was devoted to education and learning. He was passionate about knowledge acquisition and his main goal was personal and moral cultivation. Confucius was the first to advocate education for all. He was the founding father of education in China. *Second*, Confucius was deeply concerned with individual and social morality. Confucius emphasized the concept of "Ren," which means benevolence. Ren includes love, wisdom, generosity, respect and filial piety. *Third*, Confucius was a political genius. He knew the basis of political legitimacy lies in virtue. He advocated that every leader should care about the people's welfare. *Fourth*, Confucius championed the idea of social justice. He insisted that people come first. He wanted improvement in the livelihood of common people. He thought all activities should benefit everyone.

In conclusion, I think we should build a statue to honor Confucius. We must remember his inspiration and carry on his philosophy because they promote virtue, love, ethics and morality.

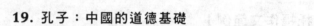

19. 孔子：中國的道德基礎

　　有史以來最偉大的中國哲學家，也許就是孔子了。他對於中國文明以及文化上的眾多貢獻，直到今日都還沒有人能夠超越。讓我藉由討論四個受他影響最大的領域，來多告訴你一些有關他的非凡才能。

　　首先，孔子致力於教育以及學習。他熱中於追求知識，而且他的主要目標是個人及道德上的教化。孔子是第一個提倡有教無類的人。他是中國教育的創始者。第二點，孔子深切地關心個人品德及社會道德。孔子強調「仁」的觀念，也就是仁慈。「仁」包括了愛、智慧、慷慨、尊重以及孝順。第三點，孔子是一個政治上的天才。他知道政權正當性的基礎是在於美德。他倡導每個領導者都應該要關懷人民的福祉。第四點，孔子支持社會正義的觀念。他堅持人民優先。他希望平民百姓的生活獲得改善。他認為所有的活動都應該要造福每一個人。

　　總之，我認為我們應該興建一座雕像來向孔子致敬。我們必須要永遠記得他帶給我們的啓示，並且讓他的哲學傳承下去，因為那些哲學提倡的是美德、愛、倫理以及道德。

【托福作文原試題】

Your city has decided to build a statue or monument to honor a famous person in your country. Who would you choose? Use reasons and specific examples to support your choice.

20. *What Makes One an Adult?*

Greetings everyone.
Welcome to everyone of any age.
Welcome to all children, adolescents
and adults.

What defines maturity?
What makes a person mature?
Maturity is my topic for today.

Let's talk about the maturation process.
Let's compare age versus experience.
Let's analyze what makes one an adult.

---

greetings ('gritɪŋz)
define (dɪ'faɪn)
mature (mə'tjʊr)
process ('prɑsɛs)
versus ('vɝsəs)

adolescent (,ædl'ɛsn̩t)
maturity (mə'tjʊrətɪ)
maturation (,mætʃu'reʃən)
compare (kəm'pɛr)
analyze ('ænl̩,aɪz)

First, *chronological age is the main determinant*.

Chronological age classifies one as an adult.

Chronological age is the physical and official
  criterion.

Governments decide adult status by birth-dates.

Governments legislate the activities of the
  underaged.

Minors are prohibited from doing a lot.

In some western countries adulthood
  is eighteen.

In some eastern countries it's twenty-one.

The age of legal adulthood varies widely.

---

chronological (ˌkrɑnə'lɑdʒɪkl̩)   main (men)

determinant (dɪ't3mənənt)   classify ('klæsə,faɪ)

physical ('fɪzɪkl̩)   official (ə'fɪʃəl)

criterion (kraɪ'tɪrɪən)   status ('stetəs)

birth-date ('b3θ'det)   legislate ('lɛdʒɪs,let)

underaged ('ʌndə'edʒɪd)   minor ('maɪnə)

prohibit (pro'hɪbɪt)   adulthood (ə'dʌlthʊd)

legal ('ligl̩)   vary ('vɛrɪ)

widely ('waɪdlɪ)

Second, life experience also determines adulthood.
People judge others by what they've accomplished.
People who have experienced a lot are often
 considered adults.

Most married people are thought of as adults.
Most parents are considered adults.
Most active soldiers and full-time employees
 are considered adults, too.

Sometimes young teens act like adults.
Some young adolescents also act very mature.
Challenging life experiences can accelerate
 adulthood.

---

determine (dɪ'tɝmɪn)	accomplish (ə'kɑmplɪʃ)
experience (ɪk'spɪrɪəns)	married ('mærɪd)
be thought of as	active ('æktɪv)
full-time ('fʊl'taɪm)	employee (,ɛmplɔɪ'i)
teens (tinz)	act (ækt)
challenging ('tʃælɪndʒɪŋ)	accelerate (æk'sɛlə,ret)

Third, successfully handling responsibility is another qualifier.

Those who are successful are seen as adults.

Those who aren't, are thought of as childlike.

Being independent is another factor.

Being financially independent is influential, too.

Being self-supporting is a main qualifier of adulthood.

Overcoming adversity facilitates adulthood.

Overcoming real hardship matures one fast.

Tough times really force people to mature.

---

handle ('hændl̩)

responsibility (rɪ,spɑnsə'bɪlətɪ)

be seen as

independent (,ɪndɪ'pɛndənt)

financially (fə'nænʃəlɪ,faɪ-)

self-supporting (,sɛlfsə'portɪŋ)

adversity (əd'vɝsətɪ)

hardship ('hardʃɪp)

tough (tʌf)

qualifier ('kwɑlə,faɪɚ)

childlike ('tʃaɪld,laɪk)

factor ('fæktɚ)

influential (,ɪnflʊ'ɛnʃəl)

overcome (,ovɚ'kʌm)

facilitate (fə'sɪlə,tet)

mature (mə'tjʊr)

force (fors)

Finally, being an adult depends on maturity.

This includes some very important intangibles.

This can be defined as being mentally or
   spiritually developed.

Being selfless and committed is important.

Being courageous and moral is, too.

Being patient and willing to sacrifice for
   others are characteristics of adults.

Adults should keep promises and loyalties.

They should say what they mean, and mean
   what they say.

They should let their actions speak for themselves.

---

depend on

be defined as

spiritually ('spırıtʃuəlı)

selfless ('sɛlflıs)

courageous (kə'redʒəs)

patient ('peʃənt)

sacrifice ('sækrə,faıs)

promise ('pramıs)

speak for oneself

intangible (ın'tændʒəbl̩)

mentally ('mɛntl̩ı)

developed (dı'vɛləpt)

committed (kə'mıtıd)

moral ('mɔrəl)

willing ('wılıŋ)

characteristic (,kærıktə'rıstık)

loyalty ('lɔıəltı)

In conclusion, adulthood is an earned status.

Many older people still act childish.

Many young people are way beyond their
   years.

Some wish to be younger.

Some wish to be older.

That's one of life's great contradictions.

I hope you all have the spirit of a child.

I wish you all have the intelligence
   of an adult.

Have a heart full of love and thank you.

---

in conclusion	earned (ɝnd)
childish ('tʃaɪldɪʃ)	way (we)
beyond (bɪ'jɑnd)	years (jɪrz)
contradiction (ˌkɑntrə'dɪkʃən)	spirit ('spɪrɪt)
intelligence (ɪn'tɛlədʒəns)	*be full of*

20. What Makes One an Adult?

什麼是成年人必備的特質？

【演講解說】

Greetings everyone.	大家好。
Welcome to everyone of any age.	歡迎任何年紀的人。
Welcome to all children,	歡迎所有的孩童、青少年和
adolescents and adults.	大人。
What defines maturity?	成熟的定義是什麼？
What makes a person mature?	是什麼讓一個人變成熟？
Maturity is my topic for today.	成熟是我今天的主題。
Let's talk about the maturation process.	讓我們來談談成熟的過程。
Let's compare age versus experience.	讓我們來比較年紀和經驗。
Let's analyze what makes one an adult.	讓我們來分析成年人應具備的特質是什麼。

**

greetings (ˈgritɪŋz) n. pl. 問候語　　adolescent (ˌædḷˈɛsn̩t) n. 青少年
define (dɪˈfaɪn) v. 定義　　maturity (məˈtjurətɪ) n. 成熟（期）
mature (məˈtjur) adj. 成熟的；成年人的
maturation (ˌmætʃuˈreʃən) n. 成熟（期）
process (ˈpɑsɛs) n. 過程　　compare (kəmˈpɛr) v. 比較
versus (ˈvɝsəs) prep. 與⋯對比；比較　　analyze (ˈænḷˌaɪz) v. 分析

First, *chronological age is the main determinant*.

首先，實際年齡是主要的決定因素。

Chronological age classifies one as an adult.

實際年齡把一個人歸類為成年人。

Chronological age is the physical and official criterion.

實際年齡是身體方面與法定上的認定標準。

Governments decide adult status by birth-dates.

政府依照出生日期確定成年人的地位。

Governments legislate the activities of the underaged.

政府立法規範未成年人的活動。

Minors are prohibited from doing a lot.

未成年者有許多事情是法律禁止從事的。

In some western countries adulthood is eighteen.

在某些西方國家，十八歲代表成年。

In some eastern countries it's twenty-one.

在某些東方國家，是二十一歲。

The age of legal adulthood varies widely.

法定年齡的定義大不相同。

** ─────────────

chronological (ˌkrɑnəˈlɑdʒɪk!) *adj.* 依時間前後排列順序的
main (men) *adj.* 主要的　　determinant (dɪˈtɝmənənt) *n.* 決定因素
classify (ˈklæsəˌfaɪ) *v.* 分類；把…歸類為 < *as* >
physical (ˈfɪzɪk!) *adj.* 身體的　　official (əˈfɪʃəl) *adj.* 官方的；法定的
criterion (kraɪˈtɪrɪən) *n.* (判斷的) 標準　　status (ˈstetəs) *n.* 身分；地位
birth-date (ˈbɝθˈdet) *n.* 出生日期　　legislate (ˈlɛdʒɪsˌlet) *v.* 用立法規定
underaged (ˈʌndɚˈedʒɪd) *adj.* 未成年的　　minor (ˈmaɪnɚ) *n.* 未成年者
prohibit (proˈhɪbɪt) *v.* (根據法律或規定) 禁止 < *from* >
adulthood (əˈdʌlthʊd) *n.* 成年 (時期)　　legal (ˈlig!) *adj.* 法定的
vary (ˈvɛrɪ) *v.* 不同　　widely (ˈwaɪdlɪ) *adv.* 遠；大大地

Second, life experience also determines adulthood.	第二，生活經驗也決定成年與否。
People judge others by what they've accomplished.	人們以他人所做過的事情來判斷。
People who have experienced a lot are often considered adults.	有許多經歷的人通常被認爲是成年人。
Most married people are thought of as adults.	大部分已婚的人被認爲是成年人。
Most parents are considered adults.	大部分的父母被人爲是成年人。
Most active soldiers and full-time employees are considered adults, too.	大部分現役的軍人和全職的員工，也會被認爲是成年人。
Sometimes young teens act like adults.	有時候，年輕的十幾歲青少年，行爲舉止像是成人。
Some young adolescents also act very mature.	有些年輕的青少年，也表現得非常成熟。
Challenging life experiences can accelerate adulthood.	充滿挑戰性的人生經驗，能夠使人很快就變成成年人。

** ————————————————————

determine〔dɪˋtɝmɪn〕v. 決定　　accomplish〔əˋkɑmplɪʃ〕v. 達成
experience〔ɪkˋspɪrɪəns〕v. 經歷　　married〔ˋmærɪd〕adj. 已婚的
be thought of as 被認爲是　　active〔ˋæktɪv〕adj. 現役的
full-time〔ˋfʊlˋtaɪm〕adj. 全職的　　employee〔͵ɛmplɔɪˋi〕n. 員工
teens〔tinz〕n. pl. 十幾歲的青少年　　act〔ækt〕v. 表現；舉止；顯得
challenging〔ˋtʃælɪndʒɪŋ〕adj. 充滿挑戰性的
accelerate〔ækˋsɛlə͵ret〕v. 加快；促進

Third, successfully handling
responsibility is another qualifier.
Those who are successful are seen
    as adults.
Those who aren't, are thought of
    as childlike.

Being independent is another factor.
Being financially independent is
    influential, too.
Being self-supporting is a main
    qualifier of adulthood.

Overcoming adversity facilitates
    adulthood.
Overcoming real hardship matures
    one fast.
Tough times really force people to
    mature.

第三，是否能夠成功地處理責
任，是另一個決定條件。
成功處理好的人被認爲是成
年人。
做不好的人則被認爲是小孩子。

獨立自主是另一個因素。
經濟上能夠獨立，也是有影響
力的。
能夠自食其力是成年的主要
條件。

克服逆境有助於長大成人。
克服眞正的困難讓一個人很快
變成熟。
苦日子眞的能迫使人成長。

** ——————————————————

handle (ˈhændḷ) v. 處理　　responsibility (rɪˌspɑnsəˈbɪlətɪ) n. 責任
qualifier (ˈkwɑləˌfaɪ∂) n. 賦予資格或權限的人或物
be seen as 被視爲　　childlike (ˈtʃaɪldˌlaɪk) adj. 孩子般的
independent (ˌɪndɪˈpɛndənt) adj. 獨立自主的　　factor (ˈfækt∂) n. 因素
financially (fəˈnænʃəlɪ,faɪ-) adv. 經濟上
influential (ˌɪnfluˈɛnʃəl) adj. 具有影響力的
self-supporting (ˌsɛlfsəˈportɪŋ) adj. 自食其力的
overcome (ˌov∂ˈkʌm) v. 克服　　adversity (ədˈvɝsətɪ) n. 逆境
facilitate (fəˈsɪləˌtet) n. 促進　　hardship (ˈhɑrdʃɪp) n. 艱難；辛苦
mature (məˈtjur) v. 使成熟　　tough (tʌf) adj. 艱苦的
force (fors) v. 迫使

Finally, being an adult depends on maturity.	最後一點，成年人必須要夠成熟。
This includes some very important intangibles.	這包括一些非常重要而無形的東西。
This can be defined as being mentally or spiritually developed.	可以定義爲是指心理上或精神上的成熟。
Being selfless and committed is important.	無私及投入是很重要的。
Being courageous and moral is, too.	具有勇氣及道德感也是同樣重要。
Being patient and willing to sacrifice for others are characteristics of adults.	有耐心，願意爲別人犧牲是成年人的特質。
Adults should keep promises and loyalties.	成年人應該信守承諾和保持忠誠。
They should say what they mean, and mean what they say.	他們說話應該要眞誠。
They should let their actions speak for themselves.	他們應該付諸行動來證明這一點。

** ─────────────

depend on 視…而定
intangible (ɪnˈtændʒəbḷ) *n.* 無形的事物　　***be defined as*** 被定義爲
mentally (ˈmɛntḷɪ) *adv.* 心理上地　　spiritually (ˈspɪrɪtʃʊəlɪ) *adv.* 精神上地
developed (dɪˈvɛləpt) *adj.* 成熟的　　selfless (ˈsɛlflɪs) *adj.* 無私的
committed (kəˈmɪtɪd) *adj.* 全心奉獻的；投入的
courageous (kəˈredʒəs) *adj.* 有勇氣的　　moral (ˈmɔrəl) *adj.* 有道德的
patient (ˈpeʃənt) *adj.* 有耐心的　　willing (ˈwɪlɪŋ) *adj.* 願意的
sacrifice (ˈsækrəˌfaɪs) *v.* 犧牲　　characteristic (ˌkærɪktəˈrɪstɪk) *n.* 特徵
promise (ˈprɑmɪs) *n.* 承諾　　loyalty (ˈlɔɪəltɪ) *n.* 忠誠
speak for oneself （事實等）不言自明

In conclusion, adulthood is an earned status.　　總之，成年是要努力才能得到的身分。

Many older people still act childish.　　很多年紀大的人，仍然顯得很幼稚。

Many young people are way beyond their years.　　很多年輕人表現得遠比他們的實際年齡成熟很多。

Some wish to be younger.　　有人希望變得年輕一點。

Some wish to be older.　　有人希望變得老一點。

That's one of life's great contradictions.　　那真是人生的一大矛盾。

I hope you all have the spirit of a child.　　我希望你們全都有小孩子的心靈。

I wish you all have the intelligence of an adult.　　我希望你們全都有大人的智慧。

Have a heart full of love and thank you.　　擁有一顆充滿愛的心，謝謝大家。

＊＊

in conclusion 總之　　earned〔ɝnd〕*adj.* 努力得來的

childish〔'tʃaɪldɪʃ〕*adj.* 幼稚的　　way〔we〕*adv.* 老遠地；非常地

beyond〔bɪ'jɑnd〕*prep.*（指範圍）越出　　years〔jɪrz〕*n. pl.* 年齡

contradiction〔ˌkɑntrə'dɪkʃən〕*n.* 矛盾　　spirit〔'spɪrɪt〕*n.* 精神

intelligence〔ɪn'tɛlədʒəns〕*n.* 聰明才智；智慧　　*be full of* 充滿

【托福作文範例】

20. What Makes One an Adult?

When we were young, how many of us wished that we would grow up soon and be treated and respected like an adult? Especially during our teenage years, we would always try to dress and act older. But what makes a person an adult? What defines maturity?

First, chronological age classifies one as an adult. Governments decide adult status by birth-dates and legislate the activities of minors. The legal age for adults varies from country to country. *Second*, life experience also determines adulthood. Most married people and parents are considered adults. Active soldiers and full-time employees are considered adults, too. *Third*, successfully handling responsibility is another qualifier. Those who are successful are thought of as adults. Being financially independent and self-supporting are other adult-like qualities. *Finally*, being an adult depends on maturity. This can be defined as being mentally or spiritually developed. Being selfless and committed is important as well as being courageous and moral. Adults should keep promises and loyalties and let their actions speak for themselves.

In conclusion, adulthood is a status we have to earn. Some wish to be younger and some wish to be older. That's the great contradiction of life.

20. 什麼是成年人必備的特質？

當我們年輕的時候，我們之中有多少人希望可以很快長大，並且能被當作成年人一樣地對待及尊重？尤其在青少年時期，我們總是試著使自己的穿著及行為看起來更成熟。但是成年人必備的特質是什麼？成年的定義是什麼呢？

首先，實際年齡決定誰被歸類為成年人。政府藉由出生日期來認定成年人的身分，同時立法規範未成年人的活動。成年人的法定年齡在每個國家都不相同。第二，生活經驗也決定了一個人是否成年。大多數已婚的人及父母，都被認為是成年人。現役軍人及全職員工，也被認為是成年人。第三，能夠成功地處理責任是另外一個決定條件。成功的人被認為是成年人。能夠在經濟上獨立，並且自食其力，也是成年人的特徵。最後，成年人必須要夠成熟。這樣的成熟可以定義為是指心智上或是精神上的成熟。能夠無私而投入是很重要的，具有勇氣及道德感也同樣重要。成年人應該信守承諾和保持忠誠，並付諸行動來證明這一點。

總之，成年是我們要努力才能得到的一個身分。有些人想要變得更年輕，而有些人想要變得更老。那真是人生中最大的矛盾。

【托福作文原試題】

People recognize a difference between children and adults. What events (experiences or ceremonies) make a person an adult? Use specific reasons and examples to explain your answer.

21. Why People Attend College or University

Ladies and gentlemen:
I'm so happy to be here.
I am happy to talk about my college experience.

Attending college was one of the best decisions
  of my life.
It opened a new world for me.
It taught me independence and changed my
  world view.

People attend college for many reasons.
Some want to explore a variety of interests.
Some want to specialize in a certain field
  of study.

---

attend (ə'tɛnd)

world view

a variety of

specialize ('spɛʃəl,aɪz)

field (fild)

independence (,ɪndɪ'pɛndəns)

explore (ɪk'splor)

interest ('ɪntrɪst)

certain ('sɝtn̩)

study ('stʌdɪ)

In college, students can prepare for a career.
They can develop self-reliance.
They can have new experiences every day.

Today's students are lucky.
Today many of us can attend college.
In the past only the rich could go to college.

Today's students are more practical.
They have to be able to compete.
Therefore, a practical education is
    very important.

Going to college is a big investment.
Students want to get everything they can
    out of it.
They want to get their money's worth.

---

career (kə'rɪr)	develop (dɪ'vɛləp)
self-reliance ('sɛlfrɪ'laɪəns)	*the rich*
practical ('præktɪkl)	compete (kəm'pit)
investment (ɪn'vɛstmənt)	*out of*
worth (wɝθ)	

It is best for them to have clear goals.

They must know what they want.

They must know what they need to learn.

Today's students know who they are.

They are not trying to find themselves
  in college.

They are trying to improve themselves.

Of course, all students want to learn.

They want to broaden their minds.

That is why they attend college.

But today's students want specific knowledge.

What they learn must be relevant.

What they learn must help them in
  their careers.

---

clear (klɪr)   goal (gol)
improve (ɪm'pruv)   broaden ('brɔdn̩)
specific (spɪ'sɪfɪk)   relevant ('rɛləvənt)

Defining their goals will help them to do that.

They will be able to target their learning.

They will be able to learn what they

   need to learn.

Today's universities are not like they were

  in the past.

Today's students are different as well.

The world has changed a great deal.

Universities are still great places to develop.

Students can acquire broad knowledge.

Students can also pursue personal

   development.

---

define (dɪ'faɪn)	target ('tɑrgɪt)
as well	*a great deal*
acquire (ə'kwaɪr)	broad (brɔd)
pursue (pə'su)	personal ('pɜsn̩l)

A college education must be balanced.

A student must balance personal development
  and specific goals.

That way higher education can be a valuable tool.

In conclusion, I hope my speech has helped you.

I hope you can get the most out of college.

I hope I have given you some ideas.

Just remember to set your goals.

Make them clear and relevant.

Make sure you know what you want and who
  you are.

Thank you for listening.

I appreciate your attention.

You've been a terrific audience.

---

balanced ('bælənst)	balance ('bæləns)
higher education	valuable ('væljuəbḷ)
tool (tul)	*in conclusion*
get the most out of	set (sɛt)
make sure	appreciate (ə'priʃɪˌet)
attention (ə'tɛnʃən)	terrific (tə'rɪfɪk)
audience ('ɔdɪəns)	

21. *Why People Attend College or University*
人們爲什麼要上大學

【演講解說】

Ladies and gentlemen:　　各位先生、各位女士：
I'm so happy to be here.　　我非常高興能夠來到這裡。
I am happy to talk about my college　　很高興可以談談我的大學
　　experience.　　經驗。

Attending college was one of the　　上大學是我這輩子最棒的決
　　best decisions of my life.　　定之一。
It opened a new world for me.　　它爲我開啓了一個新的世界。
It taught me independence and　　它讓我學會獨立自主，也改變
　　changed my world view.　　了我的世界觀。

People attend college for many　　人們因爲很多不同的理由上
　　reasons.　　大學。
Some want to explore a variety　　有些人想探索各種不同的
　　of interests.　　興趣。
Some want to specialize in a　　有些人想專攻某個研究領域。
　　certain field of study.

** ─────────────────────

attend (ə'tɛnd) v. 上（學）
independence (ˌɪndɪ'pɛndəns) n. 獨立；自主　　*world view* 世界觀
explore (ɪk'splor) v. 探索　　*a variety of* 各式各樣的
interest ('ɪntrɪst) n. 興趣　　specialize ('spɛʃəlˌaɪz) v. 專攻 < *in* >
certain ('sɝtn) adj. 某個　　field (fild) n. （知識）領域
study ('stʌdɪ) n. 研究

In college, students can prepare
　for a career.

They can develop self-reliance.

They can have new experiences.

Today's students are lucky.

Today many of us can attend college.

In the past only the rich could go
　to college.

Today's students are more practical.

They have to be able to compete.

Therefore, a practical education is
　very important.

Going to college is a big investment.

Students want to get everything
　they can out of it.

They want to get their money's
　worth.

在大學裡，學生可以為職業作
準備。

他們可以培養自立的能力。

他們可以擁有新的體驗。

現今的學生很幸運。

現在我們有許多人可以上大學。

在過去，只有有錢人才能上
大學。

現在的學生比較講求實際。

他們必須能夠競爭。

因此，實用的教育就非常重要。

上大學是一項重大的投資。

學生竭盡所能，想從中得到
一切。

他們想要每一分錢都花得值得。

**

career〔kə'rɪr〕*n.* 職業　　develop〔dɪ'vɛləp〕*v.* 培養

self-reliance〔ˌsɛlfrɪ'laɪəns〕*n.* 自我依賴；自立

the rich 有錢人 (= *rich people*)　　practical〔'præktɪk!〕*adj.* 實用的

compete〔kəm'pit〕*v.* 競爭　　investment〔ɪn'vɛstmənt〕*n.* 投資

out of 從　　worth〔wɝθ〕*n.* 價值

It is best for them to have clear goals. 他們最好有明確的目標。

They must know what they want. 他們必須知道自己想要什麼。

They must know what they need to learn. 他們必須知道自己需要學習什麼。

Today's students know who they are. 現在的學生知道自己的定位。

They are not trying to find themselves in college. 上大學並不是為了追尋自我。

They are trying to improve themselves. 他們是想努力讓自己更進步。

Of course, all students want to learn. 當然，所有的學生都想要學東西。

They want to broaden their minds. 他們希望能擴展自己的心智。

That is why they attend college. 這就是為什麼他們要上大學。

But today's students want specific knowledge. 但是現在的學生想追求特定的知識。

What they learn must be relevant. 他們所學的東西必須有關聯。

What they learn must help them in their careers. 他們所學的東西必須對他們的職業有幫助。

**

clear〔klɪr〕*adj.* 清楚的
goal〔gol〕*n.* 目標　　improve〔ɪmˈpruv〕*v.* 改進
broaden〔ˈbrɔdn̩〕*v.* 增廣（知識、經驗等）
specific〔spɪˈsɪfɪk〕*adj.* 特定的
relevant〔ˈrɛləvənt〕*adj.* 有關聯的；合適的

Defining their goals will help them
to do that.

讓目標明確將對他們想做的事
有所幫助。

They will be able to target their
learning.

他們將能夠為自己的學習設定
目標。

They will be able to learn what they
need to learn.

他們將能夠學會必須學習的
事物。

***Today's universities are not like they
were in the past.***

現今的大學和以前已經不一
樣了。

Today's students are different
as well.

現今的學生也不一樣了。

The world has changed a great deal.

這個世界已經有了重大的改變。

Universities are still great places to
develop.

大學仍然是追求發展的好地方。

Students can acquire broad
knowledge.

學生能夠獲得廣泛的知識。

Students can also pursue personal
development.

學生也能夠追求個人的發展。

**

define (dɪ'faɪn) *v.* 使明確　　target ('tɑrgɪt) *v.* 為…設定目標
as well 也　　***a great deal*** 非常
acquire (ə'kwaɪr) *v.* 獲得　　broad (brɔd) *adj.* 廣泛的
pursue (pə'su) *v.* 追求　　personal ('pɝsn̩l) *adj.* 個人的

A college education must be balanced. 　大學教育必須均衡發展。

A student must balance personal 　學生必須在個人發展和特定目
　development and specific goals. 　標之間尋求平衡。

That way higher education can be 　如此一來，高等教育才能成為
　a valuable tool. 　一種有價值的工具。

In conclusion, I hope my speech 　總之，我希望我的演說對你們
　has helped you. 　有幫助。

I hope you can get the most out 　我希望你們能夠從充分利用大
　of college. 　學教育。

I hope I have given you some ideas. 　我希望我已經提供你一些想法。

Just remember to set your goals. 　只要記得設定自己的目標。

Make them clear and relevant. 　讓目標明確而合適。

Make sure you know what you 　務必確定你想要什麼，還有你
　want and who you are. 　自己的定位。

Thank you for listening. 　感謝你們的聆聽。

I appreciate your attention. 　我很感激大家專心聆聽。

You've been a terrific audience. 　你們是很出色的聽眾。

**　balanced** (ˈbælənst) *adj.* 平衡的　　**balance** (ˈbæləns) *v.* 使平衡
higher education 高等教育　　**valuable** (ˈvæljəbl̩) *adj.* 有價值的
tool (tul) *n.* 工具　　***in conclusion*** 總之
get the most out of 充分利用 (= *make the most of*)
set (sɛt) *v.* 設定　　***make sure*** 確定
appreciate (əˈpriʃɪˌet) *v.* 感激　　**attention** (əˈtɛnʃən) *n.* 注意；專心
terrific (təˈrɪfɪk) *adj.* 很棒的　　**audience** (ˈɔdɪəns) *n.* 聽眾

【托福作文範例】

21. Why People Attend College or University

A college or university education is very important. Our parents often emphasize the importance of a good education and I'm here to tell you why.

First, in college, students can prepare for a career. They can develop self-reliance and have new experiences every day. Today's students are more practical so they can compete in today's society. *Second*, going to college is a big investment. Students want to get their money's worth so it's best for them to have clear goals. They must know what they want and need to learn. Today's students know who they are; they are not trying to find themselves in college. They are trying to improve themselves. *Third*, all students want to learn to broaden their minds; that's why they attend college. Today's universities are different because the students are different. The world has changed a great deal and universities are still great places to develop. A student can achieve personal development and specific goals while in school.

In conclusion, I hope you try your best to get into a college or university. It will be great for your development into a well-rounded person. Just remember to set clear and relevant goals.

21. 人們爲什麼要上大學

大學教育是非常重要的。我們的父母經常強調良好教育的重要性,而我現在就告訴你們爲什麼。

首先,在大學裡,學生可以爲他們的職業做準備。他們可以培養自立的能力,而且每天都能得到新的經驗。現今的學生已經更講求實際,所以能夠在現在的社會中競爭。第二點,上大學是一個重大的投資。學生希望他們的錢花得值得,所以他們最好能有清楚的目標。他們必須知道什麼是他們想要的,而什麼又是他們需要學習的。現在的學生很清楚自己的定位;他們不是努力要在大學裡找尋自我。他們是努力要讓自己變得更好。第三點,所有的學生都想要藉由學習來擴展自己的心智;那就是他們上大學的原因。現今的大學已經不一樣了,因爲學生也已經不同了。這世界已經改變很多,而大學仍然是一個值得發展的好地方。學生可以在學校中實現個人的發展,以及達到特定的目標。

總之,我希望你們盡全力進入大學就讀。那對於讓你成爲一個多元發展的人是很有幫助的。只要記住,一定要設定清楚而合適的目標。

【托福作文原試題】

*People attend college or university for many different reasons (for example, new experiences, career preparation, increased knowledge). Why do **you** think people attend college or university? Use specific reasons and examples to support your answer.*

22. *Parents Are the Best Teachers*

Ladies and gentlemen:
May I have your attention, please?
What I am about to say is very important.

It concerns our education.
It concerns the best way to learn.
I am going to tell you how to get the best
    education.

The most important thing is finding a
    good teacher.
A good teacher is the key to successful learning.
A good teacher can help us learn anything.

We all have many teachers in our lives.
They include our teachers in school,
    our classmates, and friends.
They also include our colleagues and bosses.

---

attention (ə'tɛnʃən)   *be about to V.*
concern (kən'sɜn)   key (ki)
colleague ('kɑlig)

However, our most important teachers
  are our parents.
They are our first teachers.
They are our best teachers.

Our parents teach us the most important
  things in life.
They teach us responsibility, integrity
  and compassion.
They always have our best interests at heart.

What our parents teach us is very important.
What they teach us are the basic facts of life.
It is the foundation of our education.

---

responsibility (rɪˌspɑnsəˈbɪlətɪ)
integrity (ɪnˈtɛgrətɪ)
compassion (kəmˈpæʃən)　　interest (ˈɪntrɪst)
have···at heart　　　　basic (ˈbesɪk)
facts of life　　　　　foundation (faʊnˈdeʃən)

Our parents teach us about our own culture.
They teach us what is right and wrong.
They teach us how to get along with other people.

Our parents also teach us how to be independent.
They teach us many practical skills.
They teach us how to learn.

Our parents teach us continually.
They start teaching when we are born.
They never stop educating us.

They teach us when they praise us.
They teach us when they punish us.
They teach us whether we realize it or not.

---

culture (ˈkʌltʃɚ)
independent (ˌɪndɪˈpɛndənt)
practical (ˈpræktɪkḷ)
continually (kənˈtɪnjuəlɪ)
praise (prez)
whether…or not

get along with

skill (skɪl)
educate (ˈɛdʒəˌket)
punish (ˈpʌnɪʃ)
realize (ˈriəˌlaɪz)

We learn by watching them.
We learn by listening to them.
They teach us by words and by example.

Parents are devoted teachers.
They will do anything for us.
They never stop sacrificing for us.

They always care for and protect us.
They always want the best for us.
They will let nothing hurt us.

Their motivation is to prepare us.
They want us to have a good life in the future.
No one wants our success more than they do.

---

example (ɪgˋzæmpḷ)   devoted (dɪˋvotɪd)
sacrifice (ˋsækrəˌfaɪs)   *care for*
protect (prəˋtɛkt)
motivation (ˌmotəˋveʃən)   prepare (prɪˋpɛr)

Everyone we meet can be our teacher.

Everyone has something to offer and share.

Throughout our lives we will learn from

    many people.

However, no teacher can take the place

    of our parents.

They are our first and last teachers.

They are our best and most devoted teachers.

I hope this speech was helpful to you.

I hope you appreciate your parents.

I hope you learn well from them.

---

offer ('ɔfɚ)   share (ʃɛr)

throughout (θru'aʊt)   *take the place of*

appreciate (ə'priʃɪ,et)

22. *Parents Are the Best Teachers*
父母是最好的老師

【演講解說】

Ladies and gentlemen:	各位先生、各位女士：
May I have your attention, please?	請注意聽我說，好嗎？
What I am about to say is very important.	我即將要說的話非常重要。
It concerns our education.	它和我們的教育有關。
It concerns the best way to learn.	它和學習的最好方式有關。
I am going to tell you how to get the best education.	我要告訴你們如何得到最好的教育。
The most important thing is finding a good teacher.	找到一位好的老師是最重要的事情。
A good teacher is the key to successful learning.	好的老師是學習成功的關鍵。
A good teacher can help us learn anything.	好的老師可以幫助我們學習任何事情。

**

attention〔ə'tɛnʃən〕*n.* 注意；專心
be about to V. 即將~　　concern〔kən'sɜn〕*v.* 關於
key〔ki〕*n.* 關鍵 < *to* >

We all have many teachers in our
　　lives.

我們一生當中都遇到許多老師。

They include our teachers in school,
　　our classmates, and friends.

其中包括學校的老師、同學和
朋友。

They also include our colleagues
　　and bosses.

也包括我們的同事與老闆。

However, our most important
　　teachers are our parents.

然而，我們最重要的老師是我
們的父母。

They are our first teachers.

他們是我們最初的老師。

They are our best teachers.

他們是我們最好的老師。

Our parents teach us the most
　　important things in life.

我們的父母教導我們生活中最
重要的事情。

They teach us responsibility,
　　integrity and compassion.

他們教導我們責任感、正直和
同情心。

They always have our best interests
　　at heart.

他們總是非常關心我們的利
益。

**

colleague (ˈkɑlig) *n.* 同事 (= *co-worker*)
responsibility (rɪˌspɑnsəˈbɪlətɪ) *n.* 責任感
integrity (ɪnˈtɛgrətɪ) *n.* 正直；誠實
compassion (kəmˈpæʃən) *n.* 同情 (心)
interest (ˈɪntrɪst) *n.* 利益　　***have…at heart*** 關懷；把…放在心上

What our parents teach us is very important.	父母教導我們的東西非常重要。
What they teach us are the basic facts of life.	他們教我們的是人生最基本的現實情況。
It is the foundation of our education.	是構成我們教育的基礎。
Our parents teach us about our own culture.	我們的父母教導我們認識自己的文化。
They teach us what is right and wrong.	他們教導我們明辨是非。
They teach us how to get along with other people.	他們教導我們如何與人相處。
Our parents also teach us how to be independent.	我們的父母也教導我們如何自立。
They teach us many practical skills.	他們教導我們很多實用的技能。
They teach us how to learn.	他們教導我們如何學習。
Our parents teach us continually.	我們的父母持續不斷地教導我們。
They start teaching when we are born.	他們從我們出生後，就開始教導我們。
They never stop educating us.	他們從未停止教育我們。

** ────────────────────────────

foundation〔faʊnˋdeʃən〕*n.* 基礎　　basic〔ˋbesɪk〕*adj.* 基本的
facts of life 生活中的嚴酷現實　　culture〔ˋkʌltʃɚ〕*n.* 文化
get along with 和～相處　　independent〔͵ɪndɪˋpɛndənt〕*adj.* 獨立的
practical〔ˋpræktɪkl〕*adj.* 實用的　　skill〔skɪl〕*n.* 技能
continually〔kənˋtɪnjʊəlɪ〕*adv.* 持續地　　educate〔ˋɛdʒə͵ket〕*v.* 教育

They teach us when they praise us.	他們讚美我們時，也在教導我們。
They teach us when they punish us.	他們處罰我們時，也在教導我們。
They teach us whether we realize it or not.	不論我們了不了解，他們都教導我們。
We learn by watching them.	我們也觀察他們的行為來學習。
We learn by listening to them.	我們聽從他們的話來學習。
They teach us by words and by example.	他們透過言敎及身敎來敎導我們。
Parents are devoted teachers.	父母是最盡責的老師。
They will do anything for us.	他們會為我們做任何事情。
They never stop sacrificing for us.	他們從不停止為我們犧牲。
They always care for and protect us.	他們總是照顧我們、保護我們。
They always want the best for us.	他們總是想給我們最好的。
They will let nothing hurt us.	他們不會讓我們遭受任何傷害。

**

praise〔prez〕v. 讚美　　*whether…or not* 是否
realize（'riə,laiz）v. 了解　　punish〔'pʌnɪʃ〕v. 處罰
example（ɪg'zæmpḷ）n. 榜樣　　devoted（dɪ'votɪd）adj. 全心全意的
sacrifice（'sækrə,faɪs）v. 犧牲　　*care for* 照顧
protect〔prə'tɛkt〕v. 保護

Their motivation is to prepare us.	他們的動機是要讓我們做好準備。
They want us to have a good life in the future.	他們希望我們將來有美好的生活。
No one wants our success more than they do.	沒有人比他們更希望我們成功。
Everyone we meet can be our teacher.	我們所遇到的每個人都可以成為我們的老師。
Everyone has something to offer and share.	每個人都有可以貢獻和分享的東西。
Throughout our lives we will learn from many people.	在我們的一生中，我們會向很多人學習。
However, no teacher can take the place of our parents.	然而，沒有老師可以取代父母的地位。
They are our first and last teachers.	他們是我們最初、也是最終的老師。
They are our best and most devoted teachers.	他們是我們最棒、最盡責的老師。
I hope this speech was helpful to you.	我希望這篇演講對你們有幫助。
I hope you appreciate your parents.	我希望你們對父母心存感激。
I hope you learn well from them.	我希望你們從他們身上好好學習。

** ────────────────────────

motivation (ˌmotə'veʃən) *n.* 動機　　prepare (prɪ'pɛr) *v.* 使…準備好
offer ('ɔfɚ) *v.* 提供；給予　　share (ʃɛr) *v.* 分享
throughout (θru'aut) *prep.* 遍及　　*take the place of* 取代 (= *replace*)
appreciate (ə'priʃɪˌet) *v.* 感激

【托福作文範例】

22. Parents Are the Best Teachers

A good education is important. *However*, finding a good teacher is even more important because a good teacher can help us learn anything. We all have many teachers in our lives, but I think the most important teachers are our parents and here's why.

Parents are our teachers the first day we are born and they will always have our best interests at heart. They teach us important things in life like responsibility, integrity and compassion. Our parents teach us about our own culture. They teach us what is right and wrong. Parents also teach us how to be independent by passing down to us many practical skills. They teach us how to learn. They teach us when they praise us as well as when they punish us. We learn by watching them and by listening to them. Parents are devoted teachers because they will do anything for us and they always want the best for us.

Parents are motivated to prepare us because they want us to have a good life in the future. They are our first and last teachers and they are our best and most devoted teachers. So we should all start appreciating our parents more.

22. 父母是最好的老師

　　良好的教育是非常重要的。然而，找到一位好老師更加的重要，因爲一位好老師能幫助我們學習任何事物。我們在一生中都有過許多老師，但我認爲最重要的老師是我們的父母，以下就是原因。

　　父母自我們出生的第一天起，就成爲我們的老師，他們總是爲我們著想。他們教導我們生命中許多重要的事物，像是責任感、正直以及同情心。我們的父母也教導我們認識自身的文化。他們教我們明辨是非。父母也藉由將許多實用技能傳承給我們，來教導我們如何自立。他們教導我們如何學習。無論是稱讚我們或是懲罰我們，他們都是在教導我們。我們藉由觀察他們的行爲以及聽從他們的教誨來學習。父母是最盡責的老師，因爲他們會爲我們做任何事，並且永遠希望給我們最好的。

　　父母想要讓我們做好準備，因爲他們希望我們將來能夠擁有一個美好的生活。他們是我們最初也是最終的老師，而且也是我們最棒、最盡責的老師。所以我們都應該開始更加感激我們的父母。

【托福作文原試題】

Do you agree or disagree with the following statement? Parents are the best teachers. Use specific reasons and examples to support your answer.

23. *Changing Food, Changing Lives*

Good morning, ladies and gentlemen:
Today's topic is something we are all
   familiar with.
Today I am going to talk about food.

We all eat every day.
We all enjoy eating out.
But sometimes we prefer a home-cooked meal.

Making that home-cooked meal today is a lot
   easier than it was in the past.
That is because the food we eat has
   changed a lot.
That, in turn, has changed the way we live.

---

familiar (fə'mɪljɚ)   *eat out*
prefer (prɪ'fɝ)   home-cooked ('hom,kukt)
meal (mil)   *in the past*
in turn

In the past, preparing a meal was difficult.
It took a long time.
It was a lot of hard work.

The raw ingredients had to be found.
People had to grow them.
People also had to travel a long way to buy
   some things.

Then the ingredients had to be prepared.
This was often a painstaking process.
Chickens had to be plucked; fish had to
   be cleaned.

Cooking the food was difficult as well.
There were no labor-saving devices.
Everything had to be done by hand.

---

raw (rɔ)	ingredient (ɪn'gridɪənt)
grow (gro)	prepare (prɪ'pɛr)
painstaking ('penz,tekɪŋ)	process ('prɑsɛs)
pluck (plʌk)	*as well*
labor-saving ('lebɚ,sevɪŋ)	device (dɪ'vaɪs)

In the past, preparing three meals a day
   was a big job.
It took a great deal of time.
It required a lot of skill and knowledge.

Now all that has changed.
Today it is easy to prepare a meal.
Today it's quick and convenient.

Nowadays, meals can be ready in minutes.
Now a cook no longer has to spend hours in
   the kitchen.
Convenience foods have given us all more
   free time.

Stores are filled with convenience foods.
Stores have instant foods and entire frozen meals.
All we have to do is heat them up.

---

a great deal of	skill (skɪl)
nowadays ('nauə,dez)	*no longer*
free time	*be filled with*
convenience food	instant ('ɪnstənt)
entire (ɪn'taɪr)	frozen ('frozn)
all one has to do is V.	*heat up*

All this has changed the way we live.

Many women have time to do things other
　　than cook.

Many work outside the home or pursue other
　　interests.

Now many more people are trying to cook.

Now the process is no longer a mystery.

Anyone can do it — even a child.

You just have to read the directions.

You just have to follow the instructions.

Most food products have simple pictures
　　to show you what to do.

Cooking is as easy as one two three.

Cooking is as simple as can be.

Modern cooking is a piece of cake.

---

other than	pursue (pɚˋsu)
mystery (ˋmɪstrɪ)	directions (dəˋrɛkʃənz)
follow (ˋfɑlo)	instructions (ɪnˋstrʌkʃənz)
as easy as one two three	***as…as can be***
piece of cake	

To sum up, changing food has changed

our lives.

Cooking and eating are easier today than

ever before.

We no longer have to spend so much time

and effort on them.

Without this time-consuming process, we all

have more free time.

We can work more or play more.

We have lots of time for other things.

Now I hope you have enjoyed my speech.

Now I hope you appreciate the advancements.

Remember this next time you sit down

to dinner.

---

to sum up   effort (ˈɛfət)

time-consuming (ˈtaɪmkənˌsjumɪŋ)

appreciate (əˈpriʃɪˌet)

advancement (ədˈvænsmənt)

23. *Changing Food, Changing Lives*
不同的食物，不同的生活

【演講解說】

Good morning, ladies and gentlemen: 各位先生、各位女士，早安：

Today's topic is something we are all familiar with. 今天的主題是我們都很熟悉的東西。

Today I am going to talk about food. 今天我要來談談食物。

We all eat every day. 我們每天都要吃東西。

We all enjoy eating out. 我們全都喜歡外出用餐。

But sometimes we prefer a home-cooked meal. 但是有時候我們比較喜歡在家做飯。

Making that home-cooked meal today is a lot easier than it was in the past. 現在在家裡做飯比以前容易很多。

That is because the food we eat has changed a lot. 那是因為我們所吃的食物已經改變許多。

That, in turn, has changed the way we live. 那也因此改變了我們生活的方式。

**

---

familiar (fə'mıljɚ) *adj.* 熟悉的

eat out 外出用餐　　prefer (prı'fɝ) *v.* 比較喜歡

home-cooked ('hom,kʊkt) *adj.* (食物) 在家裡烹煮的；家常的

meal (mil) *n.* 一餐　　*in the past* 在過去　　*in turn* 然後

***In the past, preparing a meal was
   difficult*.**　　　　　　　　　　以前，準備食物很困難。

It took a long time.　　　　　　　要花很長的時間。

It was a lot of hard work.　　　　要做很多辛苦的工作。

The raw ingredients had to be found.　　要找到生鮮食材。

People had to grow them.　　　　　人們必須耕種。

People also had to travel a long way　人們也必須到很遠的地方購買
   to buy some things.　　　　　　某些東西。

Then the ingredients had to be　　　然後必須把材料準備好。
   prepared.

This was often a painstaking　　　準備的過程往往是很耗費心力
   process.　　　　　　　　　　　的。

Chickens had to be plucked; fish　　要拔雞毛；要把魚洗乾淨。
   had to be cleaned.

***Cooking the food was difficult as well*.**　烹調食物也是很困難的。

There were no labor-saving devices.　沒有可以省力的設備。

Everything had to be done by hand.　每件事情都必須用手工處理。

**　**

raw〔rɔ〕*adj.*（食物）生的；未煮過的

ingredient〔ɪnˈgridɪənt〕*n.*（烹飪的）原料

grow〔gro〕*v.* 種植；栽培　　prepare〔prɪˈpɛr〕*v.* 準備；做（飯菜）

painstaking〔ˈpenz͵tekɪŋ〕*adj.* 費力氣的　　process〔ˈprɑsɛs〕*n.* 過程

pluck〔plʌk〕*v.* 拔毛　　***as well*** 也

labor-saving〔ˈlebɚ͵sevɪŋ〕*adj.* 省力的　　device〔dɪˈvaɪs〕*n.* 裝置

In the past, preparing three meals a day was a big job.	在過去，一天準備三餐是個浩大工程。
It took a great deal of time.	做飯要花很多的時間。
It required a lot of skill and knowledge.	做飯需要具備許多的技術和知識。
Now all that has changed.	現在情況完全不同了。
Today it is easy to prepare a meal.	現在做飯很容易。
Today it's quick and convenient.	現在做飯既快又方便。
Nowadays, meals can be ready in minutes.	現在做飯只需要花幾分鐘的時間就好了。
Now a cook no longer has to spend hours in the kitchen.	現在做飯的人不用再待在廚房裡好個鐘頭。
Convenience foods have given us all more free time.	便利食品已經為我們帶來更多的空閒時間。
Stores are filled with convenience foods.	商店有很多便利的食品。
Stores have instant foods and entire frozen meals.	商店有速食食品和全套的冷凍餐。
All we have to do is heat them up.	我們只要將它們加熱就好了。

** ——————————

a great deal of 大量的　　skill〔skɪl〕*n.* 技術
nowadays〔'nauə,dez〕*adv.* 現在　　*no longer* 不再
convenience food 便利食品　　*free time* 空閒時間
be filled with 充滿　　instant〔'ɪnstənt〕*adj.* 立即的；速食的
entire〔ɪn'taɪr〕*adj.* 全部的　　frozen〔'frozn〕*adj.* 冷凍的
all one has to do is V. 某人只需要～　　*heat up* 加熱

All this has changed the way we live.　　我們的生活已經完全受到改變。

Many women have time to do things other than cook.　　許多女性有時間從事做飯之外的事情。

Many work outside the home or pursue other interests.　　許多女性到外面工作，或者從事其他自己有興趣的活動。

Now many more people are trying to cook.　　現在有越來越多人想要做飯。

Now the process is no longer a mystery.　　現在做菜的過程不再是令人難以理解的事。

Anyone can do it — even a child.　　任何人都可以做飯 —— 即使是小孩也可以。

You just have to read the directions.　　你只要看使用說明。

You just have to follow the instructions.　　你只要照著指示做。

Most food products have simple pictures to show you what to do.　　大部分的食品都有簡單的圖示，告訴你要怎麼做。

**

other than 除了　　pursue 〔 pə'su 〕 *v.* 追求

mystery 〔'mɪstrɪ 〕 *n.* 難以理解的事物

directions 〔 də'rɛkʃənz 〕 *n. pl.* 指示；使用說明

　(= instructions 〔 ɪn'strʌkʃənz 〕)　　follow 〔'falo 〕 *v.* 遵守

Cooking is as easy as one two three.	做飯就像是數一、二、三一樣地容易。
Cooking is as simple as can be.	做飯很簡單。
Modern cooking is a piece of cake.	現代的烹調是件容易的事。
To sum up, changing food has changed our lives.	總之,不同的食物,不同的生活。
Cooking and eating are easier today than ever before.	現在做飯和用餐比以前容易。
We no longer have to spend so much time and effort on them.	我們不再需要那麼耗費時間和精力。
Without this time-consuming process, we all have more free time.	做飯過程不再那麼耗時,因此我們有更多空閒的時間。
We can work more or play more.	我們可以有更多時間工作或玩樂。
We have lots of time for other things.	我們有很多時間做其他事情。
Now I hope you have enjoyed my speech.	現在我希望你們喜歡我的演講。
Now I hope you appreciate the advancements.	現在我希望你們對這樣的進步心存感激。
Remember this next time you sit down to dinner.	下次你坐下來吃晚餐的時候,要記得這一點。

**

as easy as one two three 就像是數一、二、三一樣地容易;極其容易
(*= as easy as ABC*)　　*as…as can be* 非常…
piece of cake 容易的事　　*to sum up* 總之
effort (ˈɛfət) *n.* 努力　　time-consuming (ˈtaɪmkən͵sjumɪŋ) *adj.* 費時的
appreciate (əˈpriʃɪ͵et) *v.* 感激　　advancement (ədˈvænsmənt) *n.* 進步

【托福作文範例】

23. **Changing Food, Changing Lives**

There is something we need to do every day in order to survive; we all need to eat. Making meals today is a lot easier than it was in the past. That's because the food we eat has changed a lot. And that, in turn, has changed the way we live.

In the past, preparing a meal was difficult. It took time and hard work because most of the raw ingredients had to be found. People either had to catch or grow dinner themselves. Cooking the food was difficult, too. There were no labor-saving devices. Everything had to be done by hand. In the past, preparing three meals a day was a big job and required a lot of skill and knowledge. Nowadays, meals can be ready in minutes. Now a cook no longer has to spend hours in the kitchen because convenience foods have given us more free time. Stores are filled with convenience foods and all we have to do is heat them up. All this has changed the way we live, too. Many women have more time to do things other than cook. Many work outside the home or pursue other interests.

In short, changing food has changed our lives. Cooking and eating are easier today. We no longer have to spend so much time and effort on them. We now have more free time outside of the kitchen to work or play more. We have lots of time for other things.

23. 不同的食物，不同的生活

　　爲了生存，有些事情是我們每天必須做的；我們都必須吃東西。做菜在今日遠比在過去輕鬆許多。那是因爲我們所吃的食物已經改變了許多。那也因此改變了我們生活的方式。

　　在過去，準備一餐是困難的。要花時間並且很辛苦，因爲大多的生鮮食材都必須要去尋找才能獲得。人們要捕捉或是栽種自己的食材。烹煮食物也很困難。當時沒有任何可以省力的設備。所有的事情都必須要用手工做。在過去，一天準備三餐是個浩大工程，而且需要很多的技巧及知識。現在做飯只需要花幾分鐘的時間就好了。現在做飯的人不用再待在廚房好幾個鐘頭，因爲便利食品已經讓我們有更多的空閒時間。商店裡面充滿了許多不同的便利食品，我們只需要將它們加熱就好了。這一切都已經改變了我們的生活方式。有很多女性因此有了更多時間，來做烹調以外的事情。很多女性到外面工作，從事其他自己有興趣的工作。

　　簡言之，不同的食物，已經改變了我們的生活。現在做飯和用餐更容易。我們不再需要那麼耗費時間和精力。我們現在能夠在廚房之外擁有更多的空閒時間，來工作或是玩樂。我們擁有更多時間，能從事其他的事情。

────【托福作文原試題】────

Nowadays, food has become easier to prepare. Has this change improved the way people live? Use specific reasons and examples to support your answer.

24. *Book Knowledge vs. Experience*

Ladies and gentlemen:
I am happy to see you here today.
I would like to talk about knowledge.

We all know how important knowledge is.
We all know that we must work to acquire it.
But do you know what is the best way?

Knowledge can be acquired from many sources.
Knowledge can come from books, teachers,
   and experience.
Each has its own advantages.

First, *we can gain knowledge from books*.
We learn through our formal education system.
We often study books at school with the help
   of our teachers.

---

acquire (əˈkwaɪr)   source (sɔrs , sors)
advantage (ədˈvæntɪdʒ)   gain (gen)
formal (ˈfɔrml̩)

Books allow us to learn about things that we
  cannot experience.
We can study all the places in the world.
We can learn from people we will never meet.

Reading books can help develop our analytical
  skills.
Reading books can increase our powers of
  perception.
By reading, we can learn so much.

***Second**, **we can learn through practical experience**.*
It gives us useful knowledge.
It's true that one learns best by doing.

Making mistakes is a common way to improve.
Making mistakes is the best way to learn.
In order to advance, it is necessary to take action.

---

experience (ɪk'spɪrɪəns)   study ('stʌdɪ)
analytical (ˌænḷ'ɪtɪkḷ)   skill (skɪl)
increase (ɪn'kris)   power ('pauɚ)
perception (pɚ'sɛpʃən)   practical ('præktɪkḷ)
common ('kɑmən)   improve (ɪm'pruv)
advance (əd'væns)   *take action*

With trial and error, you learn fast.

With trial and error, you don't repeat mistakes.

Trial and error is the mother of wisdom.

Third, we can acquire knowledge from people.

We can learn from teachers and friends.

Most importantly, we can learn from

our parents.

Knowledge comes from observation.

Knowledge is learned through imitation.

Emulating successful people is the way.

Parents are the ultimate teachers.

Parents pass on knowledge to us every day.

We can truly learn the most from our parents.

---

trial ('taɪəl)	error ('ɛrɚ)
trial and error	repeat (rɪ'pit)
mother ('mʌðɚ)	wisdom ('wɪzdəm)
observation (ˌɑbzɚ'veʃən)	imitation (ˌɪmə'teʃən)
emulate ('ɛmjəˌlet)	ultimate ('ʌltəmɪt)
pass on	truly ('trulɪ)

***Finally, we can combine the knowledge we
get from books and from experience.***
We can apply the insights we gained from
  books to our practical experience.
This will make every experience more
  meaningful.

In fact, we must apply our book knowledge.
If we never use it, what good is it?
If we don't apply it, it's a big waste of time.

Practical experience is more meaningful
  than book knowledge.
Practical experience is far more useful.
Trying to do something is the best way
  to learn.

---

combine (kəm'baɪn)	apply (ə'plaɪ)
insight ('ɪn͵saɪt)	meaningful ('minɪŋfəl)

In conclusion, *we can gain knowledge in many ways*.

We can read books and we can try new experiences.

Both will help us a lot.

In the end, we must combine the two.

It will make our book knowledge more useful.

It will make our experiences much more meaningful, too.

However you choose to learn, remember that constant learning is the key.

Never stop learning and you will never stop progressing.

Thank you for your attention.

---

in conclusion	*in the end*
however (haʊ'ɛvɚ)	constant ('kɑnstənt)
key (ki)	progress (prə'grɛs)
attention (ə'tɛnʃən)	

24. *Book Knowledge vs. Experience*
書本知識與實際經驗

【演講解說】

Ladies and gentlemen:	各位先生、各位女士：
I am happy to see you here today.	我很高興今天能在這裡和你們見面。
I would like to talk about knowledge.	我想要談論知識。
We all know how important knowledge is.	我們都知道知識有多重要。
We all know that we must work to acquire it.	我們都知道，我們必須努力才能獲得知識。
But do you know what is the best way?	但是你知道什麼是最好的方法嗎？
Knowledge can be acquired from many sources.	可以獲得知識的來源有很多。
Knowledge can come from books, teachers, and experience.	知識可以從書本、老師，以及實際經驗中獲得。
Each has its own advantages.	每一種都有其優點。

**

acquire〔ə'kwaɪr〕*v.* 獲得　　source〔sors, sɔrs〕*n.* 來源
advantage〔əd'væntɪdʒ〕*n.* 優點

First, we can gain knowledge from books.	第一，我們可以從書本獲得知識。
We learn through our formal education system.	我們透過正規教育體制學習。
We often study books at school with the help of our teachers.	我們往往是在學校老師的協助下唸書。
Books allow us to learn about things that we cannot experience.	書本讓我們知道沒有機會親身去體驗的事。
We can study all the places in the world.	我們可以研究世界各地。
We can learn from people we will never meet.	我們可以向不曾謀面的人學習。
Reading books can help develop our analytical skills.	讀書也有助於培養我們分析的技巧。
Reading books can increase our powers of perception.	閱讀書本可以增加我們的觀察力。
By reading, we can learn so much.	藉由閱讀，我們可以學到非常多東西。
Second, we can learn through practical experience.	第二，我們可以從實際的經驗中學習。
It gives us useful knowledge.	我們會得到有用的知識。
It's true that one learns best by doing.	的確，從做中學的效果最好。

** ————————————————

gain〔gen〕*v.* 獲得　　formal〔'fɔrml̩〕*adj.* 正規的
experience〔ɪk'spɪrɪəns〕*v.* 體驗　　study〔'stʌdɪ〕*v.* 研究
analytical〔͵ænl̩'ɪtɪkl̩〕*adj.* 分析的　　skill〔skɪl〕*n.* 技巧
increase〔ɪn'kris〕*v.* 增加　　power〔'pauɚ〕*n.* 能力
perception〔pɚ'sɛpʃən〕*n.* 感知能力；認識能力；洞察力
practical〔'præktɪkl̩〕*adj.* 實際的

Making mistakes is a common way to improve.	犯錯是使人進步常見的方式。
Making mistakes is the best way to learn.	犯錯是最好的學習方式。
In order to advance, it is necessary to take action.	爲了進步，就必須要付諸行動。
With trial and error, you learn fast.	藉由嘗試錯誤，你會學得很快。
With trial and error, you don't repeat mistakes.	藉由嘗試錯誤，你不會重蹈覆轍。
Trial and error is the mother of wisdom.	嘗試錯誤是智慧之母。
Third, we can acquire knowledge from people.	第三，我們可以從別人身上獲得知識。
We can learn from teachers and friends.	我們可以從老師和朋友身上學習。
Most importantly, we can learn from our parents.	最重要的是，我們可以從父母身上學習。

** ————————————————————

common (ˈkɑmən) *adj.* 常見的   improve (ɪmˈpruv) *v.* 改善
advance (ədˈvæns) *v.* 進步   ***take action*** 採取行動
trial (ˈtraɪəl) *n.* 嘗試   error (ˈɛrə) *n.* 錯誤
trial and error 嘗試錯誤法；反覆試驗；不斷摸索
repeat (rɪˈpit) *v.* 重複   mother (ˈmʌðə) *n.* 根源 < *of* >
wisdom (ˈwɪzdəm) *n.* 智慧

Knowledge comes from observation.	知識來自觀察。
Knowledge is learned through imitation.	知識能透過模仿學習而來。
Emulating successful people is the way.	仿效成功的人就是個途徑。
Parents are the ultimate teachers.	父母是最好的老師。
Parents pass on knowledge to us every day.	父母每天傳遞知識給我們。
We can truly learn the most from our parents.	我們眞的可以從父母身上學到最多。

Finally, we can combine the knowledge we get from books and from experience.　最後，我們可以將書本上獲得的知識和實際經驗相結合。

We can apply the insights we gained from books to our practical experience.	我們可以將藉由讀書所獲得的見解，應用在實際的經驗中。
This will make every experience more meaningful.	這會讓每個經驗都變得更有意義。
In fact, we must apply our book knowledge.	事實上，我們必須將書本知識加以應用。
If we never use it, what good is it?	如果我們從來不加以運用，那學了有什麼用？
If we don't apply it, it's a big waste of time.	如果我們不加以應用，那就白白地浪費了時間。

**

observation〔͵ɑbzə'veʃən〕 *n.* 觀察　imitation〔͵ɪmə'teʃən〕 *n.* 模仿
emulate〔'ɛmjə͵let〕 *v.* 熱心學習；模仿　ultimate〔'ʌltəmɪt〕 *adj.* 最好的
pass on 傳遞 *< to >*　truly〔'trulɪ〕 *adv.* 眞實地；眞正地
combine〔kəm'baɪn〕 *v.* 結合　apply〔ə'plaɪ〕 *v.* 應用 *< to >*
insight〔'ɪn͵saɪt〕 *n.* 洞察力；見識　meaningful〔'minɪŋfəl〕 *adj.* 有意義的

Practical experience is more
   meaningful than book knowledge.

Practical experience is far more useful.

Trying to do something is the best
   way to learn.

In conclusion, we can gain knowledge
   in many ways.

We can read books and we can try
   new experiences.

Both will help us a lot.

In the end, we must combine the two.

It will make our book knowledge
   more useful.

It will make our experiences more
   meaningful, too.

However you choose to learn, remember
   that constant learning is the key.

Never stop learning and you will
   never stop progressing.

Thank you for your attention.

實際的經驗比書本知識更有意義。

實際的經驗有用多了。

試著去做某件事情是最好的學習方式。

總之，我們可以經由許多不同的方式來獲得知識。

我們可以看書，也可以嘗試新的體驗。

兩者對我們都有很大的幫助。

最後，我們必須將兩者結合。

這樣會使我們的書本知識更有用。

也會使我們的經驗更具有意義。

不管你是選擇什麼方法學習，記住不斷的學習是關鍵所在。

絕對不要停止學習，這樣你就會不斷地進步。

謝謝你們專心聽講。

**

in conclusion 總之   *in the end* 到最後
however〔hau'ɛvɚ〕*adv.* 不管用什麼方法
constant〔'kɑnstənt〕*adj.* 持續的；不斷的   key〔ki〕*n.* 關鍵
progress〔prə'grɛs〕*v.* 進步   attention〔ə'tɛnʃən〕*n.* 注意；專心

【托福作文範例】

24. Book Knowledge vs. Experience

There are different ways to gain knowledge. The most popular way is to acquire it from books, teachers and experience. But which is the best way? They each have their own advantages.

First, we can gain knowledge from books. We study books with the help of our teachers. Books let us learn things we cannot experience, like exotic places around the world and people we will never meet. *Second*, we can learn through practical experience as well. It gives us useful knowledge because we learn best by doing. *For example*, making mistakes is the best way to learn. With trial and error, you learn fast. *Third*, we learn from other people like our teachers, friends and parents. Knowledge comes from observation. Knowledge is learned through imitation and parents are the ultimate teachers. *Finally*, we can combine the knowledge we get from books and from experience. In fact, we must apply our book knowledge; if we never use it, what good is it?

In conclusion, there are many ways for us to gain knowledge. We can get it from books or we can try new experiences. In the end, we must combine the two to gain more knowledge. But you should never stop learning!

24. 書本知識與實際經驗

　　獲取知識有許多的方法。最普遍的方式就是從書本、老師及經驗中取得。但是哪一個才是最好的方法呢？它們其實都各有優點。

　　首先，我們可以從書本獲得知識。我們藉由老師的協助來研讀書本。書本讓我們學習到我們無法親身體驗的事物，像是全世界有異國風情的地方，或是我們從未見過的人們。第二點，我們也可以藉由實際的經驗來學習。它能給我們有用的知識，因為我們從做中學的效果最好。舉例來說，犯錯是最好的學習方法。藉由嘗試錯誤法，你將會學習得很快。第三點，我們從別人身上學習，像是我們的老師、朋友以及父母。知識來自觀察。知識可透過模仿而獲得的，而父母是最好的老師。最後一點，我們可以結合我們從書本以及經驗中取得的知識。事實上，我們必須要應用我們所學到的書本知識；如果我們從不用它，那學了有什麼用？

　　總之，我們有許多方法可以獲得知識。我們可以從書本中獲得，或是嘗試新的經驗。最後，我們必須結合兩者來獲得更多的知識。但是應該要不斷地學習！

──【托福作文原試題】──

It has been said, "Not everything that is learned is contained in books." Compare and contrast knowledge gained from experience with knowledge gained from books. In your opinion, which source is more important? Why?

25. A Factory in the Neighborhood

Good evening, neighbors.
I'm glad to see you here.
What we are going to talk about tonight is
  very important.

We have to make a decision.
We have to look at the pros and cons.
Then we can make the best choice possible.

This decision is important.
It will affect our neighborhood.
It will affect all of our lives.

Someone wants to build a factory.
He wants to build it here.
He wants to build it in our backyard.

---

factory ('fækt(ə)rı)	neighborhood ('nebə,hud)
pro (pro)	con (kɑn)
the pros and cons	affect (ə'fɛkt)
backyard ('bæk'jɑrd)	*in one's backyard*

We all have to decide.

We must decide together.

That's why we're here tonight.

We have to tell him yes or no.

Do we want a factory in our neighborhood?

Do we want it to change or stay the way it is?

We should talk about the advantages and disadvantages.

We should think carefully about his proposal.

Then we can make the best decision.

On the one hand, there would be some advantages
   to having a factory here.

It could help our community.

It could make our lives better.

---

stay (ste)   advantage (əd'væntɪdʒ)

disadvantage (ˌdɪsəd'væntɪdʒ)

proposal (prə'pozl̩)   ***on the one hand***

community (kə'mjunətɪ)

For example, it could bring a lot of jobs.

Many of us might find employment in the factory.

Many of us would increase our incomes.

It would be great for our kids.

It would keep the next generation close to home.

Our children wouldn't have to move away.

A factory would also bring money to our
   community in other ways.

The owner would pay taxes.

The workers might eat dinner or go shopping here.

On the other hand, the factory might cause
   some problems.

It could affect our quality of life.

It might hurt more than help.

---

employment (ɪm'plɔɪmənt)   increase (ɪn'kris)

income ('ɪn‚kʌm)   generation (‚dʒɛnə'reʃən)

close (klos)   ***move away***

owner ('onɚ)   tax (tæks)

on the other hand   cause (kɔz)

quality ('kwɑlətɪ)

For example, it might pollute the environment.

It might harm our health.

It would also bring down property values.

In addition, it would increase traffic.

It could cause a lot of congestion.

It might be unsafe for our children to
  play outside.

Obviously, there are both pluses and minuses.

We have to weigh them carefully.

We have to decide what is important to us.

---

pollute (pə'lut)

environment (ın'vaırənmənt)　　　harm (harm)

bring down　　　　　　　　　property ('prapətı)

value ('vælju)　　　　　　　　　*in addition*

congestion (kən'dʒɛstʃən)

obviously ('abvıəslı)　　　　　plus (plʌs)

minus ('maınəs)　　　　　　　　weigh (we)

As for me, I think the disadvantages
   are greater.
I think the factory would hurt more than help.
Therefore, I oppose it.

You have to make up your own minds.
You have to think about it carefully.
Let me know what you decide.

Thank you all for listening.
God bless you all for being here.
May God give us the wisdom to make the
   right decision.

---

as for   oppose (ə'poz)
make up one's mind   bless (blɛs)
wisdom ('wɪzdəm)

25. *A Factory in the Neighborhood*
住家附近的工廠

【演講解說】

Good evening, neighbors.	各位鄰居，晚安：
I'm glad to see you here.	我很高興能在這裡和大家見面。
What we are going to talk about tonight is very important.	我們今晚要談論的事情非常重要。
We have to make a decision.	我們必須做決定。
We have to look at the pros and cons.	我們必須考慮到利弊得失。
Then we can make the best choice possible.	然後我們就能夠做出最好的選擇。
This decision is important.	這個決定很重要。
It will affect our neighborhood.	會影響我們的住家環境。
It will affect all of our lives.	會影響我們大家的生活。
Someone wants to build a factory.	有人想蓋一間工廠。
He wants to build it here.	他想在這裡興建工廠。
He wants to build it in our backyard.	他想在我們的住家附近蓋工廠。

**

factory (ˈfækt(ə)rɪ) *n.* 工廠　　neighborhood (ˈnebəˌhud) *n.* 鄰近地區
pro (pro) *n.* 贊成（的論點）　　con (kən) *n.* 反對（的論點）
the pros and cons 贊成和反對的理由；利弊得失
affect (əˈfɛkt) *v.* 影響　　backyard (ˈbækˈjɑrd) *n.* 後院
in one's backyard 在某人住家的後院（這裡引申為「在住家附近」）

We all have to decide.	我們大家必須做出決定。
We must decide together.	我們必須一起決定。
That's why we're here tonight.	那就是為什麼我們齊聚在這裡的原因。

We have to tell him yes or no.	我們必須告訴他可不可以蓋工廠。
Do we want a factory in our neighborhood?	我們希望住家附近有工廠嗎？
Do we want it to change or stay the way it is?	我們希望改變，還是保持現狀？

We should talk about the advantages and disadvantages.	我們必須談論優缺點。
We should think carefully about his proposal.	我們應該仔細思考他的提議。
Then we can make the best decision.	然後我們可以做出最好的決定。

On the one hand, there would be some advantages to having a factory here.	一方面來說，在這裡蓋座工廠會有一些優點。
It could help our community.	有助於我們的社區。
It could make our lives better.	可以讓我們的生活更好。

** ————————————————

stay〔ste〕*v.* 繼續；保持　　advantage〔əd'væntɪdʒ〕*n.* 優點
disadvantage〔͵dɪsəd'væntɪdʒ〕*n.* 缺點
proposal〔prə'pozl̩〕*n.* 提議　　***on the one hand*** 一方面
community〔kə'mjunətɪ〕*n.* 社區

For example, it could bring a lot of jobs. | 例如,會帶來很多工作機會。

Many of us might find employment in the factory. | 我們當中有很多人可能會在工廠找到工作。

Many of us would increase our incomes. | 我們當中有很多人會增加收入。

It would be great for our kids. | 這對我們的孩子而言會是很棒的。

It would keep the next generation close to home. | 會讓我們的下一代不用遠離家園。

Our children wouldn't have to move away. | 我們的孩子不必搬到別的地方。

A factory would also bring money to our community in other ways. | 工廠也可能會以其他方式為我們社區增加財富。

The owner would pay taxes. | 老闆要付稅金。

The workers might eat dinner or go shopping here. | 員工可能會在這裡吃晚餐或購物。

On the other hand, the factory might cause some problems. | 另一方面,工廠可能會造成某些問題。

It could affect our quality of life. | 會影響我們的生活品質。

It might hurt more than help. | 造成的傷害可能多於助益。

**

employment (ɪmˈplɔɪmənt) *n.* 工作　　increase (ɪnˈkris) *v.* 增加
income (ˈɪn,kʌm) *n.* 收入　　generation (,dʒɛnəˈreʃən) *n.* 世代
close (klos) *adj.* 接近的 < *to* >　　***move away*** 搬走
owner (ˈonɚ) *n.* 物主;所有人　　tax (tæks) *n.* 稅
on the other hand 另一方面　　cause (kɔz) *v.* 引起
quality (ˈkwɑlətɪ) *n.* 品質

For example, *it might pollute the environment*.

It might harm our health.

It would also bring down property values.

In addition, it would increase traffic.

It could cause a lot of congestion.

It might be unsafe for our children to play outside.

Obviously, there are both pluses and minuses.

We have to weigh them carefully.

We have to decide what is important to us.

例如，工廠可能會污染環境。

有可能危害到我們的健康。

也會造成房地產價格下跌。

此外，會增加交通流量。

可能會導致交通嚴重阻塞。

小孩子在外面玩耍，可能會變得不安全。

顯然地，好處和壞處兩者都有。

我們必須仔細權衡利弊。

我們必須決定什麼對我們才是重要的。

**

pollute (pə'lut) *v.* 污染　environment (ɪn'vaɪrənmənt) *n.* 環境
harm (hɑrm) *v.* 危害　***bring down*** 使降低
property ('prɑpətɪ) *n.* 房地產　value ('vælju) *n.* 價值
in addition 此外　congestion (kən'dʒɛstʃən) *n.* 阻塞
obviously ('ɑbvɪəslɪ) *adv.* 顯然地　plus (plʌs) *n.* 好處
minus ('maɪnəs) *n.* 壞處　weigh (we) *v.* 考慮；權衡

***As for me, I think the disadvantages
   are greater.***
I think the factory would hurt more
   than help.
Therefore, I oppose it.

對我而言，我認為帶來的缺點
會比較多。
我認為工廠造成的傷害會多於
助益。
因此，我反對興建工廠。

You have to make up your own
   minds.
You have to think about it carefully.
Let me know what you decide.

你必須做出決定。
你必須仔細考慮清楚。
讓我知道你的決定。

Thank you all for listening.
God bless you all for being here.
May God give us the wisdom to
   make the right decision.

謝謝你們的聆聽。
願上帝祝福在場的所有人。
願上帝賦予我們智慧，能做出
正確的決定。

**

as for 至於　　oppose〔ə'poz〕*v.* 反對
make up one's mind 做決定
bless〔blɛs〕*v.* 祝福　　wisdom〔'wɪzdəm〕*n.* 智慧

【托福作文範例】

25. A Factory in the Neighborhood

There is an important issue that we must talk about tonight; a decision has to be made. This is very important because the decision will affect our neighborhood and all of our lives.

Someone wants to build a factory in our town. We now have to decide together on the pros and cons of this factory and tell this person yes or no. Let's talk about the advantages and disadvantages. *On the one hand*, a factory could bring many advantages to our town and make our lives better. We would have more jobs and the town could use the extra money from the taxes the factory would pay. Our kids could stay close to home and not go to the big cities to find employment. But there might be some problems the factory might bring as well. *For example*, it might pollute the environment and harm our health. Traffic would also increase and make it unsafe for our children to play outside. Our quality of life could be seriously affected by the factory.

There are both pluses and minuses for building a factory here. After weighing the pros and cons, I have decided to say no. You have to think about it carefully and make your own decisions. I hope you make the right decision.

25. 住家附近的工廠

今晚我們必須要談一個重要的議題；我們必須做出決定。這件事相當的重要，因為這個決定將會影響到附近的住家以及我們大家的生活。

有人想要在我們的鎮上建一座工廠。我們現在必須要一起來權衡利弊得失，然後告訴那個人我們是否同意。讓我們來談談這件事情的優缺點。一方面來說，一座工廠可以為我們的鎮上帶來許多好處，並且使我們的生活更好。我們能夠有更多的工作機會，而且鎮上還能夠因為工廠所付的稅金而有額外的經費。我們的孩子能夠在自家附近找到工作，而不需要跑到其他的大城市就業。但是工廠也會帶來一些問題。舉例來說，它可能會污染我們的環境，危害我們的健康。交通流量會因此而增加，我們的孩子無法在外面安全地玩耍。我們的生活品質可能會嚴重地受到工廠的影響。

此地興建一座工廠，對我們是有利也有弊。在權衡所有的利弊得失後，我決定拒絕這項提議。你們必須仔細考慮，做出自己的決定。我希望你們能夠做出正確的決定。

【托福作文原試題】

A company has announced that it wishes to build a large factory near your community. Discuss the advantages and disadvantages of this new influence on your community. Do you support or oppose the factory? Explain your position.

26. Changing My Hometown

Ladies and gentlemen:
I hope you are interested in what I have
to say.
My topic is something that affects all of us.

I am concerned about my hometown.

I love this place I call home.

But I'm not completely happy with it.

I would like to change something about

my hometown.

I would like to change it for the better.

I would like to make it a better place to live.

---

hometown ('hom'taʊn)   affect (ə'fɛkt)
concerned (kən'sɜnd)   completely (kəm'plitlɪ)
be happy with   better ('bɛtɚ)

My hometown is a large city.

My hometown has a big population.

It's a crowded and busy place.

Unfortunately, it's not very clean.

Unfortunately, too many cars and buses
   pollute the air.

People also create a lot of garbage.

That's what I would like to change.

I'd like to change the environment.

I'd like to make my town a cleaner, less
   polluted place.

Our living environment is important.

It can affect our health.

It affects us both mentally and physically.

---

population (ˌpɑpjəˈleʃən)   crowded (ˈkraʊdɪd)

unfortunately (ʌnˈfɔrtʃənɪtlɪ)   pollute (pəˈlut)

create (krɪˈet)

environment (ɪnˈvaɪrənmənt)   mentally (ˈmɛntlɪ)

physically (ˈfɪzɪkḷɪ)

Bad air contributes to many health problems.

It can cause asthma.

It can also shorten our lives.

Garbage can spread bacteria.

It is a big danger to our health.

It can make us very sick.

In addition, the environment affects the
  way we feel.

We feel better in a clean environment.

We feel optimistic about our health in
  a clean environment.

We all must work together.

Together we can improve this situation.

Together we can make it a better place to live.

---

contribute (kən'trɪbjut)

asthma ('æsmə)

spread (sprɛd)

danger ('dendʒɚ)

optimistic (ˌɑptə'mɪstɪk)

improve (ɪm'pruv)

cause (kɔz)

shorten ('ʃɔrtn̩)

bacteria (bæk'tɪrɪə)

in addition

work together

We have to do several things to accomplish
our goals.
We must enact laws to limit pollution.
We must also be responsible for ourselves.

Others must know about this problem.

Other people must realize its importance so
they will take it seriously.
We must inform people of the dangers
of a poor environment.

This problem does not only affect my
hometown.
It is a worldwide problem.
It is getting worse every day.

---

accomplish (ə'kɑmplɪʃ)   goal (gol)
enact (ɪn'ækt)   limit ('lɪmɪt)
pollution (pə'luʃən)
responsible (rɪ'spɑnsəbl)   realize ('riə,laɪz)
take ~ seriously   inform (ɪn'fɔrm)
worldwide ('wɜld,waɪd)

It affects your communities, too.

But we can change the situation.

We can do that by working together.

Let's start now to clean up our towns.

Let's spread the news.

Then we can all live happier, healthier lives.

I'm asking now for volunteers.

I'm hoping everyone here will get involved.

The time for action is upon us.

That's all I have to say.

That's how we can change our town.

Thank you all for your care and concern.

---

community (kə'mjunətɪ)   *clean up*

ask for   volunteer (ˌvɑlən'tɪr)

involved (ɪn'vɑlvd)   action ('ækʃən)

upon (ə'pɑn)   care (kɛr)

concern (kən's ɜn)

26. *Changing My Hometown*
改變我的家鄉

【演講解説】

Ladies and gentlemen:　　　各位先生、各位女士：

I hope you are interested in what　　我希望你們有興趣聽我要告訴
I have to say.　　　　　　　你們的事情。

My topic is something that affects　　我的主題和影響我們全體的事
all of us.　　　　　　　　有關。

I am concerned about my　　　　我很關心我的家鄉。
hometown.

I love this place I call home.　　　我愛這塊我稱爲家鄉的地方。

But I'm not completely happy　　　但是我對這個地方並非完全滿
with it.　　　　　　　　　意。

I would like to change something　　我想要讓我的家鄉作點改變。
about my hometown.

I would like to change it for the　　我想要加以改善。
better.

I would like to make it a better　　我想要使它成爲一個更適合居
place to live.　　　　　　　住的地方。

** ────────────

hometown (ˈhomˈtaʊn) *n.* 出生的故鄉；生長的城市

affect (əˈfɛkt) *v.* 影響　　concerned (kənˈsɜnd) *adj.* 關心的 <*about*>

completely (kəmˈplitlɪ) *adv.* 完全地　　***be happy with*** 對…滿意

better (ˈbɛtɚ) *n.* (人或事物) 較優者　*adj.* 較佳的；更好的 (good 的比較級)

My hometown is a large city.	我的家鄉是一個大城市。
My hometown has a big population.	我的家鄉人口很多。
It's a crowded and busy place.	它是個擁擠而且熱鬧的地方。
Unfortunately, it's not very clean.	遺憾的是，它不是很乾淨。
Unfortunately, too many cars and buses pollute the air.	遺憾的是，汽車及公車數量過多，污染了空氣。
People also create a lot of garbage.	人們也製造了許多垃圾。
That's what I would like to change.	這就是我想要改變的地方。
I'd like to change the environment.	我想改變環境。
I'd like to make my town a cleaner, less polluted place.	我想使我的家鄉成為一個更乾淨、更少污染的地方。
Our living environment is important.	我們的生活環境很重要。
It can affect our health.	它會影響我們的健康。
It affects us both mentally and physically.	我們在心理上和生理上都會受到影響。

** ————————————

population〔͵pɑpjəˈleʃən〕*n.* 人口
crowded〔ˈkraʊdɪd〕*adj.* 擁擠的
unfortunately〔ʌnˈfɔrtʃənɪtlɪ〕*adv.* 遺憾的是；不幸地
pollute〔pəˈlut〕*v.* 污染　　create〔krɪˈet〕*v.* 製造
environment〔ɪnˈvaɪrənmənt〕*n.* 環境
mentally〔ˈmɛntḷɪ〕*adv.* 心理上　　physically〔ˈfɪzɪkḷɪ〕*adv.* 生理上

Bad air contributes to many health problems.	空氣品質不良會導致許多健康方面的問題。
It can cause asthma.	會造成氣喘。
It can also shorten our lives.	也會縮短我們的壽命。
Garbage can spread bacteria.	垃圾會散播細菌。
It is a big danger to our health.	對我們的健康構成極大威脅。
It can make us very sick.	會讓我們病得很嚴重。
In addition, *the environment affects the way we feel*.	此外，環境會影響我們的感受。
We feel better in a clean environment.	在乾淨的環境中，我們會覺得較舒適。
We feel optimistic about our health in a clean environment.	我們在乾淨的環境中，對自己的健康會很樂觀。
We all must work together.	我們大家必須同心協力。
Together we can improve this situation.	我們要一起來改善這個情況。
Together we can make it a better place to live.	我們一起讓它成為更好的居住場所。

**

contribute〔kən'trɪbjut〕v. 促成＜ to ＞　　cause〔kɔz〕v. 引起
asthma〔'æsmə〕n. 氣喘　　shorten〔'ʃɔrtn̩〕v. 縮短
spread〔sprɛd〕v. 散播　　bacteria〔bæk'tɪrɪə〕n. pl. 細菌
danger〔'dendʒɚ〕n. 危險（物）；威脅＜ to ＞　　*in addition* 此外
optimistic〔,ɑptə'mɪstɪk〕adj. 樂觀的＜ about ＞
work together 合作　　improve〔ɪm'pruv〕v. 改善

We have to do several things to
accomplish our goals.

We must enact laws to limit
pollution.

We must also be responsible for
ourselves.

Others must know about this problem.

Other people must realize its
importance so they will take it
seriously.

We must inform people of the
dangers of a poor environment.

This problem does not only affect
my hometown.

It is a worldwide problem.

It is getting worse every day.

我們必須做些事情，來達成我
們的目標。

我們必須制定法律，限制污染。

我們也必須為自己的行為負責。

其他人必須知道這個問題。

其他人必須了解其重要性，才
會認真看待這件事。

我們必須先讓大家知道，不良
的環境可能造成的危險。

這個問題不只影響我的家鄉。

這是全球性的問題。

它正每天日益惡化。

**

accomplish〔əˋkamplɪʃ〕v. 達成
goal〔gol〕n. 目標　　enact〔ɪnˋækt〕v. 制定（法律）
limit〔ˋlɪmɪt〕v. 限制　　pollution〔pəˋluʃən〕n. 污染
responsible〔rɪˋspɑnsəbḷ〕adj. 應負責任的 < for >
realize〔ˋrɪəˏlaɪz〕v. 了解　　**take ~ seriously** 把 ~ 看得很認真
inform〔ɪnˋfɔrm〕v. 告知 < of >
worldwide〔ˋwɝldˏwaɪd〕adj. 遍及全球的

It affects your communities, too. | 它也影響到我們的社區。
But we can change the situation. | 但是我們可以改變這個情況。
We can do that by working together. | 我們可以藉由共同努力來完成。

Let's start now to clean up our | 我們現在開始打掃市容吧。
  towns.
Let's spread the news. | 我們把這個消息傳出去吧。
Then we can all live happier, | 然後我們就可以過著更快樂、更
  healthier lives. | 健康的生活。

I'm asking now for volunteers. | 我現在徵求志工。
I'm hoping everyone here will get | 我希望這裡的每個人都能參與。
  involved.
The time for action is upon us. | 該是我們行動的時候了。

That's all I have to say. | 以上就是我要說的話。
That's how we can change our town. | 那就是我們可以改變家鄉的做法。
Thank you all for your care and | 感謝大家的關心。
concern.

**

community (kə'mjunətɪ) *n.* 社區
clean up 打掃；整理　　***ask for*** 要求
volunteer (ˌvɑlən'tɪr) *n.* 志願者；志工
involved (ɪn'vɑlvd) *adj.* 有關係的；參與的
action ('ækʃən) *n.* 行動　　upon (ə'pɑn) *prep.* 在…之上
care (kɛr) *n.* 關心　　concern (kən'sɝn) *n.* 關心

【托福作文範例】

26. Changing My Hometown

All people have their own hometown in which they grew up. My hometown is still where I call home but I'm not completely happy about it. I would like to change something about my hometown to make it a better place to live.

My hometown is a large city. It's very crowded and busy. **Unfortunately**, it's not very clean. There are too many cars and buses polluting the air and people also creating a lot of garbage. That's what I want to change. A clean living environment is important. It affects our mind and body. Bad air causes asthma and can shorten our lives. **In addition**, the environment affects the way we feel. We feel better and more optimistic in a clean environment. Working together, we can improve this situation. We must enact laws to limit pollution and be responsible for ourselves. Others must know about this problem and realize its importance. This is a worldwide problem and it's getting worse every day.

Let's start cleaning up our towns. Let's work together to spread the news to get volunteers. I'm hoping everyone will get involved. It's time to protect our hometown!

26. 改變我的家鄉

　　每個人都有自己成長的家鄉。我的家鄉儘管是我稱爲家的地方，但我對那個地方並不是完全滿意。我想要將它做一些改變，使它成爲一個更適合居住的地方。

　　我的家鄉是一個大城市。那裡非常的擁擠而且熱鬧。遺憾的是，那裡不是非常乾淨。汽車和公車的數量太多，污染了空氣，而人們也製造了許多垃圾。那就是我想要改變的地方。一個乾淨的生活環境是相當重要的。那會影響我們的心理和生理。空氣品質不良會導致氣喘，也會縮短我們的生命。此外，環境會影響我們的感受。在一個乾淨的環境中，我們會感覺比較舒適，而且比較樂觀。只要我們一起努力，我們可以改善這個狀況。我們必須制定限制污染的法律，並且對我們自己負責。其他人也必須知道這個問題，並了解它的重要性。這是一個全球性的問題，而且每天日益嚴重。

　　讓我們開始打掃我們的城鎮吧。讓我們一起努力把這個消息傳出去，招募更多的志工。我希望每個人都能夠參與。保護我們家園的時候到了！

【托福作文原試題】

If you could change one important thing about your hometown, what would you change?　Use reasons and specific examples to support your answer.

27. The Influence of Television and Movies

Ladies and gentlemen:
We are a video nation.
Television and movies have become common
in our society.

I think we all like to watch television.
I think most of us probably like movies, too.
We may have a VCR or DVD player in
   our home.

It seems that everyone spends a lot of time
   watching video programs.
It must have an effect on us.
Let's talk about what these effects are.

---

influence ('ɪnfluəns)   video ('vɪdɪ‚o)
common ('kɑmən)   *VCR*
DVD   effect (ə'fɛkt‚ɪ-)

First, when we watch TV we see a lot of ads.

They make us want to buy things.

They make us think we need things.

Even movie theaters permit advertisements now.

There is no escaping advertising.

There is widespread advertising everywhere!

Seeing so many ads affects our choices.

We are induced to buy certain products.

We buy them whether we need them or not.

Second, TV and movies can affect our view
of the world.

Both can make our view broader or they
can distort it.

Both can influence us depending on what
we watch.

---

ad (æd)	permit (pɚ'mɪt)
advertisement (ˌædvɚ'taɪzmənt)	
there is no + V-ing	escape (ə'skep)
advertising ('ædvɚˌtaɪzɪŋ)	widespread ('waɪd'sprɛd)
induce (ɪn'djus)	view (vju)
broad (brɔd)	distort (dɪs'tɔrt)
depend on	

We can watch news and educational programming.

We can learn many new things from such shows.

They can open both our eyes and our minds.

The entertainment programs show us a
  different world.

The entertainment world is distorted.

It is not like the real world at all.

Third, TV is often misleading.

It's not realistic at all.

It's sensational, exaggerated entertainment.

In it, everyone possesses great wealth.

In it, everyone is very attractive.

Unfortunately, we can only find such a
  perfect world on TV.

---

educational (ˌɛdʒə'keʃənḷ)   programming ('progræmɪŋ)

show (ʃo)   entertainment (ˌɛntə'tenmənt)

not···at all   misleading (mɪs'lidɪŋ)

realistic (ˌriə'lɪstɪk)   sensational (sɛn'seʃənḷ)

exaggerated (ɪg'zædʒəˌretɪd)

possess (pə'zɛs)   wealth (wɛlθ)

attractive (ə'træktɪv)   unfortunately (ʌn'fɔrtʃənɪtlɪ)

Watching these shows may make us dissatisfied.

We may wonder why we are not rich.

We may want to look as good as the actors.

Finally, TV and movies can affect our children.

They are the most susceptible.

They are easily persuaded by what they see.

Many children cannot tell fact from fiction.

They believe what they see on the screen.

As a result, they develop a distorted view of life.

Even worse, they may imitate what they see.

They may try the stunts they have seen.

They don't realize that this can be very dangerous.

---

dissatisfied (dɪsˈsætɪsˌfaɪd)	wonder (ˈwʌndɚ)
actor (ˈæktɚ)	susceptible (səˈsɛptəbl̩)
persuade (pɚˈswed)	*tell* A *from* B
fact (fækt)	fiction (ˈfɪkʃən)
screen (skrin)	*as a result*
imitate (ˈɪməˌtet)	stunt (stʌnt)

In conclusion, *television and movies are not*
   going to go away.
Instead they are going to become more
   and more popular.
Therefore, we must pay attention to the
   effects that they have on us.

The visual media can be informative.
They can also be entertaining.
Both of these things are good.

However, they can also hurt us if we are
   not careful.
Most important of all, they cannot take the
   place of real experience.
So let's turn off the TV and experience real life.

---

in conclusion	*go away*
instead (ɪn'stɛd)	*pay attention to*
visual ('vɪʒuəl)	media ('midɪə)
informative (ɪn'fɔrmətɪv)	
entertaining (,ɛntə'tenɪŋ)	*most important of all*
take the place of	*turn off*
experience (ɪk'spɪrɪəns)	

27. *The Influence of Television and Movies*
電視和電影的影響

【演講解説】

Ladies and gentlemen:	各位先生、各位女士：
We are a video nation.	我們置身在一個充滿影像的國度。
Television and movies have become common in our society.	電視和電影在我們的社會中已經變得很普遍。
I think we all like to watch television.	我想我們全都喜歡看電視。
I think most of us probably like movies, too.	我想我們大部分的人也都喜歡看電影。
We may have a VCR or DVD player in our home.	我們可能在家裡就有一台錄影機或 DVD。
It seems that everyone spends a lot of time watching video programs.	似乎每個人都花很多時間在看電視節目。
It must have an effect on us.	這必定會對我們造成影響。
Let's talk about what these effects are.	咱們來談談這些影響是什麼。

** ───────────────

influence (ˈɪnfluəns) *n.* 影響 (= *effect*)
video (ˈvɪdɪˌo) *adj.* 電視影像的   common (ˈkɑmən) *adj.* 常見的
VCR 卡式錄放影機 (= *video cassette recorder*)
DVD 數位影音光碟 (= *digital visual disk*)

First, when we watch TV we see a lot of ads.	第一，我們在看電視的時候，也看了很多廣告。
They make us want to buy things.	廣告讓我們想買東西。
They make us think we need things.	廣告讓我們以為我們需要東西。
Even movie theaters permit advertisements now.	甚至電影院現在都允許播放廣告。
There is no escaping advertising.	要避開廣告是不可能的。
There is widespread advertising everywhere!	廣告在各地都非常普遍！
Seeing so many ads affects our choices.	看到這麼多廣告會影響我們的選擇。
We are induced to buy certain products.	我們會被誘導去買某些產品。
We buy them whether we need them or not.	不論需不需要，我們都會買下這些產品。
Second, TV and movies can affect our view of the world.	第二，電視和電影會影響我們的世界觀。
Both can make our view broader or they can distort it.	兩者都可以讓我們的視野更廣闊，或是被扭曲。
Both can influence us depending on what we watch.	兩者都可以影響我們，而這要視我們所看的東西而定。

**

ad (æd) *n.* 廣告 (= *advertisement*)　　permit (pɚˋmɪt) *v.* 允許
there is no + *V-ing*　～是不可能的　　escape (əˋskep) *v.* 逃脫；避免
advertising (ˋædvɚˏtaɪzɪŋ) *n.* 廣告 (總稱)
widespread (ˋwaɪdˋsprɛd) *adj.* 普遍的　　induce (ɪnˋdjus) *v.* 引誘
view (vju) *n.* 看法　　broad (brɔd) *adj.* 寬闊的
distort (dɪsˋtɔrt) *v.* 扭曲　　*depend on* 視～而定

We can watch news and
　　educational programming.

我們可以觀賞新聞及教育性的節
目。

We can learn many new things
　　from such shows.

我們可以從這些節目中學習許多新
事物。

They can open both our eyes and
　　our minds.

它們不僅開闊我們的視野，也開闊我
們的心胸。

The entertainment programs show
　　us a different world.

娛樂節目呈現給我們一個不一樣的
世界。

The entertainment is distorted.

娛樂世界是被扭曲的。

It is not like the real world at all.

一點都不像現實世界。

Third, *TV is often misleading*.

第三，電視通常是會誤導人的。

It's not realistic at all.

一點也不真實。

It's sensational, exaggerated
　　entertainment.

那是煽情的、誇張的娛樂。

In it, everyone possesses great
　　wealth.

在電視裡，每個人都都很有錢。

In it everyone is very attractive.

在電視裡，每個人都很有吸引力。

Unfortunately, we can only find
　　such a perfect world on TV.

可惜的是，我們只能從電視上找
到如此完美的世界。

** ――――――――――――――――――――――

educational〔͵ɛdʒə'keʃənḷ〕*adj.* 教育性的
programming〔'progræmɪŋ〕*n.* 節目　　show〔ʃo〕*n.* 節目
entertainment〔͵ɛntə'tenmənt〕*n.* 娛樂　　***not…at all*** 一點也不…
misleading〔mɪs'lidɪŋ〕*adj.* 使人誤解的；誤導的
realistic〔͵riə'lɪstɪk〕*adj.* 現實的；實際的
sensational〔sɛn'seʃənḷ〕*adj.* 煽情的；聳動的
exaggerated〔ɪg'zædʒə͵retɪd〕*adj.* 誇張的　　possess〔pə'zɛs〕*v.* 擁有
wealth〔wɛlθ〕*n.* 財富　　attractive〔ə'træktɪv〕*adj.* 吸引人的
unfortunately〔ʌn'fɔrtʃənɪtlɪ〕*adv.* 可惜的是

Watching these shows may make us dissatisfied.

看這些節目可能會讓我們不滿意。

We may wonder why we are not rich.

我們可能會納悶爲什麼自己不是有錢人。

We may want to look as good as the actors.

我們可能會希望自己看起來和那些演員一樣好看。

Finally, TV and movies can affect our children.

最後，電視和電影會影響我們的孩子。

They are the most susceptible.

他們是最容易受到影響的人。

They are easily persuaded by what they see.

他們容易相信眼睛所看到的東西。

Many children cannot tell fact from fiction.

很多孩童無法分辨眞實與虛構。

They believe what they see on the screen.

他們相信螢幕上所看到的東西。

As a result, they develop a distorted view of life.

因此，他們會產生扭曲的人生觀。

Even worse, they may imitate what they see.

更糟糕的是，他們可能會模仿所看到的行爲。

They may try the stunts they have seen.

他們可能會嘗試所看到的驚險動作。

They don't realize that this can be very dangerous.

他們不知道那可能會是非常危險的舉動。

** ──────────

dissatisfied〔ˌdɪsˈsætɪsˌfaɪd〕*adj.* 不滿意的　　wonder〔ˈwʌndɚ〕*v.* 納悶
actor〔ˈæktɚ〕*n.* 演員　　susceptible〔səˈsɛptəbl̩〕*adj.* 易受影響的
persuade〔pɚˈswed〕*v.* 說服；使相信　　***tell A from B*** 分辨 A 與 B
fact〔fækt〕*n.* 事實　　fiction〔ˈfɪkʃən〕*n.* 虛構的事
screen〔skrin〕*n.* (電影) 銀幕；(電視) 螢光幕　　***as a result*** 因此
imitate〔ˈɪməˌtet〕*v.* 模仿　　stunt〔stʌnt〕*n.* 驚險動作；特技

In conclusion, television and movies are not going to go away.

總之，電視和電影不會消失不見。

Instead they are going to become more and more popular.

反而會變得越來越普遍。

Therefore, we must pay attention to the effects that they have on us.

因此，我們必須注意電視或電影對我們造成的影響。

The visual media can be informative.

視覺媒體可以是知識性的。

They can also be entertaining.

也可以是娛樂性的。

Both of these things are good.

兩者都不錯。

However, they can also hurt us if we are not careful.

然而，如果我們不小心的話，也可能對我們造成傷害。

Most important of all, they cannot take the place of real experience.

最重要的是，它們無法取代實際的經驗。

So let's turn off the TV and experience real life.

所以我們關掉電視，體驗真實的人生吧。

**

in conclusion 總之　　*go away* 消失
instead (ɪn'stɛd) *adv.* 反而　　*pay attention to* 注意
visual ('vɪʒuəl) *adj.* 視覺的　　media ('midɪə) *n. pl.* 媒體
informative (ɪn'fɔrmətɪv) *adj.* 能增進知識的
entertaining (ˌɛntɚ'tenɪŋ) *adj.* 娛樂性的
most important of all 最重要的是　　*take the place of* 取代
turn off 關掉（電器）　　experience (ɪk'spɪrɪəns) *v.* 體驗

【托福作文範例】

27. The Influence of Television and Movies

Television and movies are two of the most popular forms of entertainment today. We spend a lot of time sitting in front of the television and in movie theaters. They must have an effect on us, so let's talk about what these effects are.

First, we are exposed to a lot of ads when we watch TV. Even movie theaters have advertisements now. All these ads influence our choices and induce us to buy certain products. *Second*, TV and movies affect our view of the world. They can broaden our view or distort it. Educational programming is very informative while entertainment programs depict a world that is not real. *Third*, TV is often misleading. It's a sensational and exaggerated form of entertainment. In it, everybody is wealthy and beautiful. In other words, it's not real life. But it affects us by making us dissatisfied with our own wealth and looks. *Finally*, TV and movies can affect our children. Many children cannot tell fact from fiction. They believe what they see on the screen. They may even imitate some of the stunts they see, not realizing it is very dangerous.

In conclusion, television and movies are not going to go away. They are going to become more popular. So we have to pay attention to the effects they have on our children and us. But television can't replace real experience, so turn off that TV and go for a walk!

27. 電視和電影的影響

電視和電影是現今最受歡迎的兩種娛樂形式。我們花費相當多時間坐在電視機前面或是電影院裡面。它們對我們一定有影響，所以讓我們來談談這些影響是什麼。

第一，我們在看電視時會接觸到許多的廣告。現在連電影院都會播放廣告。這些廣告會影響我們的選擇，並誘導我們去購買某些產品。第二，電視和電影影響了我們的世界觀。它們可以擴展我們的視野，或是加以扭曲。教育性的節目就非常具有知識性，而娛樂性節目所描繪的是一個不真實的世界。第三，電視節目常會誤導我們。那是一種煽情而誇大的娛樂型式。在電視裡，每個人都非常富有，而且漂亮。換句話說，那並不是真實的人生。但是它會影響我們，讓我們對自己的財富及外表不滿意。最後，電視和電影會影響我們的孩子。很多小孩無法分辨真實和虛構。他們相信他們在螢幕上所看到的東西。他們甚至還會模仿一些他們看到的驚險動作，不知道那是非常危險的事情。

總之，電視和電影不會消失。它們會變得越來越普遍。所以我們必須要注意它們對我們的孩童，以及我們自身的影響。但電視永遠無法取代真實生活的經驗，所以關掉電視，出去走走吧！

【托福作文原試題】

How do movies or television influence people's behavior? Use reasons and specific examples to support your answer.

28. The Effects of Television on Communication

Ladies and gentlemen:
I'm glad to see you here tonight.
I'm happy you came out.

I know you had a choice.
You could be doing something else right now.
You could be at home watching TV.

That's what I would like to talk about.
I'd like to discuss television.
I'd like to discuss the effect it has on us.

***There is no doubt that television affects all
of our lives***.
There is a TV in nearly every home.
It has become an indispensable part of most
households.

---

effect (ə'fɛkt,ɪ-)
communication (kə,mjunə'keʃən)   ***right now***
no doubt   affect (ə'fɛkt)
indispensable (,ɪndɪs'pɛnsəbḷ)
household ('haʊs,hold)

Many families have more than one TV.

Many may have two or three.

Now every family member can watch whatever
   he wants.

Spending so much time watching TV has
   changed us.

It has reduced the amount of time that we
   spend with each other.

It has caused us to communicate less often
   with our family and friends.

Television wasn't always around.

Long ago people did not have this amusement.

Long ago people did other things instead.

---

member ('mɛmbɚ)	reduce (rɪ'djus)
amount (ə'maunt)	cause (kɔz)
communicate (kə'mjunə‚ket)	
around (ə'raund)	*long ago*
amusement (ə'mjuzmənt)	instead (ɪn'stɛd)

In the past, people played cards and other games.
They listened to the radio together.
They went out to see their friends.

Those were the "good old days."
Families spent the evenings together.
Families interacted more and shared stories
   and tales.

Now television is widely available.
There are a variety of program choices.
There are programs that appeal to almost
   everyone.

Now, we spend more time alone.
We no longer have to look to others for
   entertainment.
We don't even have to watch TV together.

---

cards (kɑrdz)	*good old days*
interact (ˌɪntɚˈækt)	share (ʃɛr)
tale (tel)	widely (ˈwaɪdlɪ)
available (əˈveləbḷ)	*a variety of*
appeal (əˈpil)	*no longer*
look to	entertainment (ˌɛntɚˈtenmənt)

We are also less active.

Television is like a sedative.

Television makes us passive and lazy.

We are spending increasing amounts of time
  on television.

We watch more and more.

We do less and less.

But it doesn't have to be this way.

We have a choice.

We can turn off the TV.

Or we can watch something together.

The program should be meaningful.

It should provoke discussion.

---

active (ˈæktɪv)   sedative (ˈsɛdətɪv)

passive (ˈpæsɪv)

increasing (ɪnˈkrisɪŋ)   **turn off**

meaningful (ˈminɪŋfəl)   **provoke** (prəˈvok)

In conclusion, there is no doubt that television

   has changed us.

There is also no doubt that TV is here to stay.

We must change ourselves to make viewing

   worthwhile.

We must be selective and conscientious.

We must control the quality of the programs

   we watch.

We have to stop watching "junk" TV programs.

Thank you all for listening.

I wish you all the best.

Please don't let TV make you lazy!

---

in conclusion

be here to stay   view (vju)

worthwhile ('wɜθ'hwaɪl)   selective (sə'lɛktɪv)

conscientious (ˌkɑnʃɪ'ɛnʃəs)   quality ('kwɑlətɪ)

junk (dʒʌŋk)   wish (wɪʃ)

all the best

28. The Effects of Television on Communication
電視對溝通的影響

【演講解說】

Ladies and gentlemen:	各位女士，各位先生：
I'm glad to see you here tonight.	很高興今晚能在這裡看到你們。
I'm happy you came out.	我很高興你們能出門參與。
I know you had a choice.	我知道你們有選擇的機會。
You could be doing something else right now.	你們現在本來可以做其他事情。
You could be at home watching TV.	你們本來可以在家裡看電視。
That's what I would like to talk about.	那就是我想談的東西。
I'd like to discuss television.	我想要討論電視。
I'd like to discuss the effect it has on us.	我想要討論電視對我們的影響。

** ————————————

effect (ə'fɛkt, ɪ-) *n.* 影響 <*on*>
communication (kə,mjunə'keʃən) *n.* 溝通
right now 現在　　***no doubt*** 無疑地
affect (ə'fɛkt) *v.* 影響

***There is no doubt that television
affects all of our lives*.**　無疑地，電視影響我們大家的生活。

There is a TV in nearly every home.　幾乎每一戶人家都有一台電視。

It has become an indispensable part
of most households.　電視已經成為大多數家庭中，不可或缺的一部份。

Many families have more than
one TV.　很多家庭擁有一台以上的電視。

Many may have two or three.　他們可能擁有兩、三台。

Now every family member can
watch whatever he wants.　現在每個家庭成員都可以看自己想看的節目。

Spending so much time watching
TV has changed us.　花這麼多的時間看電視，已經使我們有所改變。

It has reduced the amount of time
that we spend with each other.　它減少了我們彼此相處的時間。

It has caused us to communicate less
often with our family and friends.　它使我們較少和家人及朋友溝通。

***Television wasn't always around*.**　電視並不是一直存在的。

Long ago people did not have this
amusement.　很久以前，人們並沒有這項娛樂。

Long ago people did other things
instead.　很久以前，人們會從事其他活動。

**　**————————————

indispensable〔͵ɪndɪsˈpɛnsəbl̩〕*adj.* 不可或缺的
household〔ˈhaʊs͵hold〕*n.* 家庭　　member〔ˈmɛmbɚ〕*n.* 成員
reduce〔rɪˈdjus〕*v.* 減少　　amount〔əˈmaʊnt〕*n.* 數量
cause〔kɔz〕*v.* 導致　　communicate〔kəˈmjunə͵ket〕*v.* 溝通
around〔əˈraʊnd〕*adj.* 存在的　　***long ago*** 很久以前
amusement〔əˈmjuzmənt〕*n.* 娛樂　　instead〔ɪnˈstɛd〕*adv.* 作為替代

In the past, people played cards and other games.	以前，人們玩撲克牌，還有其他遊戲。
They listened to the radio together.	他們一起聽收音機。
They went out to see their friends.	他們外出拜訪朋友。
Those were the "good old days."	這是「美好的舊日時光」。
Families spent the evenings together.	全家人晚上聚在一起。
Families interacted more and shared stories and tales.	全家人有更多互動，並且會一起分享故事。
Now television is widely available.	現在電視很普及。
There are a variety of program choices.	有各式各樣的節目可供選擇。
There are programs that appeal to almost everyone.	幾乎每個人都可以找到自己感興趣的節目。
Now, we spend more time alone.	現在，我們獨處的時間比較多。
We no longer have to look to others for entertainment.	我們不再仰賴他人尋求娛樂。
We don't even have to watch TV together.	我們甚至不需要一起看電視。

** ───────────────

cards (kɑrdz) *n. pl.* 紙牌遊戲   ***good old days*** 美好的往日；從前的好日子
interact (ˌɪntəˈækt) *v.* 互動   share (ʃɛr) *v.* 分享
tale (tel) *n.* 故事   widely ('waɪdlɪ) *adv.* 廣泛地
available (əˈveləbḷ) *adj.* 可獲得的   ***a variety of*** 各式各樣的
appeal (əˈpil) *v.* 吸引 <*to*>   ***no longer*** 不再
look to 指望；依靠   entertainment (ˌɛntəˈtenmənt) *n.* 娛樂

We are also less active.	我們變得比較不主動。
Television is like a sedative.	電視就好像鎮靜劑一樣。
Television makes us passive and lazy.	電視讓我們變得被動，而且懶惰。
We are spending increasing amounts of time on television.	我們花越來越多的時間看電視。
We watch more and more.	我們越看越多。
We do less and less.	我們越做越少。
But it doesn't have to be this way.	但是並不一定非要如此。
We have a choice.	我們可以選擇。
We can turn off the TV.	我們可以關上電視。
Or we can watch something together.	或者我們可以一起觀看。
The program should be meaningful.	電視節目應該是有意義的。
The program should provoke discussion.	電視節目應該要能引發大家的討論。

**　——————————

active (ˈæktɪv) *adj.* 主動的；積極的
sedative (ˈsɛdətɪv) *n.* 鎮靜劑
passive (ˈpæsɪv) *adj.* 被動的；消極的
increasing (ɪnˈkrisɪŋ) *adj.* 越來越多的　　***turn off*** 關掉（電器）
meaningful (ˈminɪŋfəl) *adj.* 有意義的　　provoke (prəˈvok) *v.* 引起

In conclusion, there is no doubt that television has changed us.	總之,電視無疑地已經改變了我們。
There is also no doubt that TV is here to stay.	也毫無疑問地,電視會一直存在下去。
We must change ourselves to make viewing worthwhile.	我們必須改變自己,讓看電視變成是件值得做的事情。
We must be selective and conscientious.	我們必須要精挑細選,而且謹慎。
We must control the quality of the programs we watch.	我們必須控制所收看節目的品質。
We have to stop watching "junk" TV programs.	我們必須停止收看「垃圾」電視節目。
Thank you all for listening.	謝謝你們大家的聆聽。
I wish you all the best.	我祝福大家順心如意。
Please don't let TV make you lazy!	請不要讓電視使你自己變懶惰了!

**
in conclusion 總之　　*be here to stay* 得到公眾的承認;被普遍接受
view〔vju〕*v.* 觀看　　worthwhile〔'wɜθ'hwaɪl〕*adj.* 值得做的
selective〔sə'lɛktɪv〕*adj.* 選擇的;精選的
conscientious〔‚kɑnʃɪ'ɛnʃəs〕*adj.* 謹慎的
quality〔'kwɑlətɪ〕*n.* 品質
junk〔dʒʌŋk〕*n.* 垃圾　*adj.* 破爛的;無用的　　wish〔wɪʃ〕*v.* 祝福
all the best (敬酒、告別等時候說)祝一切順利

【托福作文範例】

28. The Effects of Television on Communication

Television has become a part of our lives. Most people can now afford a TV, even two or three. As we spend more time in front of the TV, it's beginning to affect our communication and here's how.

Television has affected our lives for the worse. It has become an indispensable part of most households and spending too much time watching TV has changed us. It has caused us to communicate less often with our family and friends. Television wasn't always around, though. Long ago, people did other things instead, like playing cards and other games. People listened to the radio together; they went out to see friends. Now, television is widely available with an amazing variety of program choices. There are programs that appeal to everyone. *As a result*, we spend more time alone. We no longer interact with others; we don't even watch TV together. We are watching more and more TV and doing less and less. Television has made us passive and lazy.

In conclusion, television has changed us, but we must change ourselves to make viewing worthwhile. We must be selective and conscientious and control the quality of the programs we watch. We have to stop watching "junk" TV programs.

28. 電視對溝通的影響

　　電視已經成爲我們生活的一部份。現在大部分的人都買得起一台電視，甚至能買得起兩到三台。隨著我們花在電視機前面的時間越來越多，電視也開始影響我們的溝通方式。以下就是它影響我們的方式。

　　電視已經負面地影響了我們的生活。它已經成爲大多數家庭中，不可或缺的一部份，而花這麼多的時間看電視，也改變了我們。它使我們和家人或是朋友較少溝通。不過，電視並不是一直都存在的。很久以前，人們從事其他活動，像是玩撲克牌或其他遊戲。人們會一起聽收音機；他們也會外出拜訪朋友。現在，電視很普及，而且很驚人地，有各式各樣的節目可供選擇。每個人都能夠找到自己所喜歡的節目。因此，我們獨處的時間變多了。我們和其他人不再有互動；我們甚至沒有一起看電視。我們電視越看越多，做的事情卻越來越少。電視使我們變得既被動又懶惰。

　　總之，電視已經改變了我們，但是我們也必須改變自己，讓看電視成爲是值得做的事。我們必須要精挑細選，並且謹慎，同時也要控制我們所收看的節目品質。我們一定要停止收看「垃圾」節目。

【托福作文原試題】

Do you agree or disagree with the following statement? Television has destroyed communication among friends and family. Use specific reasons and examples to support your opinion.

29. The Advantages of City Life

Ladies and gentlemen:
I'm happy to be here.
I'm glad to have this chance to talk to you.

Tonight's topic is important.
It concerns our home.
It is about the best place to live.

Some prefer the country, and some prefer
  the city.
Both have many advantages.
But for me there is just one choice: the city.

You may ask why I prefer city life.
After all, the country is cleaner, quieter,
  and often friendlier.
Here are the many reasons why.

---

advantage (əd'væntɪdʒ)	concern (kən'sɜn)
prefer (prɪ'fɝ)	*the country*
after all	friendly ('frɛndlɪ)

*First, **the city is more convenient***.

More goods are available in the city.

More stores are open later.

A city is a shoppers' paradise.

A city is a consumers' mecca.

A city offers everything from A to Z.

Cities are commercial havens.

Cities have so much to offer.

Cities offer variety and diversity.

*Second, **there is better public transportation***.

There are subways and ferries.

There are buses, trains, and taxis, too.

---

goods (gʊdz)

shopper ('ʃɑpɚ)

consumer (kən'sjumɚ)

from A to Z

haven ('hevən)

variety (və'raɪətɪ)

public transportation

ferry ('fɛrɪ)

available (ə'veləbḷ)

paradise ('pærə،daɪs)

mecca ('mɛkə)

commercial (kə'mɜʃəl)

offer ('ɔfɚ)

diversity (də'vɜsətɪ ،daɪ-)

subway ('sʌb،we)

Everything is faster in a city.
Everything is more efficient.
It's always easier to get around.

City transportation is safer.
City transportation is more interesting.
It's always reliable and on time.

Third, *there are more ways to spend*
   leisure time.
There are many places to go.
There are many places to have fun.

Cities have excellent parks.
Cities have fascinating museums.
Cities have cultural activities galore.

---

efficient (ə'fɪʃənt, ɪ-)

reliable (rɪ'laɪəbḷ)

leisure ('liʒɚ)

excellent ('ɛksḷənt)

cultural ('kʌltʃərəl)

galore (gə'lor, -'lɔr)

get around

on time

have fun

fascinating ('fæsn̩,etɪŋ)

activity (æk'tɪvətɪ)

You can see great live performances.

You can view quality entertainment.

A city offers many ways to relax.

Finally, there is more opportunity in the city.

The city attracts the best teachers and the

   best companies.

We can get a better education and find a

   better job.

For all these reasons I prefer the city.

It provides everything I need.

It offers almost everything I want.

---

live (laɪv)

performance (pɚˈfɔrməns)   view (vju)

quality (ˈkwɑlətɪ)

entertainment (ˌɛntɚˈtenmənt)   relax (rɪˈlæks)

attract (əˈtrækt)   provide (prəˈvaɪd)

I admit I sometimes miss the fresh air and
  quiet of the country.
But I think I would miss the city more.
Nothing can make up for all the opportunities
  it offers me.

Before you choose a place to live, consider
  carefully.
Are you a city person or a country person?
Think about it and then make the best choice.

Good luck to you all.
I want to thank you for listening so politely.
I hope you find a wonderful place to live!

---

admit (əd'mɪt)	fresh (frɛʃ)
quiet ('kwaɪət)	*make up for*
consider (kən'sɪdɚ)	politely (pə'laɪtlɪ)

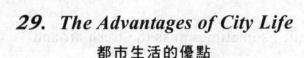
29. *The Advantages of City Life*
都市生活的優點

【演講解說】

Ladies and gentlemen:	各位先生，各位女士：
I'm happy to be here.	我很高興能夠來到這裡。
I'm glad to have this chance to	我很高興有這個機會能和你們
talk to you.	談談。
Tonight's topic is important.	今晚的主題很重要。
It concerns our home.	和我們的家有關。
It is about the best place to live.	是關於最適當的居住場所。
Some prefer the country, and	有些人比較喜歡住在鄉下，而
some prefer the city.	有些人比較喜歡住在都市裡。
Both have many advantages.	兩者都有許多優點。
But for me there is just one choice:	但是對我而言，只有一個選
the city.	擇：都市。

**

advantage〔əd'væntɪdʒ〕*n.* 優點
concern〔kən'sɝn〕*v.* 關於
prefer〔prɪ'fɝ〕*v.* 比較喜歡
the country （對都市而言的）鄉下；郊外

You may ask why I prefer city
　life.

After all, the country is cleaner,
　quieter, and often friendlier.

Here are the many reasons why.

你可能會問我爲什麼喜歡都市
生活。

畢竟，鄉下比較乾淨、安靜，
而且比較舒適。

以下就是衆多理由。

First, *the city is more convenient*.

More goods are available in
　the city.

More stores are open later.

首先，都市生活比較方便。

在都市裡可以買到比較多的
商品。

比較多商店會營業到比較晚。

A city is a shoppers' paradise.

A city is a consumers' mecca.

A city offers everything from A
　to Z.

都市是購物者的天堂。

都市是消費者的朝聖地。

都市會提供各式各樣的東西，
應有盡有。

Cities are commercial havens.

Cities have so much to offer.

Cities offer variety and diversity.

都市是商業的避風港。

都市可以提供非常多的東西。

都市提供變化和多樣性。

**────────────────

after all 畢竟　　friendly〔'frɛndlɪ〕*adj.* 舒適的

goods〔gʊdz〕*n. pl.* 商品　　available〔ə'veləbḷ〕*adj.* 可獲得的

shopper〔'ʃɑpɚ〕*n.* 購物者　　paradise〔'pærə,daɪs〕*n.* 天堂

consumer〔kən'sjumɚ〕*n.* 消費者

mecca〔'mɛkə〕*n.* 許多人拜訪之地；衆人憧憬之地；…的麥加

　(Mecca 是回教聖地「麥加」)　　***from A to Z*** 從頭到尾；完全地

commercial〔kə'mɝʃəl〕*adj.* 商業的　　haven〔'hevən〕*n.* 避風港

offer〔'ɔfɚ〕*v.* 提供　　variety〔və'raɪətɪ〕*n.* 變化；多樣性

diversity〔də'vɝsətɪ,daɪ-〕*n.* 多樣性

Second, there is better public
  transportation.

There are subways and ferries.

There are buses, trains, and taxis, too.

第二，都市有較好的大眾運輸。

有地下鐵和渡輪。

也有公車、火車和計程車。

Everything is faster in a city.

Everything is more efficient.

It's always easier to get around.

都市裡的一切都比較快速。

每件事都更有效率。

要去哪裏都比較容易。

City transportation is safer.

City transportation is more
  interesting.

It's always reliable and on time.

都市交通比較安全。

都市交通更有趣。

總是很可靠，而且準時。

Third, there are more ways to
  spend leisure time.

There are many places to go.

There are many places to have fun.

第三，有比較多的方法，可以
消磨空閒時間。

有很多地方可以去。

有很多地方可以玩得很開心。

＊＊ ——————————————

public transportation 大眾運輸工具

subway (ˈsʌbˌwe) *n.* 地下鐵　　ferry (ˈfɛrɪ) *n.* 渡輪

efficient (əˈfɪʃənt, ɪ-) *adj.* 有效率的　　**get around** 到處走動

reliable (rɪˈlaɪəbḷ) *adj.* 可靠的　　**on time** 準時

leisure (ˈliʒɚ) *adj.* 空閒的　　**have fun** 玩得開心

Cities have excellent parks.　都市有很棒的公園。

Cities have fascinating museums.　都市有很棒的博物館。

Cities have cultural activities
　galore.　都市有豐富的文化活動。

You can see great live performances.　你可以看到精采的現場表演。

You can view quality entertainment.　你可以觀看高品質的娛樂活動。

A city offers many ways to relax.　都市提供很多放鬆的方法。

***Finally*, *there is more opportunity
　in the city*.**　最後，都市裡的機會較多。

The city attracts the best teachers
　and the best companies.　都市能吸引最好的老師和最棒
　的公司。

We can get a better education and
　find a better job.　我們可以獲得較好的教育，找
　到更好的工作。

** ─────────────────

excellent〔ˈɛkslɪnt〕*adj.* 很棒的

fascinating〔ˈfæsn̩ˌetɪŋ〕*adj.* 迷人的；極好的

cultural〔ˈkʌltʃərəl〕*adj.* 文化的　　activity〔ækˈtɪvətɪ〕*n.* 活動

galore〔gəˈlor,-ˈlɔr〕*adj.* 大量的；豐富的（用在名詞後）

live〔laɪv〕*adj.* 現場的　　performance〔pəˈfɔrməns〕*n.* 表演

view〔vju〕*v.* 觀看　　quality〔ˈkwɑlətɪ〕*adj.* 有品質的

entertainment〔ˌɛntəˈtenmənt〕*n.* 娛樂

relax〔rɪˈlæks〕*v.* 放鬆　　attract〔əˈtrækt〕*v.* 吸引

For all these reasons I prefer the city.

基於這些理由,我比較喜歡住在都市。

It provides everything I need.

它提供我所需要的一切。

It offers almost everything I want.

它幾乎可提供我所想要的任何東西。

I admit I sometimes miss the fresh air and quiet of the country.

我承認有時候,我會想念鄉下新鮮的空氣及安靜的生活。

But I think I would miss the city more.

但是我想我會更想念都市生活。

Nothing can make up for all the opportunities it offers me.

沒有什麼可以彌補都市生活提供給我的機會。

Before you choose a place to live, consider carefully.

在你選擇居住場所前,要仔細考慮。

Are you a city person or a country person?

你比較適合住在都市,還是鄉下呢?

Think about it and then make the best choice.

考慮一下,然後做出最好的選擇。

Good luck to you all.

祝大家好運。

I want to thank you for listening so politely.

我想謝謝大家如此有禮貌地聽講。

I hope you find a wonderful place to live!

我希望你們能找到很棒的居住地點!

**　

provide〔prə'vaɪd〕v. 提供　admit〔əd'mɪt〕v. 承認
fresh〔frɛʃ〕adj. 新鮮的　quiet〔'kwaɪət〕n. 安靜　*make up for* 彌補
consider〔kən'sɪdɚ〕v. 考慮　politely〔pə'laɪtlɪ〕adv. 有禮貌地

【托福作文範例】

29. The Advantages of City Life

Some people prefer to live in the country and others prefer to live in the city. Whichever is your preference, both places offer advantages and disadvantages. I prefer to live in the city and here are my reasons why.

First, the city is more convenient. More goods are available in the city and stores are open later. A city is a shoppers' paradise and they offer everything from A to Z. *Second*, there is better public transportation in cities. There are subways, ferries, buses, trains and taxis. Everything is faster in a city and more efficient. It's easier to get around. *Third*, there are more ways to spend leisure time. Cities have excellent parks, fascinating museums and cultural activities galore. You can see great live performances, view quality entertainment and find many ways to relax. *Finally*, there are more opportunities in the city. The city attracts the best teachers and the best companies. We can get a better education and find better jobs.

These are the reasons why I prefer the city. I do miss the fresh air and quiet of the country sometimes, but I still prefer the city. So before you choose a place to live, consider carefully if you are a country person or a city person.

29. 都市生活的優點

　　有些人比較喜歡住在鄉下，而有些人比較喜歡住在都市。無論你的喜好是什麼，兩種地方都各有優缺點。我比較偏好住在都市，以下就是我的理由。

　　首先，住在都市比較方便。你可以在城市中買到更多的商品，而且商店營業到比較晚。都市是購物者的天堂，它提供了各式各樣的東西，應有盡有。第二，在都市中有較好的大眾運輸系統。有地下鐵、渡輪、公車、火車，還有計程車。都市裡的一切都比較快速，而且更有效率。要去哪裡都會比較容易。第三，有比較多的方法，可以消磨你的空閒時間。都市中有很棒的公園、迷人的博物館，還有豐富的文化活動。你可以看到精彩的現場表演、觀賞高品質的娛樂活動，而且找到許多可以放鬆的方法。最後，都市裡有更多的機會。都市會吸引最好的老師和最棒的公司。我們可以在這裡得到較好的教育，並找到更好的工作。

　　基於這些理由，我比較喜歡住在都市。我的確有時候會想念鄉下新鮮的空氣及安靜的生活，但是我還是比較喜歡都市生活。所以在你選擇居住場所之前，要仔細考慮你是適合住在都市，還是鄉下。

【托福作文原試題】

Some people prefer to live in a small town. Others prefer to live in a big city. Which place would you prefer to live in? Use specific reasons and details to support your answer.

30. *The Role of Luck in Success*

Ladies and gentlemen:
I have a question for you all.
Do you want to succeed in life?

I think everyone's answer must be yes.
We all dream about our future success.
We all wonder how to achieve it.

People say that only hard work can lead
  to success.
People say that luck has nothing to do with it.
However, I disagree with that.

Luck is important, too.
There is no denying the role of luck.
It has been responsible for many success stories.

---

dream about	wonder ('wʌndɚ)
achieve (ə'tʃiv)	*lead to*
have nothing to do with	*there is no + V-ing*
deny (dɪ'naɪ)	responsible (rɪ'spɑnsəbḷ)
be responsible for	*success story*

For example, some discoveries are made by
　accident.
Some scientists trying to solve one problem
　find the solution to another.
These breakthroughs are the result of
　good luck.

Other people are simply in the right place
　at the right time.
They happen to meet the right person.
They come across a good opportunity
　by chance.

Luck is a wonderful thing.
Its influence cannot be ignored.
However, it can't be counted on, either.

---

discovery (dɪ'skʌvərɪ)	***by accident***
solve (sɑlv)	solution (sə'luʃən)
breakthrough ('brek͵θru)	***happen to V.***
come across	***by chance***
influence ('ɪnfluəns)	ignore (ɪg'nor)
count on	

It's not easy to win the lottery.

It's almost impossible to get rich quick.

It happens but it's extremely rare.

So what can we do?

We can work hard!

If we work hard, we will eventually succeed.

Hard work can make us lucky.

Hard work is often the essential ingredient

  of luck.

It enables us to take advantage of luck.

It may be slow, but it's sure.

We can succeed some day.

And we can do it with or without good luck.

---

lottery ('lɑtərɪ)	quick (kwɪk)
extremely (ɪk'strimlɪ)	rare (rɛr)
eventually (ɪ'vɛntʃʊəlɪ)	essential (ə'sɛnʃəl)
ingredient (ɪn'gridɪənt)	enable (ɪn'ebl̩)
take advantage of	sure (ʃʊr)
some day	

Let me explain with this example.

A scientist must work hard to develop his
  knowledge.

If he does not, he cannot recognize that lucky
  breakthrough when it comes.

Finally, luck is important.

Both luck and hard work are important.

Both of them can help us succeed.

My suggestion is to work as hard as you can.

My advice is don't count on luck to bring
  you success.

It's not a sure thing.

At the same time, keep your eyes open.

Always look for that lucky break.

When you see it, grab it.

---

explain (ɪk'splen)   develop (dɪ'vɛləp)
recognize ('rɛkəg,naɪz)   suggestion (sə'dʒɛstʃən)
as…as one can   advice (əd'vaɪs)
a sure thing   break (brek)
a lucky break   grab (græb)

In conclusion**, **your future is all up to you.

It's all in your hands.

It's necessary to work hard and create

   good luck.

You must combine luck with hard work.

Give great effort and fortune will follow.

Give it all you've got and luck will be

   a companion.

Do both of these things and you will succeed.

I wish everyone success in the future.

God bless you all and good luck.

---

in conclusion

combine (kəm'baɪn)

effort ('ɛfət)

follow ('falo)

companion (kəm'pænjən)

up to sb.

give (gɪv)

fortune ('fɔrtʃən)

have got

30. *The Role of Luck in Success*
運氣在成功裡所扮演的角色

【演講解說】

Ladies and gentlemen:	各位先生、各位女士：
I have a question for you all.	我有一個問題要問大家。
Do you want to succeed in life?	你想要成功嗎？
I think everyone's answer must be yes.	我想每個人的答案一定都是要。
We all dream about our future success.	我們全都夢想未來能夠成功。
We all wonder how to achieve it.	我們全都想知道如何獲得成功。
People say that only hard work can lead to success.	有人說只有努力才能成功。
People say that luck has nothing to do with it.	有人說運氣和成功是一點關係也沒有。
However, I disagree with that.	然而，我不同意那樣的說法。
Luck is important.	運氣很重要。
There is no denying the role of luck.	運氣所扮演的角色是不可否認的。
It has been responsible for many success stories.	運氣是很多人成功的原因。

**

dream about 夢想　　wonder ('wʌndɚ) v. 想知道
achieve (ə'tʃiv) v. 達到　　lead to 導致
have nothing to do with 與～無關　　**there is no + V-ing** ～是不可能的
deny (dɪ'naɪ) v. 否認　　responsible (rɪ'spɑnsəbl̩) adj. 是…原因的
be responsible for 是…的原由　　**success story** 一個人的成名史

For example, some discoveries are
　　made by accident.

Some scientists trying to solve one
　　problem find the solution to
　　another.

These breakthroughs are the result
　　of good luck.

例如，有些發現是意外獲得的
結果。

有些科學家原本試圖解決某個
問題，反而找到另一個問題的
解決方法。

這些突破是好運的結果。

Other people are simply in the
　　right place at the right time.

They happen to meet the right
　　person.

They come across a good
　　opportunity by chance.

其他人則只是掌握了天時和地
利的時機。

他們碰巧遇到對的人。

他們偶然遇到好機會。

***Luck is a wonderful thing*.**

Its influence cannot be ignored.

However, it can't be counted on,
　　either.

運氣是很棒的東西。

它的影響力不容忽視。

但是，人也不能只靠運氣。

**

---

discovery〔dɪ'skʌvərɪ〕*n.* 發現　　***by accident*** 偶然地（= *by chance*）
solve〔sɑlv〕*v.* 解決　　solution〔sə'luʃən〕*n.* 解決（辦法）< *to* >
breakthrough〔'brek,θru〕*n.* 突破　　***happen to V.*** 碰巧
come across 偶然遇到　　influence〔'ɪnfluəns〕*n.* 影響力
ignore〔ɪg'nor〕*v.* 忽視　　***count on*** 依靠；指望

It's not easy to win the lottery. | 要中樂透彩不是一件容易的事情。
It's almost impossible to get rich quick. | 要馬上致富幾乎是不可能的。
It happens, but it's extremely rare. | 這種事情會發生，但是機率非常低。

So what can we do? | 所以，我們能怎麼辦？
We can work hard! | 我們可以努力！
If we work hard, we will eventually succeed. | 如果我們努力，我們最後就會成功。

Hard work can make us lucky. | 努力可以讓我們幸運。
Hard work is often the essential ingredient of luck. | 努力通常是好運的必要因素。
It enables us to take advantage of luck. | 它能讓我們充份利用幸運。

It may be slow, but it's sure. | 這樣可能很慢，但卻很確實。
We can succeed some day. | 我們總有一天會成功。
And we can do it with or without good luck. | 而且不論運氣好不好，我們還是會成功。

**

lottery (ˈlɑtərɪ) n. 彩券   quick (kwɪk) adv. 快；迅速地
extremely (ɪkˈstrimlɪ) adv. 非常   rare (rɛr) adj. 稀有的；罕見的
eventually (ɪˈvɛntʃʊəlɪ) adv. 最後   essential (əˈsɛnʃəl) adj. 必要的
ingredient (ɪnˈgridɪənt) n. 因素   enable (ɪnˈebl̩) v. 使能夠
take advantage of 利用   sure (ʃʊr) adj. 確實的；可靠的
some day 總有一天 (= someday)

Let me explain with this example.　讓我用這個例子說明。

A scientist must work hard to develop his knowledge.　科學家必須努力豐富自己的知識。

If he does not, he cannot recognize that lucky breakthrough when it comes.　如果不這麼做的話，在某個幸運的突破出現時，他可能也看不出來。

***Finally**, **luck is important**.*　最後，運氣是很重要的。

Both luck and hard work are important.　運氣和努力都很重要。

Both of them can help us succeed.　兩者都能幫助我們成功。

My suggestion is to work as hard as you can.　我的建議是，你要竭盡所能地努力。

My advice is don't count on luck to bring you success.　我的勸告是，不要指望運氣能帶給你成功。

It's not a sure thing.　那並不是百分之百的事情。

At the same time, keep your eyes open.　同時要張大眼睛。

Always look for that lucky break.　要隨時尋找幸運。

When you see it, grab it.　一看見它，就要好好把握。

** ————————————

explain〔ɪkˈsplen〕*v.* 解釋；說明　develop〔dɪˈvɛləp〕*v.* 發展；啓發

recognize〔ˈrɛkəɡ͵naɪz〕*v.* 認出　suggestion〔səˈdʒɛstʃən〕*n.* 建議

as…as one can 儘可能…；儘量…（ *= as…as possible* ）

advice〔ədˈvaɪs〕*n.* 勸告　***a sure thing*** （成功、勝利等）確實的事

break〔brek〕*n.* 機會；好運　***a lucky break*** 幸運

grab〔græb〕*v.* 抓住；把握（機會）

In conclusion, your future is all up to you.	總之，你的未來全靠你自己決定。
It's all in your hands.	全都掌握在你的手中。
It's necessary to work hard and create good luck.	必須要努力，並且創造好運。
You must combine luck with hard work.	你必須結合運氣和努力。
Give great effort and fortune will follow.	努力付出，好運就會隨之而來。
Give it all you've got and luck will be a companion.	全力以赴，好運就會成為你的朋友。
Do both of these things and you will succeed.	如果這兩件事都做到，那麼你就會成功。
I wish everyone success in the future.	我希望每個人未來都能成功。
God bless you all and good luck.	願上帝保佑你們，祝大家好運。

**

in conclusion 總之　　*up to sb.* 由某人決定

combine (kəm'baɪn) v. 結合　　give (gɪv) v. 付出

effort ('ɛfət) n. 努力　　fortune ('fɔrtʃən) n. 好運

follow ('falo) v. 隨之而來　　*have got* 有

companion (kəm'pænjən) n. 同伴；朋友

【托福作文範例】

30. The Role of Luck in Success

Do you want to be successful? Of course you do! Some people say that only hard work can lead to success and that luck has nothing to do with it. I disagree with that.

Luck is important, too. It has been responsible for many success stories. *For example*, some discoveries are made by accident when scientists trying to solve one problem find the solution to another. Other people are simply in the right place at the right time. Luck is a wonderful thing. Its influence cannot be ignored. *However*, it can't be counted on, either. It's not easy to win the lottery; it happens, but it's extremely rare. So what can we do? Work hard! Hard work can make us lucky. Hard work is the essential ingredient of luck. It may be slow, but it's sure. Let me explain with this example. A scientist must work hard to develop his knowledge. If he does not, he cannot recognize that lucky breakthrough when it comes. *Finally*, luck is important. We need both luck and hard work to help us succeed.

In conclusion, your future is up to you. It's necessary to work hard and create good luck. Give great effort and fortune will follow. Do both of these things and you will succeed.

30. 運氣在成功裡所扮演的角色

你想要成功嗎？你當然想要！有人說只有努力才能導致成功，而運氣和成功則是一點關係也沒有。我不同意那樣的說法。

運氣也是很重要的。它是很多人成功的原因。舉例來說，有些發現是偶然的，是因為科學家原本想解決某個問題，卻發現另一個問題的解決方法。而另外有些人則是掌握了天時和地利。運氣真是一個很棒的東西。它的影響力是不容忽視的。然而，我們也不能完全依賴它。要中樂透彩不是一件容易的事，那的確會發生，但是機率非常低。所以我們能怎麼辦呢？努力！努力可以讓我們幸運。努力是好運的必要因素。也許很慢，但卻很確實。讓我用這個例子來說明。科學家一定要努力豐富自己的知識。如果他不這麼做，在某個幸運的突破出現時，他可能也看不出來。最後，運氣是相當重要的。我們需要運氣和努力，來幫助我們成功。

總之，你的未來都是取決於你自己。努力和創造好運都是必須的。努力付出，好運就會隨之而來。如果這兩件事都做到，那麼你就會成功。

【托福作文原試題】

"When people succeed, it is because of hard work. Luck has nothing to do with success." *Do you agree or disagree with the quotation above?* *Use specific reasons and examples to explain your position.*

31. *Money for Sports Activities*

Hello, everyone.

It's great to see you here.

I'm so glad to have your support.

I'd like to talk to you about our school.

I want to discuss our sports program.

I think sports activities are so important.

Our education consists of many things.

We not only study academics, but also

   learn life skills.

We develop teamwork and healthy habits.

---

sports (sports , spɔrts)	activity (æk'tɪvətɪ)
support (sə'port)	program ('progræm)
consist of	academics (,ækə'dɛmɪks)
not only···but also	develop (dɪ'vɛləp)
teamwork ('tim,wɜk)	healthy ('hɛlθɪ)

The goal of education is to develop your mind.

The road to learning must be mental, spiritual and physical.

Today I'd like to discuss and support physical education.

Sports activities are important for students.

Therefore, the sports facilities should be good.

They should be as good as the library.

A library enriches the mind.

A sports arena stimulates the body.

Together they promote physical and mental health.

---

goal (gol)   road (rod)

mental ('mɛntl̩)   spiritual ('spɪrɪtʃʊəl)

physical ('fɪzɪkl̩)   *physical education*

facilities (fə'sɪlətɪz)   enrich (ɪn'rɪtʃ)

arena (ə'rinə)   stimulate ('stɪmjə,let)

promote (prə'mot)

We all know the school library is important.

We have to invest and maintain a top
  quality library.

But we also have to invest in sports.

Library resources are long-lasting.

They don't wear out too fast.

They don't need to be replaced so often.

***In addition*, *students have other academic resources*.**

Many have their own computers.

They can access the Internet at any time.

Sports, however, require some investment
  every year.

Equipment wears out quickly.

Equipment needs to be replaced.

---

invest (ɪn'vɛst)

top (tɑp)

resources (rɪ'sorsɪz)

wear out

in addition

access ('æksɛs)

investment (ɪn'vɛstmənt)

maintain (men'ten)

quality ('kwɑlətɪ)

long-lasting ('lɔŋ'læstɪŋ)

replace (rɪ'ples)

academic (,ækə'dɛmɪk)

Internet ('ɪntɚ,nɛt)

equipment (ɪ'kwɪpmənt)

Right now we need money badly.
We need to renovate our athletic facilities.
We need to purchase more modern equipment.

Good equipment encourages more students to play.
They will be happy to participate in games and
  competitions.
This is an important part of their education.

A school should provide a well-balanced education.
Students should have the opportunity to develop
  all of their skills.
Students' education includes both academics
  and personal development.

Sports play an important role in education.
Sports must not be ignored.
Therefore, they deserve our attention.

---

badly ('bædlɪ)　　　　　renovate ('rɛnə,vet)
athletic (æθ'lɛtɪk)　　　purchase ('pɝtʃəs)
encourage (ɪn'kɝɪdʒ)　　play (ple)
participate (pɑr'tɪsə,pet)　competition (,kɑmpə'tɪʃən)
well-balanced ('wɛl'bælənst)
play an important role in
ignore (ɪg'nor)　　　　　deserve (dɪ'zɝv)

We must develop our sports programs.

It is our responsibility.

Let's give it our full support.

In conclusion, *I advocate a fund drive*.

Let's try to raise money for our sports program.

Let's ask our school community for help.

We can encourage donations.

We can hold fundraisers.

We can upgrade our sports program by

   doing this.

I want to thank you all for listening.

I hope I've persuaded you to support sports.

Let's take action and make our sports program

   great.

---

responsibility (rɪˌspɑnsə'bɪlətɪ)

in conclusion   advocate ('ædvəˌket)

fund (fʌnd)   drive (draɪv)

raise (rez)   community (kə'mjunətɪ)

donation (do'neʃən)   fundraiser ('fʌndˌrezɚ)

upgrade (ʌp'gred)   persuade (pɚ'swed)

take action

31. *Money for Sports Activities*
資助體育活動

【演講解說】

Hello, everyone.	哈囉,大家好。
It's great to see you here.	很高興能在這裡看到你們。
I'm so glad to have your support.	我很高興能有你們的支持。
I'd like to talk to you about our school.	我想要和大家談談我們的學校。
I want to discuss our sports program.	我想討論我們的運動課程。
I think sports activities are important.	我認為體育活動非常重要。
Our education consists of many things.	我們的教育包含很多東西。
We not only study academics, but also learn life skills.	我們不僅要研讀學業,還要學習生活技能。
We develop teamwork and healthy habits.	我們要培養團隊合作的精神,以及健康習慣。

**

sports (sports, spɔrts) *adj.* 運動的   activity (æk'tɪvətɪ) *n.* 活動
support (sə'port) *v. n.* 支持;資助   program ('progræm) *n.* 課程
consist of 由~組成   academics (,ækə'dɛmɪks) *n. pl.* 學科
not only…but also 不僅…而且   develop (dɪ'vɛləp) *v.* 培養;發展
teamwork ('tim,wɜk) *n.* 團隊合作
healthy ('hɛlθɪ) *adj.* 健康的;有益的

The goal of education is to develop
your mind.

教育的目標是發展你的心智。

The road to learning must be mental,
spiritual and physical.

學習之道必須是心智、心靈
和身體並重。

Today I'd like to discuss and support
physical education.

今天我想要討論，並且支持
體育。

***Sports activities are important for
students***.

體育活動對學生而言是重
要的。

Therefore, the sports facilities
should be good.

因此，體育設施應該要完善。

They should be as good as the library.

應該就像圖書館一樣好。

A library enriches the mind.

圖書館能豐富心靈。

A sports arena stimulates the body.

運動場能促進體能。

Together they promote physical
and mental health.

它們能共同促進身體和心理
的健康。

**　*

goal〔gol〕*n.* 目標　　road〔rod〕*n.* 道路；途徑＜*to*＞
mental〔'mɛntḷ〕*adj.* 心智的；心理的
spiritual〔'spɪrɪtʃʊəl〕*adj.* 精神上的；心靈的
physical〔'fɪzɪkḷ〕*adj.* 身體的　　***physical education*** 體育
facilities〔fə'sɪlətɪz〕*n. pl.* 設施　　enrich〔ɪn'rɪtʃ〕*v.* 使豐富
arena〔ə'rinə〕*n.*（周圍有觀眾席的）比賽場；競技場
stimulate〔'stɪmjə,let〕*v.* 刺激　　promote〔prə'mot〕*v.* 促進

We all know the school library is important.	我們都知道，學校圖書館很重要。
We have to invest and maintain a top quality library.	我們必須投資，並且維持圖書館的頂尖品質。
But we also have to invest in sports.	但是我們也必須花錢投資體育活動。
Library resources are long-lasting.	圖書館的資源是可長期使用的。
They don't wear out too fast.	不會太快就耗損。
They don't need to be replaced so often.	不需要那麼常更換。
In addition, students have other academic resources.	此外，學生還有其他的學術資源。
Many have their own computers.	許多學生自己都有電腦。
They can access the Internet at any time.	他們可以隨時使用網際網路。
Sports, however, require some investment every year.	然而體育每年都需要一些投資經費。
Equipment wears out quickly.	器材很快就會耗損。
Equipment needs to be replaced.	器材需要更換。

** ————————————

invest (ɪn'vɛst) v. 投資　　maintain (men'ten) v. 維持
top (tɑp) adj. 最高的　　quality ('kwɑlətɪ) n. 品質
resources (rɪ'sorsɪz) n. pl. 資源　　long-lasting ('lɔŋ'læstɪŋ) adj. 持久的
wear out 耗損　　replace (rɪ'ples) v. 更換　　*in addition* 此外
academic (ˌækə'dɛmɪk) adj. 學術的　　access ('æksɛs) v. 使用
Internet ('ɪntɚˌnɛt) n. 網際網路　　investment (ɪn'vɛstmənt) n. 投資
equipment (ɪ'kwɪpmənt) n. 設備；器材

Right now we need money badly.	現在我們非常需要資金。
We need to renovate our athletic facilities.	我們需要更新我們的運動設施。
We need to purchase more modern equipment.	我們需要採購更多的現代設備。
Good equipment encourages more students to play.	完善的器材能鼓勵學生多參加競賽。
They will be happy to participate in games and competitions.	他們會很樂意參與運動及競賽。
This is an important part of their education.	這是他們的教育中很重要的一環。

A school should provide a well-balanced education.　　好學校會提供學生均衡發展的教育。

Students should have the opportunity to develop all of their skills.	學生應該有機會發展他們各方面的技能。
Students' education includes both academics and personal development.	學生的教育包括學業和個人發展兩方面。
Sports play an important role in education.	體育活動在我們的教育中扮演一個重要的角色。
Sports must not be ignored.	體育活動不容忽視。
Therefore, they deserve our attention.	因此，體育活動值得我們的注意。

**　——————————

badly (ˈbædlɪ) *adv.* 很；非常　　renovate (ˈrɛnəˌvet) *v.* 更新
athletic (æθˈlɛtɪk) *adj.* 運動的；體育的　　purchase (ˈpɝtʃəs) *v.* 購買
encourage (ɪnˈkɝɪdʒ) *v.* 鼓勵　　play (ple) *v.* 參加競賽
participate (parˈtɪsəˌpet) *v.* 參加　　competition (ˌkɑmpəˈtɪʃən) *n.* 競賽
well-balanced (ˈwɛlˈbælənst) *adj.* 均衡的
play an important role in 在…扮演重要角色
ignore (ɪgˈnor) *v.* 忽視　　deserve (dɪˈzɝv) *v.* 應得

We must develop our sports programs.	我們必須發展體育課程。
It is our responsibility.	那是我們的責任。
Let's give it our full support.	我們來全力支持體育活動吧。

In conclusion, I advocate a fund drive.	總之,我提倡舉辦一個資金募款活動。
Let's try to raise money for our sports program.	我們努力為我們的體育課程籌款。
Let's ask our school community for help.	我們來向學校團體尋求協助。

We can encourage donations.	我們可以鼓勵捐款。
We can hold fundraisers.	我們可以舉辦募款活動。
We can upgrade our sports program by doing this.	我們可以藉由這麼做,使我們的體育課程升級。

I want to thank you all for listening.	我想要感謝大家的聆聽。
I hope I've persuaded you to support sports.	我希望我已經說服你們資助體育活動。
Let's take action and make our sports program great.	我們來採取行動,讓我們的體育課程更完善吧。

** ————————————————

responsibility (rɪ͵spɑnsə'bɪlətɪ) *n.* 責任　***in conclusion*** 總之

advocate ('ædvə͵ket) *v.* 提倡　　fund (fʌnd) *n.* 資金;基金

drive (draɪv) *n.* (籌募慈善捐款等的) 活動;宣傳

raise (rez) *v.* 籌 (款)　　community (kə'mjunətɪ) *n.* 社區;團體

donation (do'neʃən) *n.* 捐獻　　fundraiser ('fʌnd͵rezə) *n.* 資金籌集活動

upgrade (ʌp'gred) *v.* 使升級;提升

persuade (pə'swed) *v.* 說服　　***take action*** 採取行動

【托福作文範例】

31．Money for Sports Activities

Education serves a purpose in our life. The goal of education is to develop our minds. Our education consists of many things. The road of learning must be mental, spiritual and physical. So today, I would like to talk about supporting physical education in our school.

Sports activities are important for students. *Therefore*, the sports activities should be good. A library enriches the mind and a sports arena stimulates the body. Library resources are long-lasting; they don't wear out too fast and don't need to be replaced so often. Sports, *however*, require some investment every year. Equipment wears out quickly and needs to be replaced. Right now we need money badly. We need to renovate our athletic facilities and purchase more modern equipment. Good equipment encourages more students to play. A school should provide a well-balanced education. Students should have the opportunity to develop all of their skills. Students' education includes both academics and personal development.

In conclusion, I advocate a fund drive. We can encourage donations and hold fundraisers. We can upgrade our sports program by doing this.

31. 資助體育活動

　　教育在我們人生中是有用途的。教育的目標是要發展我們的心智。我們的教育是由許多方面組成的。學習之道必須心智、心靈和身體並重。所以今天,我想要討論資助我們學校的體育教育。

　　體育活動對學生來說是重要的。因此,體育活動應該要很好。圖書館豐富心靈,而運動場則能促進體能。圖書館資源是可以長期使用的;不會很快就耗損,而且也不需要那麼常更換。然而,體育則是每年都需要一些投資。器材很快會耗損,並且需要更換。現在我們非常需要資金。我們需要更新我們的運動設施,並且購買更多現代的設備。完善的設備能鼓勵更多的學生參與競賽。學校應該提供讓學生均衡發展的教育。學生應該要有機會發展他們各方面的技能。學生的教育包含學業及個人發展這兩方面。

　　總之,我提倡舉辦一個資金募款活動。我們可以鼓勵捐款,並且舉辦募款活動。我們可以藉由這麼做,使我們的體育課程升級。

【托福作文原試題】

Do you agree or disagree with the following statement? Universities should give the same amount of money to their students' sports activities as they give to their libraries. Use specific reasons and examples to support your opinion.

32. Why People Visit Museums

Ladies and gentlemen:
Do you like to travel?
I bet most of you do.

What do you like to do when you travel?
Many people like to see the sights.
Many like to visit palaces and scenic places.

I know many people like to go to museums.
I'm one of those people.
There are many reasons why we should
  visit museums.

For one thing, museums are great places.
Museums are repositories of artifacts and art.
We can see wonderful things in them.

---

visit ('vɪzɪt)	museum (mju'ziəm)
bet (bɛt)	sights (saɪts)
palace ('pælɪs)	scenic ('sinɪk)
for one thing	repository (rɪ'pazə,tori)
artifact ('artɪ,fækt)	art (art)

We can also learn in a museum.

We can learn about the past.

We can learn about other cultures.

That is why I like to visit museums.

I can find out something about other people there.

I can understand other cultures better.

Most people travel because they are interested
   in new things.

They want to see a different place.

They want to experience another way of life.

A museum is the perfect place to visit.

It is informative and enlightening.

It can also be interesting, fascinating
   and exciting.

---

culture ('kʌltʃɚ)   *find out*

experience (ɪk'spɪrɪəns)   *way of life*

informative (ɪn'fɔrmətɪv)

enlightening (ɪn'laɪtṇɪŋ)

fascinating ('fæsṇˌetɪŋ)

That is another reason I like to go to museums.

I am inspired by my new environment.

I want to find out more about it.

To visit a foreign museum is to see something
  special.

There are many things we cannot see at home.

There are many famous works of art in
  museums overseas.

Foreign museums show things in a different
  perspective.

They are like windows for observing a country.

They can present and teach so much in such
  a short time.

---

inspire (ɪn'spaɪr)   *at home*
work of art   overseas ('ovɚ'siz)
perspective (pɚ'spɛktɪv)   observe (əb'zɝv)
present (prɪ'zɛnt)

Finally, we can pursue a special interest.

We may find a museum related to our hobby.

We should take advantage of the opportunity.

There is a museum for almost every interest.

I prefer history and science museums the most.

I enjoy art museums, too.

It is impossible for every community to support
  every interest.

There may be only a few butterfly museums
  in the world.

If we have the chance to visit one, we should
  take it.

---

pursue (pə'su)	related (rɪ'letɪd)
hobby ('hɑbɪ)	*take advantage of*
prefer (prɪ'fɝ)	community (kə'mjunətɪ)
support (sə'port)	butterfly ('bʌtɚ͵flaɪ)

***In conclusion, a journey often offers the
   opportunity to visit a museum.***
It can give us a better understanding of a culture.
It can also help us see the world more clearly.

I recommend that everyone visit a museum.
Never miss a chance to learn more.
Never pass up the opportunity to increase your
   knowledge.

That's all I have to say about museums.
I hope I've persuaded you that museums are great!
I know that museums are super places.

Have a wonderful day.
I'll be here for a while to answer your questions.
I wish everyone here the best of luck.

---

in conclusion	journey ('dʒɜnɪ)
recommend (ˌrɛkə'mɛnd)	*pass up*
increase (ɪn'kris)	persuade (pə'swed)
super ('supə)	

32. Why People Visit Museums
人們爲什麼要參觀博物館

【演講解説】

Ladies and gentlemen:	各位先生，各位女士：
Do you like to travel?	你們喜歡旅行嗎？
I bet most of you do.	我相信你們大部分人都喜歡旅行。
What do you like to do when you travel?	你在旅行的時候，喜歡做什麼呢？
Many people like to see the sights.	很多人喜歡遊覽觀光名勝。
Many like to visit palaces and scenic places.	很多人喜歡參觀宮殿和景點。
I know many people like to go to museums.	我知道很多人喜歡去博物館。
I'm one of those people.	我就是其中之一個。
There are many reasons why we should visit museums.	我們應該參觀博物館的理由很多。

** ——————————————————

visit ('vɪzɪt) v. 參觀；遊覽
museum (mju'ziəm) n. 博物館
sights (saɪts) n. pl. 名勝；觀光地
palace ('pælɪs) n. 宮殿　　scenic ('sinɪk) adj. 風景優美的

For one thing, museums are great places.

首先，博物館是很棒的地方。

Museums are repositories of artifacts and art.

博物館是人類歷史文物及藝術品的寶庫。

We can see wonderful things in them.

我們可以在那裡看到很棒的東西。

We can also learn in a museum.

我們也可以在博物館中學習。

We can learn about the past.

我們可以得知過去的事情。

We can learn about other cultures.

我們可以認識其他文化。

That is why I like to visit museums.

那就是爲什麼我喜歡參觀博物館的原因。

I can find out something about other people there.

我可以知道關於當地人們的事情。

I can understand other cultures better.

我可以更了解其他的文化。

Most people travel because they are interested in new things.

大部分的人去旅遊，是因爲對新事物有興趣。

They want to see a different place.

他們想看看不一樣的地方。

They want to experience another way of life.

他們想要體驗另一種生活方式。

**

for one thing 首先；一則　　repository (rɪ'pɑzə,torɪ) *n.* 寶庫
artifact ('ɑrtɪ,fækt) *n.* 手工藝品　　art (ɑrt) *n.* 藝術品
culture ('kʌltʃə) *n.* 文化　　*find out* 找出；發現
experience (ɪk'spɪrɪəns) *v.* 體驗　　*way of life* 生活方式

A museum is the perfect place to visit.	博物館是供人參觀的絕佳地點。
It is informative and enlightening.	它具有知識性及啓發性。
It can also be interesting, fascinating, and exciting.	也是個有趣、迷人和刺激的地方。
That is another reason I like to go to museums.	那是另外一個我喜歡去博物館的理由。
I am inspired by my new environment.	我會受到新環境的啓發。
I want to find out more about it.	我會想要發掘更多的東西。
To visit a foreign museum is to see something special.	我想參觀外國博物館,是爲了看看特別的東西。
There are many things we cannot see at home.	有很多東西是我們在國內無法看到的。
There are many famous works of art in museums overseas.	國外的博物館有很多有名的藝術品。
Foreign museums show things in a different perspective.	國外的博物館會以不同的角度來展示物品。
They are like windows for observing a country.	它們就像是觀察一個國家的窗口。
They can present and teach so much in such a short time.	它們可以在如此短暫的時間內,呈現出並教導人們很多東西。

＊＊ ─────────────────────

informative〔ɪnˋfɔrmətɪv〕*adj.* 知識性的
enlightening〔ɪnˋlaɪtṇɪŋ〕*adj.* 啓發性的
fascinating〔ˋfæsṇ͵etɪŋ〕*adj.* 迷人的;極好的
inspire〔ɪnˋspaɪr〕*v.* 啓發　***at home*** 在國內;在本國
work of art 藝術品　overseas〔ˋovɚˋsiz〕*adv.* 在海外;在國外
perspective〔pɚˋspɛktɪv〕*n.* 觀點
observe〔əbˋzɝv〕*v.* 觀察　present〔prɪˋzɛnt〕*v.* 呈現

Finally, *we can pursue a special interest.*	最後，我們可以追求特別的興趣。
We may find a museum related to our hobby.	我們可以尋找和我們的嗜好相關的博物館。
We should take advantage of the opportunity.	我們應該好好利用機會。
There is a museum for almost every interest.	幾乎每一種興趣都有專門的博物館。
I prefer history and science museums the most.	我最喜歡歷史和科學博物館。
I enjoy art museums, too.	我也喜歡藝術博物館。
It is impossible for every community to support every interest.	並非每一個社區都可以資助每一種興趣。
There may be only a few butterfly museums in the world.	全世界的蝴蝶博物館可能只有一些。
If we have the chance to visit one, we should take it.	如果我們有機會去參觀，就應該把握機會。

** ─────────────

pursue〔pə'su〕*v.* 追求　　related〔rɪ'letɪd〕*adj.* 有關的 *< to >*

hobby〔'hɑbɪ〕*n.* 嗜好　　***take advantage of*** 利用

prefer〔prɪ'fɚ〕*v.* 偏愛　　community〔kə'mjunətɪ〕*n.* 社區

support〔sə'port〕*v.* 支持；資助　　butterfly〔'bʌtɚ,flaɪ〕*n.* 蝴蝶

In conclusion, a journey often offers the opportunity to visit a museum.	總之,旅行常能提供參觀博物館的機會。
It can give us a better understanding of a culture.	它能讓我們對某個文化有更深入的了解。
It can also help us see the world more clearly.	也有助於我們更清楚地認識這個世界。
I recommend that everyone visit a museum.	我建議每個人都去參觀博物館。
Never miss a chance to learn more.	絕不要錯過能多學習的機會。
Never pass up the opportunity to increase your knowledge.	絕不要放棄能增進知識的機會。
That's all I have to say about museums.	關於博物館,我所要說的話就是這些了。
I hope I've persuaded you that museums are great!	我希望我已經說服你們,認為博物館很棒!
I know that museums are super places.	我知道博物館是最棒的地方。
Have a wonderful day.	祝你們有個美好的一天。
I'll be here for a while to answer your questions.	我會待在這裡一下子,回答你們的問題。
I wish everyone here the best of luck.	我祝福在場的每個人好運。

** ───────────────

in conclusion 總之   journey〔'dʒɜnɪ〕*n.* 旅行
recommend〔ˌrɛkə'mɛnd〕*v.* 推薦;建議
pass up 拒絕;放棄   increase〔ɪn'kris〕*v.* 增加
persuade〔pə'swed〕*v.* 說服   super〔'supə〕*adj.* 極好的

【托福作文範例】

32. **Why People Visit Museums**

People like to travel to see different sights. Many may like to visit palaces and scenic places and some people may like to go to museums. I am one of those people. There are many reasons why we should visit museums.

For one thing, museums are great places. They are repositories of artifacts and art. We can learn about the past and about other cultures. That is why I like to go to museums. I can find out something about other people there. A museum is the perfect place to visit. It is informative and enlightening. That is another reason I like to go to museums. My new environment inspires me. Visiting a foreign museum is to see something special. There are many things we cannot see at home. There are many famous works of art in museums overseas. Foreign museums show things in a different perspective. *Finally*, we can pursue a special interest. We may find a museum related to our hobby. We should take advantage of the opportunity. There is a museum for almost every interest. If we have the chance to visit one, we should take it.

In conclusion, a journey often offers the opportunity to visit a museum. It can give us a better understanding of a culture. It can help us see the world more clearly. So the next time you are in a foreign country, take some time out and stop by a museum. You will learn something new!

32. 人們為什麼要參觀博物館

　　有人喜歡旅行，遊覽各種不同的觀光名勝。很多人喜歡參觀宮殿和景點，而有些人則喜歡去博物館，我就是其中之一。我們應該參觀博物館的理由很多。

　　首先，博物館是很棒的地方。博物館是人類歷史文物及藝術品的寶庫。我們可以在博物館中學習到過去的事情，以及認識其他文化。那就是為什麼我喜歡去博物館的原因。在那裡我可以知道關於當地人們的事情。博物館是一個非常適合參觀的地方。它具有知識性及啟發性。那是另一個我喜歡去博物館的理由。新的環境能夠啟發我。參觀國外的博物館，可以看到特別的事物。有非常多的東西是我們在國內看不到的。國外的博物館收藏了許多有名的藝術品。國外的博物館會以不同的角度來展現事物。最後，我們可以追求特別的興趣。我們可以尋找和我們的嗜好有關的博物館。我們應該好好利用機會。幾乎每一種興趣都有專門的博物館。如果我們有機會去參觀，我們應該要把握機會。

　　總之，旅行常常能提供參觀博物館的機會。它能夠讓我們對某個文化更加瞭解。它能夠使我們更清楚地認識這個世界。所以下一次你去國外時，花點時間去參觀博物館吧。你會學到新的東西！

─────【托福作文原試題】─────

Many people visit museums when they travel to new places. Why do you think people visit museums? Use specific reasons and examples to support your answer.

33. Home Cooking

Ladies and gentlemen:
I'm glad to see you here.
I think you'll like what I have to say.

I'd like to talk about food.
More specifically, I want to talk about
   home-cooked food.
In my opinion, it's the best kind.

We all love to eat.
We probably like to eat different things.
As for me, I like home cooking.

I don't dislike restaurants.
In fact, I often eat out.
It's a way of life here.

---

specifically (spɪ'sɪfɪklɪ)
home-cooked ('hom,kʊkt)
as for
way of life

in one's opinion
eat out

Our country is famous for its good food.

There is a delicious variety available all

over town.

There is something for every taste

and every wallet.

However, I most enjoy eating at home.

I like to cook with my family.

We enjoy sharing the food we make.

None of us are master chefs.

The food we make is nothing special.

The food is certainly not elegant enough

for a fine restaurant.

I like the taste of my mother's cooking best.

My mom is the head chef in our house.

My mom's cooking tastes like home.

---

variety (və'raɪətɪ)   available (ə'veləbl̩)

all over   town (taʊn)

taste (test)   master ('mæstɚ)

chef (ʃɛf)   elegant ('ɛləgənt)

fine (faɪn)   *head chef*

Although my mother is the chef, we all like
   to help out.
Preparing food together is fun.
Preparing food together brings us closer.

We enjoy eating at home, too.
We can talk more freely at home.
The atmosphere is quiet and personal.

Most important of all, we don't have to
   pay a big bill.
However, we do have to wash up.
We all pitch in and help.

 I love to eat.
And I love to eat with my family.
Having dinner at home is so comfortable.

---

help out

close (klos)

atmosphere ('ætməs,fɪr)

bill (bɪl)

pitch in

prepare (prɪ'pɛr)

freely ('frilɪ)

personal ('pɜsn̩l)

wash up

We enjoy the time we spend together.

It's a peaceful time.

It's a nice change of pace after a busy day.

Families today are so busy.

Families rarely have lots of time together.

Therefore, a meal together is a precious
  opportunity.

We must appreciate home cooking.

We should always assist with every meal.

A home-cooked meal should be a family-team
  effort.

---

peaceful ('pisfəl)	pace (pes)
rarely ('rɛrlɪ)	meal (mil)
precious ('prɛʃəs)	
appreciate (ə'priʃɪˌet)	assist (ə'sɪst)
team (tim)	effort ('ɛfət)

A home-cooked meal is a special treat.
A home-cooked meal should never be taken
   for granted.
It's one of the fondest home memories
   we'll ever have.

I hope you enjoy your dinner tonight.
Whether you eat out or eat at home,
   bon appetit.
Whether you are with family or friends,
   enjoy your meal.

That's all I wanted to say.
Thank you for being so attentive.
Let's all go find some delicious home-cooked
   food.

---

treat (trit)

fond (fɑnd)

appetite ('æpə,taɪt)

attentive (ə'tɛntɪv)

take…for granted

memory ('mɛmərɪ)

bon appetit

33. *Home Cooking*
在家做飯

【演講解說】

Ladies and gentlemen.　　　　　各位女士，各位先生。
I'm glad to see you here.
I think you'll like what I have　　我很高興能在這裡看到大家。
　　to say.　　　　　　　　　　我想你們會喜歡我要說的話。

I'd like to talk about food.　　　　我想談談食物。
More specifically, I want to talk
　　about home-cooked food.　　　更明確地說，我想談談在家裡
In my opinion, it's the best kind.　　做的飯。
　　　　　　　　　　　　　　　依我之見，那是最棒的食物。

We all love to eat.　　　　　　　我們全都喜歡吃東西。
We probably like to eat different
　　things.　　　　　　　　　　我們大概會喜歡吃不一樣的東西。
As for me, I like home cooking.

　　　　　　　　　　　　　　　至於我，我喜歡在家做飯。

** ————————————————

specifically〔spɪˈsɪfɪkl̩ɪ〕*adv.* 明確地
home-cooked〔ˈhomˌkʊkt〕*adj.* (食物) 在家裡烹煮的；家常的
in one's opinion 依某人之見　　　*as for* 至於

I don't dislike restaurants.	我並不是不喜歡餐廳。
In fact, I often eat out.	事實上，我常常出去吃飯。
It's a way of life here.	那是這裡的生活方式。
Our country is famous for its good food.	我國以美食聞名。
There is a delicious variety available all over town.	市區到處有各式各樣好吃的食物。
There is something for every taste and every wallet.	每一種口味和價位的東西都有。
However, I most enjoy eating at home.	然而，我還是最喜歡在家裡吃飯。
I like to cook with my family.	我喜歡和家人一起做菜。
We enjoy sharing the food we make.	我們喜歡分享我們所做的食物。
None of us are master chefs.	我們當中沒有人是技術高超的大廚師。
The food we make is nothing special.	我們所做的食物沒什麼特別。
The food is certainly not elegant enough for a fine restaurant.	當然沒有高級餐廳那麼精緻。

** ───────────────

eat out 外出用餐　　*way of life* 生活方式
variety〔vəˈraɪətɪ〕*n.* 變化；多樣性　available〔əˈveləbḷ〕*adj.* 可獲得的
all over 遍及　　town〔taʊn〕*n.* 市中心
taste〔test〕*n.* 口味　*v.* 吃起來；嚐起來
master〔ˈmæstɚ〕*adj.* 熟練的；師傅的
chef〔ʃɛf〕*n.* 廚師（尤指餐館的主廚）
elegant〔ˈɛləgənt〕*adj.* 精緻的　　fine〔faɪn〕*adj.* 上等的

I like the taste of my mother's cooking best.	我最喜歡我媽媽烹調的口味。
My mom is the head chef in our house.	我媽媽是我們家的主廚。
My mom's cooking tastes like home.	我媽媽煮的東西，嚐起來有家的味道。
Although my mother is the chef, we all like to help out.	雖然我媽媽是主廚，但是我們都喜歡幫忙。
Preparing food together is fun.	一起做飯很有趣。
Preparing food together brings us closer.	一起做飯讓我們更加親密。
We enjoy eating at home, too.	我們也喜歡在家吃飯。
We can talk more freely at home.	我們可以在家裡自在地聊天。
The atmosphere is quiet and personal.	氣氛安靜又隱密。
Most important of all, we don't have to pay a big bill.	最重要的是，我們不用付大筆的帳單。
However, we do have to wash up.	不過，我們必須洗碗。
We all pitch in and help.	我們全都會動手幫忙。

**

head chef 主廚　　***help out*** 幫忙
prepare〔prɪˈpɛr〕*v.* 做（飯菜）　　close〔klos〕*adj.* 親密的
freely〔ˈfrilɪ〕*adv.* 自在地　　atmosphere〔ˈætməsˌfɪr〕*n.* 氣氛
personal〔ˈpɜsn̩l〕*adj.* 私人的　　bill〔bɪl〕*n.* 帳單
wash up 洗碗　　***pitch in*** 動手做；使勁做

I love to eat.	我喜歡吃。
And I love to eat with my family.	而且我喜歡和我的家人一起吃。
Having dinner at home is so comfortable.	在家吃晚餐是非常舒服的事情。
We enjoy the time we spend together.	我們享受在一起的時光。
It's a peaceful time.	那是非常安詳的時光。
It's a nice change of pace after a busy day.	在忙碌的一天後，能改變步調很不錯。
Families today are so busy.	現在的家庭成員都很忙碌。
Families rarely have lots of time together.	人很少有很多時間聚在一起。
Therefore, a meal together is a precious opportunity.	因此，在一起吃飯是珍貴的機會。
We must appreciate home cooking.	能吃到家常菜，我們一定要心存感激。
We should always assist with every meal.	我們一定要幫忙準備每一餐。
A home-cooked meal should be a family-team effort.	在家用餐應該是全家人團隊努力成果。

**

peaceful ('pisfəl) *adj.* 平靜的；安寧的
pace (pes) *n.* 步調　rarely ('rɛrlɪ) *adv.* 很少
meal (mil) *n.* 一餐　precious ('prɛʃəs) *adj.* 珍貴的
appreciate (ə'priʃɪˌet) *v.* 感激　assist (ə'sɪst) *v.* 協助 <*with*>
team (tim) *n.* 團隊　effort ('ɛfət) *n.* 努力

A home-cooked meal is a special treat.	在家用餐是特別的享受。
A home-cooked meal should never be taken for granted.	在家用餐絕不該被視為理所當然。
It's one of the fondest home memories we'll ever have.	那將是我們擁有的家庭回憶中，令人最喜愛的一部份。
I hope you enjoy your dinner tonight.	我希望你們能好好享受今晚的晚餐。
Whether you eat out or eat at home, bon appetit.	不論是外出用餐或在家吃飯，都祝你胃口大開。
Whether you are with family or friends, enjoy your meal.	不論你是和家人或是朋友在一起，都要好好享用這一餐。
That's all I wanted to say.	那就是我所想說的話了。
Thank you for being so attentive.	謝謝你們如此專心聆聽。
Let's all go find some delicious home-cooked food.	我們都去找一些好吃的家常菜吧。

**

treat〔trit〕*n.* 難得的樂事　　*take…for granted* 視…為理所當然
fond〔fɑnd〕*adj.* 喜歡的　　memory〔'mɛmərɪ〕*n.* 回憶
bon appetit【法文】祝你胃口大開（法文 appetit 就是英文 appetite
〔'æpə,taɪt〕*n.* 食慾；胃口）
attentive〔ə'tɛntɪv〕*adj.* 專注的；傾聽的

【托福作文範例】

33. Home Cooking

"What's for dinner?" is often a question many people ask at the end of the day. We all need to eat. Some people like to eat out and some people prefer home cooking. I prefer home cooking the most.

I like to cook with my family. None of us are master chefs, but we enjoy the food we make. I like the taste of my mother's cooking best. My mom is the head chef in our house. My mom's cooking tastes like home. Although my mother is the chef, we all help out in the kitchen. Preparing food together is fun and brings us closer. We enjoy eating at home more because we can talk freely at home. Most important of all, there are no bills to pay! *However*, we do have to wash up. We all pitch in and help. I love to eat with my family because having dinner at home is so comfortable. Families today are so busy and they rarely have lots of time together. *Therefore*, a meal together is a precious opportunity. We should appreciate home cooking and help out whenever we can. A home-cooked meal should never be taken for granted.

I hope you enjoy your home-cooked meal tonight. Whether you are with friends or family, enjoy your meal.

33. 在家做飯

「晚餐吃什麼？」常常是許多人在一天結束時會問的問題。我們都需要吃東西。有些人喜歡在外面用餐，有些人喜歡在家自己煮。我個人最喜歡的是在家做飯。

我喜歡和家人一起煮飯。雖然我們當中沒有人是技術高超的大廚師，但是我們都很享受我們自己烹調的食物。我最喜歡我媽媽烹調的口味。我媽媽是我們家的主廚。我媽媽做的菜，總是有家的味道。雖然我媽媽是主廚，我們在廚房裡都會幫忙。一起做飯很有趣，也讓我們更加親密。我們比較喜歡在家用餐的感覺，因為在家裡，我們可以自在地談話。最重要的是，沒有帳單要付！然而，我們必須自己洗碗。我們全部都會一起動手幫忙。我喜歡和家人一起吃飯，因為在家吃晚餐非常舒服。現在的人都太忙碌了，家人很少有很多時間聚在一起。因此，能夠一起吃飯是個珍貴的機會。能夠在家吃飯，我們應該要心存感激，而且能幫忙就多幫忙。不應該把在家吃飯視為理所當然。

我希望你們今晚都能在家好好享受一餐。無論你是和朋友還是和家人一起吃飯，祝你用餐愉快。

【托福作文原試題】

Some people prefer to eat at food stands or restaurants. Other people prefer to prepare and eat food at home. Which do you prefer? Use specific reasons and examples to support your answer.

34. Class Attendance

Ladies and gentlemen:
Thank you for your attendance tonight.
I really appreciate your attention.

There is a proposal for a new regulation.
It states that all university students must
    attend classes.
It has some flaws that I'd like to point out.

Everyone knows that class attendance is important.
Everyone knows that we should all take our
    studies seriously.
However, I don't think a regulation is necessary
    or wise.

There are several reasons why I feel this way.
As a student myself, I have an interest in this.
The regulation will affect me personally.

---

attendance (ə'tɛndəns)

appreciate (ə'priʃɪ,et)

proposal (prə'pozl̩)

regulation (,rɛgjə'leʃən)

state (stet)

flaw (flɔ)

point out

take ~ seriously

wise (waɪz)

interest ('ɪntrɪst)

have an interest in

personally ('pɜsn̩lɪ)

One reason I disagree with it is that students
    should take their schoolwork seriously.
They should not need a regulation to remind
    them to do so.
They should be motivated to do it on their own.

Please remember that university students are adults.
They are responsible for their own actions.
They should make their own decisions.

Of course, students should attend their classes.
They should not only attend, but also actively
    take part.
They should pursue every opportunity to learn.

Therefore, attending their classes is of benefit
    to them.
They are only hurting themselves if they do
    not attend.
They will have no one else to blame.

---

schoolwork ('skul,wɜk)   remind (rɪ'maɪnd)

motivate ('motə,vet)   *on one's own*

responsible (rɪ'spɑnsəbl̩)   *take part*

pursue (pə'su)   benefit ('bɛnəfɪt)

blame (blem)

As adults, the students must learn to manage
   their own time.
They must learn to be responsible.
They cannot depend on others to make their
   arrangements for them.

Another reason I object to the regulation is
   that it does not benefit professors.
Professors want students to attend their classes.
Professors want students to come because
   they want to, not because they must.

Class attendance can be a good indication
   of how a professor is doing.
If attendance falls off, perhaps he should
   consider making some changes.
If class size gets smaller, students may be
   having trouble with the material.

---

manage ('mænɪdʒ)   *depend on*
arrangement (ə'rendʒmənt)   object (əb'dʒɛkt)
indication (ˌɪndə'keʃən)   *fall off*

Finally, I think the proposed regulation is a bad idea.

It will prevent students from developing responsibility.

It will prevent professors from honestly evaluating their courses.

It doesn't make sense to me.

It defeats the purpose of education.

There is nothing educational about a mandatory regulation.

Students in a free society must learn good judgment.

Students must exercise that freedom.

Students should never be forced to attend class.

---

proposed (prə'pozd)   prevent (prɪ'vɛnt)

responsibility (rɪ,spɑnsə'bɪlətɪ)

honestly ('ɑnɪstlɪ)   evaluate (ɪ'væljʊ,et)

make sense   defeat (dɪ'fit)

educational (,ɛdʒə'keʃənḷ)   mandatory ('mændə,torɪ)

judgment ('dʒʌdʒmənt)   exercise ('ɛksə,saɪz)

freedom ('fridəm)   force (fors)

In my opinion, there is no reason to require

   class attendance.

University students are not children.

University students should be allowed to grow up.

Class attendance should be optional.

Class attendance is a privilege and a

   guaranteed right.

It's the best opportunity and method to improve.

Thank you for your attention today.

I hope you will seriously consider what I

   have said.

Please make the best decision for all concerned.

Please remember what I've said.

Please value and cherish the gift of education.

God bless you all, good luck and attend class!

---

optional ('ɑpʃən!)	privilege ('prɪvl̩ɪdʒ)
guaranteed (ˌgærən'tid)	right (raɪt)
concerned (kən's3nd)	value ('vælju)
cherish ('tʃɛrɪʃ)	gift (gɪft)

34. *Class Attendance*
上課出席

【演講解說】

Ladies and gentlemen:	各位先生，各位女士：
Thank you for your attendance *tonight.*	感謝你們今晚出席。
I really appreciate your attention.	我眞的很感謝你們注意聽我說。
There is a proposal for a new regulation.	有人提出一個新規定。
It states that all university students must attend classes.	內容是所有的大學生，上課必須出席。
It has some flaws that I'd like to point out.	這項提議有些缺點，是我想要指出來的。
Everyone knows that class attendance is important.	每個人都知道上課出席的重要性。
Everyone knows that we should all take our studies seriously.	每個人都知道我們應該認眞看待自己的學業。
However, I don't think a regulation is necessary or wise.	然而，我不認爲規定是有必要或明智的。

** ───────────────

attendance〔əˈtɛndəns〕 *n.* 出席（人數）
appreciate〔əˈpriʃɪˌet〕 *v.* 感激　　proposal〔prəˈpozḷ〕 *n.* 提議
regulation〔ˌrɛgjəˈleʃən〕 *n.* 規定　　state〔stet〕 *v.* 陳述
flaw〔flɔ〕 *n.* 缺點　　*point out* 指出
take ~ seriously 認眞看待　　wise〔waɪz〕 *adj.* 明智的

There are several reasons why I feel this way.	我會這麼覺得是基於好幾個理由。
As a student myself, I have an interest in this.	我自己身為學生，和這一點有利害關係。
The regulation will affect me personally.	這項規定會影響到我個人。
One reason I disagree with it is that students should take their schoolwork seriously.	我不同意的一個理由是，學生應該認真看待自己的學業。
They should not need a regulation to remind them to do so.	他們不需要規定來提醒他們要這麼做。
They should be motivated to do it on their own.	他們應該自己主動去做到。
Please remember that university students are adults.	請記住一點，大學生是大人了。
They are responsible for their own actions.	他們要對自己的行為負責。
They should make their own decisions.	他們應該自己做決定。
Of course, students should attend their classes.	當然，學生應該上課要出席。
They should not only attend, but also actively take part.	他們不應該只有出席，也要積極參與。
They should pursue every opportunity to learn.	他們應該追求各種學習機會。

** ————————————

interest (ˈɪntrɪst) *n.* 利害關係　　***have an interest in***　和…有利害關係
personally (ˈpɝsn̩lɪ) *adv.* 針對個人地　　schoolwork (ˈskulˌwɝk) *n.* 學業
remind (rɪˈmaɪnd) *v.* 提醒　　motivate (ˈmotəˌvet) *v.* 給…動機；刺激
on one's own 靠自己　　responsible (rɪˈspɑnsəbl̩) *adj.* 應負責任的
take part 參加　　pursue (pɚˈsu) *v.* 追求

Therefore, attending their classes is of benefit to them.	因此，上課對他們是有益的。
They are only hurting themselves if they do not attend.	如果他們不上課的話，他們只會害到自己。
They will have no one else to blame.	他們不能怪別人。
As adults, the students must learn to manage their own time.	身為大人，學生必須學會管理自己的時間。
They cannot depend on others to make their arrangements for them.	他們不能依賴別人為他們做安排。
They must learn to be responsible.	他們必須學會負責任。
Another reason I object to the regulation is that it does not benefit professors.	我反對這項規定的另一個理由是，這對教授沒有好處。
Professors want students to attend their classes.	教授希望學生來上課。
Professors want students to come because they want to, not because they must.	教授希望學生出席，是因為他們想要來，並不是必須來。
Class attendance can be a good indication of how a professor is doing.	出席率是教授表現得如何的一個很好的指標。
If attendance falls off, perhaps he should consider making some changes.	如果出席率下降，或許他就應該考慮做些改變。
If class size gets smaller, students may be having trouble with the material.	如果上課人數減少，學生可能是覺得上課內容有問題。

** ――――――――――――

benefit (ˈbɛnəfɪt) *n.* 好處　*v.* 對⋯有益　　blame (blem) *v.* 責備
manage (ˈmænɪdʒ) *v.* 管理　***depend on*** 依靠
arrangement (əˈrendʒmənt) *n.* 安排　object (əbˈdʒɛkt) *v.* 反對 <*to*>
indication (ˌɪndəˈkeʃən) *n.* 表示；指標 <*of*>　***fall off*** （數量）減少

Finally, I think the proposed regulation is a bad idea.	最後，我認為所提議的規定是不好的點子。
It will prevent students from developing responsibility.	那會妨礙學生培養負責感。
It will prevent professors from honestly evaluating their courses.	那會妨礙教授誠實評估自己的課程。
It doesn't make sense to me.	對我而言，那是不合理的。
It defeats the purpose of education.	那會違反教育的目的。
There is nothing educational about a mandatory regulation.	強制規定毫無教育意義可言。
Students in a free society must learn good judgment.	身處自由社會的學生必須學習做出明智的判斷。
Students must exercise that freedom.	學生必須行使那樣的自由權。
Students should never be forced to attend class.	學生絕對不應該被強迫上課必須出席。

**

proposed (prə'pozd) *adj.* 被提議的
prevent (prɪ'vɛnt) *v.* 妨礙 < *from* >
responsibility (rɪˌspɑnsə'bɪlətɪ) *n.* 責任感
honestly ('ɑnɪstlɪ) *adv.* 誠實地
evaluate (ɪ'væljuˌet) *v.* 評估　　***make sense*** 合理；有意義
defeat (dɪ'fit) *v.* 使 (計畫、希望等) 受到挫折；推翻
educational (ˌɛdʒə'keʃənļ) *adj.* 有教育意義的
mandatory ('mændəˌtorɪ) *adj.* 強制的
judgment ('dʒʌdʒmənt) *n.* 判斷 (力)
exercise ('ɛksəˌsaɪz) *v.* 運用；行使
freedom ('fridəm) *n.* 自由 (權)　　force (fors) *v.* 強迫

In my opinion, there is no reason to require class attendance.	依我之見，沒有理由要求上課一定要出席。
University students are not children.	大學生不是小孩子。
University students should be allowed to grow up.	應該讓大學生長大了。
Class attendance should be optional.	上課要不要出席應該是非強制性的。
Class attendance is a privilege and a guaranteed right.	上課出席是個基本權利，是受到保障的權利。
It's the best opportunity and method to improve.	是追求進步的最佳機會和方法。
Thank you for your attention today.	謝謝你們今天專心聽講。
I hope you will seriously consider what I have said.	我希望你們認真考慮我所說的話。
Please make the best decision for all concerned.	請為所有相關的人做出最好的決定。
Please remember what I've said.	請記住我所說的話。
Please value and cherish the gift of education.	請重視並且珍惜教育這項恩惠。
God bless you all, good luck and attend class!	願上帝祝福大家，祝各位擁有好運，並且去上課！

**

optional (ˈɑpʃən!) *adj.* 可選擇的；非必須的
privilege (ˈprɪvḷɪdʒ) *n.* (憲法保證公民享有的)基本權利
guaranteed (ˌgærənˈtid) *adj.* 保障的   right (raɪt) *n.* 權利
concerned (kənˈsɝnd) *adj.* 有關的   value (ˈvælju) *v.* 重視；珍視
cherish (ˈtʃɛrɪʃ) *v.* 珍惜   gift (gɪft) *n.* 所賜之物；恩惠

【托福作文範例】

34. Class Attendance

The university is proposing to pass a new regulation to make class attendance mandatory for students. There are some flaws to that proposal that I would like to point out.

Everyone knows that class attendance is important. And *one* reason I disagree with the proposal is that students should take their work seriously. They should not need regulations to remind them to do so. University students are adults. They are responsible for their own actions and they should make their own decisions. As adults, the students learn to manage their own time. They must learn to be responsible. They cannot depend on others to make arrangements for them. *Another* reason I object to the regulation is that it does not benefit professors. Professors want students to attend their classes because they want to, not because they must. Class attendance can be a good indication of how a professor is doing. *Finally*, I think the proposed regulation is a bad idea. It will prevent students from developing responsibility. Students in a free society must learn good judgment. Students should never be forced to attend class.

In conclusion, class attendance should be optional, because university students are not children. We should allow them the freedom to make their own decisions, whether to attend class or not.

34. 上課出席

　　大學在提議，要通過一項新規定，要求所有的學生上課必須出席。我想要指出這項提議的一些缺點。

　　每個人都知道上課出席非常重要。而我不同意此項提議的其中一個原因是，學生應該要自己認眞看待他們的課業。他們不應該需要靠規定來提醒自己這麼做。大學生都是成年人了。他們應該要爲自己的行爲負責，並且自己做決定。身爲成人，學生應該要學習管理自己的時間。他們必須要學會負責任。他們不能依靠別人來替他們做安排。另外一個我反對的原因是，這麼做對教授並沒有好處。教授會希望學生上課，是學生出於自願的，而不是被強制要求的。課堂的出席率可以是教授表現如何的一個良好指標。最後，我認爲這個所提出的這項規定是個不好的主意。那會阻礙學生培養責任感。在自由社會中的學生，應該要學習做出良好的判斷。學生不應該被逼迫去上課。

　　總之，上課是否出席應該是可選擇的，因爲大學生也不是小孩子了。我們應該讓他們有自己決定要不要去上課的自由。

【托福作文原試題】

> *Some people believe that university students should be required to attend classes. Others believe that going to classes should be optional for students. Which point of view do you agree with? Use specific reasons and details to explain your answer.*

35. *Good Neighbors*

Welcome ladies and gentlemen.
Welcome friends and neighbors.
It's so nice to see your friendly faces.

I would like to talk about neighbors.
Do you have good neighbors?
Do you get along well with them?

It's important to establish good relationships
    in our neighborhoods.
Someday, we may need our neighbors.
And, like it or not, they are a part of our lives.

Therefore, it is very important to get along
    well with our neighbors.
To do that we have to be good neighbors
    ourselves.
If we are good neighbors, chances are that
    we will have good neighbors.

---

get along with
relationship (rɪˈleʃənˌʃɪp)
neighborhood (ˈnebɚˌhʊd)

establish (əˈstæblɪʃ)

chances are that

There are several things we can do to be good
  neighbors.
Let me tell them to you in detail.
Let me list them now for your better understanding.

***First of all*, *we should get along with others*.**
That is rule number one.
That is the minimum requirement.

Respect everyone all the time.
Be considerate of others all the time.
Be sensitive and alert when around other people.

***Second*, *we must not disturb our neighbors*.**
We cannot be too noisy.
We shouldn't block our neighbors' parking spaces.

---

detail ('ditel)	***in detail***
list (lɪst)	***first of all***
minimum ('mɪnəməm)	
requirement (rɪ'kwaɪrmənt)	***all the time***
considerate (kən'sɪdərɪt)	sensitive ('sɛnsətɪv)
alert (ə'lɜt)	disturb (dɪ'stɜb)
block (blɑk)	***parking space***

We must treat neighbors with kindness.
We should treat them the way we want to
  be treated.
That's the golden rule of getting along.

Third, we should take care of the neighborhood.
We all have to work together.
We should keep the place clean.

The neighborhood is everyone's community.
The community is like one big family.
Everyone has to care about and support each other.

Fourth, we should watch out for our neighbors.
We should report suspicious people.
We should care about the safety of our
  neighborhood.

---

treat (trit)	*golden rule*
get along	*take care of*
work together	community (kə'mjunətɪ)
care about	support (sə'port)
watch out for	report (rɪ'port)
suspicious (sə'spɪʃəs)	

Safety is everyone's responsibility.

Neighbors must protect fellow neighbors.

Neighbors must share the duty of public safety.

Finally, we should help our neighbors when

   they are in trouble.

Often we are the closest help available.

We should do all we can 24/7.

If we can do all of those things above, I believe

   we can be good neighbors.

Then we will be blessed with good neighbors

   in return.

That will result in a happy and safe

   neighborhood.

---

responsibility (rɪ,spɑnsə'bɪlətɪ)

protect (prə'tɛkt)   fellow ('fɛlo)

share (ʃɛr)   duty ('djutɪ)

in trouble   help (hɛlp)

available (ə'veləbḷ)   *24/7*

bless (blɛs)   *in return*

result in

People say good fences make good neighbors.

I really don't agree with that statement.

I think kindness is repaid with kindness.

If we respect others, they will respect us.

If we want good neighbors we must do one

  important thing.

We must be good neighbors.

It sounds simple to do.

It is very easy to be a good neighbor.

Just give, support, share and care!

---

fence (fɛns)
repay (rɪ'pe)

statement ('stetmənt)
care (kɛr)

35. *Good Neighbors*
好鄰居

【演講解説】

Welcome ladies and gentlemen.	各位先生、各位女士，歡迎大家。
Welcome friends and neighbors.	歡迎各位朋友及鄰居。
It's so nice to see your friendly faces.	看到你們親切的臉真好。
I would like to talk about neighbors.	我想要談談鄰居。
Do you have good neighbors?	你有好鄰居嗎？
Do you get along well with them?	你和他們處得好嗎？
It's important to establish good relationships in our neighborhoods.	在鄰近地區建立良好的關係是很重要的。
Someday, we may need our neighbors.	將來有一天，我們可能會需要我們的鄰居。
And, like it or not, they are a part of our lives.	而且，不論你喜不喜歡，他們是我們生活的一部份。
Therefore, it is very important to get along well with our neighbors.	因此，和我們的鄰居處得好是非常重要的。
To do that we have to be good neighbors ourselves.	為了做到這一點，我們必須自己先是好鄰居。
If we are good neighbors, chances are that we will have good neighbors.	如果我們是好鄰居，我們可能就會有好鄰居。

** ――――――――――――――

get along with 和～和睦相處　　establish ﹝ əˋstæblɪʃ ﹞ *v.* 建立
relationship ﹝ rɪˋleʃən͵ʃɪp ﹞ *n.* 關係
neighborhood ﹝ˋnebɚ͵hud ﹞ *n.* 鄰近地區　　*chances are that* 可能

There are several things we can do
　to be good neighbors.
Let me tell them to you in detail.
Let me list them now for your better
　understanding.

要成為好鄰居，有好幾件事情
我們可以做。
讓我詳細地告訴你們。
讓我現在把它們列舉出來，讓
你們更加了解。

**First of all, we should get along
　with others.**
That is rule number one.
That is the minimum requirement.

首先，我們應該和別人和睦相
處。
那是第一條規則。
那是最起碼的必備條件。

Respect everyone all the time.
Be considerate of others all the time.
Be sensitive and alert when around
　other people.

隨時尊重每個人。
隨時為他人著想。
和別人相處時，要夠敏感和
謹慎。

**Second, we must not disturb our
　neighbors.**
We cannot be too noisy.
We shouldn't block our neighbors'
　parking spaces.

第二，我們絕不能打擾鄰居。
我們不能太吵鬧。
我們不應該堵住鄰居的停車位。

** ─────────────

detail (ˈditel) *n.* 細節　　*in detail* 詳細地　　list (lɪst) *v.* 列舉
first of all 第一；首先　　minimum (ˈmɪnəməm) *adj.* 最低限度的
requirement (rɪˈkwaɪrmənt) *n.* 必要條件　　*all the time* 一直；始終
considerate (kənˈsɪdərɪt) *adj.* 體貼的 < *of* >
sensitive (ˈsɛnsətɪv) *adj.* 敏感的
alert (əˈlɜt) *adj.* 警覺的　　disturb (dɪˈstɜb) *v.* 打擾
block (blɑk) *v.* 阻塞　　*parking space* 停車位

We must treat neighbors with kindness. | 我們必須友善地對待鄰居。
We should treat them the way we want to be treated. | 我們應該以自己希望被對待的方式來對待他們。
That's the golden rule of getting along. | 那是要和別人相處的不二法則。

Third, we should take care of the neighborhood. | 第三，我們應該要關照住家附近的地區。
We all have to work together. | 大家必須合作。
We should keep the place clean. | 我們應該維護環境的整潔。

The neighborhood is everyone's community. | 附近地區是大家的社區。
The community is like one big family. | 社區就像是一個大家庭。
Everyone has to care about and support each other. | 每個人都必須彼此關心並且互相支持。

Fourth, we should watch out for our neighbors. | 第四，我們應該要與鄰居守望相助。
We should report suspicious people. | 發現可疑人士，我們應該要加以舉發。
We should care about the safety of our neighborhood. | 我們應該關心鄰近地區的安全。

**

treat (trit) v. 對待　　*golden rule* 金科玉律　　*get along* 和睦相處
take care of 照顧　　*work together* 合作
community (kə'mjunətɪ) n. 社區　　*care about* 關心
support (sə'port) v. 支持　　*watch out for* 留意
report (rɪ'port) v. 告發　　suspicious (sə'spɪʃəs) adj. 可疑的

Safety is everyone's responsibility.

安全是每個人的責任。

Neighbors must protect fellow
　　neighbors.

鄰居必須保護自己的鄰居。

Neighbors must share the duty of
　　public safety.

鄰居必須共同分擔公共安全的
責任。

Finally, we should help our
　　neighbors when they are in trouble.

最後一點，當鄰居有困難時，
我們應該幫助他們。

Often we are the closest help
　　available.

我們往往是距離最近的幫手。

We should do all we can 24/7.

我們應該盡量幫忙，全年無休。

If we can do all of those things
　　above, I believe we can be good
　　neighbors.

如果我們可以做到上面所有的
事情，我相信我們可以成為好
鄰居。

Then we will be blessed with good
　　neighbors in return.

然後我們就能夠有幸得到好
鄰居。

That will result in a happy and safe
　　neighborhood.

那樣就會擁有快樂而且安全的
居住環境。

**　　——————————————

responsibility〔rɪ͵spɑnsə'bɪlətɪ〕*n.* 責任
protect〔prə'tɛkt〕*v.* 保護　　fellow〔'fɛlo〕*adj.* 同伴的
share〔ʃɛr〕*v.* 分擔　　duty〔'djutɪ〕*n.* 責任
in trouble 處於困難中　　help〔hɛlp〕*n.* 幫忙者
available〔ə'veləbḷ〕*adj.* 可獲得的
24/7 一個禮拜七天，一天二十四小時；全年無休（唸成：twenty-four seven）
bless〔blɛs〕*v.* 使有幸得到＜*with*＞
in return 作為回報　　*result in* 導致

People say good fences make good
　　neighbors.

有些人說籬笆築得牢，鄰居處
得好。

I really don't agree with that
　　statement.

我真的不同意這樣的說法。

I think kindness is repaid with
　　kindness.

我認為好心會有好報。

If we respect others, they will
　　respect us.

如果我們尊重別人，別人就會
尊重我們。

If we want good neighbors we must
　　do one important thing.

如果我們想要有好鄰居，我們
必須做到一件重要的事情。

We must be good neighbors.

我們必須先當好鄰居。

It sounds simple to do.

這聽起來很容易做到。

It is very easy to be a good neighbor.

要做個好鄰居非常容易。

Just give, support, share and care!

只要付出、支持、分享和關心！

** ───────────────────

fence〔fɛns〕*n.* 籬笆；圍牆
Good fences make good neighbors.【諺】籬笆築得牢，鄰居處得好。
statement〔'stetmənt〕*n.* 陳述；說明
repay〔rɪ'pe〕*v.* 報答　　care〔kɛr〕*v.* 關心

【托福作文範例】

35. Good Neighbors

We all have neighbors regardless of where we live. It's important to establish good relationships in our neighborhoods. To do that, we have to be good neighbors ourselves. There are several things we can do to be good neighbors.

First, we should get along with others. Respect everyone all the time. Be sensitive and alert when around other people. *Second*, we must not disturb our neighbors. We cannot be too noisy and we shouldn't block our neighbors' parking spaces. We must treat neighbors with kindness. That's the golden rule of getting along. *Third*, we should take care of the neighborhood. We all have to work together. The neighborhood is everyone's community. Everyone has to care about and support each other. *Fourth*, we should watch out for our neighbors. We should report suspicious people. We should care about the safety of our neighborhood. Safety is everyone's responsibility. Neighbors must protect fellow neighbors.

Finally, we should help our neighbors when they are in trouble. We are often the closest help available. If we want good neighbors, we have to be good neighbors ourselves. If we respect others, they will respect us.

35. 好鄰居

　　無論我們住在哪裡，我們都會有鄰居。和我們的鄰居建立良好的關係是一件很重要的事。爲了達成這個目標，我們自己必須先做別人的好鄰居。要成爲好鄰居，有幾件事情我們可以做。

　　首先，我們應該要和其他人和睦相處。隨時都要尊重他人。和別人相處時，要能敏感和謹慎。第二，我們絕不能打擾鄰居。我們不能太吵鬧，也不應該堵住鄰居的停車位。我們應該要親切地對待鄰居。那是要和別人相處的不二法則。第三，我們應該要關照我們住家附近的地區。我們應該要共同合作。附近地區是大家的社區。大家應該要彼此關心並且互相支持。第四，我們應該要與鄰居守望相助。如果看到可疑的人一定要舉發。我們應該要關心整個鄰近地區的安全。安全是每個人的責任。鄰居們彼此之間一定要互相保護。

　　最後一點，我們應該在鄰居有困難時提供幫助。我們是鄰居有難時最近的幫手。如果我們想要有好的鄰居，我們自己就得先當好鄰居。如果我們能尊重別人，他們一定也會尊重我們。

【托福作文原試題】

Neighbors are the people who live near us. In your opinion, what are the qualities of a good neighbor? Use specific details and examples in your answer.

36. *A New Restaurant*

Ladies and gentlemen.
Thank you for coming tonight.
We have a lot to discuss.

I have some important news about our
  neighborhood.
I've learned someone wants to open a
  restaurant here.
We must give him an answer as soon as
  possible.

We have to think about the advantages.
We also have to consider the disadvantages.
Then we can make a good decision.

---

neighborhood ('nebɚ͵hud)   learn (lɜn)
as soon as possible
advantage (əd'væntɪdʒ)   consider (kən'sɪdɚ)
disadvantage (͵dɪsəd'væntɪdʒ)

Having a restaurant in the neighborhood could
   be wonderful for us all.
It could benefit us in many ways.
Let me tell you a couple of reasons right now.

***First*, *it would be convenient*.**
We all could save a lot of time.
We wouldn't have to cook every night.

We all work hard every day.
We all feel too tired to cook sometimes.
Having a restaurant nearby would be a big help.

The women would appreciate a break from
   the kitchen.
The men would appreciate a meal out
   of the house.
Everyone would enjoy a little variety and a
   night out.

---

benefit ('bɛnəfɪt)	*a couple of*
right now	nearby ('nɪr'baɪ)
appreciate (ə'priʃɪˌet)	break (brek)
out of	variety (və'raɪətɪ)

***Second**, it would give us a place to go*.

We would have a nice place to meet our friends.

We could enjoy our leisure time there.

Eating together is an important social activity.

It gives us time to relax and catch up.

It also adds variety to our routine.

A new restaurant could bring us closer together.

A new restaurant could strengthen our
   community.

It could become a meeting place for both
   young and old.

***However**, restaurants have their drawbacks, too*.

They may cause noise or traffic problems.

These things could disturb the peace of our
   neighborhood.

---

leisure time

activity (æk'tɪvətɪ)

catch up

routine (ru'tin)

community (kə'mjunətɪ)

drawback ('drɔ,bæk)

disturb (dɪ'stɝb)

social ('soʃəl)

relax (rɪ'læks)

add (æd)

strengthen ('strɛŋθən)

young and old

cause (kɔz)

peace (pis)

We might have parking problems.

We might have additional pollution problems.

We'll definitely have more strangers temporarily
   in our neighborhood.

I think we could avoid these problems.

I know we could work them out with the
   restaurant managers.

After all, they want to keep us — the customers —
   happy.

In conclusion, I think the advantages outweigh

   the disadvantages.

A restaurant would benefit us more than it
   hurts us.

It would be worth any small problems it brings.

---

parking ('pɑrkɪŋ)

pollution (pə'luʃən)

temporarily ('tɛmpə,rɛrəlɪ)

manager ('mænɪdʒɚ)

in conclusion

worth (wɝθ)

additional (ə'dɪʃənl)

definitely ('dɛfənɪtlɪ)

work out

after all

outweigh (aʊt'we)

Therefore, I support the proposal.

I think it will be good for all of us.

I vote yes to having a restaurant in our

   neighborhood.

I hope that you agree with me.

I hope that you support it, too.

Let's say yes to a new restaurant.

It will spice up our neighborhood.

It will be healthy for our local economy.

It will be interesting and more fun for all of us.

You've heard all the good reasons.

You've heard many pros and possible cons.

Please make the right choice and have

   a good day!

---

support (sə'port)　　　　　proposal (prə'pozḷ)

vote (vot)　　　　　　　　yes (jɛs)

say yes　　　　　　　　　spice (spaɪs)

healthy ('hɛlθɪ)　　　　　　local ('lokḷ)

economy (ɪ'kɑnəmɪ)　　　　pro (pro)

con (kɑn)

36. *A New Restaurant*
一家新餐廳

【演講解說】

Ladies and gentlemen ;	各位先生，各位女士：
Thank you for coming tonight.	謝謝你們今晚來到這裡。
We have a lot to discuss.	我們有很多事情要討論。

I have some important news about our neighborhood.	關於我們的鄰近地區，我有些重要的消息。
I've learned someone wants to open a restaurant here.	我得知有人想在這裡開餐廳。
We must give him an answer as soon as possible.	我們必須儘快給他一個答案。

We have to think about the advantages.	我們必須考慮有什麼好處。
We also have to consider the disadvantages.	我們也必須考慮有什麼缺點。
Then we can make a good decision.	然後我們可以做出適當的決定。

** ——————————————————

neighborhood (ˈnebɚ͵hud) *n.* 鄰近地區
learn (lɝn) *v.* 得知　　***as soon as possible*** 儘快
advantage (ədˈvæntɪdʒ) *n.* 優點
consider (kənˈsɪdɚ) *v.* 考慮
disadvantage (͵dɪsədˈvæntɪdʒ) *n.* 缺點

Having a restaurant in the neighborhood could be wonderful for us all.	住家附近有一間餐廳，對我們大家而言很不錯。
It could benefit us in many ways.	它在很多方面都對我們都有益。
Let me tell you a couple of reasons right now.	現在讓我來告訴你們幾個原因。
First, it would be convenient.	第一，這樣會很方便。
We all could save a lot of time.	我們都可以省下很多時間。
We wouldn't have to cook every night.	我們不用每天晚上煮飯。
We all work hard every day.	我們每天都工作很辛苦。
We all feel too tired to cook sometimes.	有時候，我們都覺得太累了，沒辦法煮飯。
Having a restaurant nearby would be a big help.	附近有家餐廳會是一大幫助。
The women would appreciate a break from the kitchen.	婦女會很感謝有機會可以遠離廚房。
The men would appreciate a meal out of the house.	男性會感謝有機會可以到外面用餐。
Everyone would enjoy a little variety and a night out.	每個人都會很高興有點變化，晚上到外面吃飯。

**

benefit〔ˈbɛnəfɪt〕v. 對…有益　　*a couple of* 幾個

right now 現在；馬上　　nearby〔ˈnɪrˈbaɪ〕adv. 在附近

appreciate〔əˈpriʃɪˌet〕v. 感激　　break〔brek〕n. 斷絕 <*from*>

out of 自…離開　　variety〔vəˈraɪətɪ〕n. 變化

**Second, it would give us a place
to go.**

We would have a nice place to meet
our friends.

We could enjoy our leisure time
there.

	第二，這樣我們會有個地方可以去。
	我們會有和朋友見面的好地方。
	我們可以在那裡享受空閒時光。

Eating together is an important
social activity.

It gives us time to relax and
catch up.

It also adds variety to our routine.

和他人一起用餐是一項重要的
社交活動。

這樣能讓我們有時間放鬆，並
知道別人的近況。

也爲我們例行的生活增添變化。

A new restaurant could bring us
closer together.

A new restaurant could strengthen
our community.

It could become a meeting place
for both young and old.

新餐廳可以使我們彼此之間的關
係變得更親密。

新餐廳可以鞏固我們的社區。

它可以成爲男女老少聚會的地方。

**

leisure time 空閒時間　　social (ˈsoʃəl) *adj.* 社交的
activity (ækˈtɪvətɪ) *n.* 活動　　relax (rɪˈlæks) *v.* 放鬆
catch up 向…提供最新消息　　add (æd) *v.* 添加 < *to* >
routine (ruˈtin) *n.* 例行公事　　strengthen (ˈstrɛŋθən) *v.* 增強；鞏固
community (kəˈmjunətɪ) *n.* 社區
young and old 無論老少；不論男女老幼

However, restaurants have their drawbacks, too.

They may cause noise or traffic problems.

These things could disturb the peace of our neighborhood.

然而，餐廳也有缺點。

可能會造成噪音或交通問題。

這些問題會擾亂我們居住地區的安寧。

We might have parking problems.

We might have additional pollution problems.

We'll definitely have more strangers temporarily in our neighborhood.

我們可能會有停車問題。

我們可能會有額外的污染問題。

一定會有更多的陌生人暫時湧進我們附近的地區。

I think we could avoid these problems.

I know we could work them out with the restaurant managers.

After all, they want to keep us — the customers — happy.

我認為我們可以避免這些問題。

我知道我們可以和餐廳經理一起解決這些問題。

畢竟，他們會希望我們——這些顧客群——感到滿意。

In conclusion, I think the advantages outweigh the disadvantages.

A restaurant would benefit us more than hurt us.

It would be worth any small problems it brings.

總之，我認為優點勝過缺點。

餐廳對我們的益處，多於帶給我們的害處。

所造成的小問題都是值得承擔的。

**

drawback (ˈdrɔ,bæk) *n.* 缺點　　cause (kɔz) *v.* 引起
disturb (dɪˈstɝb) *v.* 擾亂　　peace (pis) *n.* 寧靜
parking (ˈpɑrkɪŋ) *n.* 停車　　additional (əˈdɪʃənḷ) *adj.* 額外的
pollution (pəˈluʃən) *n.* 污染　　definitely (ˈdɛfənɪtlɪ) *adv.* 肯定地；當然
temporarily (ˈtɛmpə,rɛrəlɪ) *adv.* 暫時地　　***work out*** 解決 (= *solve*)
manager (ˈmænɪdʒɚ) *n.* 經理　　***after all*** 畢竟　　***in conclusion*** 總之
outweigh (aʊtˈwe) *v.* 勝過　　worth (wɝθ) *adj.* 值得…的

Therefore, I support the proposal.　　　因此，我支持這項提議。
I think it will be good for all of us.　　　我認為對我們全體而言，會有好處。
I vote yes to having a restaurant　　　在附近地區開餐廳，我投贊成票。
　　in our neighborhood.

I hope that you agree with me.　　　我希望你們同意我的看法。
I hope that you support it, too.　　　我希望你們也支持我。
Let's say yes to a new restaurant.　　　我們來贊成一家新餐廳的開幕吧。

It will spice up our neighborhood.　　　它將為我們的鄰近地區增添趣味。
It will be healthy for our local　　　它將對我們本地的經濟有益。
　　economy.
It will be interesting and more　　　它將對我們大家而言是有趣的，
　　fun for all of us.　　　會帶來更多樂趣。

You've heard all the good reasons.　　　你們已經聽到所有充分的理由。
You've heard many pros and　　　你們已經聽到許多贊成的原因與
　　possible cons.　　　可能有的反對理由。
Please make the right choice and　　　請做出正確的選擇，祝大家有個
　　have a good day!　　　美好的一天！

** ────────────────

support〔sə'port〕v. 支持　　proposal〔prə'pozl〕n. 提議
vote〔vot〕v. 投（票）　　yes〔jɛs〕n. 贊成票
say yes 同意；贊成　　spice〔spaɪs〕v. 使增添趣味＜*up*＞
healthy〔'hɛlθɪ〕*adj.* 有益的　　local〔'lokl〕*adj.* 當地的
economy〔ɪ'kɑnəmɪ〕n. 經濟
pro〔pro〕n. 贊成的論點　　con〔kɑn〕n. 反對的論點

【托福作文範例】

36. A New Restaurant

Our neighborhood is about to have a new addition. Someone wants to open a restaurant here and we have to give him an answer as soon as possible. We have to consider the advantages and disadvantages this restaurant would bring. I think it could benefit us in many ways and here are my reasons.

First, we could all save a lot of time. We wouldn't have to cook every night. The women would appreciate a break from the kitchen and the men would appreciate a meal out of the house. *Second*, it would give us a place to go. Eating together is an important social activity. It adds variety to our routine. A new restaurant could bring us closer. *However*, restaurants have their drawbacks, too. They may cause noise or traffic problems. These things could disturb the peace of our neighborhood. We might have parking problems and additional pollution. We'll definitely have more strangers temporarily in our neighborhood.

I think we can avoid these problems by speaking with the restaurant managers. *In conclusion*, I think the advantages outweigh the disadvantages. The new restaurant can help spice up our neighborhood and help our local economy.

36. 一家新餐廳

　　我們的住家附近即將要有新成員。有人想在這裡開餐廳,而且我們必須盡快給他答覆。我們必須考慮這間餐廳會帶給我們的好處和壞處。我認為住家附近有一間餐廳,在很多方面對我們都有益,以下就是我的理由。

　　第一點,我們大家可以省下很多時間。我們不需要每天晚上自己煮飯。婦女會很感謝有機會可以遠離廚房,而男性也可以享受在外用餐的樂趣。第二點,那會提供我們一個去處。一起吃飯是一項重要的社交活動。那會為我們例行的生活中增添變化。一間新的餐廳可以使我們彼此更親密。然而,餐廳也有缺點。它可能會帶來噪音或是交通的問題。這些問題會干擾我們鄰近地區的安寧。我們還可能會面臨停車問題和額外的污染。一定會有更多的陌生人暫時湧進我們附近的地區。

　　我認為我們可以和餐廳經理談一談,來避免這些問題。總之,我認為優點勝過缺點。一間新的餐廳可以為整個鄰近地區增添趣味,也對本地的經濟有幫助。

【托福作文原試題】

It has recently been announced that a new restaurant may be built in your neighborhood. Do you support or oppose this plan? Why? Use specific reasons and details to support your answer.

||||||||||||●學習出版公司門市部●|||||||||||||||

台北地區：台北市許昌街 10 號 2 樓 TEL：(02)2331-4060・2331-9209
台中地區：台中市綠川東街 32 號 8 樓 23 室
　　　　　TEL：(04)2223-2838

|||||||||||||||||||||||||||||||||||||||||

托福、演講、英作文

編　　著 ／ 劉　毅
發 行 所 ／ 學習出版有限公司　　　　　☎ (02) 2704-5525
郵 撥 帳 號 ／ 0512727-2 學習出版社帳戶
登 記 證 ／ 局版台業 2179 號
印 刷 所 ／ 裕強彩色印刷有限公司
台 北 門 市 ／ 台北市許昌街 10 號 2 F　　　☎ (02) 2331-4060・2331-9209
台 中 門 市 ／ 台中市綠川東街 32 號 8 F 23 室　☎ (04) 2223-2838
台灣總經銷 ／ 紅螞蟻圖書有限公司　　　　☎ (02) 2795-3656
美國總經銷 ／ Evergreen Book Store　　　☎ (818) 2813622
本公司網址　www.learnbook.com.tw
電 子 郵 件　learnbook@learnbook.com.tw

售價：新台幣四百八十元正

2004 年 10 月 1 日初版

ISBN 957-519-751-8